THE YOUNG WEREWOLF!

Lisa is a twelve-year-old girl with all the worries and troubles and angst of any normal girl just beginning the slow transition into womanhood. Her mother is gone, so she has only her father—a man who doesn't really know how to talk to a young girl about personal things—to advise her.

She's frightened by the changes that are happening to her body—the budding breasts, the hint of a menstrual cycle, the stiff black hairs that appear on the back of her hands and the way her nails twist to look like claws during the full moon. Is this normal? And if not, how is she different, *why* is she different, and *why* doesn't her dad want her to go to the harvest moon dance?

"One of the first books of its type, a young adult novel with serious thoughts and reasoning about what it means to be that different...a good book...which does not deserve to be forgotten."—Scott A. Culp.

LISA KANE

A NOVEL OF WEREWOLVES

RICHARD A. LUPOFF

THE BORGO PRESS

MMXI

LISA KANE

SECOND EDITION

Published by Wildside Press LLC

www.wildsidebooks.com

DEDICATION

For the One whom I have loved so long,
And love now more than ever.

CONTENTS

FOREWORD

by

Michael Kurland

Since dinosaurs walked the earth have Richard Lupoff and I been friends. Or at least since the Beatles came to New York to appear on the Ed Sullivan Show. I don't know what Dick gets out of the relationship, since I am notoriously grumpy, unkempt, pedantic, neurotic, and irascible, but what I get is a wise, patient, tolerant comrade and advisor who, despite his sweet disposition, is a master of satire and parody and a pastiche artist of the first water. And he seems to know quite a bit about any subject that might come up. Comic books? He wrote the book. Edgar Rice Burroughs? He wrote the book. Science fiction? He wrote the book—and one of the leading fan magazines in the field. Paperback book publishing? He wrote the book, and illustrated it with a fine selection of covers from every genre you can think of. Memory? He wrote the book—well, half of the book—and taught a course on it in the Army. And did I mention horror (the genre I mean—I don't know what's making those strange noises in your attic)? He wrote the book. *Marblehead: A Novel of H. P. Lovecraft*, to be exact. And, as is fitting with the subject, the unpublished manuscript was believed lost for over thirty years before it turned up in the library of a private collector.

And so, when Lupoff turned his hand to writing a young

adult novel, he produced *Lisa Kane,* a story of those fierce and evil creatures, dripping gore from fang and claw, that mothers in the Carpathians frighten their children with at bedtime. Werewolves! Men who are tortured by the gods for their heinous crimes by being, against their will, turned into fearsome savage lupine killers at the full of the moon.

But perhaps there's another side to their story—perhaps these creatures are misunderstood and unjustly feared and spurned.

Nonsense!

But wait.... No one had even imagined such a possibility until 1976 when Dick Lupoff wrote *Lisa Kane: A Novel of the Supernatural* and, further, turned it into a morality tale and a plea for tolerance.

Lisa is a twelve-year-old girl with all the worries and troubles and angst of any normal girl just beginning the slow transition into womanhood. And her mother is gone so she has only her father—a man who doesn't really know how to talk to a young girl about personal things—to advise her. She is frightened by the changes that are happening to her body, the budding breasts, the hint of a menstrual cycle, the stiff black hairs that appear on the back of her hands and the way her nails twist to look like claws during the full moon. Is this normal? And if not, how is she different, why is she different, and why doesn't her dad want her to go to the harvest moon dance?

Her dad, a professor at Howard Phillips University (there's a hidden reference there, in the best tradition of hidden references—if you get it you chuckle and feel superior, and if you don't you don't know you're missing anything so you don't feel dumb and out of the loop), decides it's time to tell her, in his bumbling way, the facts of life.

Lisa laughs. She's twelve, she knows all that stuff.

"Not those facts of life...," her father says.

But enough about the plot of the story you're about to read. I don't want to take away any of your pleasure in seeing the development of each new twist on this ancient theme. As you read on, reflect on the effortless way in which Lupoff spins his simple tale of an almost-teen-age girl, and allows the reader to consider things that she didn't know were in question and thus grow in wisdom and understanding, through this exploration of lycanthropy, of what it is to be human.

(Oh, yes—that hidden reference: Howard and Phillips are the first two names of horror writer H. P. Lovecraft.)

Michael Kurland

AUTHOR'S NOTE

The original publisher of this book cut it without the authorization of the writer. This Borgo Press edition restores the authentic, original text of the novel.

Richard A. Lupoff

CHAPTER ONE

Lisa piled her books together and balanced them carefully against her hip amidst the usual bustle and confusion of the end of school. Mr. Barton's biology class was the last of the day and today, Friday, was the last of the week. Lisa found herself smiling happily at the cheerful prospect of two full days to do only the things she wanted—and no grammar, no algebra, no French I, no English lit.

She linked arms with her best pal, Toni MacPherson, and they made their way between rows of desks, casually dressed boys and girls gathering their belongings to carry home with them.

They nearly collided with one tall, skinny boy who turned crimson when he saw them. "Hi Toni, hi Lisa," he said.

Lisa said, "Hi Billy," and Toni added "Hi," as they kept on going.

"Isn't he cool?" Toni asked as they reached the hallway, "Isn't he bad?"

"I think he has a crush on you," Lisa told her friend. "Did you see the way he blushed?"

Toni made a partial shrug, tossing her curly dark hair nonchalantly, but partway through she burst into uncontrollable giggles and the two girls exchanged a wriggly hug, their stacks of schoolbooks clashing between them and then tumbling to the composition floor.

While they squatted gathering up loose-leaf binders and text books, Billy Cantor came ambling out of the classroom on his long, gangly legs. He was talking with Chris Simmons. Billy and Chris shared a paper route. They stopped walking and watched Lisa and Toni fumbling for their belongings on the floor.

Chris said, "You need some help, girls?"

Now it was Lisa's turn to blush. She kept her eyes on her task—but couldn't help seeing Chris's and Billy's identically scuffed old shoes and faded blue jeans.

"No thank you, we can pick up our own books," she replied levelly.

The scuffed shoes and faded jeans moved away without another word. Lisa looked up and saw that both boys were wearing quilted ski jackets. That was what all the boys were wearing this year: battered shoes, faded jeans and quilted jackets.

Chris Simmons was inches shorter than Billy Cantor. Lisa thought he was altogether better looking although she didn't say so to Toni. Chris did seem upset that he was shorter, not merely than his friend Billy, but than Lisa as well. But she was certain that he would grow soon and be taller than she was.

The two boys were gone now, and Lisa and Toni had their books back in order. They stood up and halted in front of the glass-covered bulletin board where the Harvest Moon Ball poster advertised the coming event. Mainly, they used the glass front of the bulletin board for a mirror.

They were about the same height and general size, but where Toni's hair was curly and almost black, and her skin was pale in contrast, Lisa had long, straight hair, rust-red in color, and a ruddy, freckled complexion. They were both wearing jeans and boy's or man's shirts, Toni got hers from her older brother Jeff: Lisa, from her father who was fortunately a compactly built man whose shirts fit his daughter without her having to make too many tucks and pleats in them.

Lisa looked down at her hands holding the load of books she was carrying home for the weekend. They were long, slim hands with rounded fingernails. There was nothing the matter with them. They were perfectly normal hands, with no suggestion of stiff, dark hair on their backs and no sign of claws or pads.

Lisa and Toni went through the lobby of the Whitbridge Consolidated School and down the front steps in warm October sunlight waving to friends as they walked. When they reached Centre Avenue, the street in front of the school, they turned toward Toni's house. Lisa lived in the same direction, beyond the little concentration of buildings that made up Whitbridge's small, sleepy downtown district.

They passed Dave's soda and sandwich shop—Whitbridge was essentially too small a town to attract most of the modern fast-food franchises, and the Board of Selectmen had passed a resolution to make it clear that none would be welcome if they tried to open in the town.

So the old-style snack shop remained, a favorite hangout for school kids of all ages in the afternoons, the young kids from the elementary school coming in for ice cream and cookies and the older ones, from the consolidated junior-senior high school, coming in on dates. Young Dave—he wasn't yet forty—had taken over the shop when his parents had retired a few years before. Old Dave and Irene, Dave's dad and mom, still came in to lend a hand when business got heavy.

"Want to stop for a soda?" Lisa asked as she and Toni walked past the big window of Dave's.

Toni shook her head. "No money today. We can get a snack at my house, though."

Lisa said okay and they kept walking. She did turn her head to look through the window of the shop, and see which boys and girls were inside.

At Toni's house they stopped and watched Toni's little brother playing with a bright yellow dump truck, "Bruce Dan, is Mom home?" Toni asked. He said she was shopping for groceries. The girls dropped their books on the window-seat near the front door, then went up to Toni's room and put one of Toni's record albums on the turntable.

"Are you going to the dance at the school?" Toni asked Lisa.

Lisa took a bite of her sandwich, then washed it down with a mouthful of chocolate milk. "I don't know. I haven't asked my father yet. I don't know if he'll let me."

Toni scowled. "All the kids are going, Lisa. What's the point of being in junior high if you have to stay home when there's a dance?"

"I know," Lisa said. "But my dad—he acts like he has to keep the old eagle eye on me all the time. Sometimes I wish we still lived in the city. You know, we lived in the city when I was really little."

"I know that." Toni took a bite of her own sandwich. "You told me before."

"Yeah."

There was a moment of silence between the two girls, with only the sound of the record player to fill the gap. Lisa bit off some more of her peanut butter and jelly sandwich and munched on it for a few seconds.

Then she said, "He thinks it's too dangerous in the city. Kids get into trouble there, or criminals attack them. He says that's why we have to live in Whitbridge."

"Don't you like Whitbridge? I've lived here all my life and I think it's fine."

Lisa shrugged her shoulders carelessly. She was better at it than Toni. "I don't know. I guess it's okay. It just isn't very exciting, is all."

"Well," Toni said, swinging the subject back to the Harvest Moon Ball, "my big brother Jeff is going to be back from college for a few days. I'll bet I can get him to drive us to the dance and back home. I'll bet Billy Cantor and Chris Simmons would go with us."

"You really like Billy?" Lisa asked.

Toni said, "And you like Chris?"

Lisa swallowed a mouthful of cold chocolate milk. "I guess so."

"What? Don't you know?"

"Well, he's nice. But he's kind of—strange. I mean, he doesn't hang around like the other kids. And sometimes he acts—you know. Funny. Sad. Or worried. And then he just goes off to his house, way on the other side of town."

"You think he's creepy!" Toni accused.

"No I don't! He's nice. And I like him. A lot."

Toni jumped up and hugged Lisa. "You have a crush on him! You have a crush on little Chris Simmons!"

Lisa flared angrily "I don't either! I don't have any crush on anybody! Chris is just a nice boy, and he isn't little either. He just needs some more time to grow."

"I'll bet you wish he'd hang around more. Like at Dave's."

"I have to get home now," Lisa said. "Daddy will start to worry about me."

"I don't see why he has to keep such a close watch on you, you know. You're almost as old as I am, and my mom and dad trust me. They let me baby-sit with Bruce Dan and everything."

"Well, you're thirteen."

"You're nearly thirteen."

"Then maybe he'll trust me more after I have my birthday, "And—" She stood up and twined her fingers together, twisting them uncomfortably. "—and after I start—"

She stopped again, felt herself blushing hotly, her usually cool face and neck beginning to feel all tingly.

Toni jumped up and squealed. "Did you get your—?" She left the last word of the question hanging, knowing that Lisa would know what she meant to say.

Lisa stared down at her hands, turning them this way and that. "I think I got it just a little bit. Does that happen at first?" She looked at her friend. "You're older, Toni, you must have yours."

Now Lisa saw that Toni was blushing. Toni said, "Yes, my mom told me what would happen. At first you can hardly tell if it's there. Then after that it starts to come, you know, every month. I guess if you had a mom to tell you about it you'd know."

Lisa's face grew hotter, then cold. She ran across the room and grabbed her jacket. "I'll see you," she said. She headed for the door leading to the stairway and downstairs.

"At Dave's tomorrow afternoon?" Toni called after her. "Or how about the spook show? Want to watch the spook show together tonight?"

"I don't know," Lisa threw back over her shoulder. She was halfway down the stairs now. She reached the bottom of the flight, gathered up her books and was out of the house, down the cement pathway to the sidewalk and on her way home, running.

Soon she stopped running and began to walk slowly. She was very upset and she knew why. The problem was that if she was going to do anything about it she'd have to ask her father, and then there would be an unpleasant scene.

Not that Dad would be angry with her, exactly. But he'd be annoyed in his own way. He'd sit and smoke his pipe and bury himself in his work, and then Lisa would feel angry with him for not paying attention to her and guilty, herself, for bothering him. And everything would be horrible.

But she knew she had to try.

CHAPTER TWO

Lisa ran up the steps of her house, opened the old carved wooden door with its cut-glass panels and dumped her books. Then she tiptoed into Dad's workroom.

He was buried in papers as usual, stacks of manuscripts covering the top of the huge old desk where he worked on days when he wasn't in Stonesboro teaching or searching for things in the library. There was a thick manuscript before him and low piles of even thicker reference books to either side.

On the small table behind his desk there were the usual signs that he was deeply engrossed in his work: a dead pipe and a cup of coffee left half filled, cold and forgotten.

Lisa crossed the room quietly and gave her father a kiss on the cheek.

He looked up for a moment, gave her a distracted smile and grunted, then turned back to his work.

Lisa sighed and walked from the room. She closed the door behind her and went to her own room to change clothes. She came back downstairs and took her books to the pantry where she usually did her homework.

The pantry was a light room, filled with cheery spirits. Lisa thought the whole house was light and pleasant. Old as it was, the builders of a century before had provided many tall windows that let in a good supply of sunlight and provided the house itself with a nice supply of fresh air. And when they had moved from the city her dad had had the old peeling paint on the house's outer walls done over completely in fresh white, and the interiors done in cream and pastels so the rooms had a feel of lightness to them.

Lisa finished all her French homework—at least she wouldn't have to worry about cases and tenses all weekend—and left her other assignments for later on.

She looked at the clock, went into the back yard and called her fluffy gray afghan Lucy for a romp, then returned to the kitchen and made dinner for herself and dad. There was plenty of room for everything she wanted to do in the house. Only the two of them lived in it, plus Lucy. Lucy slept on the foot of Lisa's bed—or the pillow, if Lisa let her get away with it.

Dad had said any number of times "It's a big house for just us but we can afford it here in Whitbridge. We never could in the city, and it's a nicer place than Stonesboro. It's just a lucky break that I can do most of my work here and just drive into Stonesboro to meet my classes. Good thing old Fineman isn't tough about office hours."

As he spoke he nodded vaguely in the direction of Stonesboro, the town where he drove three times each week to teach his classes at Howard Phillips University. Most of his work, dad had explained to Lisa, was research, studying, writing. He could do a lot of it at home, and the rest of it at the Gamwell Library at the university.

Lisa did love the big house, and she liked Whitbridge well enough. She had plenty of friends at school and she enjoyed living with her dad and Lucy. She had few memories of the city where she'd lived as a small child.

But there were things that she thought were strange, and others that made her feel shy. She wished that she had a mother she could talk to about those things, but there was only Dad, and he was stuck in his journals and reference books and manuscripts, seemingly all the time.

And he didn't like her to discuss what he called *private matters, family matters,* with outsiders. Not even with Mrs. Harkins, her home room and guidance teacher. Not even with her best friend Toni, and Lisa shared secrets with Toni anyhow.

Dad might know all about *family matters* but Lisa and Toni shared girl matters, and her father couldn't share in those.

* * * * * * *

Lisa lifted the lid on the pot of ravioli she'd made and took a final sniff of the little dumplings bubbling in their sauce of mushrooms and tomatoes. Then she put the lid back on the pot, turned off the stove and went to call her father for dinner.

She knocked on the door of his study and heard him grunt, then she walked away. She took Lucy by the collar, tossed a snack for her into the back yard, and closed the door. Then Lisa went back to her father's workroom and took the pen gently from his fingers.

"Oh, is dinner ready?" he asked.

Lisa said she'd called him earlier.

"Of course, of course," Dad said. "Must not have heard. Well."

He disappeared to wash up, then returned and Lisa brought the food from the stove and set it out. Her father went to the cupboard and fetched himself a half-bottle of red wine. He offered a sip to Lisa and she wrinkled her nose with distaste. She'd tasted wine before and found its flavor sharp and unpleasant. But Dad insisted that there should be no mysteries —what he called "no forbidden fruit"—so Lisa had dutifully sampled and rejected wine, brandy, caviar, tobacco and coffee.

But she liked tea and brought a cup of it for herself to sip with her dinner.

She waited until Dad had sampled the ravioli, the salad, and the hot garlic bread before she raised the subject that was bothering her.

"All the kids are going to the Harvest Moon Ball at school," Lisa started. Dad had a mouthful of ravioli and she knew he couldn't stop her in the middle of what she was saying because he had a rule against talking with food in your mouth.

Lisa went on, "And I can't be the only one who misses it. And

Toni MacPherson says her big brother's going to be home from college and he'll drive us in his car. Toni and me and, ah...."

Dad swallowed his food with a gulp of wine. "And some boys?" he completed the sentence for Lisa.

She blushed and nodded, keeping her gaze on her own plate. She felt her dad's hand close over hew own and squeeze gently.

"That's perfectly all right," she heard him say, "About boys, I mean. It's perfectly natural for a girl of your age to start liking boys. Which boys did you and Toni have in mind?"

Lisa looked up and saw her father smiling at her reassuringly. "Billy Cantor and Chris Simmons," she said. "Do you know them?"

"Billy and little Chris? They're fine youngsters. No, that isn't the problem." He released his grip on her hand and seemed to search for something in his pockets. He fumbled at one, found nothing, pulled a pencil stub from another and returned it after studying its pink eraser for a few seconds. Finally he picked up his wine glass and held it in both hands.

"Lisa, when is this dance?"

"It's the Saturday of the full moon in October." She allowed herself a small glow of hope. At least he hadn't said no right off. If he was interested in the details of the dance he might be planning to let her go to it. "At the school gym," she added, "and the committee is getting a band to come up all the way from the city."

She had trouble sitting still as she explained to him. "Big Stew and the Studebakers. They have a record album and every-thing. They play all those real old songs like when you were young, Dad, 'Louie Louie' and neat songs like that!"

She watched a series of expressions rapidly cross her father's face. For a second he looked as if he was going to laugh out loud and Lisa felt encouraged but then he looked sad and she knew that the worst was coming.

"I'm afraid not, baby," he said.

She felt as if her chair, the floor, and the whole house had fallen out from under her.

"I wish I could let you go," Dad continued. "But I just don't think it would be a good idea. Not that night, anyway."

"But why not?" She felt tears rising in her eyes and tried to squeeze them away. She knew a trick—if she chewed on her lower lip it sometimes kept her from crying. "All the kids are going," she said. "There'll be parents there, nothing bad will happen."

"I know that, darling."

"Don't you trust me?"

He looked as if she had struck him. Then after a moment he said steadily "I trust you. Lisa, you are my only child. I have no one else. If I didn't trust you I would have nothing." He looked vaguely past her and heaved a sigh, then continued. "But you can't go to this dance. Not—how old are you now?"

Why had he changed the subject so oddly? And didn't he know his own daughter's age, Lisa wondered. But she said, "Twelve, Daddy. Almost thirteen."

Her father pushed his chair away from the table and stood up looking troubled. He paced once to the doorway that led into the big dining room that they almost never used, seemed to be gazing into the growing darkness of that room, then walked back and stood over the kitchen table, gazing down at Lisa.

"If only your mother were—" he started, then stopped himself and started again. "Lisa, you're learning to grow up now. You aren't just a little girl any more. It's time for you to learn, ah—" He stopped for a moment, really just a pause, then continued what he had been saying. "—what we used to call the facts of life." He stopped and cleared his throat. Lisa watched him. He looked around the room, looked at everything in it but her.

Lisa laughed.

"If you mean where babies come from and things like that, Daddy, I've known about that for years. All the kids know about that. If they didn't Mrs. Harkins had a special class at school for all the girls and Mr. Barton had one for the boys. But everybody knew everything already."

He looked at her, now, his eyebrows raised in a peculiar expression. "Well," he said. "Well, hmm. I really haven't been keeping up, have I? But that's all for the best, all for the best. Youngsters should have full information, no use to fill their heads with fairy tales about sex."

Lisa said, "Are you finished with dinner, Dad?"

"Eh? Oh, yes, thank you, dear. That was very good, ah, very good—what did we have tonight?"

"Ravioli."

"Ah, yes, thank you. Here, let me lend a hand."

They cleared the table and cleaned up together, carefully putting the china away in the old tall cabinets that lined the pantry. The special china that was reserved for guests stood in glass-fronted breakfronts in the dining-room.

They had hardly spoken while they cleaned up, but as they finished Dad said, "Lisa, dear, despite what you've learned in school, I think we should still, ah—if you don't mind. This is really very, very important."

He took both of her hands in his, but before she could make any reply the telephone rang. It was Toni MacPherson,

Did Lisa want to come over tonight? They could watch the Great Friday Night Spook Show on the Stonesboro TV channel. Lisa could bring Lucy along to keep her company and they could stay over in Toni's room.

Lisa told Toni to wait while she asked her father if it was all right. He said that it was and she told Toni she'd be over in a while with her pajamas and toothbrush and Lucy. Lisa hung up the phone and found her father sitting in the living room, perched at one end of the old-fashioned sofa that he'd found to match the period and the style of the house.

Lisa went and sat on the sofa too. She thanked her dad for permission to stay over at her friend's house.

"Lisa," he tried again, "we really ought to have a serious, ah, chat. Are you leaving right away?"

She shook her head. "Not for a while. The spook show doesn't come on till late."

He nodded his understanding, "Well, we should have time," He looked away from her, seemed to study the ceiling, fidgeted with his hands. Finally he got started.

"You know, ah, when a child gets to be, ah, around the beginning of her teens—" He rubbed his hands once over his face "—she begins to, ah, to mature."

He paused and looked at Lisa.

"Yes," she said.

"That is, ah, her body begins to change. To develop. And, ah, one of the things that occurs is what we call menarche. That is, ah, the beginning of the monthly cycle."

For the first time Lisa felt embarrassed, but also relieved. This was her chance to talk about what was bothering her. She'd tried, indirectly, to ask Toni about it, since Mrs. Harkins had very obviously memorized a lecture and wasn't prepared to do anything but recite it.

But either Toni had missed the point or Lisa had been too indirect and had not asked properly. And she'd been too frightened that time to say anything more.

She knew what was supposed to happen, or thought she knew anyway, and that was not what had happened to her. It was very upsetting.

She started to look into her father's face, then dropped her gaze to her own lap, "I think I started once," she said. "It went away, though."

"Not unusual," Dad said kindly.

"But it was," Lisa whispered. "I think it was unusual, anyway. It was—it isn't supposed to make your hands change, is it? Make your hands get all hairy and your fingernails like claws? I was so scared! What if it comes back?"

Suddenly she threw herself into her father's arms and felt him holding her as he had when she was little. He patted her on the back of her head and she felt her tears, hot and stinging, wetting the shoulder of his plaid shirt. He didn't speak, but seemed to be humming to her, something that she remembered vaguely his doing years before when she took naps on his lap.

Finally she pulled away from him a little bit and looked into his face. "I'm not normal, am I?" she asked, "There's something terribly wrong with me and that's why we moved to Whitbridge and why we live here all alone in this house! That's all so, isn't it?"

She waited for him to say she was wrong. She wanted desperately to hear him tell her that she was normal, that she was a normal girl just like her friends and that there was nothing the matter with her.

But he didn't answer for a long time and when he finally spoke each word struck her like an icy slap, "There is something, Lisa. I had hoped it wouldn't happen to you. I thought it might pass with your mother, and you could have a life like any other girl. I even let myself think that everything was all right, all the years here in Whitbridge. Letting you make friends with other children. Letting you go to public school.

"But I'm sorry I was wrong. It was my fault and I'm sorry."

Lisa's ears rang, her stomach felt as if she'd swallowed a block of solid ice and was freezing from the inside out.

"What's the matter?" she screamed at her father. She wrenched herself completely away from his touch, jumped to her feet and stood over him. For the moment everything seemed frozen and she noticed for the first time things she had never noticed before. That her father was a rather small man, shrunken and somehow sad looking. She'd always thought he was very strong. That his hair was thinning on top.

That there were spots on the backs of his hands and that those hands, that she had always thought of as steady and powerful, trembled slightly.

She shook herself and felt time begin to flow again. She demanded of her father, "Tell me what's wrong with me!"

He dropped his face into his hands and seemed to be staring straight at the floor between his feet. He whispered some syllables that she couldn't understand. Then he looked up at her, an expression of despair etched on his face.

"Last month when you—when you told me that you'd had

that strange experience—when you felt strangely, and your body felt as if it was changing—"

"It was!" Lisa interrupted. "My hands were turning into paws, my whole body felt so—" she stopped for breath, left words unsaid, then continued "—and then it just went away again."

Her father nodded. "I hoped that that was the normal onset of menarche," he said. "That everything else was just upset on your part. But I knew I was deceiving myself. I wanted for you what any father would want for his daughter. A normal life. Growing up. Yes, having fun with boys. But you cannot have that, Lisa. Your mother tried and—no, you cannot have that."

Suddenly he began to weep into a handkerchief he pulled from his trousers pocket. It was the first time Lisa had ever seen her father crying. Maybe there had been a time, when her mother had... whatever had happened to her mother. But she'd been too small then to have any clear recollection. And now her father was sitting doubled forward on the old horsehair sofa he'd bought for their hundred year old house, crying.

"You still haven't told me what's wrong with me," Lisa insisted

Her dad looked up at her, his face wet. He repeated the word she hadn't quite made out before. "Lycanthropy," he said. Then he provided herewith another word of the same meaning. "Werewolfery."

Lisa's eyes opened wide in horror and amazement but her father seemed not to notice. He went on talking to her as he always did when he explained this: kindly, sympathetically, but somehow wrapped up in what he was saying, as if he'd half-forgotten that she was even there.

"When you were born you seemed to be quite normal except for—you know, the two rows of little dots running from your chest to your belly. They looked almost like extra pairs of, ah, nipples." It was a word she'd never heard her father use before. He'd always advised Lisa not to be prudish about her body or her speech, but he himself had always dodged around such words.

Until now.

"You know, they didn't amount to anything," her dad was rambling on. "On newborn babies they're just little pink dots on the skin anyhow. And the doctor assured me that the condition was really quite common, that the extra mammaries almost never developed and they faded away to barely noticeable spots as the child grew.

"I wanted very much to believe that, Lisa. You can't imagine, there is simply no way for you to understand how your mother and I lied to each other in those days. Trying to make ourselves believe.

"And at the same time we didn't want to say too much. To the pediatrician or to anyone else. We just hoped, and lied to each other. And then after your mother...died—"

He stopped talking and shook himself, shook his head as if clearing it of unwanted pictures. He appeared to try again to speak but he was unable to get his thoughts in order. At least, that was Lisa's perception.

She dropped to her knees beside her father and took his hands in her own. "You mean," she said quietly, "you mean that I'm one of those creatures, like in the Lon Chaney movies? That I'm going to turn into a hairy monster and run around biting people when it's a full moon outside? The old gypsy and the foggy moors and all of that stuff? How can you say that, Father? It's crazy! I won't believe it!"

He shook his head and smiled at her sadly.

"I know it's hard to believe, darling. It sounds like something out of—yes, out of a crazy, cheap motion picture. Or out of some lurid old magazine.

"But it's real," he insisted. "We have to face it. It was my fault, my fault that I kept it from you. I thought it might never happen to you. But it is beginning. We must face it."

Lisa looked into his face, "But I was never bitten by a wolf. Nothing ever happened to me."

She released his hands and jumped up, unable to stay still any longer, unable to remain by the couch calmly discussing the fact that she was some kind of monster.

She faced her father, feeling a terrible upsurge of anger with him for saying what he had. If it was all lies she was furious—and if it was true she was even more furious.

"You're the monster!" she shouted at him. "You're the monster for saying this to me, doing this to me!"

She ran at him.

Be stood up in front of the couch.

Lisa started to beat at him with her fists but he caught her by the wrists and she found herself staring into his face, realizing that he wasn't much taller than she any more.

He released her and stood, not saying anything.

"It's not true, is it?" Lisa pleaded desperately, "Aren't you lying to me for some reason I don't understand? Is it something about the dance? I won't go if it's so important. I—"

Suddenly she was crying again, and Dad had fumbled his handkerchief back out of the pocket where he'd stuffed it and was helping her to dab at her eyes with it.

He led her by the hand into his study and sat her down in a big leather chair. He walked around behind his desk as if he was going to sit down there to talk to her but then he changed his mind and came back . He pulled up another small armchair and sat in it facing her.

"I'm sorry that it's true," he said calmly.

She looked at him but she didn't have anything to say now, so he went on instead.

"Lisa, we have to sit here like two adults and talk this through, and we have to decide what to do about it. If we turn our backs and pretend that it will go away by itself, it will only grow worse. Then we'll have to face it later on."

He sat up straighter than he had been. "So let's face it now,"

She nodded her willingness.

"Now then, we first have to get our facts together. All these years that I've worked at the university I've been accumulating information against this very possibility." He gestured to the shelves piled with oddly assorted books, to the stacks that contained the overflow from the shelves.

"I thought that was all for your classes," Lisa said, surprised.

"Partly it is, of course. But I've always been on the lookout for information that might help you, dear, should you ever need that help. I am not saying this to paint myself in virtuous colors. It is simple truth."

Lisa nodded, understanding, not knowing what else to do. Slowly she realized that she was feeling sorry less for herself than for her father.

"And all of the information that I've been able to gather adds up to very little of value," he said sadly.

Lisa was bewildered. "I just can't—Daddy, I always thought that werewolves were make-believe. Like vampires and living mummies and—you know. Just scary stories. Just for fun. Not for real!"

"I know, I know." He reached behind him onto the big desk and picked up a cold, empty pipe. He turned it over in his hands, looking into it as if to find something helpful in its dark bowl. "The idea of, as you put it, just scary stories, is one of the places that my research has always led me, dear."

He seemed to be lapsing into his abstracted professorial tone. Oddly, Lisa felt better for it, more comfortable, less frightened. It was her dad explaining something the way he always did when she asked him questions—with a long, rambling kind of lecture that wandered through miles of back roads before it arrived at what she needed to learn. But he always seemed to know, to get to the real answer if she could just keep up with his reply.

"Werewolves have been taken over by Hollywood, to be sure," Dad was saying. "But for once they did some homework—at least a little. The films you see are a mixture of authentic folklore and creepy-crawly flummery. All of the screen versions are based on two of the more serious explanations traditionally given for lycanthropy. And for those, why, we begin our search with that most useful of research tools, a good dictionary."

Lisa glanced across the room at the huge unabridged dictionary lying open on its rack. She started to move toward it but her father put his hand on her arm and stopped her.

"I've looked it up a thousand times," he said. "Let me save you the trouble just this once." He looked at her inquiringly. "Do you know where the word lycanthrope comes from, Lisa?"

She shook her head,

"It's an old word. Greek. It is formed from the Greek words for wolf and man. What the Greeks called the lycanthropos, the werewolf. The original wolfman. You see—nothing mysterious."

He gestured with his hands, the way he always did when he explained things to her. When he explained, things usually wound up being nothing mysterious.

"The book gives two definitions," Lisa's dad went on. "One says that lycanthropy is the assumption of the form of a wolf through witchcraft or magic. The other defines it as a form of insanity in which the patient imagines himself a wolf."

He gave Lisa a sharp look, then continued.

"We don't believe in magic these days, and I certainly know that you are sane, Lisa. You are as strong and healthy and lovely a daughter as any parent could ever hope for. In every way. Except...."

Lisa made a gesture of puzzlement.

"If neither, uh, explanation is right, then how can you, ah—" she found that she couldn't even get the question formed sensibly. It wasn't exactly the shock of what her father had said to her—it was more the opposite of shock, the confirmation of what she had already feared and suspected was true—and had hoped would be proven false.

But it was not false.

"Well," her dad was saying in his professor's voice again, "there is a good deal of evidence that lycanthropy is a real phenomenon. Not merely an emotional problem, much less a form of insanity. Although I would imagine that there might be terrible psychic shock associated with the condition.

"In that case the physical symptoms would reinforce the psychic ones—and vice versa. You'd have a vicious circle. There are enough ailments that work that way, and nothing mysterious about them." He sat and nodded at her, as if agreeing with his own words.

"But what about the full moon, and the silver bullets, and wolf bane and all of that stuff?" Lisa asked. She wasn't really seeking information now so much as she was struggling desperately for something she could cling to. Something sensible, something involving neither witchery nor madness.

Her father made a characteristic shrug and walked to his desk again. He put down the pipe he'd been holding, selected another from a maple rack, filled and lighted it. Lisa liked it when he did that—there was a kind of familiar comfort in watching him, and she liked the odor of his pipe smoke.

Some of the kids at school smoked cigarettes, Lisa knew, because it made them feel very sophisticated and mature to do it. She had tried it a few times and found the experience thoroughly unpleasant.

"The full moon and the rest of that business, eh?" her father asked around the stem of his pipe.

Lisa could imagine him sitting in front of his classroom at the university. Professor Leo Kane, anthropology 101. She pretended she was a college student.

"Well, I suppose it's a matter of mixing authentic facts—as far as those can be found," Professor Kane lectured, "and superstition and folklore. And of course some pure Hollywood invention thrown in to make the films more appealing."

"And the biting part," Lisa exclaimed suddenly, the thought shattering her classroom fantasy and bringing her back to her father's study. "Don't you have to be bitten by a werewolf to become a werewolf?"

"The biting part," her dad repeated, "Lycanthropy transmitted by the bite of the werewolf. And you've never been so bitten. Therefore...." He let his voice trail away and looked at Lisa inquiringly.

"Therefore—how could I be—what?" she asked.

Dad sighed.

"There's so little solid information, so much hearsay and folklore and outright fantasy. Of course the folklore is of the highest value—but how to separate it from the fantasy? Every writer of sensational horror stories for the past hundred years seems to have tried his hand at a werewolf yarn, and they're all tangled into the same skein as the little real data we have. The literature goes back even to old Herodotus twenty-five hundred years ago. It's a long tradition."

He leaned back and puffed on his pipe, then continued. "But the condition does seem to run in families. And it seems to be transmitted by heredity—from parent to child—rather than by contact. The old notion—" He paused and ran his hand down the spine of an ancient, brown-covered book that lay on his desk. "—the old notion of satanic pacts is of course nonsense. Although within a coven," he mused aloud, "within a cult of witches, if there were a virus associated with the condition, it could be transmitted from master to neophyte just as in a family it was transmitted from parent to child."

He looked at his daughter almost angrily, and Lisa was more upset than ever until she realized that his annoyance was not directed at her. It was directed at her condition, and at his own helplessness to come to her aid.

He drew on his pipe, blew a cloud of smoke at the ceiling and talked to her through its lower wisps, once more the calm professor, "As for wolf bane, I have not been able to find any explanation for that belief. All of these books, everything I can find. No help. The silver bullet—well, someone may once have killed a werewolf with a silver bullet or with a silver sword or whatever. It wasn't the silver that did it, it was the bullet or the sword.

"But the moon, now, that's another matter."

He stood up and began to pace, pipe held in one hand like a lecturer's classroom pointer.

"For a long while the moon was associated with oddities of human behavior, eh? Hence the very word lunatic. And then self-styled wiser heads prevailed and we decided that that was a lot of rubbish. Mmm—until the science of statistics came along."

He stopped pacing beside his desk, opened a huge volume to a section of tables and charts. "Crime rates vary with the phases of the moon. Outbreaks of violence in asylums correlate with the phases of the moon. Even the stock market moves with the phases of the moon!"

"Why?" Lisa asked as her father paused between statements.

"Why?" he echoed. "Why? We don't know! Differences in illumination. As yet undetected radiations. Tidal forces. Yes, very likely it has to do with tidal forces. Women's monthly cycles correspond to the lunar month, not the calendar or solar month."

He interrupted himself and looked down at Lisa, "I did not mean to embarrass you, my dear."

Lisa laughed nervously. She was feeling a little better now. Dad was explaining things in his drowsy, comforting manner. Somehow, she felt, everything might still be all right.

Dad came back to where she was sitting and planted himself in the chair facing hers. "I am convinced that the correlation of the full moon and outbursts of lycanthropy is a real phenomenon. It involves a triggering effect, probably tidal in nature. There is nothing magical to it!"

Lisa felt that she had heard all she could of the subject. She felt better and worse at the same time—better to hear her father talk, to know that he cared and was involved with her problem. But she wanted to get away from the subject, too, away from her father's theories, away from herself and the terrible things she was learning about herself. All she wanted was to be like other girls!

"Can we talk some more another day, Dad?" she asked. "I promised Toni that I'd come over to her house tonight to watch the spook show."

Her father laughed and said of course, he'd even drive her.

Lisa bounded upstairs and grabbed her toothbrush and pajamas and called Lucy to her. They ran back downstairs and out the front door. Lisa and her afghan piled into the family car, an old round-backed Volvo that Andy Frayne down at East Street kept in running order.

Dad drove them over to Toni's house. He gave Lisa a kiss and shooed her out of the car. Lucy jumped out behind her, gray tail wagging.

CHAPTER THREE

Inside Toni's house they lay on the floor in front of the TV set and watched the spook show. Toni's little brother was in bed as were her parents, and Jeff wasn't back from college. The TV host Gil Ghoul introduced the movie, a Karloff and Lugosi team-up called *The Invisible Ray*, and Lisa and Toni watched, giggling at the silly dialog.

Then they went to bed, Lisa and Toni and Lucy all in one big old featherbed that belonged to Toni, and whispered and giggled about school and horror movies and boys and the Harvest Moon Ball until they all fell asleep.

In the morning they had a big breakfast and Toni walked back to Lisa's house with her and Lucy. When they arrived Lisa put her dog's food in her dish outside and penned her in the yard. Than the girls went back inside the house,

Lisa's dad, Leo Kane, was working in his study. When the two girls stuck their heads inside he looked up, said, "Hello, Lisa, Antonia," and returned to his papers. The girls went to Lisa's room and played some records, practiced dance steps, and decided to save money by skipping Dave's for the day even though it was Saturday.

The Harvest Moon Ball was in two weeks—the October full moon would come on a Saturday and the juniors and seniors at the Whitbridge Consolidated School were working to get things set up.

Toni suggested that they spend a while calling their friends to talk about things like the football team and the dance, and when Lisa agreed Toni dialed Billy Cantor's house. She giggled into the phone when he came on the line and started to push Lisa away. When Lisa started to leave the room Toni ran and pulled her back to sit with her on the edge of Lisa's bed while she talked with Billy.

When they finished Lisa demanded to know what Billy had said.

"Oh, he says he wants to go to the dance with me. He has a Big Stew and the Studebakers album and he says we can come over and listen to it any time we want to. I didn't tell him that we both have it too!" She laughed out loud.

Then she jumped up and ran over to the window, looked out as if she could see Billy Cantor's house from Lisa's window even though Lisa knew that was impossible. All you could see from her window was a bunch of trees and their garage.

"You ought to call up Chris Simmons," Toni said. "I called Billy."

Suddenly, Lisa felt shy. She'd phoned boys before and boys had phoned her. And she and Toni had shared phoning like this. But she'd never actually asked a boy about going to a dance. It was—almost like asking him for a date. But then Toni said that Lisa was afraid to call Chris Simmons, and for that very reason—Lisa knew that Toni was right—she took the telephone and dialed.

Chris answered himself and Lisa couldn't think of a single word to say. Chris kept saying hello, hello, sounding puzzled and then annoyed, and just when Lisa thought he was going to hang up she managed to gasp "Uh, hi. Chris, this is Lisa Kane. You know. From school."

Chris admitted that he knew her. They talked about their teachers and the subjects that they both had, the football team, and Big Stew and the Studebakers. Finally Lisa asked Chris if he was going to the Harvest Moon Ball.

He didn't know.

All the kids were going, she reminded him.

He said he'd like to go, he just didn't know.

Lisa said he must have a date or else that he just didn't like her.

"I like you a lot," Chris said. Then he made a choking sound and didn't say anything else.

Lisa felt a marvelous tingling all down her arms to her fingertips and back up again. "You really do?" she said.

There was a pause. Then Chris said, "Yes. But I have to go now."

He hung up.

Lisa said, "Did you hear, Toni? Chris Simmons likes me. He likes me a lot. He said so himself!"

"Is he going to the dance?" Toni demanded.

"He didn't say. But he said he likes me."

After lunch Lisa and Lucy walked Toni home, then made their way back to their own house. It wasn't a long walk—they could either go back to Centre Avenue from Toni's house on Blackwood Street, and then to Psalter Street where Lisa lived, or go the other way, Blackwood to Farnsworth and over to Psalter. This time they took the quieter way, by Farnsworth Street.

At home Dad was sitting in the living room, a few papers spread before him on the coffee table. He looked up from his papers and smiled at her.

"Lisa dear," he said. "About the things we discussed last night"

Lisa's heart sunk a little. She said, "Yes, Dad?"

"Ah, I don't wish to upset you," he said, "but we didn't quite finish with the topic, ah, the topic of lycanthropy."

Lisa knew what was coming. She'd had such a nice time at Toni's house, and then back at home this morning, playing records and phoning boys. Now it was back to this frightening topic. She wished they didn't have to get back to it, and yet underneath she realized that Leo was right, they would have to face it and there was nothing to gain by delay.

"Ah, I believe I mentioned, dear, that lycanthropy tends to run in families," her dad was saying in the same voice he used to explain who the Boston Braves had been or why Franklin

Roosevelt was an important president. "The records are far from complete, and those we have are often unreliable," he went on, gesturing to the papers on the low table.

"But there do seem to be suggestions of the, ah, conditions in the family. In your mother's side of the family, specifically. She was a Talbot, you know. And there was once some sort of scandal covered up, in that family. They're from Wales, you know."

"No, Daddy, I don't know. You never talk about Mother. I don't know anything about her. You have that baby picture of me on your desk, but I can't see her face in it."

"She was a beautiful woman, Lisa, but camera-shy."

"Well you never told me about her. I think anybody has a right to know about her parents."

He looked troubled. With hands that trembled slightly he lifted off his rimless eyeglasses and laid them carefully on the stack of papers nearest his knees. He rubbed his temples with his hands then picked up the glasses and put them back on, adjusting them carefully.

"I'm sorry, Lisa dear. I thought—but you see, I loved her very deeply and—and it is a painful subject for me. We weren't married for many years. She was very lovely, perfect in every way except for the, ah, the very minor abnormality which you share with her."

He looked up at her, his eyes clearly begging her to say that she understood. She nodded to show that she did.

"Your mother used to be gone for a few days each month." He was on his feet now, pacing nervously, looking at the carpet, up at the wainscoted ceiling, the old tall windows, anywhere but at Lisa.

"She and I both worked," he continued, "and occasionally each of us would have to be away on business. Our marriage was based on mutual trust." He exhaled heavily.

"I don't know if this means anything to you, Lisa, you are still so very young. But I thought your mother was away on business. Actually she was staying with relatives. They—they took care of one another. The, ah, condition didn't strike everyone in her family, and not each person every month.

"So they would protect the ones who did, ah, who did change. People are so afraid of lycanthropes." He laughed bitterly.

"It's the lycanthropes who need protection, not the people around them! They don't become man-slayers. Even natural wolves aren't interested in man, no less lycanthropes. But—" he stopped as if he'd lost the thread of his own idea.

"But Mother," Lisa prompted.

"Yes." He turned his glance onto Lisa, then away and out the window, then back to her again. "When your mother became pregnant we were both delighted. We both wanted a child very badly. And for those nine months your mother made no more mysterious trips.

"You see—" and he was the professor again "—this is evidence that the various phenomena are somehow connected. The lunar cycle, the menstrual cycle, the lycanthropic cycle. A woman's menstruation ceases during pregnancy—you understand what I mean?"

Lisa nodded.

"And so did your mother's lycanthropy during pregnancy! And there seem to be no post-menopausal female lycanthropes, no pre-pubescent ones." He stopped talking and looked at Lisa. "I'm afraid this is over your head. Do you follow—?"

"Most of it," she said.

"Yes. Well, essentially there are no she-werewolves among small children or old women, you see. That's all I was saying."

"And what about men?" Lisa asked. "I always thought werewolves were men until, ah, until—" She stopped.

"Oh, yes," her father supplied. "There are as many men as women affected with this. Just as men are affected by the lunar cycle, you know, although not as overtly as women. It's still there, absolutely."

Suddenly Lisa jumped to her feet. "What does it mean, though?" she demanded. "You talk about it like some kind of geography lesson or something. What am I going to do?"

And even before he answered, another thought struck her, a thought that hit her almost like a physical blow, leaving her stunned and aching.

"And what happened to my mother after I was born?"

"Ah, child," her father said, "your mother was—was—" He stopped speaking and came to take her by the hands, raising her from her chair. Again Lisa noticed that he was not much taller than she was—a small man, gentle, who had held his worries and his grief inside for years while his daughter had grown, happily unaware that anything was wrong.

Now Dad's eyes looked wet behind the rimless glasses, and for an instant Lisa felt strangely as if their roles had been exchanged. She was the comforting parent, he was the sad, frightened child.

And then Dad said, "Your mother died, child. She cared for you for three years. Her—condition—gradually returned after your birth. At first she'd thought it was gone for good, but it came back. And she—finally she decided that she couldn't live that way."

"What happened to her?" Lisa demanded again. She had learned the worst, now there was nothing left to be afraid of. Now she wanted to hear everything.

"It was winter," her father told her. "Your mother and I had rented a cabin in the mountains. Not too far from Whitbridge, in fact. We skied and snow-shoed, sat before an open fire at night. You stayed with our neighbors in the city. For your mother and me it was like a second honeymoon.

"Honeymoon!" He repeated the word as if it had a bitter taste to it. "One night I awoke and heard her moving about. Suddenly I realized that we'd forgotten the calendar. It was the night of the full moon.

"I called to your mother but she didn't answer. The cabin was dark—there was no electricity and the fire by then was only embers.

"There was a scratching sound, and the cabin door opened and something dark moved through it. I jumped out of bed and ran to the doorway, and the snow outside seemed as bright in the glaring moonlight as a white sandy beach on a summer's day."

He stopped to draw a deep breath, still holding both Lisa's hands with his own.

"And there I saw a wolf not twenty yards away. Beautiful. The wolf is a beautiful creature, Lisa, which has got a bad reputation from fairy tales. But it is a lovely creature, strong and graceful. The wolf is a noble beast."

He pulled his hands from Lisa's and covered his face with them for a moment, then went on.

"I called to—to the wolf. She looked back at me for a flash—somehow I knew the wolf was female—and then she was gone."

He sat down and remained motionless, gazing through the window into the trees that stood outside their house, into the dark shady glen under the branches and leaves.

"They never found Mother?" Lisa asked.

Dad shook his head.

"Didn't they even try? Didn't *you* even try?" she demanded angrily.

He turned toward her with a wan smile. "Yes, I tried. I stayed and searched until my food ran out, and then I went back into town and got help. There was even a sheriff's posse—you know, vacationers get lost in the mountains every now and then.

"But they never found her. Some tracks—but wolves were not uncommon in those mountains. Fewer of them now, but they're still there. But we never knew about your mother."

Lisa said, "Then you don't know that she died! She might still be alive even now. She might be anywhere! She might need help!"

Her father sighed. "It's been nine years, Lisa. Nine years. If your mother were alive—I am convinced she is not, and believe me, I resisted that conviction for as long as I could—but if she were alive, wouldn't she have contacted me? Contacted us? She loved us both, I know that."

"Maybe she can't contact us. How do you know? It's never

happened to you, you're—you're—" Lisa struggled to find the right way to say what she meant. "You're just a human," she finally managed. "You can't understand. What if Mother got, uh, stuck? And couldn't change back! She might still be out there, living in the mountains."

Her dad shook his head, and she saw a weariness in his face that she had never noticed there before. "This might be and that might be," he answered vaguely. "I have worked for these nine years, and I can only go on doing my best, Lisa. And that has to be my best for you, not for your mother who is dead and gone."

The conversation ended there, and they did not discuss the matter again that weekend. Monday morning Lisa went back to school and everything seemingly returned to normal. Classes and homework, chattering with her friends, alternately teasing and turning shyly from boys. Sodas at Dave's after school or going out to the football field to watch the senior team practice.

And the Harvest Moon Ball came closer.

CHAPTER FOUR

Thursday afternoon Lisa went to Dave's along with Toni MacPherson and Billy Cantor and, rarity of rarities, Chris Simmons. Chris kept saying things about having to go home but he didn't go. Instead he stayed with the group, stayed closest to Lisa, even held her hand once for a few seconds. When the kids had got their food from Dave, Toni jumped up and gasped, "It's Jeff! It's my big brother!"

Toni's big brother was tall and broad-shouldered. He wore a white tee-shirt and jeans. He looked incredibly old—probably close to twenty. He walked over and said hello to Dave first, then to Toni and the other kids.

He sat down with them and ordered a cup of coffee. After he had drunk half of it he said, "Hey, anybody want a ride in my Mustang?"

Toni and her friend Billy jumped at once. Lisa started to follow but she felt Chris's hand tightening on her wrist. She turned and saw a serious look on his face. He shook his head nervously.

Lisa turned to Jeff and said, "You guys go ahead. We'll come another time."

As soon as Jeff was gone with Toni and Billy, Lisa turned to Chris and asked, "What is it?"

He flushed and looked away, then said, "You want to go for a walk together, Lisa?"

She stood up and they left Dave's snack shop. They walked slowly along Centre Avenue away from the section where Lisa and Toni both lived. Past the Congregational Church and just before Andy Frayne's garage they cut across Centre Avenue and started up Mountain Road. After a while they could see the old stone textile factory, long vacant, ahead of them.

They were no longer walking down Whitbridge's maple and elm lined streets, but were on old semi-rural road, one almost untraveled since the days of the textile mill. They stopped walking and sat in a grassy field beside the road, watching the infrequent passage of cars.

"Lisa," Chris said after they'd watched a dust-coated Porsche creep past on the uneven surface, "Um, I know that all the kids have been talking about the Harvest Moon Ball."

She said nothing.

"I mean, I kind of think, you know, that you might have thought that we were all, ah, you know, Antonia and Billy and..."

He turned his face away.

"My dad said I can't go," Lisa told him simply.

He stared at her. "He did? I mean, he says you can't?"

Lisa nodded.

To her astonishment Chris made a huge, face-splitting grin.

"Uh, my aunt says the same thing," he spluttered. "I mean, that's what she said. That I can't go. You know, I live with my Aunt Stella."

Lisa said "I know. The kids told me. You never did."

"Well, I don't have kids over much to visit."

Lisa knew that too, "In fact," Chris said sadly, "I don't really have many friends. Billy shares my paper route but that's mostly for the money, you know. Aunt Stella doesn't have much money and I have to help."

Lisa nodded, Yes,

"Um, I guess I just don't—I mean—" Chris stopped again.

Lisa turned to face him. She felt very strange, somehow frightened but oddly happy. She put her hand on his and said, "I like you very much, Chris."

He appeared startled by that but after a minute he said, "I like you too. I think I like you better than anybody. So that's why

I—" He stood up.

Lisa stood up too.

They started walking down the road again, not talking. Soon they were in front of the old stone factory.

"Do you think the mill is haunted?" Chris asked. "Some of the older kids told me that there was something in the cellar. A coffin. A vampire's coffin."

Lisa shuddered. She looked up into the clear sky, at the warm, early-autumn sun. "I don't believe in vampires," she said.

"Or any of that stuff, Lisa? I mean—oh, ghosts, zombies, any of that stuff?"

"None of it," she said as firmly as she could. But she felt her jaw tremble a little. "No," she said angrily, "none of it. No mummies or monsters or any of that movie stuff." She found that she was almost shouting at Chris. She stopped to catch her breath, and suddenly, amazed, found that she was crying. And she was leaning on Chris, her face bent to the collar of his shirt, crying stinging tears that she could not stop from coming.

She felt his hands, light and uncertain, holding her by the shoulders.

She pushed him away and looked defiantly into his face. "You knew," she spat the words. "Somebody told you about me and you're teasing me. I hate you, Chris Simmons!"

He stepped back as if she had punched him in the chest. His face was utterly blank. "Nobody told me anything," he protested, "I don't know—I mean—" He stood staring at her.

Lisa said, "You did this whole thing just to be cruel. Bringing me out here by the mill, saying that about vampires—"

"No I didn't. Really."

"You didn't know about me?"

"No!"

He shook his head in puzzlement.

"I'm a werewolf!" she blurted.

The instant the words were spoken she regretted them. If only she could call them back, make them unsaid, she would. But she couldn't. And now Chris would whoop with laughter and run back into town, back to Dave's. In an hour everybody would be laughing....

But Chris didn't laugh.

He said, "That's a genetic abnormality. My aunt told me, my Aunt Stella, so I wouldn't be upset about it. I have it, too, Lisa. Aunt Stella said that it doesn't show up in children, little children I mean. Only when you start to grow up, it comes out. It has something to do with tides, I think, with the moon and all. That's why people think that moonlight causes it, it doesn't."

Lisa herself had fallen back a step. She was pressing one hand to her mouth and chewing her knuckles, something she hadn't done since she was a very little girl.

"You—you're a—you have lycanthropy?" she asked him.

Chris nodded. "That's why I have to share my paper route with Billy Cantor. I mean, in the winter when it gets dark early and the moon is full—can you imagine a wolf delivering the *Whitbridge Express* to people?"

"But—you don't seem upset about it or anything. It's a terrible thing, it's worse than a disease."

"No it isn't."

"But people—"

"People think it's awful but they're wrong. I mean, it's kind of fun. People just don't understand. So we have to stay in hiding for now. But someday people will know. You'd be amazed how many of us there are. And others, too!"

"Others?"

"Sure. I mean, other kinds of, ah, special people. You know. *Weres.*"

"But I don't know. I don't. This is too much for me, Chris. I can't, uh—"

"Sure you can. Want to come and meet my Aunt Stella? She knows all about this stuff. She can talk to you about it."

"I don't know your aunt. Nobody does. She always stays out in the country at your house, nobody in town even knows what she looks like."

"She's kind of shy," Chris shrugged. He put his hands on

Lisa's shoulders again and looked straight into her face, standing close to her.

She felt very strange for a moment, lightheaded and with her heart fluttering in her chest. It was a very nice feeling.

"You mustn't tell, Lisa, but I know I can trust you. My aunt is a lycanthrope, too. And she had a terrible experience once, with, ah, people who didn't understand. So she's very shy, but I'll explain to her about you. I know she'll talk to you."

"Maybe she should talk to my father," Lisa said. Chris looked very doubtful at that.

"I think they might—" Suddenly Lisa found herself crying again, but this time not the hot, hurt tears of anger and shame she had cried before. Instead she felt happy, unbelievably happy, and she couldn't understand why that should make her cry, but it did.

She barely managed to get her words out through the tears. "I think they might already know each other."

* * * * * * *

It was the first time Lisa had ever seen Chris Simmons' house on Mountain Street. She'd been out to the east end of Whitbridge a few times—times when she'd come on her bike with friends like Toni, just for a ride after school or with a picnic in the summer.

But they'd never ridden farther than the stone mill. Its thickly overgrown yard was a perfect picnic ground, and its cool shady walls were a good place to avoid the hottest August sun. But now with autumn drawing on and the afternoon sunlight coming pale and weak across the hills, the mill suddenly became a chilly and uncomfortable place.

Lisa kept her thick, quilted jacket pulled snug around her as she walked with Chris. The sidewalks of town had long since disappeared, now the paving ended too as Mountain Street turned into an ancient dirt road. It was line with neglected, over-grown fields that gave way to old, tangled woods and finally the low, round-topped rows of hills that gave Mountain Street its somewhat overstated name.

Then they came to Chris's house.

Lisa stood looking at it, aware suddenly of all the questions she should have asked Chris before they ever got there. What was his house like inside? Did he like it? Why did he live alone with his Aunt Stella, and what sort of person was she? An image of a cruel old woman flashed through Lisa's brain—why didn't Chris's aunt ever come to town? There must be something the matter with her, something so horrid that Chris had never spoken of it, and seldom enough of Aunt Stella at all, except to say that she was a shy woman who liked to be by herself.

The house itself was ordinary looking—a low, old structure of some uncertain color between gray and brown. There was grass around it, tall and uneven, and a few trees with signs of old fallen branches and leaves around their roots. There was a low iron fence around the place, and Chris opened a creaking gate in it for Lisa.

"Kind of rusty," he said. "I promised Aunt Stella I'd scrape it and paint it and oil the hinges but I haven't done it yet."

Lisa stepped through the opening and walked toward the front of the house. She trembled despite the quilting of her heavy jacket. She heard Chris shut the gate again with a creak and a clatter, then hurry up the path until he was beside her. She looked into his face, at the eyes just a trifle lower than her own, and he smiled at her. She grabbed Chris's hand and they went up to the door.

He didn't knock or ring a bell or use a key—just pressed the door latch and pushed the door open. They stepped inside together.

"Come on," Chris said, "let's get a snack." He led the way across a vestibule and old-fashioned parlor into the kitchen. Lisa stood looking at the old furnishings of the house while Chris fixed then both sandwiches. An old print hanging above the kitchen table fascinated Lisa—it showed a snowy scene of a hillside overlooking some buildings with a vaguely European look to them, like stage sets in some of the movies she'd seen on the Friday Night Spook Show. The snow and the houses looked so bright that it took a minute to realize that the picture was of a night scene, the bright light coming from a giant cream-colored moon.

The houses looked comfortable and warm. A thin wisp of smoke rose from a stone chimney into the night air. And standing on a snow-covered hill overlooking the houses was a pack of wolves. Lisa could see the eyes of one wolf—all the others were turned toward the buildings in the picture but the largest of the animals was glancing toward the viewer with a disquieting look in its eyes. For a long while Lisa tried to figure out what was odd about these eyes, and then she realized what it was: they were not the eyes of an animal. No, there was something in their expression that spoke of intelligence, of a human awareness. They seemed to be saying something. Lisa looked for a title on the print but there was none.

She heard Chris speaking to her, started and said, "What, Chris, I didn't hear—"

"I just asked if you like hot chocolate," he said. "What's the matter, Lisa?"

She shook her head. "Sure, hot chocolate is fine."

He made it and they sat down at the table beneath the print of the snowy scene to eat their sandwiches and sip their hot drinks.

"Isn't your aunt at home?" Lisa asked.

Chris said, "She must be, I—" He stopped, looked toward the doorway behind Lisa, the doorway they'd come through from the old parlor. Lisa turned in her chair, following Chris's eyes.

The woman standing in the doorway was the most beautiful person Lisa had ever seen. She was tall and slim. Lisa couldn't be sure how tall, certainly she would rise over Lisa's dad. Her face was pale and thin, with high arched cheekbones and a straight nose that might have been carved from soft limestone, brilliant green eyes of a riveting intensity and a shade that Lisa had never seen before, and warm, full lips.

Her hair was the same dark red shade as Lisa's, and it hung

straight and glistening over her shoulders. She wore a long, dark, warm-looking dress.

Suddenly Lisa realized that she had been staring at Chris's aunt—but also that the tall beautiful woman had been staring at her! Lisa heard Chris speaking. "Aunt Stella, this is my friend from school. Uh—Lisa Kane. Lisa, this is my Aunt Stella.

A distant corner of Lisa's mind flew back to a schoolroom, to a bit of English class where they were learning to make introductions: younger to older, man to woman except a woman being introduced to the President of the United States....

"Lisa Kane," Chris's aunt said. Her voice was a beautiful as her face, strong and almost as deep as a man's but there was no questioning the feminine tone. It was exactly the voice Lisa had always hoped to have someday, and always despaired of even coming close to.

She stood up beside the table and fought down an impulse to curtsy the way children did in movies when they were introduced to the king or queen. Instead she reached to shake hands, taking her eyes from Aunt Stella's for one panic-stricken look at her own hand—it mustn't have peanut butter smeared on it... and it didn't!

Aunt Stella stepped from the doorway into the kitchen, and Instead of taking Lisa's one extended hand she took both of them in her own, and drew Lisa close to her so she could look down into Lisa's face. Aunt Stella's hands were warm. They made Lisa feel good to hold them.

"Come along now," Aunt Stella said. "Bring your snacks along. She released Lisa's hands, turned and led Lisa and Chris into the parlor. "Here, Lisa," she said, "sit with me here," and they settled onto a high-hacked settee. Lisa put her cup and dish onto a low table. Chris sat opposite them in a big easy-chair. Aunt Stella turned to Lisa. "You are—Leo Kane's daughter, then?"

Lisa nodded, yes. There was an odd expression in Aunt Stella's eyes. Lisa watched them, wondering why they seemed so familiar.

"Would you tell me about your father, Lisa? You and he live by yourselves? He never remarried, did he?"

Lisa told Aunt Stella about herself and her father. How they had moved to Whitbridge when Lisa was a little girl, how they got along in their house. She told about Lucy, how the afghan had become hers as a puppy and how Lisa had wanted to name her after herself, and finally settled on Lucy because it was next closest.

Aunt Stella laughed at that and suddenly Lisa knew what it was about her eyes, They were the same as the glowing, intelligent eyes of the great wolf in the print. Lisa decided not to mention that.

But she liked Chris's aunt, liked her hugely. It wasn't like meeting a stranger, especially an older person. Meeting Aunt Stella was more like a reunion with an old acquaintance. More than an acquaintance, Lisa suspected that she knew who Aunt Lisa really was, but—she was afraid to say what she thought.

Instead she chattered about Whitbridge, about her friends at school and her teachers, her favorite places around the town like Dave's sandwich shop, and about her father and his teaching job at Howard Phillips University over in Stonesboro. Chris added a comment or two of his own, now and then, but mostly he kept out of the conversation, letting Lisa and Aunt Stella get to know each other.

Finally Aunt Stella took Lisa's two hands again, as she had in the kitchen, and Lisa found herself wondering what this woman was going to do. Their eyes met, and Lisa saw once more the person she most wanted to be like in the world. Her heart was beating fast and she couldn't decide whether she felt ice cold or hot.

"Lisa," Aunt Stella said to her, "Lisa Kane. Has your father ever talked to you about—yourself? Or your mother? Have you ever noticed anything unusual about yourself, or did Leo Kane say anything?"

This was it! Lisa knew that she could deny everything, say that she had to go home now and never come back to this house on Mountain Street, never again. Or she could trust this woman, Chris's aunt, and her own—her own friend, at least. She could tell her what Chris already knew....

"Yes! I'm a—a lycanthrope!" She blurted it out, stopped in the middle because it was so hard to say the word that everyone either hated or laughed at, werewolf. At least the other made it sound like a disease, something that could happen to anyone instead of a dreadful curse that only fell on people in horror stories.

Aunt Stella nodded, that beautiful dark red hair glistening as it moved up and down.

"Of course," she said, smiling at Lisa.

Of course? No surprise, no revulsion? But then Lisa realized that Stella's own nephew Chris was also a—lycanthrope. A werewolf, Aunt Stella must be accustomed to dealing with the changes that came, with the fur and the fangs. And if she was who Lisa suspected she was...

There were the things that Lisa's father had told her, told her about her mother. About the disappearances, and about that final trip they had taken together to the cabin in the woods. Chris's Aunt Stella would surely not be shocked to hear about lycanthropy.

Stella was asking a question. "Have you had the change, Lisa?"

Lisa shook her head uncertainly. "Only—only a little. I thought it was just part of growing up. You know." She felt herself blushing. She really blushed much too easily. She wished she could control it, but the more she thought about it and tried to stop it, the worse it got. She kept her eyes strictly away from Chris, looked down at the cushion between herself and Aunt Stella, then up again, into Stella's fascinating green eyes.

Patiently, Stella asked "What exactly happened?"

Lisa told her, and Stella nodded and asked what Lisa's dad had done when she told him.

"Well, he didn't exactly do anything," Lisa explained. "He told me what it was. I mean, that it wasn't just growing up, like a normal girl. Like my friend Toni, she's thirteen. He said that it was a kind of disease that came from my—" She stopped for a few seconds, then when no one else said anything, continued "—from my mother."

Stella said, "I see. But he didn't do anything? Didn't give you anything for it?"

Lisa shook her head, no.

What was she doing? she suddenly wondered. Talking about this most private and most important thing in her life, with a woman she had only just must. But of course, this wasn't just any woman, not at all.

Aunt Stella asked "Did your father give you any kind of medicine or ointment? A kind of salve to rub on yourself?"

Lisa's eyes opened wide. "No! I never heard of—is there a medicine for it—for lycanthropy?"

Stella nodded, smiling.

"It—what does it do?" Lisa asked. "Does it make it go away? Keep you from changing? Make you like—normal people?"

"Why no, Lisa," Stella smiled broadly. "Nothing like that at all, oh no! It helps us. It helps us change, and then later on it helps us change back. It's really quite wonderful! I feel so sorry for ordinary people who can't change, they just don't know what it is that they miss!

"Of course, your father wouldn't know that," she ended.

"No," Lisa agreed. "He—he wouldn't know about that. But you would, Aunt Stella? You said that it helps us. Us. Then you must be—"

Stella nodded, smiling still.

An old clock standing on a mantelpiece at the far side of the room began to chime. Lisa looked at it, then out the window at the fast gathering night. She jumped from the couch and said, "Thank you very much. I loved the snack. Ah—daddy doesn't like me to stay out after dark, and I have to cook dinner for him. He'll be back from Stonesboro by now and I don't want him to worry about me.

She started to run from the room, realized that she'd dropped her coat somewhere in the house and asked for it. Chris found it for her and handed it to her. "Uh, thank you," she said again.

"See you in school," Chris said.

And Aunt Stella said, "I'm sure we'll see you again very soon, Lisa."

Lisa slammed the door shut as she went out, ran down the path and jumped over the iron fence without opening it.

She ran down the edge of Mountain Street as long as it was a dirt road, then slowed down at the start of the paved section and walked on, past the deserted mill, back to where Mountain Street ended at Centre Street. Now there were houses on both sides, and soon there were shops and filling stations and then the Whitbridge Consolidated School came into sight and Lisa stopped for a minute, leaning against a shop-front, catching her breath.

She had never met anyone like Aunt Stella before. She had been drawn to the woman: there was some kind of bond between them that Lisa could feel even though she hadn't said anything about it. She knew that she would see Stella again. She had to find out about the salve that Stella had spoken of, and she had to find out how many lycanthropes there were.

A week ago she would have said that there were no such creatures, that werewolves were only something that you saw in movies or read about in horror stories. Then a few days later she had known that they were real—and that she was one of them!—but that they must be very rare creatures. Perhaps that she was the only one.

But now?

Now she had learned from her father that were-beings were fairly numerous, and today she had learned that her friend Chris and his aunt were both werewolves.

How many were there?

And what was going to happen to her?

CHAPTER FIVE

She felt herself beginning to tremble from the chill of the evening. A few street lamps had gone on along Centre Street, and a couple of restaurants had turned on their lights. She started walking again and felt better almost at once.

She passed Dave's sandwich shop, then Blackwood Street where her friend Toni MacPherson lived, then turned at the corner of Psalter Street toward her own house.

She heard a high-pitched yelping and caught a fifty-pound gray bundle of fur and bones that came flying to greet her. "Lucy, Lucy," Lisa said. She rubbed the afghan's skinny flanks, let her stand up with her paws on Lisa's shoulders and give her a kiss, then shoved her off. They walked home together, Lucy staying close by, wagging her tail and hitting it softly on the side of Lisa's leg with each wag.

Dad's car was standing in the driveway when they got home. It wasn't late enough in the year to need the garage, and there was a summer's accumulation of clutter in it, so Dad left the car on the rough blacktop surface outside.

Up on the front porch Lisa pushed the door open. Lucy shoved past her and into the house, then Lisa went in and hung her warm jacket in the closet. Dad had built a small fire in the living-room fireplace and was sitting near it, reading a newspaper in his favorite chair.

Lisa bent over him and kissed him on the forehead.

He put his newspaper down and turned to her. "Hello, dear," he smiled, "I missed you. Stay at school late?"

Lisa said, "No, I was visiting Chris Simmons. I ought to go make dinner now."

"Nice boy, Chris," Lisa's dad mumbled. She looked back at him as she left the room to head for the kitchen. He had picked up his newspaper and was deeply immersed in it already. Lisa got a snack for her dog and shut her out of the kitchen.

She looked in the refrigerator and cupboard, got together some food and began to cook dinner for herself and her father. Tomorrow was the last school day of the week and Lisa would spend her evening doing homework. Maybe she'd phone Toni to talk about assignments and they could talk about other things.

But she knew that she had to face her father during dinner. What would he say about her having visited Chris's Aunt Stella? There was so much that Lisa had learned—and so much more that she suspected, half hoping and half-fearing to learn the truth. Had her father told her everything that he knew about her mother and herself, or was there more?

What would he say about her telling Chris that she was a— lycanthrope? And about his being one also?

She sat down at the kitchen table while the food was cooking, then remembered that she had not set places for them to use and made herself busy with dishes and silver.

Finally she called her father and they sat down to their meal. "Stay late at school today?" Dad asked absent-mindedly. Lisa told him again that, No, she had been visiting Chris Simmons' house. "I met his aunt," she added. "Chris's aunt. She's beautiful, Daddy! She has hair like mine, only long and straight. I hope I look like her when I grow up."

Her dad smiled at that. "You're beautiful to me, darling, and I'm sure you will be a very beautiful woman."

Lisa blushed, took a mouthful of food and a swallow of milk. "We had a nice talk. Chris's aunt and I, I mean. It was like— almost like having a mother to talk to. Not that I don't love talking to my father, but—"

He reached across the table and patted her hand. "I understand. A child should have—it would be better if you had two parents, I know." He looked sad, his eyes watery behind rimless eyeglasses.

"Please don't feel bad, Daddy," Lisa pleaded. "I'm sorry for what I said."

He shook his head. "No, you're right. We all do our best, that's all. I wish I could do better. You must be lonely."

Lisa watched him pick at the food on his dish. Their dinner was almost over, and she did have homework to catch up on.

Dad looked up and smiled at her, "I'll tell you what, Lisa, how would you like to go to Stonesboro with me? On Saturday? We both have to go to school tomorrow, eh? You to learn and I to teach. But on Saturday I will be at the library at HPU." That was how he always referred to the university, by its initials, like an old friend or a famous politician.

"I don't know what it's like," Lisa stalled. Now that her father offered the opportunity, she found herself almost frightened of what might happen, what he might say. Perhaps, she thought, it would be a good idea to invite Toni along. Dad wouldn't say anything horrible in front of her friend. But he spoke again before she had a chance to make the suggestion, and she realized with a small sinking feeling that it was too late.

"Just the two of us," he smiled again. "I'm afraid that I cut myself off from you too much. I know I'm involved in my work, preparing lectures, grading student work, writing articles for the journals. You know, it's publish or perish at HPU, not the secure cloistered life it looks like from the outside."

"But what will it be like?" Lisa asked desperately. "I've never been there." She wanted to add, *and I'm afraid,* but she was afraid even to say that. She felt herself growing angry with herself, with the monster that she was.

Her father didn't notice. He just answered her question. "It's a very pretty campus. Old buildings, trees, stately halls of ivy kind of place." He smiled at that and Lisa smiled too, uncertainly. She'd heard the expression *halls of ivy* before but didn't see any humor in it.

"What can I do there?"

"Oh, bring a book if you want to. Or take a walk around, see the famous buildings. We can have lunch together at the faculty club. I'm supposed to meet Old If for lunch there, I think you'll like him. I only have a few hours work to do at the library."

"Who's Old If?"

"*Heh*—of course you don't know him. Fine man, *hah*, that's a bit of a joke too, you know."

Lisa didn't, and was growing confused and annoyed.

"Fine man," her father explained, "Isaac Fineman, you see. That's his real name, but he has a brilliant mind. Made great contributions to the field, years ahead of his time. Still has a sharp mind, old as he is. They call him Old If because of his initials, I. F. Isaac Fineman, you see."

Lisa shook her head. "I guess I do. I'm afraid I don't quite, ah—" How could she say it?

"Don't quite see the point in academic humor," her father supplied. "Well, don't let that worry you, my dear. It's a rather esoteric topic. We professors tend to get very specialized and we end up talking only to each other like the Cabots and the Lodges used to." He looked up at her, then said, "Oh, I don't suppose that means anything either."

She shook her head, No.

"Let it be," Daddy said. "Anyway, it will be a nice opportunity for us to chat, you and I. About anything you wish. And you'll enjoy the campus, I promise that. Will you join me?"

Lisa said, "Yes," and got up to clear their dishes. They had their after-dinner tea together in the living room, Lisa struggling with her algebra text, her father buried in an anthropology journal. Lisa had some trouble getting the algebra problems right, but she didn't ask for help. Her father was wonderful with anything to do with people, history, languages, literature. But when she had asked him for help earlier in the term with algebra, all he'd wanted to talk about was the spread of culture, the early Greek and later Arab mathematicians. He knew all about algebra except how to solve equations,

"Not my field, I'm afraid," he'd finally said, and Lisa had

gone over to Toni's house and Mr. MacPherson who was an engineer at the computer works down in Parkhurst had helped them both with their work.

Lisa went back in the kitchen and called Toni about the homework. They solved some problems together, then Lisa told Toni about going to Stonesboro on Saturday. Toni said that she would go to Howard Phillips University if her father was a professor there. Her brother Jeff didn't go to HPU, he went to the state university, but he'd told her all about college and it sounded marvelous.

And no, she wasn't mad because she wasn't invited, but maybe Lisa's dad would ask them both another time, or she could get Jeff to take her to the state university some time, if she could get rid of Bruce Dan for a day.

After the call Lisa felt tired. She went back to the living room and found her father still studying his journal, a lined pad on the table beside his easy chair. He was mumbling to himself, scribbling notes with a worn stub of a pencil that Lisa would have been ashamed to use in school. His cup of tea stood full and cold beside the lined pad.

Lisa took it away and put it in the kitchen so it wouldn't spill, brought her dog Lucy in from the yard and went to say goodnight to her father.

He looked up, surprised, when she came up behind him and put her hands on his shoulders. "Going to bed already?" he asked.

She said she was.

"All your homework finished?"

"Yes," she said impatiently. Then, "All except a little reading. American history. I can do that in the morning."

Her father lowered his journal. "If you must. But you'd do better to finish it before you go to sleep. Let your subconscious work it over, you know."

She said all right and called Lucy to go upstairs.

She sat up in bed, snuggled with her warmest quilt, Lucy sprawled across the bottom of the bed keeping her feet warm for her. Her history book was telling about the colonial period in New England, and the Salem witch burnings of Cotton Mather and others. They used the Bible to justify killing witches, people they accused of making deals with the devil, of casting spells, of having familiars, of turning themselves into cats or mice or other animals.

She shivered and closed the book and slid down under the warm heavy quilt and went to sleep. Lucy was still lying across her legs.

She had a dream about the old days, about being a girl in the American colonies back in the days of the witch-hunters. She tried to be a good girl, she went to church every Sunday and worked hard the other six, she tried always to be kind and honest and not even to think wicked thoughts.

But when the moon was full her hands changed and her feet, her teeth grew long and sharp and she went on all-fours. They caught her and put her on trial and called her werewolf, witch, devil's slut. She denied everything but they said she had made a pact with Satan.

They took her out and tied her to a wooden post and heaped dry brush around her and lit fire to it. She felt as if she were being crushed and burned and she screamed that she wasn't a witch, she wasn't, and she cried for help and suddenly—

Her father was with her.

She was in her own bed, in her own house and the light was on. Her father was sitting beside her wearing an old woolen robe and Lucy was crouching on the floor shaking because she was afraid.

The first thing Lisa did was call Lucy to come back to bed and not be afraid.

Then her father said, "You must have had a bad dream. You were crying and calling for help."

Lisa was shaking and clutching one of her father's hands in both of hers while he stroked her hair with the other, soothing her. She said, "Yes. I had a terrible dream. I was being crushed and burned."

"Poor child. It must have been that dog lying on top of you."

Lisa looked at Lucy. The afghan gazed back at her with giant liquid eyes, pleading not to be sent away. Lisa took one hand and soothed the trembling, whimpering dog. "Poor Lucy. I must have frightened her. She doesn't understand." She ran her hand through the dog's gray coat. "Poor skinny thing. Maybe I don't give her enough to eat."

Her father shook his head. "Nothing of the sort. That's just the way afghans are, you know. If you wanted a fat dog you could have got a mastiff." He laughed to show that he didn't mean to scold.

"I wouldn't want any other kind of dog. I think Lucy is perfect. Well, maybe not too smart, but I love her."

"Yes. She is as she is, we can't make her something else and we mustn't condemn her for her hereditary nature."

"Daddy," Lisa said. "I dreamed I was being burned as a witch." She reached down to the floor beside her bed and picked up her American History book. "Did they really kill people for that? Why did they do that? Did they really believe in witches?"

"Oh, yes." Her father looked very serious behind his rimless glasses, even sitting on the edge of her bed in his old blue robe. "They meant well, I suppose. Well, everybody means well, I suppose. They were religious fanatics. Warped, wicked men who thought they had to hate and destroy everything they didn't understand, everything that was different from themselves.

"They thought that witches were real and that they had made deals with the devil. It's a very old tradition in the church, the killing of witches. Probably came about as a means of suppressing the older religions In Europe."

He stopped all at once, patted Lisa's hand that still lay in the silky gray fur of her pet. "Time for cultural anthropology when you get to college, my dear," he smiled, "I'm sure your history teacher can tell you all you wish to learn about Cotton Mather and his colleagues."

He stood up and started for the door.

"Daddy," Lisa called. He stopped and turned back.

"Yes, dear?"

"Daddy, they burned witches for turning into cats and things."

He nodded soberly.

"Did they burn werewolves?"

He hesitated a moment before answering.

Lisa tensed, waiting.

"Yes, Lisa. They burned werewolves."

Lisa lay down and called her dog Lucy onto the pillow with her. She buried her face in the dog's bony shoulder, pressing so the sharp bone hurt her cheek and made her think about that little comfortable pain instead of other things. Lucy squirmed and Lisa loosened her grip but didn't let go until she fell asleep.

CHAPTER SIX

She woke up early in the morning and had breakfast with her dad before he left for Stonesboro, then walked up Psalter Street that ran in front of their house, to Centre Avenue. By the time she turned onto Centre she was full of the morning. Autumn was one of her favorite seasons in Whitbridge: the leaves were golden and yellow and red, the grass still green, and the clear, chilly air had an actual taste to it as well as a clean, strong smell.

She stopped at the corner of Blackwood Street and waited for Toni MacPherson to come up the street from her house. Lisa wanted to tell her about visiting Chris Simmons and his aunt. She didn't want to tell too much—not even to Toni, which surprised her. Toni was her best friend in the world, they told each other everything, but somehow Lisa found that she wanted to keep Aunt Stella all to herself.

Well, not quite all. She could tell Toni about meeting Stella, and how beautiful she was, and how Lisa wanted to look like that some day. That was all right.

But not about the lycanthropy. That was a secret not to be shared, not beyond the circle of herself and Chris and Aunt Stella. And maybe Dad. Lisa wondered about that. Stella hadn't asked her not to tell him, but she didn't know how much she ought to say.

She herself, and Chris and Aunt Stella were all werewolves. There, face it. And her dad wasn't. At least—she was pretty sure he wasn't. Could they share everything? Could she be closer to Stella than to her own father, who had raised her and loved her and cared for her all these years?

Toni was here now, and they walked along Centre Avenue, past Dave's opposite the gym building that Lisa's school shared with the Whitbridge elementary school she'd attended until last year. The two girls crossed Centre Avenue at the corner of Thomas Street where the two churches faced each other across the way.

Lisa and Toni crossed the schoolyard and went into the big building for their classes.

The day passed, and Friday night Toni came to Lisa's house to watch the Spook Show with Gil Ghoul as host. Toni stayed over and they talked until Lisa's dad reminded them of the late hour; then they went to bed.

At breakfast Dad said, "I'm off to HPU in a little while. You never said whether you were planning to join me or not."

Lisa looked at Toni hoping for some kind of support, but Toni said, "Jeff has to go back to college tomorrow and he's taking me for a ride today."

Lisa shrugged and said she'd go to Stonesboro.

They all piled into the black Volvo—Toni in the front seat beside Lisa's dad, Lisa and Lucy in the back. They dropped Toni off at her house on Blackwood, then headed through town on Centre Avenue toward the old turnpike. Everybody said that you could make better time to Stonesboro by heading out to 909 and heading east, the opposite direction from Parkhurst and the computer works, but Dad said he wasn't in that much of a hurry and preferred the old, narrow turnpike.

They stopped at Frayne's gas station opposite the Mountain Road turnoff. While Andy Frayne pumped gas into the car Lisa pointed up Mountain Road. "Chris's house is up there."

"Eh?" her father said. He had a leather folder in his lap, was looking through some sheets of notes. He closed the folder and turned to Lisa. "I'm sorry, what did you say?"

"That Chris Simmons lives up Mountain Road. Along with his aunt that I was telling you about. His Aunt Stella."

Lisa's dad said, "Yes," very seriously. She watched him

looking in the direction of Mountain Road although she knew it was impossible to see the house from here at Andy's.

"Dad," Lisa said, her voice quivering, "what was mother's name?" She reached into the back seat with one hand and grabbed a fistful of Lucy's fur. Lucy pushed her cold black nose up inside Lisa's quilted jacket sleeve.

Her father said, "Talbot. Your mother was a Talbot, descended from the Welsh Talbots."

"You told me before. I meant, what was her first name?"

He didn't answer for what seemed like a long time. Andy Frayne had finished pumping the gasoline into the car, and had come to stand beside the open window and collect his money for the fuel.

Lisa's dad counted his change, put his wallet back into his pocket and started up the car's engine. He pulled out into Centre Avenue, passed East Street and drove steadily until Centre Avenue swerved away to the right, dividing into an unpaved road and a narrow old blacktop highway marked Stonesboro Pike.

There was hardly any traffic on the Stonesboro Pike.

Dad turned his face partway toward Lisa so he could see her and the turnpike at the same time, and said very softly, "Your mother's name was Stella Talbot. Stella Talbot Kane if she still wishes." He turned back and faced the road.

"If she wishes," Lisa cried. "Then she isn't dead! You always said she was never found, that she might be alive. Couldn't she be Chris Simmons' Aunt Stella? She has to be! She had red hair like mine and eyes like mine and she's—she's—she said that she had lycanthropy too. Like me. And you said that my mother did. That can't all be a coincidence!"

Her father didn't answer.

"Daddy? Can it be? Tell me!"

He kept his hands on the steering wheel and his face toward the car's old-fashioned two-piece windshield. "I never saw your mother again after that vacation in the mountains. You know all about that. If Stella—if Chris's aunt is the same woman, she has her reasons for acting as she does. We must respect those reasons."

He drew a deep breath and exhaled almost with a sigh. "She must know where we are, who we are. She must have reasons for acting as she does."

"Then she is my mother," Lisa exclaimed.

A cluttered van passed them headed In the opposite direction. Lisa's dad held the wheel of the Volvo, not answering her at first. Then he said, "I haven't seen your mother in nine years, Lisa. Your friend's Aunt Stella might—might—be your mother. If she is, there must be some reason for her choosing not to reveal herself. I don't know what it is."

Now Lisa pondered for a minute, ruffling the soft, feather-like crest on top of her dog's head. Finally she asked, "Do you mind that I saw her? She told me a lot of interesting things about—werewolves. I know you're a great authority, Daddy, but Stella is—"

She paused in mid-sentence, hoping that her father would pick up the statement. When he did it was to say, "Yes, your mother is a lycanthrope. Was or is. So are you, of course, and so you tell me are the Simmons boy and his aunt."

Lisa said, "Yes."

"And I am not," Dad resumed. "That is a barrier that must separate us, do you think? For all that I study and learn and write on the subject, it still amounts to less than one experience beneath the full moon, your skin covered with a bristling coat, your senses sharpened to lupine acuteness."

Lisa shuddered. She was sitting in the front seat now, beside her father. She reached into the back seat and clutched Lucy tightly. She said, "I didn't mean to—to shut you out, Daddy. I mean—well, Toni and I were talking about it one night. She doesn't know about—about me. But we were just talking, and we thought it was a shame that we could never know what it was like to be some other kind of person, I mean—we could never know what it was like to be boys, and boys can never know what it's like to be girls. Or white people and black people. Or cave men. Or people who get to go into space. Or—you see?"

"I think I do. You're quite right, dear," He turned toward her and gave a reassuring smile before he turned back to the road. The Volvo climbed smoothly across an old drawbridge that crossed the White River. Halfway across there was a green rectangular sign that announced they were crossing the county line.

"Are we almost there?" Lisa asked.

Her father said they would reach Stonesboro in a few minutes. Then he added, "I understand what you mean about never really knowing. Yes, I will never know what your experience is. Stella surely does, and so does Chris."

He geared down and braked to avoid hitting an old horse and wagon plodding along the edge of the turnpike. Then as they pulled past the wagon Lucy saw the horse and started jumping up and down with excitement. Lisa turned around and calmed the dog, then turned back. They were at the edge of Stonesboro, a real city compared to tiny, quiet Whitbridge. The road wound through neighborhoods of big old Victorian and colonial houses, past a gloomy dock area where the river they had earlier crossed wound lazily through town, then uphill to the university campus.

"Here it is," Dad said. The previous topic had been dropped. Lisa wasn't sure whether they had accomplished anything or not, during their drive. Her father pulled the car into a reserved space beside a big stone building covered with thick growths of old ivy. "Surely you've heard of this," Lisa father said, half in question,

"Heard of it?"

"The famous halls of ivy. They really exist, you know. On scores of campuses. Wonderful old tradition." He undid his seat belt and started to open his door. "This is the Gamwell Memorial Library. I have about an hour before I'm supposed to meet old Fineman at the faculty club. You could let Lucy out of the car for a romp, then just explore if you'd like or come into the library and ask for me. Everybody here knows me, just use my name and they'll direct you."

Lisa said all right, and climbed out of her side of the car, pulling the seat-back down so Lucy could jump out. Dad was disappearing into the library already, and Lucy was running in circles, happy to be freed from her confinement in the car. Lisa looked around the quadrangle upon which the library faced. Howard Phillips University looked largely deserted—on a Saturday morning students would be in downtown Stonesboro catching up on a week's worth of errands, or home visiting their families as Jeff was back in Whitbridge with the other MacPhersons.

Tall trees dotted the grass, and as Lisa watched her dog she saw Lucy heading rapidly away from the library. She followed and found the dog lapping delightedly from a clear, running stream. Lucy's tail was waving back and forth, its letter-C curve maintained as it always was except when she was frightened or sad, and the tail drooped behind her hind legs like a limp gray rope.

Lisa went and sat on the stream-bank, watching Lucy drink, Lisa had forgot to bring along a school book as her father had suggested, but the sunlight filtered beautifully down between tree-leaves and the water made a soothing, gurgling sound as it bubbled over smooth old rocks in its bed. Lisa stretched on the grass and turned her face away from the sun's rays. She hadn't slept very well since her nightmare about the witch-burners. She closed her eyes.

Cold water was dripping on her face and she opened her eyes, startled, to look up at a shiny black nose, long gray snout and huge, liquid brown eyes. "Lucy, wow! I was sound asleep! What time is it, I have to meet Daddy!"

She jumped to her feet and sprinted back toward the black Volvo, Lucy scampering around her legs. When they got to the car Lisa opened the door and Lucy jumped in. Lisa left the window open a ways so Lucy could get air, then locked the door and pounded up the library steps, slowing to pull open the heavy metal door of the building.

She ran inside, saw a desk with somebody sitting at it—some

kind of assistant librarian or student worker, she guessed—and ran over to get help. "I'm looking for Professor Kane," she gasped, still out of breath from her run from the stream.

The librarian—a woman of around twenty, Lisa guessed—looked up, startled. Her face showed alarm. "What's the matter? Did something happen to you?"

Lisa saw her face in a display mirror near the desk. Her red hair was standing up in all directions and her face looked as if she had just rolled it in grass and dirt. "Oh!" she exclaimed. She fished around in her pockets and turned up a wrinkled handkerchief and a comb. She wiped her face as best she could and tried to pull her hair into place.

"No, I'm Professor Kane's daughter," she told the librarian. "I'm supposed to meet him here. Do you know where he is?"

"Rare books and manuscripts," the librarian said, relaxing, "Down this hall, look for a marked door."

Lisa started out of the room, found the door she'd been sent to and pushed it open.

The room was tall and hushed. Light streamed through tinted windows that ran the full distance from floor to ceiling, admitting a spray of autumn colors. The walls were covered with glass-cased book shelves, everything labeled with little index tags, and a lock conspicuous on every case.

Lisa found her father seated at a long, gleaming table, stacks of musty papers and volumes around him, his yellow note-pad in its leather cover opened before him. Seated at the huge table in the high-ceilinged room he looked almost tiny to Lisa, but he looked up and smiled when she came and stood opposite him. He looked at his watch, grunted, and began to gather his materials. Soon they were walking across the campus to the faculty club for their luncheon date with "Old If," Isaac Fineman.

The faculty club was another impressive building, not very different from the Gamwell Library except for its smaller size. Lisa's dad checked his message box as they entered the front door, then led Lisa down a corridor toward the dining room. He walked with his arm around her shoulders and Lisa felt warm and loved.

She stopped at the ladies room, then went on into the dining room where her father was sitting at a linen-covered table with glittering china and crystal and silver on it. The room was decorated with heavy curtains and old paintings on its dark, wood-paneled walls

A very tall, very thin white-haired man was sitting with Lisa's dad. He rose carefully as Lisa approached. Lisa's dad looked a bit flustered and stood up too. He said, "Isaac, this is my daughter Lisa. Then, turning, "Lisa, this is Dr. Fineman."

The old man leaned forward slightly and Lisa realized she was expected to shake hands with him. His hand was very thin, and she touched it carefully, afraid to hurt him.

"So this is the famous Miss Kane," the old man was saying. His voice sounded dry and low, yet Lisa was surprised at how easily she understood him. "A most charming young lady. I think your father has been unfair, keeping you all to himself out there in—in—"

He faltered.

"In Whitbridge?" Lisa tried to help. Then she added, "Sir?"

Old Dr. Fineman chuckled, nodded. "Will you join us?" He moved as if to hold a chair for Lisa but instead a waiter appeared and held the chair for her. She felt uncomfortable being pampered like some kind of old-time princess.

"I have heard a good deal about you," Dr. Fineman continued. "I hope that you will honor us with your presence here at Howard Phillips in a few years. Have you thought about your field of study, Miss Kane?"

Lisa blushed and shook her head.

The waiter was back, and handed each of them a menu. Lisa discovered that she didn't know what most of the dishes were and asked her father to order for her. Soon food came—delicious—and tall glasses of deep red wine for the men and a glass of milk for Lisa.

Dr. Fineman returned to his questioning, and Lisa tried to answer between mouthfuls of food. Had she considered anthropology as a field? Actually she didn't really know very much about it. Was she aware that her father was one of the most distinguished youngsters in his field? Lisa found it hard to think of him that way, but compared to Dr. Fineman she supposed he was young.

"And will you give us the pleasure of your company at the IAS this year?"

"IAS?" Lisa asked. She had no idea what IAS was—probably some kind of initials like HPU for Howard Phillips University. She waited for someone to tell her what this new term meant.

Her father supplied the information, looking and sounding slightly uncomfortable. "The IAS is the International Anthropological Society. It's a kind of trade association that we professors have. The American section of IAS is holding its annual meeting in northern California this year."

Now Lisa remembered. "Those are your business trips. When I stay over at Toni's house for a few days every fall. You never told me that it was a kind of club, Daddy!"

Dr. Fineman looked at Lisa's dad, his expression one of mild condemnation. "The child will never make an anthropologist that way, Leo. We need good minds in this field, now more than ever! If we don't come to a better understanding of man than we've had, we're going to run ourselves right off this planet, and there are no others nearby where we can live just now."

Lisa said, "I know what anthropology is, Dr. Fineman. Daddy has told me some things about it." She hoped that she hadn't got her father in hot water with his boss by showing her ignorance of their specialty!

The old man turned his face to her and smiled encouragingly. "And just what is anthropology, child?"

Lisa tried to compose her answer to sound very intelligent, very scholarly. She cleared her throat and began "Anthropology is the study of Man, that is of the human species. It is divided into two major divisions, physical and cultural." She stopped for breath and hoped that she wasn't turning red. At once her face began to feel hot, as it did whenever she blushed.

"That's very good!" Dr. Fineman exclaimed.

Lisa looked at her father out of the corner of her eye. He appeared very pleased and proud of her—and more than a little bit relieved.

"That's more than some of our entering freshmen know, Miss Kane. Leo, I congratulate you. Now, Lisa, you said that anthropology falls into physical and cultural divisions. Do you know the difference between them?"

Lisa wracked her brain. How many nights had her dad droned on about his field of study while Lisa listened or dozed in the big easy chair near his desk? It all had to be somewhere inside her head, if only she could dredge it up!

"Ah, physical anthropology," she said, "is the study of relics and artifacts. Mostly old bones, skulls and things. From this we learn about the development of the human organism." Did she have it right? She must have heard this a hundred times—now it had to come back to her!

Professor Fineman was nodding and grinning widely. She must be doing all right!

"And cultural anthropology," Lisa continued, "is the study of human customs and societies. From this we learn about the nature and development of...of...human customs and societies," she finished with a rush. Was that all right? she wondered.

"A trifle circular," Professor Fineman was saying, still with a smile for her. "But actually not bad. Not bad at all. Leo, I think your young lady is going to be an ornament to the profession, should she choose to follow it."

He turned back toward Lisa. "Very good, young lady, very good. But now, back to my original inquiry, Miss Kane. Don't tell me that your father hasn't even invited you along!"

Lisa looked helplessly from Dr. Fineman to her father and back. She didn't know what to say. Was she going to get her dad into trouble by giving a wrong answer to the old professor?

Her father saved her from answering by taking over. "I haven't invited the child—hadn't, I should say, Isaac. After all, she's only twelve. But as a matter of fact—"

"As a matter of fact," Dr. Fineman said, "there are going to be some excellent papers this year. You've seen the advance program Leo. Stewart is going to be there from New Mexico. And Raphael from Oklahoma—the southwest will be well represented! And none other than Anthony Holmes White himself is going to give a paper. That will be something to hear!"

"A lot of dry academics," Lisa's dad protested. But she could tell that he was getting ready to go along with Dr. Fineman's wishes.

"I'll admit that Stewart gets a little dry sometimes," the old man said in his near-whisper of a voice. "But he does good, solid work. And as for the others—" he reached with a pale, bony finger and tapped Lisa's dad on the wrist "—you know they're spellbinders, Leo! Why, you'd think that Raphael was there to save all our souls from eternal hell-fires, the way he orates! And Anthony Holmes White, ah—" Lisa noticed that Dr. Fineman used that full name each time he mentioned the person, and smiled as if it conjured happy memories "—you know, it would be worthwhile to hear Anthony Holmes White buy a loaf of bread at the grocery store. What a mind! What a wit!"

The old man smiled broadly. "Leo, you can't deny the experience to this child."

Lisa's dad held his hands out over the pure white tablecloth— and she was grateful that she hadn't spilled anything on it—as if he were surrendering to Dr. Fineman. "Lisa dear," he addressed himself to her, "how would you like to attend the IAS conference with me?"

"In California?" Lisa exclaimed. She'd never been farther west than a trip to Philadelphia her dad had taken her on. "With the palm trees and surfers and movie stars?"

"Not quite. The conference will be at Berkeley, in northern California. They have rather a chilly climate, and it can be damp as well this time of year."

"I don't care!" Lisa exclaimed. "When is it?"

Her father reeled off the dates.

"But that includes the Harvest Moon Ball," Lisa said softly, feeling disappointed. He had said that she couldn't go to the dance, but there was always the chance he'd change his mind. But if she was thousands of miles away from Whitbridge there would be no question of attending.

"That cannot be helped," her father said rather sternly.

Dr. Fineman smiled his great-grandfatherly smile and reached his long, pale hand across the table to touch Lisa's wrist. She marveled again at the lightness of his hand—like a paper-thin model rather than a person. He said, "An unusual opportunity, Miss Kane, I wouldn't pass it up if I were you."

Somehow Lisa felt that the old man could be trusted but still she asked, "Isn't it awfully expensive? I mean, we'd have to buy airplane tickets all the way to California and—"

"Not to worry, my child. There will be a charter flight sponsored by the society. Howard Phillips has a block of seats being held, there's plenty of room. And a youngster like you should find this conference fascinating. There will be an unusual colloquium—you know what that is?—an exchange of views and information, on the topic of lycanthropic traditions in divergent cultures. Fascinating, utterly absorbing!"

He chuckled happily, looking forward to the meeting.

For an instant Lisa stiffened inwardly. She exchanged a look with her father, trying to gather her courage to ask for something very important that he would almost certainly refuse her. But there was nothing to do for it but try, she decided.

"Is there really plenty of room on the plane?" she asked.

"Well, I would not care to invite the entire University marching band along," Dr. Fineman chuckled, "but within limits, yes. Don't worry about crowding someone else off, child, there's room."

"I wasn't thinking about that," Lisa told him. "I just wondered if I could invite a friend from school to go along. I mean, if there's room anyway, it wouldn't do any harm. Could I do that?"

"Antonia?" Lisa's dad exclaimed in surprise.

Lisa felt herself reddening once again. She lowered her eyes to her plate and pushed her food around a little with her fork. The meal was nearly over and she was eating a little piece of delicate, sweet cake for dessert.

"Toni is nice but I wanted to invite Chris," she mumbled into her dessert. She was sorry she'd said anything, sorry she had come to Stonesboro at all today. She could be at home in Whitbridge sitting in Dave's talking to her friends, or maybe Toni's brother Jeff would have given them a ride in his car.

She waited for her father to say something, but the silence grew longer and more upsetting with every second. Finally Dr. Fineman said, "I don't see why the young lady shouldn't have a companion of her own age, Leo. And there's space enough."

Her dad coughed and sipped at a cup of coffee that the waiter had brought him. "I'm not so sure it's a good idea to invited this particular friend of Lisa's. He's a nice enough lad, but—" He let the sentence stop there.

Lisa saw Dr. Fineman's white eyebrows rise and his old, pink face wrinkle in a grin.

"Ah, Leo, Leo," he tapped Lisa's dad on the wrist with that long, bony finger, "in this day and age. Surely an entire ISA conference can provide enough chaperones for two young people. What an enlightened era we have the pleasure to live in."

For the first time in Lisa's recollection she saw her father blush. She'd always thought that the embarrassed coloration had come with her ruddiness, from her mother, but now she saw that he too could suffer from it. "We'll have to see," he said, dividing his words equally between Lisa and Professor Fineman.

The conversation turned to university topics and Lisa had little more to say. When they finished Professor Fineman shook Lisa's hand again, beaming, and said that he hoped to see her again soon, perhaps during the flight to the conference.

She left the faculty club with her father. He had a little more work to do in the library so Lisa let her dog out of the car again and they ran to the stream where Lucy drank some more water. Together they walked up and down the edge of the flowing brook, then Lucy plunged excitedly into the stream.

Lisa barely caught a glimpse of a huge frog sitting on a smooth rock, sunning itself and waiting for a fly to buzz past and provide a tasty snack. Instead a skinny gray creature yelping and bounding had launched herself toward the poor frog, and the frog wasted no time in springing from its rock into the deepest water around and disappearing.

Lucy thrashed around, jumping from rock to shallow stream bed, finally giving up on her pursuit of the frog. She struggled back out of the stream and onto the grassy bank and stood, shaking herself so that water sprayed in all directions.

"You look like a lawn-sprinkler gone wild," Lisa told her. "You'd better run around and dry off some before we start for home or Dad will be angry." Lucy looked up with her brown eyes as if she understood everything that Lisa was saying to her, and Lisa looked back and thought to herself, I wonder what will happen when I change some time, change completely into a wolf. Will you still know me, Lucy? Will we still be friends?

Or will I feel some terrible urge to kill and tear? I could never hurt my own dog, could I? Or would my mind change, too, when my body does?

She shoved her hands into the pockets of her quilted jacket and wandered up and down the stream bank, under the trees that had stood at Howard Phillips University for a hundred years or more, wondering what lay ahead for her.

She had come here today hoping to work things out with her father. Somehow she felt that she had failed. She just hadn't known what to tell him, or what to ask him either. The whole thing about not being able to understand—would that keep the two of them from ever really talking to each other about Lisa's troubles?

Maybe she could try again, she thought, on the way home in the car or afterwards, tomorrow. Sunday was always a quiet day at their house. Maybe they could sit down together and Lisa could talk to her father about the things that really mattered to her, and he would really hear her, not just grunt and nod and wander off into his books and his notepad. And then, if that happened, he might tell her something that would make everything all right.

Like what?

Lisa had no idea. Only—only her life was getting to be such a tangled, confusing mess. For as long as she could remember, her dad had always been able to take care of things for her, but that just didn't seem to be true any more.

She saw Lucy bound from behind a tree twenty or thirty yards ahead. Lisa called her and the afghan ran back, jumped and threw her paws around Lisa's shoulders, wanting a hug and a romp. Lisa scratched the dog all along her skinny neck and watched Lucy run away again, emerging from the trees in front of a low, tan-stone building.

There was music coming from the building—Lisa recognized Big Stew and the Studebakers' monster hit. She told Lucy to stay outside and clambered down the stairs that led into the building. It was a student restaurant and sundries shop. Lisa saw a snack bar, a few tables and a juke box. There were a few people around, students who had nothing better to do. A cluster of them were leaning over the juke box, a few others danced.

A couple of boys looked up at Lisa as she crossed the room and she started to smile but they looked back when they saw how young she was. Well, junior high wasn't that far from college! A few years from now they'd be fighting for her attention!

She stopped in front of a magazine rack and looked at the colorful covers. She realized that she was starting to feel better now—werewolf or not, she would have her friends and she would make her life. If her father or Aunt Stella or Professor Fineman or anybody else could help, that was fine. But if they couldn't she'd just have to do it herself. And she would!

She looked at the magazines. There were a lot of them there about politics and world problems that didn't interest her much, and some about music or clothes that did. She started to reach for one with a picture of a singing star on the cover and then saw a whole row of comic books behind the magazines. Comic books in a college store!

Everybody in Whitbrldge always said that comics were for little kids; by the time you got to sixth or seventh grade you should have outgrown them. And here were—there must be thirty different ones—comics where college students must be the ones who read them! She looked at the titles, most of them were about super-duper people with all sorts of magical powers to them.

She ran her eye past Captain Cosmos, The Mystic Eight, The Avenging Nereid—she wondered what a Nereid was—and then came to the horror comics. There, right in the middle, was one with a picture of a horrible werewolf standing over a bleeding victim, surrounded by enemies who held forward weapons and religious symbols to keep the werewolf at bay.

Lisa stuck her tongue out at the comic and went back to the snack bar. She drank an ice cream soda and listened to records till she began to feel restless again, then went and called Lucy once more. She put Lucy in the car, met her father in the Gamwell Library, and waited while he bundled up his papers and checked in her pass to the rare books and manuscripts room,

The short autumn day was over and the night sky was dotted with stars as they started back along the Stonesboro Pike to Whitbridge. Halfway home Dad pulled the car into the parking lot of an old roadhouse overlooking the White River that was indirectly responsible for Whitbridge's name. He invited Lisa to have dinner in the roadhouse, and then they'd go on the rest of the way.

Inside Lisa sat yawning and rubbing her eyes before the food came. "A long day," her father commented. "I hope you're not sorry you came along, dear,"

Lisa tried to perk up a little and answer. It was such an effort to stay awake and speak! "I hope I didn't get you in trouble with—with Dr. Fineman," she managed to get out.

Her father looked surprised. "In trouble? Isaac was absolutely charmed, Lisa. I've never seen him take to anyone like that in all the years I've known him. Whatever made you think there was anything wrong?"

"Oh—only about that conference, that trip. And wanting to invite Chris Simmons instead of Toni. I'm sorry, Dad. Toni's always been my best friend."

"Yes. That's why I should have thought..." He reached across the table and put his hand on hers. "You're so tired, maybe you'd rather not discuss it now."

"No," Lisa struggled. She took a sip of cold water and found that it woke her up a little. "I know Toni is my friend but Chris is—is the same thing I am. And Toni isn't."

"And that makes the whole difference," her father said. He seemed to be thinking very seriously about it. "That's so very important to you. I really should have understood that." He shook his head slowly. "I really should have.

"All right, Lisa. I suppose you and Fineman win, you were really right. You can ask Chris to come along, rather than Toni. I know that it will work out somehow."

But Lisa was so sleepy she could hardly hear anything her father said. She didn't even know whether she ate her dinner or not, or anything about the rest of the drive back to Whitbridge. The next thing she knew it was Sunday morning, and she was in her own bed. The day was bright, there was a wonderful smell of food coming up the stairs, and she jumped out of bed and pulled on her woolen slippers to run down to the kitchen.

Her father was standing by the stove with a big smile on his face, "Ready for a hearty breakfast?" he asked.

Lisa stood still, "I didn't know you knew how to cook, Daddy!"

He pointed a spatula at her. "Now young lady, I realize that you are a very old twelve and you've been keeping house for me for as long as you can recall."

She nodded, waiting for what he would say next.

"But I want you to think back a few years, Lisa. Just who exactly taught you how to cook a meal, or do all the other things you do so well?"

She hadn't thought about that for a long time. "I—uh—why,

you did!" She found herself giggling,

"That's right!" her father agreed. "And I'm afraid I've been getting too lazy and turning into a complete, stodgy old professor of late. Well, I'm going to turn over a new leaf, and the first line on it says: get the breakfast every other day. Is that fair?"

"It's perfect!" Lisa gave him a big kiss on the cheek and sat down to a platter of beautiful eggs (well, a couple of them were broken) and lovely toast (well, it was only a little burned).

CHAPTER SEVEN

It wasn't Lisa's first time on an airplane—at least her father insisted that she'd flown a number of times when she was a baby—but it was the first that she could remember. The ride from Whitbridge to Stonesboro had been a repeat of the earlier one, when Dad had spent Saturday at the Gamwell Library and Lisa had had lunch at the faculty club with him and Dr. Fineman.

This time they'd climbed in the Volvo and driven as far as Toni MacPherson's house on Blackwell Street while Lisa delivered her dog to Toni. One gray afghan and enough cans of food to last her while Lisa was gone across the country. Lisa and Toni had exchanged hugs and giggles and Lisa promised for the four zillionth time to remember everything about California and tell Toni each tiny detail as well as bringing her a souvenir.

Even Lisa's dad had got out of the car and walked to Toni's house. He shook hands with Mr. MacPherson, asked if he was sure Lucy wouldn't be too much trouble, and thanked both of Toni's parents for letting her take the dog.

Then they drove to pick up Chris Simmons at the old house on Mountain Road, beyond the abandoned mill. Getting everything worked out for Chris to come on the trip had been the hardest part of it. Lisa had not met any problems getting permission from her school. Even Mrs. Harkins agreed that the trip was a good idea.

Attending a real academic conference, Mrs. Harkins had put it, was an enhancement to Lisa's education, not an interruption.

Of course, she would be expected to write a report on what she had learned, as soon as she got back. The editor of the school paper—a senior Lisa had never even met—said that she'd like to see an article about the trip too. With more attention paid to the local color and less to the big-dome professors, of course.

But getting it worked out for Chris Simmons to come, that was a different story.

First, Lisa's dad wrote a letter to Chris's Aunt Stella.

No, he wouldn't go to see her and he wouldn't telephone her, it had to be a note. He wrote it and gave it to Lisa and she handed it to Chris to give to his aunt. Of course Lisa told him what it was all about, and Chris wanted to go right then, more than anything else in the world.

Billy Cantor could handle the paper route while Chris was in California. Billy could have the paper route if he wanted it!

But what would Aunt Stella say?

The same night there was a phone call after dinner and Lisa's dad happened to pick up the telephone. He listened for a minute, then he said something into the receiver about waiting, then he asked Lisa if she would go in the other room until he called her.

Dad had never done that!

Lisa knew it was discourteous to listen in on other people's telephone conversations, and she always went away when Dad was on the phone. Sometimes he even motioned for her to stay, but she'd long since learned that the conversations were totally boring: things about committee meetings and budget problems and journal deadlines and library reports.

But this time he wanted her out of the room while he spoke!

Okay, Lisa went out of the room. She picked up a stiff wire brush and cleaned some burrs out of Lucy's coat—there was always work to be done on an afghan's coat, and Lucy just sank down and sighed with pleasure when Lisa worked on hers.

By the time she had worked up Lucy's legs, the gray fur standing up burr-less and as fluffy as the so-called "feathers" on a cocker spaniel, she detected her father sitting near-by, watching her. He'd finished with his telephone call and come out of his study, into the high-ceilinged living room where Lisa had brought her dog to groom her.

He looked odd to Lisa—very serious, yet at the same time also very happy, and yet again, very concerned.

Lisa looked up at him, not knowing what to say.

Her father spoke first. "That was—" he paused "—Chris Simmons' Aunt Stella."

Lisa shooed the dog away from her and began cleaning accumulated fluff and burrs out of the brush.

"Ah, we were discussing the anthropology conference," dad resumed. "You know, I'd sent Stella a note asking if it would be all right for Christopher to attend."

Lisa merely nodded. She had the feeling that her father didn't really want a dialog with her, not right now. He wanted to tell her the things he had to tell her, and she was more than willing to listen she was relieved to be able, merely, to listen and nod and absorb the things he was saying.

"Ah, Stella is—is a remarkable woman." He sat hunched forward toward Lisa, his shirt sleeved elbows on his knees. He removed his glasses carefully with one hand and rubbed his forehead and eyes with the other, the way Lisa had seen him do so many times when he was either tired or worried or nervous.

He put his glasses back on and sat up straight. "Ah—what I want to tell you, dear, is that Stella says it's all right for Chris to attend the conference. He'll travel with us, we can pick him up on the way to Howard Phillips and then we can all ride on."

He smiled at Lisa. "I thought you would be pleased."

She jumped up from the rug where she'd knelt to groom Lucy to the couch where her father sat, and threw her arms around him, "Oh, Daddy, thank you! Thank you for letting him come along!"

"Well, don't thank me entirely," he said. "Thank yourself and Isaac Fineman. And Stella. And Stella," he repeated, then drew another breath. "And thank Chris himself. Everyone seems to agree that he's a fine, responsible boy or we wouldn't have been able to take him anyway. As it is, I'm sure he'll be all right."

He pulled a stub of a pencil from his shirt pocket, and a scrap of battered cardboard, and began making marks. "Ah—we'd better begin to pack, don't you think? It's just a few days. We'll be leaving Thursday afternoon and the conference runs through Monday. Have you thought about taking things to wear?"

Lisa laughed out loud. "I've packed five times already. First I packed my swimsuits and shorts and all my summer things, then Toni came over and we put that all away and I packed all my fancy clothes, then—" She stopped as she saw her father's smile.

"What did you finally decide?" he asked. Lisa had been picking her own clothes, with only an occasional word of advice, for years. For a while, she remembered, the results had sometimes been very strange: polka-dot shirts with striped jackets and plaid skirts. But after a while she'd learned what went with what, and now a lot of girls at school came to her for advice about things to wear.

"My best jeans and my good work shirt," she said, "and my heavy sweater and my quilted jacket, and my corduroys and my plain jeans. And my red shirt and my Magniffy Kat shirt. And hiking boots and a lot of socks."

Her dad nodded. "That sounds like enough for five days. Eh—what kind of shirt did you say you were taking? The last one."

"Oh," Lisa said, "Magniffy Kat."

"I thought you said that. Since when are you interested in Bach? Or have I missed something?"

"Magniffy Kat is a comic book. All the kids read it. I don't read many comics but I adore that one. It's all about this beautiful cat, you see, who's a big rock star, something like Big Stew and the Studebakers only Magniffy's just a comic. And when she hits this magical D minor chord there's a great burst of music and she changes—

"Yes, yes, enough, thank you." Her father was laughing.

"Don't you think I should take that shirt?"

"No," he chuckled, "it's quite all right, really. I just—you see, thirty years ago I used to read the same kind of, ah, well let's just say the same kind of thing. We didn't have your Magniffy Kat then—actually, that's quite ingenious, you know—but we had others just as far-fetched.

"My parents had fits, said I'd never learn to read if I just stuck my nose in cartoon books, they worried so. And at school—I must have had scores of the things taken away from me for reading them when I was supposed to be doing geometry or physics. I suppose my teachers were right, I never did learn very much geometry or physics.

"But I got through school somehow, and here I am. No, I'm sure that comics won't do you any harm at all, none at all. And I'm sure that when the time comes you'll outgrow them too."

He stood up, and Lisa stood with him. They were almost the same size.

"Come, let's bundle up and take your Miss Lucy for her goodnight walk." Dad put his arm around Lisa's shoulders and squeezed.

She put on a scarf and jacket and woolen hat while he climbed into his own warm clothing, then Lisa called her dog and they went down the front steps of the old house, pulling the cut-glass front door shut behind them.

It was a chilling night. Their breath stood in white streamers before their faces. The sky was utterly black, the stars and planets gleaming brilliantly in their places. The moon was nearing full and shone brightly enough to light their walk as if it had been daylight.

Lisa looked up at the moon and felt an odd stirring inside her. Her heart seemed to beat more rapidly, her blood to surge and race in her veins. There was a warm, tight feeling in her chest despite the cold night.

Something struck her leg and she looked down to see Lucy poking at her blue jeans with her long thin nose. "Oh, you want me to throw something, baby?" Lisa searched the ground, turned up a dry stick and threw it into the trees for Lucy. The dog disappeared after it and Lisa walked on down Psalter Street with her dad.

At the corner they turned into Farnsworth, headed over toward Blackwell Street.

Lisa's dad said, "You were gazing at the moon for quite a while there, before Lucy came and distracted you."

Lisa nodded. "Mm," she said.

Dad laughed. "You're picking up all my bad habits. Grunting instead of answering."

"Oh." Lisa looked back the way they'd come. A slim gray shape zoomed out from between two maples and leaped high into the air as it shot past them. Lisa reached out and grabbed the stick from Lucy's panting mouth, then threw it on past the dog who bolted on along the moonlit roadway. "I just was watching it," Lisa finally answered her father. "I think it's very beautiful. I think if I ever have a little girl I'll name her Diana, after the moon."

Now it was Dad's turn to say "Mm, mm." Lisa giggled at him and he stopped, shrugged, said, "Oh, ah, I think that's fine, ah, that you can appreciate nature that way. We overlooked the beauties of nature for too long. Now we seem to be regaining our appreciation." They went on a little farther, then he said, "It wasn't anything to worry you, I hope. I mean, about the moon and that other matter, you know. Lycanthropy."

Lisa said, "I want to learn about it. That's why I'm going to California. Uh—I mean, I'm glad you asked me along, I know I'll have a lot of fun out there. But—"

"But you want to understand yourself. No, nothing wrong with that in the least. Lisa, dear—" He stopped walking and faced her, took her two warmly-mittened hands in his own "—if anything can be done to help you, to cure you of this—afflic- tion—then we must do it. And meanwhile, I'll do everything I can to help you, to keep your secret so you can live like other children, other young people.

"I want to help your friend Chris, also. And as for Chris's Aunt Stella, why—"

"Yes?" Lisa prompted.

"Well," he sighed, "she has to make her own decisions."

They finished their walk and went on home. Lisa's dad kissed her good-night and went off to his study to do some more work before bed. Lisa and Lucy went upstairs and climbed into bed. Lisa ran her hands over Lucy's coat and muttered "Oh, Lucy, you're all full of burrs again. Now I'll have to brush you out again."

But not now.

Now she lay back with her head on her pillow, her hands clasped under her neck, gazing up at the ceiling and wondering who else had ever slept in this room, gazed at the same ceiling and wondered what their lives held in store for them.

It was an old house.

The moon was high now, and although Lisa couldn't see it directly from her bed its rays came through the window and lighted her room so she could see her furniture and belongings, her quilt and the skinny dog sleeping at the bottom of the bed. She thought about her trip to California, the things she would see and the things she would learn about herself.

Somehow the conversation she'd had with her father kept rising in her mind. Not the part about Magniffy Kat, that was just fun. But the part during their walk, when he'd said that he wanted to help her. He would help her find a cure if he could, for lycanthropy. So she wouldn't have to live with it throughout her life, like the poor wolfman in the old movies, hating himself and searching out help from scientists and gypsy witches and never really finding it.

Maybe there was a cure. Or—maybe there needn't be one. If a werewolf did no harm, why should it be so horrible to be one? Did a werewolf have to be a brutal, murdering beast? Weren't wolves part of nature's plan? That was part of her dad's conversation, too—that for too long we hadn't appreciated nature, and now we were beginning to do so again.

She turned over and buried her face in her pillow. Lucy kicked and complained at the disturbance. Lisa closed her eyes and dreamed about running. The ground was steep and covered with snow that glittered like diamonds in the moonlight. She trotted along with her sensitive nostrils attuned to the breeze, picking up every scent and every hint of life—a partridge had nested nearby and flown, a rabbit had crouched and trembled and bolted to its warm nest deep in the earth.

She felt each icy intake of air filling her deep, strong lungs to their limit, each breath delivering a hundred subtle messages about her surroundings. Her sharp, gleaming eyes picked out her companions from among the trees and the drifted snow, gray forms mostly but touched with black, with reddish-brown, even with a patch of pure white that blended into the white drifts.

The pack stopped at the crest of a hill. Below them the slope was too steep and its snowy mantle too rocky to sustain trees.

The view was clear. Below them stood a few houses, old and comfortable looking. Lights gleamed yellow and orange from their windows. Smoke rose from chimneys. The scents that wafted from them were incredibly varied, with the odors of men mixing with those of horses and dogs, wood smoke and cooking odors, cloth and metals and something else, something pungent and strange that made Lisa's nostrils quiver and her lips curl away from strong, curving teeth.

The dream faded into blackness. In the morning she could remember it only vaguely. Something she had dreamed, something she remembered had been vivid at the time, sharply outlined and almost painfully strong to the senses, but now vague and faint and fading.

CHAPTER EIGHT

She rose and dressed, made breakfast for Dad and herself and Lucy, and went off to school meeting Toni on the way and chattering and giggling all the way up Centre Avenue, and fidgeting and squirming through all her classes as she waited and waited and waited for the end of the school day to come.

Then home. Dad was already there. Oh, that was a relief! If he'd been in Stonesboro or anywhere else she would have burst, but he was sitting at his desk, shuffling final papers in and out of his brief case. They loaded their valises into the Volvo and dropped Lucy off at Toni's house, and drove out to pick up Chris Simmons.

Leo waited in the car. Lisa opened the stiff, rusted gate and walked to the house. She went inside and Chris was ready. He and Lisa smiled at each other—they were both wearing heavy quilted jackets of a dull orange color and faded jeans and low hiking boots.

Aunt Stella was standing in the parlor, well back from the front window, looking out. She looked beautiful to Lisa. She came across the carpet and embraced Lisa and told her to have a lovely time on the trip. Lisa promised to tell her about it when they got back, and Stella embraced her and kissed on the cheek, and Lisa and Chris ran out of the house and jumped into the car and they were off with Lisa's dad driving to Stonesboro.

A group of professors and their families and some graduate students from Howard Phillips University all met at the Gamwell Library parking lot in Stonesboro. They rode by bus all the way down to the big airport, and climbed onto the jet. Lisa got to sit by the window. Chris had the seat beside her. Leo Kane sat with Isaac Fineman talking intently and taking manila folders from his brief case, turning pages of typewritten papers and pointing to things, murmuring and gesturing with the old man.

The plane rose into the air and Lisa watched the ground disappear from beneath them. They climbed and climbed until they drove upward right through a thick layer of clouds. Up above the clouds Lisa clutched Chris's shoulder and pointed out the window.

It was full night, a night that had been gray and misty on the ground but that here, above the clouds, was bright. The moon was high and within a day or two of being full. Once more Lisa's eyes were drawn to it and her body felt strange, warm and almost flowing. But she made herself look away from the moon, first to some stars, then down at the clouds beneath the plane's wings.

The jet engines gave off a ghostly glowing exhaust like cold flame, and the cloud layer rippled and billowed like a living landscape of heaving, fluffy white dunes. Lisa felt Chris's face close to hers as he leaned over to see the sight she had called his attention to. He was warm and Lisa didn't move away.

After a few minutes a stewardess came by with sandwiches and hot drinks—Lisa and Chris both had hot chocolate—and they settled back in their seats to eat. After they'd finished the stewardess took away the trays and empty cups and papers, and Lisa watched the sight outside the plane for a while, then felt herself growing drowsy. She slid down in her seat and fell asleep.

When she opened her eyes she found that she was leaning on Chris's shoulder and sat up quickly, embarrassed. He didn't say anything about it so she didn't either.

The plane landed and the pilot announced that the local time was nine o'clock. Chris said that it was really midnight for them, they'd saved three hours by crossing time zones and would have to pay them back on the flight home. Lisa felt drowsy and only half aware of what was going on as they climbed onto another charter bus that took them from the Oakland Airport to a hotel. She climbed straight into bed and her dad tucked her in and went to talk about anthropology and Lisa fell asleep at once.

The next day there was a sight-seeing bus tour in the morning, then lunch, then the opening session of the conference. Lisa's dad suggested that she and Chris might want to attend some of the sessions. If they were bored, he said, they could leave and walk around the town, but be careful. The meeting was in Berkeley, at the University of California. There was a big art museum at the university, and a special anthropology museum, and the town itself was colorful and could be exciting.

Lisa and Chris both said that, Yes, they'd heard of Berkeley.

Then they should also know, Leo added, that the same free atmosphere that drew so many colorful people also attracted some odd and even dangerous ones. They must promise to be careful, not go off with strangers, not accept any kind of pills or other things that people offered them.

Lisa said she understood, they'd be careful, if they ran into any problems they would call the conference at the university and ask for Leo.

Chris added that his Aunt Stella had given him the same kind of warning before they'd ever left Whitbridge.

Leo said that was good, he trusted them both, they were responsible young people, but just be careful, please.

They were already at the university campus and had to walk across a wide plaza to reach the conference hall. What seemed to Lisa like thousands of students were walking around the campus, going from class to class carrying books, chatting with each other, stopping at dozens of food stands to buy things that Lisa had never imagined even existed.

In the middle of the plaza they passed a group of a dozen or so people wearing pale orange robes, jumping up and down and chanting. Some of them had pairs of little cymbals they played in time with the chanting, or roughly in time with it. Somebody had a set of little drums and was playing them too.

Lisa stopped and stared. The people in the robes all had bald heads—no, she realized, not bald, shaven. All except for a little knot of hair that they left growing from the back of their scalps. All of the hundreds of other people around the chanters were ignoring them except for a few who stood and watched or listened to the music for a little while, then went on their ways.

"An interesting group," Lisa's dad told her and Chris. "One of the Eastern religious movements that have been taken up by young people here. They offer answers that our Western society seems not too." He moved away from them, Lisa and Chris following close behind. Lisa looked at Chris. He shrugged. They both stayed with Leo.

On the steps of the conference hall were more knots of people. Three or four seemed to be making speeches all at once. Idle listeners—Lisa guessed they were students on break periods between classes—seemed to drift from one speaker to another, listen for a short time, then shake their heads and go to another speaker or leave altogether. People came and went constantly, but the size of the crowd didn't change.

A couple of the speech-makers were shouting about revolution and destroying the state and replacing it with a perfect society. Lisa and her dad and Chris stopped again and Lisa listened. The two speakers seemed to be saying almost exactly the same thing, yet they frequently exchanged angry glances and gestures at each other.

Another man was waving his arms and shouting at a small group of listeners. Lisa's dad stopped, along with Lisa and Chris, to listen for a few minutes. It was hard to follow the man's shouts but every so often a sentence or two would pop out of the gabble. The man held a slim book in one hand and was waving it, slapping it into the palm of his other hand. He was tall and wore dark-framed glasses, and his hair kept slipping down onto his forehead so he had to interrupt himself to shove it back.

Lisa realized why her father had stopped here to listen: the man was talking about the anthropologists' meeting. He objected to their being at the university but he seemed to want to do more than chase them away.

"...Book warns us about them," he roared at a handful of bored-looking listeners. "Idolaters and witches, magicians and familiar spirits, listen to Samuel," he ranted, "'Behold, there is a woman that hath a familiar spirit, yea, these very people who come here today, they must be destroyed, they shall be smitten!' Leviticus tells us as clear as day, 'Seek not after wizards! These wicked ones pretend to be learned people but they are the wicked! They shall burn! They shall burn!'"

As the shouting man turned his wild-looking, crazed eyes from listener to listener, Leo started to tug Lisa and Chris away but Lisa pulled back at his hand. She wanted to hear more of what the man was shouting.

"Even in Acts we read that Simon Magus used sorcery, yea, he used sorcery and he bewitched the people of Samaria, and he gave it out that he was a great one, yea, a great one, just as these so-called scholars would call themselves great ones, but what are we told? What are we told?" He held his book up in one hand, raised the other into the air, glared triumphantly at the few people paying attention to him.

"You all know it, you all know it," he gloated. "The Book tells us, and these so-called great ones who talk about folklore and lycanthropy, they mean werewolfery, that's what they mean, they're afraid to call it by its right name! Werewolfery and warlockery and witchcraft is what it is! Witchcraft and deals with the enemy, and the book tells us what we shall do with those who deal with the enemy! Burn them! Crush them! 'Thou shalt not suffer a witch to live,' may...."

And the man babbled on, but this time when Leo pulled Chris and Lisa away they went with him, and inside the conference hall they all stopped, and Leo drew them aside.

He looked very serious, and very unhappy. "Children, I'm sorry that happened," he said. "But maybe it was for the best. Inside here, in this hall, in this conference, we hear the voice of reason, the finer voice of the human spirit. But that one—" he gestured back toward the door, back toward the tall, glaring, arm-waving shouter "—there is what you have to contend with outside. You have to learn to hide from his kind, because they really mean it. Everything they say. They want to kill you."

Lisa and Chris exchanged a look. They nodded to Leo Kane and then the three of them went on, stopped at the registration desk and picked up badges to show that they were part of the conference, and into the afternoon session in the big air-conditioned meeting hall.

Leo made his way toward the front of the room to sit in the reserved section where the speakers and officers of the association sat. Lisa and Chris found a couple of comfortable seats together near the back of the room. They watched the opening ceremonies, heard the first speaker of the afternoon introduced. He was a jolly looking man with a squarish face and a fringe of dark hair going to gray. The chairman introduced him as Professor Anthony Holmes White and his topic was "The Magical Tradition in Lycanthropic Lore."

Lisa and Chris were looking around at the rest of the audience.

There must have been a couple of hundred people in the room, mostly professors from the looks of them with a heavy scattering of college students in their twenties. But there seemed to be a few kids near their own age. Wherever they picked up a glance from somebody who looked anywhere between ten and fifteen years old they'd exchange grins and waves and some sort of vague, wordless agreement would pass among them. Maybe they could all get together outside the hall later on, and have some fun together, away from the dull speeches.

Professor White was talking now about some old paper he'd written years before. "...former colleague at the University of California whom I disguised ingenuously under the name of Wolfe Wolf, since deceased. In my monograph I made reference to the use of a magical word for transformations between the anthropoid and lupine configurations. Learned colleagues will recall that the cantrip invoked was Absarka. Of course rejecting the intervention of supernatural entities we still entertain the notion of such charms as psychological triggers for the invocation of psychogenerated physiological manifestations of the order...."

Lisa felt Chris leaning over and heard him whisper in her ear "I don't know what this professor is talking about. What's a psychogenerated physiological whatchamacallit?"

Lisa giggled and a stern-looking woman sitting in front of her turned around and frowned at her and Chris. Lisa put her two hands around Chris's ear and whispered back. "I don't know exactly either. In fact I don't know at all. But don't you think he's cute?"

Chris looked up at Professor White and then turned back to Lisa and whispered loudly, "No, I don't!"

The woman in front of them turned around and glared at them so Lisa and Chris got up and left the room quietly. They went for a walk outside. They couldn't tell whether all the people making speeches in the plaza were the same ones or not. The man who had been shouting about killing witches and werewolves was still there and seemed to be making the identical speech.

"Maybe he's like a permanent exhibit," Chris said to Lisa. "You know, he stays there all the time hollering the same guff and people just come up and listen till they're bored and go away, then other people come."

They went over to the food stands at the curb and studied all the things there were to eat. Lisa looked in her pockets and found a little money. Chris had some too, so they bought snacks.

Chris had something called an organic chow mein falafel sandwich with a drink called a strawberry-avocado smoothie. Lisa bought herself a pizza-pretzel eggplant sandwich.

"I don't see why we can't get good stuff like this in Whitbridge," Chris complained.

Lisa took a big chew of her sandwich and borrowed a swallow of Chris's drink to help her get it down. "Maybe Daddy would give us both a ride over to Howard Phillips University some time. I think they have a little stuff like this. College kids get to eat all the really great food."

They walked around the university campus for a while. There were dozens of dogs wandering around, and people with puppies and kittens to give away, sitting in the afternoon sunlight holding the animals in big cardboard boxes. Lisa petted a puppy for a few minutes and talked to the older girl giving it away.

"Yeah, my dog had these pups and I can't keep them," the girl told her. "I wish I could, they're so pretty."

The puppy was gray and fluffy. It reminded Lisa of her dog at home except that it was fat and Lucy was skinny, but the pup had big dark eyes that made Lisa want to take it with her. "I think we'd better go before I can't leave at all," Lisa said. She took Chris by the hand and started away from the girl.

"Yeah, well have a nice life anyhow," the girl said.

After a while they wandered back into the conference hall and found a different pair of seats, away from the woman who had glared at their whispering. Somebody else was making a speech now.

Chris scurried away, then came back a few seconds later with a printed program for Lisa and one for himself. This speaker, she decided, had to be Professor Will Stewart. He was a tall, dignified man with gray hair and a leathery, wind-burned look to him.

The people around Lisa and Chris—in fact, Lisa noticed, the whole audience—seemed fascinated by Professor Stewart's speech. After the first few minutes the room was darkened and a series of colored slides appeared on a screen behind Professor Stewart, illustrating his talk.

Lisa listened closely, trying as hard as she could to understand all that Professor Stewart was saying.

"These are the slides made by the classic Mondrick-McLaurin expedition to the Ala-Shan region of Mongolia. Mondrick pointed out in his own memoir that the modern physicist interprets the entire universe in terms of probability, and suggested that the direct mental control of probability would surely open terrifying avenues of power.

"Mondrick Insisted that nothing at all was completely impossible in this statistical universe. The remotest impossibility became merely remotely improbable.

"McLaurin's related work in the area of space-time tensors and the mathematics of interlocking universes further support the Mondrick theories." Professor Stewart signaled the slide-projector operator and the picture on the screen—a crude cave carving that seemed to show a person turning into a tiger or jaguar—was replaced by one of a table with various ingredients spread on it.

"The use of ointments to promote such alterations," Professor Stewart said, "is very widespread. This fits in well with the Mondrick-McLaurin idea, if we assume that molecular bonds can be loosened so as to make the shape-shifting easier.

"At Clarendon College we have prepared a number of ointments, using the recipes given in folklore of various regions."

Lisa gasped and clutched Chris by the arm. "You hear that," she whispered fiercely to him, "that sounds just like what your aunt told about. The salve for changing!"

Chris nodded and hissed, "Exactly!"

"Sabine Baring-Gould believed that the transformation was merely an illusion or illness. He cites a salve of narcotic ingredients: solanum somniferum, aconite, hyoscyamos, belladonna and the like."

"I never heard of that stuff!" Chris whispered to Lisa.

"Neither did I, but let's listen anyhow!" Lisa replied.

Professor Stewart had a different picture on the screen now, a lot of things that looked liked shredded leaves and ground-up plant roots. "Montague Summers, for all that he was a credulous superstition-monger, was still a good folklorist in his way. His formula included mandrake, stramonium, belladonna and henbane. He also makes note of users of hemlock, aconite, poplar leaves, soot, cowbane, cinquefoil, sweet flag, bat's blood, and oils.

"Our modern herbalists," Professor Stewart smiled as the lights came back up, "might find a number of effective substances in these lists. Others are probably there merely for the sake of melodrama. I don't think that bat's blood, for instance, would do much for a lycanthrope.

"But," he made a gesture like a witch casting a spell, "it was certainly effective for the spook factor."

Everyone in the room laughed, including Lisa and Chris.

"I might mention," the professor said when the laughter had quieted down, "that we have brought along a sample supply of the formula from Clarendon. Anyone who wishes can have a little rubbed on the back of their hand on the way out. Since we're almost up to the full moon, you might develop fangs and fur though, so don't do it lightly."

There was another ripple of laughter through the room, and then a loud outburst of applause as Professor Stewart walked from the platform.

The chairman announced a break for dinner, to be followed by informal sessions for the rest of the evening.

Everybody got up and started shuffling toward the big doors at the back of the room. As Lisa and Chris got there they noticed people standing on either side of each doorway with little tubs of yellowish-brown stuff, and cotton swabs for rubbing it in. They were all wearing heavy-looking rubber gloves, and looked friendly but quite serious.

Chris buzzed into Lisa's ear: "Looks like chunky peanut butter to me!"

Lisa laughed. Then, when it was her turn at the doorway she saw a young woman holding a jar of the ointment and a swab in her gloved hands. She looked about twenty, and had long pigtails hanging over the shoulders of a Ludwig Beethoven sweatshirt. Lisa thought she was beautiful.

Lisa stopped in front of her and held out one hand, its palm down toward the floor.

The young woman took her hand and held it firmly, then dipped the swab in the ointment and held it out for Lisa to smell. It had a sharp, piercing odor that seemed to penetrate high into her head. The young woman pressed the swab to Lisa's wrist and rubbed.

For an instant the stuff seemed icy cold but almost at once it seemed to sink in, and a terrific feeling of warmth spread up and down Lisa's arm, from the tip of her fingers nearly to her elbow. A cramp seized Lisa's hand and her fingers curled over involuntarily. She felt her fingernails growing long and thick, curving around like claws. She looked down at her hand and wrist.

They were covered with thick, bristly fur.

CHAPTER NINE

The young woman with the Beethoven sweatshirt grabbed Lisa's hand and rubbed it over with a heavy, moist towel that appeared from somewhere behind her. Lisa felt her muscles relaxing, her fingers and nails returning to normal. The back of her hand and her wrist that had appeared furry were now smooth and freckled-looking.

Lisa felt herself propelled through the doorway into the foyer outside the conference room. Puzzled, she looked down and realized that an envelope was in her hand.

She turned and looked back to see Chris coming after her, He had an envelope, too.

Before she could look inside the little packet or say anything to Chris, her father arrived and clapped her lightly on the shoulder. With his other hand, he did the same to Chris. "You youngsters enjoy the sessions?" he asked. "Brilliant papers this afternoon. And the Ala-shan materials from Mondrick and McLaurin—pity they couldn't be here today. Hey?"

Lisa said, "Well, some of it was a little hard to understand, Dad. Some of the words they used...."

"Yes, of course. Still—what's that you have?" He pointed to the white envelope in Lisa's hand.

She shrugged and opened the flap. There was a printed card inside. It looked like an invitation. Lisa held it up and read it aloud.

"You are cordially invited to attend the special interest group on authentication. Eight-thirty, Maturin Room, by invitation only, non-transferable,"

"Oh," Leo said, "the authentication group. I think Al Raphael is running that, Good man. From Tulsa. Invitational only, that's a little bit stuffy I'd say."

"Weren't you invited, sir?" Chris asked.

Leo flushed. "In any case, I'll be at a board meeting tonight. Both you children received these cards, did you? Well, you'll be in good hands with Aloysius Raphael, and the conference is running shuttle vans back to the hotel. Do you want to attend that group?"

Lisa looked at Chris and saw him looking back at her. They both shrugged. "I think you'll find it worth your time," Leo said.

"Want to go, Chris?" Lisa waited for his vague nod. "Okay, sure, we'll go."

"Oh, just a moment." Lisa looked in surprise at her father. He had taken a step away from them, grasped a dashing-looking, handsome man by the elbow. The two men exchanged some words briefly, then Leo led the newcomer back to where Lisa and Chris stood.

"This is my daughter, Lisa," he said, "and our young friend Chris Simmons. Children, you'll want to meet this gentleman. You just received his invitation. This is Dr. Raphael of Tulsa, the very same Aloysius Raphael who's running the authentication group."

They all shook hands.

Aloysius Raphael was another elderly professor, not much taller than Leo Kane although some years older. Like Professor Stewart, Raphael had the handsome, vigorous look of a person who had spent most of his life outdoors.

"I've persuaded Dr. Raphael to share our dinner," Leo stated, "Then we'll go our separate ways afterwards. But I was wondering, Aloysius," he turned toward his colleague, "why Chris and Lisa were both invited to your group and I wasn't."

He said it in a friendly, half-joking way, but Lisa thought that he must be a little bit hurt, too. She waited for Aloysius Raphael's answer.

"Didn't you test the salve, Leo? That Will Stewart's kids brought along?"

Lisa's dad said he had tried it.

"And?" Dr. Raphael prompted.

Leo shrugged now. "Liniment. Felt rather warm. Not unpleasant. I can understand its use at Shabbats if Stewart's formula was authentic. My reading suggests that it was."

"Yes, yes," Dr. Raphael was nodding impatiently. "Well, but you see, Leo—I shouldn't tell you this I suppose, but I know you to be a man of discretion—those invitations went only to people who showed a positive reaction to the salve."

"Pos—" Leo Kane stopped. Then he said, "Oh, I see. Of course. Well, Aloysius, you and Will have taken quite a responsibility upon yourselves. I hope that you know what you're doing."

Now it was Aloysius Raphael who took Leo Kane by the elbow and began to steer him away from the milling crowd, Lisa and Chris following closely behind. "We've given it a lot of thought, Leo, I assure you."

They wound up in an Italian restaurant where Lisa ordered eggplant parmigiana and Chris got scampi and they traded half of their portions. They didn't talk much, mostly listened to Lisa's dad and Dr. Raphael. They were talking about Dr. Raphael's special interest, what he called authentication—testing out various beliefs to see what amount of truth there was behind them.

"There are so many congruent traditions," Dr. Raphael was saying, "so many widespread beliefs that fit together so neatly. Aside from Mondrick's reports of were-tigers and were-jaguars and all the rest, we have the parallel notions that my people have been tracking down."

Lisa's dad said, "These are—?"

Raphael Aloysius drank down a huge glass of red wine. "Listen, Leo, Velikof Vonk has statistics for the abominable snowman, for the hairy woodman, for the wild man of Borneo, for the sasquatch who's been seen within a hundred miles of this very spaghetti-vendery!"

"Hmm, you mean Bigfoot?" Leo asked.

"Who else! We have the booger-man, the missing link, the nine-foot-tall giant things—"

"Now, really," Leo interrupted.

"Nine feet tall or not," Raphael replied, "the reports are almost certainly distorted but they aren't all invented! Reports of surviving Neanderthals! It is believed by some that all of these beings are the same. It is believed by most that these things are no thing at all, nowhere, not in any form.

"That's why we need an authentication group!"

He reached for a straw-covered bottle and refilled his wine glass, topping off Lisa's dad's with a few drops of red.

"Do you—just think that there might be truth behind all the traditions?" Leo asked.

Lisa knew that he, her father, knew better. He must be trying to find out how much Dr. Raphael knew.

"That was the purpose of the salve this afternoon, Leo."

So he knew!

They finished the meal, and afterwards Leo kissed Lisa, gave Chris a rub on the head, and said he'd see them later on at the hotel. He went off to his own meeting. Dr. Raphael excused himself and went to prepare for the authentication group session.

CHAPTER TEN

Lisa and Chris made their way to the street that led from the main entrance of the university. It was called Telegraph Avenue and it was lined with odd shops and restaurants. It was brightly lighted and people were strolling up and down as if it were the middle of the day.

Lisa held onto Chris's hand as they passed through the milling crowd. She didn't want them to become separated. Chris squeezed her hand back and smiled at her.

They strolled down Telegraph Avenue for a while, then stopped at a building with an amazing painting on its outer wall. Chris said, "Will you look at that! They have everything! Flying saucers, people in work clothes, farmers, musicians, all in one giant picture."

"What do think it means?" Lisa asked.

Chris shrugged his shoulders and said, "Huh! No idea in the world. It says, ah, Universal Revolutionary Temple of the Salvation from Space."

"I don't have any idea either, Chris. Do you think it's a show? Or a joke of some sort?"

He shook his head. "Don't see how it could be a joke. Maybe a show. Let's see."

They walked around to the front of the building and peered in through the door. Inside the building looked as if it were partially darkened but colored lights were weaving in patterns or flashing on and off. There was a general hum of voices and noise.

A young man sat behind a table partly blocking the doorway. He wore a close-fitting helmet completely covered with silver sparkles, Only the lower half of his face was visible and that was covered with silver sparkles too.

He looked up at Lisa and Chris and said, "Come on in. Welcome to the Temple of Salvation. You're just in time."

Lisa said, "Just in time? For what?"

The young man grinned hugely. "Just in time for the free rock dance. Flash Rogers and the Lensmen. They're all members of the revolution, dynamite musicians. Free admittance tonight!"

Lisa and Chris looked at each other for an instant, then passed the desk. As they entered the building a young woman in a set of shiny black coveralls and wearing a blue-black glitter helmet took their hands and pressed a rubber stamp on them. "Prove you didn't crash the gate," she smiled,

"But if it's free anyhow?" Lisa asked.

"We charge after nine o'clock."

Chris and Lisa found their way into a huge room. Just as they got inside there was a stupendous crash of sound and a puff of bright orange smoke went up in the front of the room.

Lisa blinked, dazzled for a moment. Then she realized that there were a hundred or more people in the room, and that there was a band on the stage—a live rock band!

"Chris," she squealed, grabbing him by the arm, "look!"

There were five people on a stage holding instruments, all of them with electrical cables running to huge amplifiers. There seemed no way to tell which of the musicians were men and which were women—they all wore sparkling tights and helmets, the only difference among them the color. They were red, blue, green, gold, and the leader was in dazzling sparkling white.

The leader stepped up to a microphone and strummed a guitar chord. "Welcome to the Universal Revolutionary Temple of the Salvation from Space! We just want you all to have a good time here, away from the pressures and the problems of the big cold street.

"We're all a family here. We all share. The message comes

from our holy leader Zen-zek Belter through his handmade unique electronic computer and we learn everything from him. He is all-wise, all-knowing, and through him the Saviors from the Stars work to save us all. So just set your feet to moving and have fun! That's the message for tonight!"

Another guitar chord and the band began to play, weird organ chords and guitar wails, deep throbbing notes from an amplified bass.

In the flashing, wavering lights Chris and Lisa exchanged a look and began to dance like the other people around them. The band played two or three numbers and then the music ended and a squad of people wearing badges and armbands began to drift through the crowd in the room.

A tall, bearded man came up to Lisa and Chris and said, "We were watching you dance. You look like a couple of fine, talented young people. We'd like to talk to you about Zen-zek Belter's message and the Universal Revolutionary Temple. Won't you sit down over here?"

He led them over to the side of the room. There was a small table there, along with a few chairs. The bearded man told Lisa and Chris to have a seat. He sat down with them.

"I know that everyone is searching for answers," he said, smiling at them. "The world is so full of questions and so lacking in answers these days, everyone is running around, using up a lot of energy and not accomplishing anything. Isn't that so? Don't you agree?"

Lisa shot a look at Chris. "I guess so," she said.

"Of course, of course," the bearded man beamed. "But we're the lucky ones, aren't we? We have the answers! Isn't it wonderful to be one of the few who know when everybody else just wonders?"

"Uh, I'm not really, ah—"

Chris said, "What do you know? What answers? What questions?"

"Zen-zek loves you, little brother and sister! That's where true peace and happiness lie, you see?"

He didn't wait for their answers. "The space people tell Zen-zek everything through his computer, then he tells us. We don't have to wonder! We don't have to ask questions! We just glow and grow in the love of our master and savior, and he gives us everything we need."

"You don't have to give him anything?" Chris said. "You just get, ah, stuff from this Zenny whoever?"

"Zen-zek." There seemed to be a scowl in the thick beard. "Zen-zek Belter. The greatest single organism living on the face of the earth today. But someday we will all be as one, and Zen-zek will be as our heart. You see, little brother and sister?" He smiled happily at them both,

"You don't have to pay him or anything, right?" Chris Insisted.

"Well," the bearded man said, "we all make voluntary offerings of love. I wouldn't call that paying, would you?"

Lisa waited for Chris to answer but he didn't.

"Well we don't consider it paying," the man supplied his own answer. "We give everything to Zen-zek. How else could he carry on his holy task, eh?" He chuckled. Lisa thought the chuckle was rather thin.

Chris said, "So you have to give this guy everything you have to get his love and his what-you-call answers."

The bushy-bearded man said, "I wouldn't put it that way, you wise punk! We've got a—"

Suddenly he stopped.

Lisa looked up. A very tall, very thin man in plain clothes was standing behind the bushy-bearded man. He had placed a hand on the bearded man's shoulder. He said something in a very low, chill voice. Lisa couldn't make it out but the bearded man got up without a word and disappeared through a back doorway.

The thin man looked icily at Lisa and Chris and said, "It is very clear that you have improper attitudes. Your hearts are not prepared to receive my message. Your spirits are not ready to receive my peace. Leave!" He pointed imperiously toward the door.

Chris reached across to Lisa and grabbed her hand and they started for the door. By the time they got there they were almost running.

At the door the friendly man with the sparkle helmet who had invited them in clanked a metal bar across their path. "Entertainment fee," he said neutrally.

"Entertainment fee?" they asked together.

"Two dollars a head." The man held out a silver-sparkled hand.

Lisa said, "You told us it was free!"

"Free entrance, of course. But once you were inside there's an entertainment fee. Didn't you listen to the Lensmen? Didn't you dance? Two dollars a head. Unless you want to join the Revolutionary Temple, of course. It's free for members."

Lisa looked at Chris. "What should we do?" she asked.

Chris looked angry and started to raise his fist. Lisa put her hand on it and said, "No, Chris! We'll get in trouble!"

He grumbled "I guess you're right. Okay then, okay!" He reached for his wallet and pulled out two dollars and paid.

Lisa found two dollars in her own pocket and handed it to the man in the sparkle helmet. He said, "Thank you very much. Do come again any time."

He opened the barrier and they ran out of the building.

"What a gyp!" Chris exclaimed.

Lisa said, "I think we'd better get back to the meeting hall. I think it's safer there."

They started walking along the sidewalk silently. When they reached the university again they sat down on a grassy slope. Chris said, "What do you think they're going to do in there now?"

"In that phony temple or in the meeting?"

Chris said, "Huh! I guess in the meeting."

"I think it has to do with that stuff they rubbed on our wrists this afternoon. That peanut-butter stuff."

Chris asked "What did happen? To you, I mean."

Lisa wondered if she should tell him everything and then she decided that, yes, she would. He was like her, a lycanthrope. She would trust him, she wouldn't hide.

"When they rubbed that stuff on my whole arm up to the elbow started to change. Then that woman rubbed something else on me with a towel and I changed back. But it really worked. It must have been the same stuff Aunt Stella has in Whitbridge."

Chris said, "The same thing happened to me. I've never changed completely, at home. But I've changed a little. Aunt Stella says I'm almost old enough."

"And Dr. Raphael and Dr. Stewart have the salve too, Chris. Whatever they're going to do at that meeting, I don't think we should miss it." She shook her head to emphasize the point. "After all, we didn't come all the way to California just to, you know, mess around."

"Yeah, or nearly get caught by a bunch of phony crooks. I'm so mad about that four bucks!" Chris ground his heel into the earth.

Lisa said, "Well, anyhow. I think we ought to go into the meeting. Do you still have your invitation?"

They both dug theirs tickets out of their jacket pockets and headed into the big meeting hall.

The Maturin Room was a comfortable, old-fashioned kind of place where Lisa felt much more at home and relaxed than she had in the giant meeting hall. The room had old wood paneled walls and paintings of people in the dress of past centuries hung on them; the furniture was soft leather rather than hard folding chairs, and there was even a fireplace with some logs blazing in it.

Their invitations were checked at the door and Lisa and Chris walked in to find only about twenty people scattered around the room. Lisa recognized the young woman in the Beethoven sweatshirt and they exchanged friendly smiles. Lisa thought she saw Professor Stewart, too, and then, just as Lisa and Chris were starting to look around for seats Aloysius Raphael stood up in front of the fireplace and began to speak.

"Before we begin the work of the authentication group," he said, "you can all find some refreshments on the sideboard."

Lisa and Chris went and stood with the other people—they were the youngest present, but they saw several teenagers and people of every age in the room. Chris took a cup of hot chocolate and Lisa poured herself some tea, then they sat down.

Professor Raphael took his place, again, a hot steaming mug in his own hand. "This is by far the most exclusive group at the entire conference," the professor said, "and if we were known to the world, we might face dire peril. So I will ask only that you exercise thought and care in the business of our group.

"And now—" He gestured with his mug "—may I present our most distinguished member, Dr. Isaac Fineman of Howard Phillips University."

The older people in the room, who must know better what was expected or them, applauded. Lisa joined in uncertainly.

Dr. Raphael took a seat and in his place stood white-haired "Old If," slim and dignified.

He looked around the room, nodded to some people, then began to speak in his dry, whispery tones. His voice was so quiet that Lisa could hear the fire crackling cheerily behind him, and yet she could understand every word that was spoken.

"You are all were-beasts," he said seriously.

There was a rustle in the room. Lisa looked around—these ordinary, pleasant-looking people, men and women, professors and college students—all were what she was! At the end of looking around she locked eyes with Chris Simmons. He looked very serious. He put his free hand—the one not holding his cup of cocoa—on hers, and she smiled at him, feeling suddenly shy.

"Lycanthropes, werewolves," Dr. Fineman resumed, "Will Stewart and Al Raphael showed me their statistics. I'm a little surprised at the lack of variety—" He paused and laughed a soft, dry laugh that a few in the audience answered nervously "—but I suppose that should be expected in this conformist, homogenized country.

"A truly global sampling," he smiled, "I hope would provide

us with a wider selection of were-beings.

"Now any of you who have looked at your calendars know that the full moon for this month is due tomorrow. And I imagine that persons like us attend to their calendars far more conscientiously than the average citizen." He smiled thinly. "Of course, that is based on Greenwich time. The phase becomes complete at 6:53 tomorrow morning, local time."

Again, there was a rustling of sound around the room, as people shifted in their seats. Lisa found herself leaning forward, straining not to miss a word of Dr. Fineman's speech. This wasn't like the dull papers that were read during the day. He seemed to be speaking directly to each person in the room, not making an oration for a big, solid audience.

"Making allowances for differences in time zones," the old man went on, "that is the same as 1:53 tomorrow morning, Eastern time. Or 10:53 tonight—" He paused to look at his wristwatch "—less than two hours from now for us in the Pacific zone."

Again he paused and looked around the room, smiling. "Dr. Raphael and the authentication group have arranged with the park service for a visit to Mt. Tamalpais for us. That is, for those of us in this room. A bus will leave from in front of this building in a few minutes. Of course, no one need participate who does not wish to.

"But Mt. Tamalpais is the highest point in the area, a beautiful spot less than thirty miles from here. It is closed to the public after ten o'clock, so we will be the only ones there, except for a few forest rangers on fire lookout."

He looked at the people in the room again, and pointed a finger that made Lisa feel as if he were boring into her with his sharp old eyes and his bony, pointing finger.

"Everyone here tested positive this afternoon, using the classic salve. We will reach the mountain shortly before the moon achieves its full phase. This will be an historic moment." Again he paused and smiled, and then said, "Those of you who wish to participate in the authentication, please bring your invitations as boarding passes for the bus. Anyone who wishes to remain behind...." His whispery voice trailed away.

Lisa and Chris exchanged looks.

"What do you think, Lisa?"

She started to shrug, then said, "I guess I trust Dr. Fineman. Daddy thinks he's so marvelous. And Daddy said we could stay with this group."

Chris said, "Okay." They went outside with the rest of the people from the Maturin Room. As they climbed on board the bus Lisa decided that the driver must think he was doing an odd job. But she looked around, inside the bus, and realized that everyone from the authentication group was on the bus—no one had left. Then she was relieved that she and Chris had stayed, too.

CHAPTER ELEVEN

They had what seemed like a long ride on a freeway alongside San Francisco Bay, then turned west and crossed a long bridge. As they rode silently, a few quiet conversations drifting from other seats, Lisa turned to Chris and said, "I just had a funny thought! Daddy invited me on this trip just so I wouldn't go to the Harvest Moon Ball on the night of the full moon. At least, I think that was how he got the idea."

Chris said, "So?"

"So—the Harvest Moon Ball isn't really on the night of the full moon! It's that Greenwich time that Dr. Fineman was talking about. The full moon is tomorrow by the calendar, but that's because of Greenwich—that's an observatory in England, somebody told me."

"I thought it was a village in New York. Or Connecticut someplace."

"Well, maybe there's more than one Greenwich. But the one where they count time from is in England, and the difference in time zones means that it's morning there, now, and the moon must be setting, and it's full. And it's after midnight in Whitbridge, and it's full moon there now. And it's Saturday there, too, you see?

"But here in California it's still Friday night, and it's full moon, too! Don't you see?"

Chris only said, "Hmph," and Lisa left him alone.

They left the bridge and drove on back roads, climbing slowly. Lisa leaned her head on the window glass, watching the world outside. To one side she could see a glittering display of lights like a thousand Christmas trees. In silence she wondered where they were until she realized suddenly that they were in San Francisco.

Above them the night sky was dark. Patchy clouds and wisps of fog like torn cloth drifted across the stars. Part of the time she could see the moon and part of the time it was hidden.

Finally the bus pulled to a halt. Everyone sat quietly while the driver and Dr. Raphael went to check with the ranger. Then they came back and Dr. Raphael signaled to everyone to climb off the bus. Lisa saw that the driver wasn't there, then she looked up and saw a lighted cabin. Inside were two men, the ranger and the bus driver, sitting over a table, drinking coffee and talking.

The ranger looked out the window at all the people climbing off the bus, smiled and waved, and turned back to talk to the driver.

Lisa and Chris held hands and looked around. The people were trooping across an open area where the bus had parked and down a trail that led into the woods. Suddenly Lisa felt cold and a little bit afraid.

Then she saw the young woman with the Beethoven sweatshirt. The young woman looked at Lisa and Chris, smiled reassuringly and strode over to them. She took Lisa's hand—the one Chris wasn't holding—and they walked down the trail with the others.

Soon they came to another clearing. Some of the people Lisa recognized as Dr. Stewart's helpers had brought big containers like cooking pots and were setting them down on the ground. They opened them up and everyone made a rough circle. Dr. Fineman stood in the center of it, looked at his watch, and spoke.

"The moon will be full in just a few minutes," the clear whisper came. "Let us apply the salve so we can obtain the doubled effect of lunar and chemical influence."

He looked around, just the way teachers do when they talk to students and have an important point to make, then cleared his throat. "This is still the authentication group, of course. We have a scientific purpose, and you are all requested to make mental notes and observations for later recording. But we can all make this a vivid, memorable experience, an esthetic experience if you will."

He smiled, "Please do not stray to far or stay away too long—no one, I am sure, would want to miss the ride back to our hotel."

He gestured toward the people standing behind the huge containers of salve and everyone else began to line up. Professor Stewart's assistants were there to help people apply the stuff. Lisa stood in line where the young woman with the Beethoven sweatshirt was helping to apply the salve. She didn't see Chris or anyone else she knew, and she wanted desperately to have someone nearby whom she knew, even just by sight. She was glad that Chris was there somewhere, and Professor Fineman, but for some reason, she was most strengthened by knowing that the woman in the sweatshirt was there.

Everyone was taking off his or her clothes to apply the salve all over their bodies. Lisa felt a sudden wave of shyness and embarrassment. She knew what people looked like, of course. And she wasn't ashamed of her body. She'd been skinny-dipping in the summer, along with Toni MacPherson and some other girls from school. And Lucy, she remembered with a secret grin. All of them jumping in and out of a little pond, splashing and swimming and then drying off in the sunshine afterward, everybody running away from Lucy so they wouldn't get drenched all over again when she shook out her coat and sprayed water in all directions.

But here—in front of all these people? Men, women, girls, boys....

Lisa was at the front of her line now, and the young woman with the sweatshirt gave her an encouraging grin. It helped and Lisa started to get undressed. She thought of leaving on just her underwear, then thought of running on all fours, all covered with thick fur. If that was what was coming....

In underwear?

She slipped out of all her clothes, folded them in a neat pile on the ground, and stood shivering while the young woman helped her to spread the salve all over herself. At first, as the ointment covered her, Lisa felt even colder than she did from the damp, chilly night air. She looked at herself and saw that she was covered with goose bumps!

But then a marvelous warmth started to spread through her. A great warm energy coursed through her arms and legs and seemed to penetrate into her belly and her chest. She stared at herself: a heavy coat of red-gray fur was appearing all over her!

She looked away, up at the sky, and watched the full moon blaze huge and bright over the trees.

Suddenly Lisa felt giddy, off-balance, as if she had been standing on her toes for a long time, and had begun to teeter and sway back and forth.

She settled into a steadier, more comfortable posture, and realized to her surprise that she was on all fours! A ripple of pleasure swept from the tip of her nose to the tip of her tail. She looked around and saw that she was surrounded by beautiful, graceful, powerful wolves.

Males and females, young and old, large and small. Some were reddish-brown, as she was. Others were gray, black, silvery. She saw one old, slim wolf and realized with a start that he must be—Dr. Fineman himself!

Lisa trotted forward to the edge of the clearing where she had stood. She realized that the other wolves were doing the same. A huge old tawny male had taken the lead, and the others were following with the instinct of a well-trained pack.

They entered the woods again, this time not following a trail but making their own way through low underbrush.

As they trotted along Lisa realized that her senses had all sharpened a hundredfold at the very least. The bright moonlit night which had been clear before seemed now as bright as daylight.

But if Lisa's eyes had sharpened, her ears and nostrils had grown incredibly acute. She could hear the soft padding of scores of feet as the pack made its way along the hillside.

She could hear the sounds of small animals and birds in the woods—rabbits, field-mice, a few woodchucks, owls nesting in the trees overhead.

She looked up and saw the black shape of a great hawk floating slowly, gracefully in the sky.

And the trees and grasses and shrubs that covered the mountainside, that had been a vague green-black blur before, now stood out, a hundred varieties of plant, each with its own shade of color and form and scent, some sharp and pungent, some sweet and heavy, some light and delicate, no two alike. Although she didn't know the names of more than two or three kinds of trees, Lisa realized that she had no difficulty in distinguishing them from one another by their odors or their forms.

And all the time that she was noticing all this she was trotting, trotting tirelessly. Her wolf-lungs pulled in the delicious moist air in effortless, endless doses. There was no way she could run short of breath! And her wolf-heart beat like a mighty power in her chest, pumping strong, thick blood to her four legs as they covered ground without effort, ground that would have taken her long, hard struggles to cover in her normal shape.

There was a flash of gray and white from beneath a bush, and Lisa realized that a rabbit had been flushed from cover. Almost without thinking she sprinted after it. The little animal raced between trees, up and down the rocky slope, cutting this way, dodging that way, while Lisa's mighty wolf-legs devoured the distance between them.

The joy that she felt in the chase was something she had never experienced before. It wasn't just the exhilaration of straining her mighty body to its utmost speed and skill, matching the rabbit maneuver for maneuver. It was the sheer joy of living completely, naturally, of being all that she was and all that nature told her to be, without the thousand little rules and limits of ordinary life.

After the first few seconds Lisa realized that she was playing with the rabbit. There was nothing that she could do with it, really, unless she chose to kill it. She could devour the raw, hot flesh of the rabbit and draw pleasure and nourishment from it. As a wolf she could do that. As a wolf it was her nature to hunt and kill and consume.

But inside she was still Lisa Kane, and to Lisa Kane the rabbit was not just a meal—it was a living being with some degree, however little, of consciousness, awareness.

She let it escape.

Perhaps some of those thousands of rules had stayed with her after all, even when she had become a wolf.

She slowed her chase, began walking instead through the woods. She had become separated from the pack, but she wasn't worried. She trotted forward once more, then halted when she saw that she had come to a break in the foliage.

She stood looking through the break. The mountainside was steep here. As a human she would have had no chance to keep her balance; even as a wolf she had to be careful to avoid tumbling down the rocky slope.

But beyond the mountain she could see the Pacific Ocean. The waters were black by night, their surface textured by countless tiny wind-driven wavelets that lapped at the rocky shore. The moon was still high, huge and brilliant in the blackness above the ocean. Its brilliant reflection bounced off the black water, making what looked like a long, silvery road that led from the mountainside, across the ocean and up to the moon itself. To Diana the Huntress of the night.

Suddenly Lisa found herself hunching back on her hindquarters. The moon seemed to pull her to it, pull every cell in her strong wolf body. She threw back her head and closed her eyes and without conscious will began a high, trembling howl that echoed across the face of the mountain and out over the sea.

It was like shouting, like singing, like crying in joy. Somehow it was even like praying. And in Lisa's ears there was suddenly the sound of padded feet scratching on the rocky slope, and then a second voice blending with her own, howling, howling, howling at the great silvery globe that hung so near overhead it must be possible to reach it with one mighty leap. Finally Lisa stopped.

The second voice dropped away.

Lisa opened her keen wolf eyes and looked. There was another beast standing beside her, silver and black with bright, gleaming eyes. She sniffed the clear air and without a moment's hesitation she knew who the other wolf was—Chris.

They stood together and Lisa realized that the wolf Chris was just a little taller than she was. Somewhere, deep inside, she laughed, softly and warmly.

Chris held his face close to hers, brushed his nose against her muzzle, then nipped her playfully on the neck.

Lisa spun and scrambled away from him, looking back over her shoulder as she slipped away into the woods. Chris was running close behind her.

She dodged between tree trunks, running up and down the steep slope, hearing Chris chasing her and happy now that she had let the rabbit go. Once again she picked up dozens, hundreds of little odors and sounds as she raced along. Once she cut around a clump of bushes and caught Chris unawares. She jumped from behind him knocking him off balance, and, laughing her wolf laugh, raced away as she heard him scrambling to his feet in confusion before he was able to follow behind.

She sniffed a warm trail—the pack!

She waited there, at the edge of the trail of wolf scents, until Chris trotted up and stood beside her sniffing at the ground. She could recognize Dr. Raphael's presence, and Professor Stewart's, and the young woman with the Beethoven shirt. She whined something to Chris and he replied.

They set off at a rapid trot, back up the trail.

In a short time they were back at the clearing where they had left their clothing and the containers of salve. A few other wolves had arrived ahead of them, and they circled each other, sniffing, rubbing, walking around the little piles of belongings identifying their own and the owners of others by their scents.

Then Lisa heard the padding and breathing of the pack as the rest of the wolves returned. The ones who had dispensed the salve earlier walked to the containers and sniffed at them. Lisa watched closely as one of Dr. Stewart's assistants dipped a paw hesitantly into the ointment, then withdrew it again.

He shook the paw a few times but then Lisa saw it begin to change. The fur drew back, faded, the strong claws shriveled into puny human fingernails. The wolf with one human hand dipped the hand into the ointment again, began to spread the stuff all over himself and to change wherever he rubbed it in. Before long he was a young man standing upright beside the container.

He dressed quickly and then began helping others, spreading the salve over them. Soon there were only a few wolves left, then none at all. The entire authentication group stood around quietly until the leaders, Professors Fineman, Stewart, and Raphael, led the way back along the trail through the trees, to the bus.

Lisa felt warm and happy inside, but sleepy. So sleepy.

On the bus she and Chris didn't say a word. They just leaned on each other. Lisa felt Chris's hand reach across and hold hers, and that made her feel even happier.

She was overcome by a powerful need to yawn, and when she gave in to it Chris did the same thing. They laughed together, and that was all Lisa remembered before she fell asleep.

She didn't know how she got to her room at the hotel, or into her bed, but in the morning she woke feeling marvelous, and hungrier than she could remember ever having been before.

Her father had got up first, and was sitting fully dressed on the edge of her bed. The sun was shining brightly into her room and it was a warm, clear day.

"Must be the jet-lag finally catching up with you," her father said. "You had a good sleep."

Lisa stretched and said, "Uh-huh," emphasizing the second half of the sound, and rubbed her head on her dad's shoulder.

"Well, what about a little breakfast?" Leo asked.

"Uh-huh!" Lisa repeated. "I feel starved!"

CHAPTER TWELVE

Saturday was a drowsy kind of day for Lisa.

The air seemed warm and heavy even though the sky was clear and the sun bright. There was a pleasant, damp breeze in the air that reminded her of an occasional Whitbridge day, the kind that came every so often toward the end of April or in May, when the spring was well along, the earth had thawed from its New England winter freeze, and new life was growing everywhere.

It was marvelous to have that kind of day at the end of October and Lisa envied the people who had this climate to live with, even if it meant sacrificing the fun of real snow in winter.

She did have a huge breakfast with her father in a restaurant they walked to. Leo had brought along a folder full of papers, journals and reports that he had picked up at the previous day's sessions of the conference. He put on his glasses and worked over the documents, keeping up half a conversation with Lisa as she ate her ham and eggs, muffins, cocoa and grapefruit. Halfway through the meal she said, "Where's Chris, Dad?"

Leo looked up from his work, said, "I think he's with some of the Tulsa people. They wound up with a spare bed, you know, so he's bunking with them at the hotel. I'm sure we'll see him today." He smiled at her as if to say that he understood more than he wanted to put in words.

Lisa smiled back gratefully and returned to her meal.

Afterwards they strolled on Telegraph Avenue opposite the university, looking at the street artists' wares. The sidewalk was covered with tables and blankets displaying things that people had made themselves and brought there to sell, and there were crowds of shoppers moving up and down the pavement, looking at the artists' wares and trying things out and making purchases.

Lisa looked at everything: one-of-a-kind belt-buckles and jewelry, beautiful hand-painted or tie-dyed shirts, denim hats, hand-tooled leather belts, beautiful silver and turquoise rings and pins, candles in every imaginable shape and color, paintings and mirrors and clothing and hand-carved flutes and home-printed books of poetry and the unavoidable boxes of free puppies and kittens.

Lisa stopped to look at one display and held up a silver pin with a design in blue turquoise. "Isn't this beautiful, Daddy?" she asked her father.

He looked at it and said, "Is it for you?"

"No," she shook her head, "I promised Toni MacPherson I'd bring her a souvenir. There's nothing like this in Whitbridge. I guess I kind of kept her from getting this trip when I wanted Chris to come instead, so I thought I'd at least get her a present."

Leo smiled and said he thought that was a fine idea, and that it was, indeed, a lovely pin.

Lisa paid for it and zipped it into the pocket of her quilted orange jacket. Then they walked on.

After a while they doubled back and found themselves at the university's anthropology museum. Leo seemed fascinated by the displays and wandered off to have a long talk with one of the curators while Lisa crossed the street and spent her time in the art museum looking at beautiful paintings and strange sculptures. There was nothing like this in Whitbridge, either— or even in Stonesboro, she thought.

The rest of the day passed.

Lisa went back to the conference with her father, sat through some papers that were either beyond her understanding or crushingly dull, then started thinking about dinner. The last session of the afternoon had ended and Lisa was standing with Chris, waiting for her father to come along, when a boy of about fifteen walked up. He was much taller than either Chris or Lisa—and would actually be bigger than Lisa's dad, she realized. She recognized him from the wolf pack on Mt. Tamalpais the night before—he'd been a light-colored, thin wolf with yellowish-gray fur.

He said, "I know you guys."

Lisa thought about running on the mountainside, chasing the rabbit, playing tag with Chris in the full moonlight. She blushed.

They all introduced themselves. The boy's name was Marc. His skin was a light tan color and he had his hair brushed up like some of the black people Lisa saw occasionally on television.

Marc said that he was from Berkeley, his father was attending the conference so he came along just for something to do. He'd tried the test the day before just for fun—and was amazed when his hand changed. He'd never shown any signs of lycanthropy before, and as far as he knew nobody in his family ever had.

"I talked to Professor Stewart about it on the bus last night," he said, "The prof says it sometimes skips generations. Maybe my grandmom or grandpa was a werewolf. Maybe somebody a couple hundred years ago in France or in Africa—my people came from both places. Nobody knows. You guys want to go out for some chow?"

Lisa's father arrived before they decided. Lisa introduced him to Marc and said they might go eat together. Leo Kane said that was fine, he wanted to have a working dinner with some colleagues anyway, the children would have been bored. They could go on to the authentication group meeting afterwards, and Leo would see them at the hotel later.

Marc led Lisa and Chris to an Indian restaurant upstairs over a Persian hamburger stand in a little building around the corner from Telegraph Avenue. Lisa tried a meal of papadoms and dhal and a vegetable curry that burned her mouth but tasted wonderful. They talked about life in Whitbridge and going to the Whitbridge Consolidated School, and Marc told about life in Berkeley and all the schools he had attended in that town, changing every few years because each school only offered classes for a few years to each generation of students.

Marc told about his father, an anthropology professor at the University of California, and Lisa told about her dad, Leo, who did the same work at Howard Phillips University. Lisa and Chris told about building snowmen and sledding and ice skating and about their friends Toni MacPherson and Billy Cantor and Toni's two brothers Jeff and Bruce Dan.

The only topic that nobody raised was lycanthropy.

After dinner they battered their way through the sidewalk crowds, back to the university and to the conference hall. They went to the Maturin room and found most of the authentication group already there, clustered into small groups—clustering mostly by age—sipping at coffee or tea or cocoa or other things, and talking quietly.

In a few minutes Professor Raphael took the speaker's place in front of the hearth, and everyone found seats and quieted. There was a different feeling in the room, Lisa noticed, from the meeting the night before. At the first meeting most of the people in the Maturin room were strangers to one another, brought together by a common interest in lycanthropy. All of them were lycanthropes but they didn't all know it about one another. It was as if each of them had a secret that he kept to himself.

Now they knew that they were all the same, in a way. For all the differences they might have in age, in home, in outside interests—their experience together on the mountain and what they had all learned from it had taught them an important lesson. They were all sisters and brothers, Lisa thought, all a family who must help one another in dealing with the rest of the world.

Professor Raphael sipped from a steaming mug and gestured for silence and attention. "I don't need to say anything about last night. We all know what it meant. To the extent that we are a recognized group within the anthropological society, we will send out questionnaires, gather statistics, write our dull learned papers."

He gave a warm grin to the people in the room and sipped at

his mug. "But the real question we ought to discuss here—the real question is, now that our true identity and nature have been made clear to us, what do we do about it on the, ah, human level?"

There was a vague stir in the room as Professor Raphael looked around, waiting for someone to take up the discussion. But before anyone could there was a disturbance at the door. There was a crash as a chair was knocked over and a figure came bounding across the carpet, waving and shouting, and stood in front of Professor Raphael to face everybody else.

"You shall die! You shall burn! Witches! Idolaters!" the newcomer shouted.

People in the room were leaping to their feet, peering and jostling to see who it was and what was happening.

Lisa stood up and recognized the preacher from the plaza, the man with the plaid clothes. He was wearing the same outfit, his hair was tangled and his face looked wild.

"I know you!" he shouted. "Sinners! Consorters with the evil one! Wielders of dark forces! Thou shalt not suffer a witch to live! Thou shalt smite the wicked and exalt the holy!"

Professor Raphael and Professor Stewart were talking to the excited man, trying to calm him down, but he was shrinking away from their touch, trying to avoid them. "Warlocks and demons!" he shouted, "Werewolves and devils!"

Some people came rushing up from the back of the room and took the man by the elbows. Lisa saw that they were wearing tan uniforms.

"Cops!" Marc whispered. "University fuzz!"

In a minute the man was gone. One of the policemen stayed behind talking to Professor Raphael and Professor Stewart, a pad and pen in the policeman's hand. Finally Professor Stewart went out with him and the door was closed.

Professor Raphael said, "We won't press charges—apparently that fellow is a harmless character who likes to crash meetings and rant at people. He draws emotional satisfaction from the attention he garners."

He pulled a handkerchief from his pocket and wiped his forehead. "But even so, we have to consider—how many are there like him? It might be best to issue a report stating that lycanthropy is a tradition in folklore only. Dredge up the traditional explanations. Predatory animals, superstition, so on. Perhaps leaven it with some references to psychological disorders."

He looked around and pointed at someone in the audience.

Lisa turned to see who it was standing up to answer him. She was surprised to see her friend—the young woman with the pigtails and the Beethoven sweatshirt, although tonight she was wearing a rather severe sweater and jeans...and her pigtails had been brushed up into a great fluffy halo of hair similar to Marc's only far bigger.

"We can't do that, Professor," the young woman said.

Raphael said, "Please—come up here and express yourself."

The young woman strode forward to stand in front of the fire. Professor Raphael took his mug and sat down. Lisa looked at the young woman and thought that she was beautiful—as beautiful, even, as Aunt Stella, although in a different way, and much, much younger.

"You know," the young woman said, "everybody has to liberate himself." She gazed around the room, her eyes shining. Lisa thought they might be green. "Everybody who tries to please an oppressor, to appease—you know what happens. Study history!

"As long as we try to hide, as long as we try to pretend we're something we aren't, try to be something we aren't, we'll never get anywhere!"

Somebody from the audience called out "People need education!"

"I'll say they do!" the young woman answered. "All they need is to understand us, right? And they'll be our friends, right? Like that chapter-spouting creep in the plaid jacket? Like that Bible-thumping hate-monger? He'll be our friend? All he wants to do is burn us at the stake, that's all!

"Listen," she said, seeming to lean forward and point a finger at every person in the room, "we'd better start getting ready to come out, that's what! We'd better get ready to take care of ourselves."

"Good people will help," the voice from the audience interrupted again. "We have friends. Look at Anthony Holmes White, look at Leo Kane!"

Lisa felt a bright thrill go through her at the mention of her father's name.

But the young woman said, "No way! Oh, it's nice to know that everybody isn't against you, and it's okay to have a Holmes White or a Leo Kane for a friend. But nobody ever liberated anybody else! Lincoln didn't do it and Congress didn't do it. Nobody did it for anybody else. Nobody can!

"The whole women's movement didn't amount to anything until women stood up and took their rights! Nobody in the world could help the Jews until they took Israel and made a country and defended it! And then nobody did anything for the Palestinians, either, till they fought for their rights!

"And right here at home, nobody ever paid any real attention—not any real attention—to the black struggle...." She put her hands on the sides of her great halo of fluffy hair. "...until we took our own leadership. Then we heard about black power, and everybody got scared, and then we decided that black is beautiful, and it got okay again. Well, I say it's time for a Lycanthrope's Lib!"

Suddenly Lisa felt herself jumping to her feet. Somewhere inside she knew that she was shy and terrified to be standing in front of all these people, most of them adults, every one of them older than she was. But at the same time she was happy and excited, and filled with some kind of bright, hot energy that wouldn't let her sit quietly as an observer any longer.

She knew that she was a werewolf. And she was among werewolves. Just the night before they had all been a pack, racing up and down the wooded, steep side of Mt. Tamalpais. And now—they had to make themselves live as werewolves.

She had to shout something, and the words seemed almost to

come into her head from somewhere else.

"Were is wonderful!" she shouted.

"Perfect, sister!" the young woman by the fireplace answered. She ran across the room to Lisa and embraced her, and Lisa suddenly felt her shoulders shaking, a lump in her throat, tears in her eyes. Marc and Chris were standing on either side of her, patting her. She wiped her eyes as best she could. She could hear the sound of people clapping, and as she looked around the room she could see that the applause was spreading. At first only the youngest people were clapping—the few teenagers in the group—then the college students, then the younger instructors. The older professors held back at first, then joined in too.

A tall, white-haired figure strode slowly to the front of the room. Lisa gasped as she realized that it was Dr. Fineman— the chief of the anthropology department at Howard Phillips University, her father's boss.

"William, Aloysius," Dr. Fineman's paper-thin voice sounded, "we're the elder statesmen of this bunch. We've been playing a cautious, close-to-the-vest game for decades. Yes, back to the days of Mondrick and McLaurin, and our departed colleague whom Anthony White Holmes called Wolf Wolfe. And farther than that."

He looked around the room.

Lisa and the others had resumed their seats, and Lisa could see how old Dr. Fineman really was, how tired he must still be after last night's changes and activities on Mt. Tamalpais. He was clearly making a great effort, even a sacrifice, to stand here and speak to the authentication group.

He whispered. "These children are showing us the way. I hope they don't mind my calling them children. But our friend who burst in here before, who wanted to burn us all—he might have supplied us with another verse, one about a little child leading them."

Fineman paused, tall and gaunt and with his white hair turned into a rosy halo by the light of the fireplace behind him. He looked straight at Lisa—it was no illusion this time, he was not glancing around the room trying to pierce each person in turn with his look—and addressed her and all the others.

"Miss Kane is the youngest person in our group, the daughter of one of our distinguished friends, although Professor Kane is not himself were. And Miss Kane has cut through all of our encrusted learnedisms and theorizings. I applaud you, Miss Kane." He leaned back against the carved mantelpiece, holding onto it with one outstretched hand.

Someone in the front row rushed forward with a chair for Dr. Fineman and he slid into it, a look of gratitude on his face. "At my age," he whispered, "I'm afraid my mountain runs are about over. But you cannot imagine how precious was last night to me—to be one among my own people, innocent and unashamed."

He took several deep breaths, as if gathering his strength. Then he continued, addressing the room full of people. "We have tried for decades to make our cause understood. All to no effect. People read our reports as sensational fiction, as medical or psychological aberrations, as religious and cultural survivals.

"Even the direct, literal truth, told directly and unambiguously is avoided. I refer you to the works of Castaneda, himself a perfect corvanthrope if I may coin a word—a were-crow. A fascinating case by the way, one which I have commended to Stewart and to Raphael for study, especially regarding the apparent alteration in body-mass.

"But the man himself seems to interpret his experiences alternately in terms of narcotic hallucinations and mysticism. He cannot accept the literal reality of his own were."

He shook his head slowly a few times, an old, old man near the end of his strength, but he managed to raise his face once more and say to the others "Into your hands, children. And yes, Miss Kane, cling to your conviction, do not let yourself be swayed ever. You are completely in the right.

"Were is wonderful!"

The whole room echoed to the sound of every voice repeating the slogan. *Were is wonderful.*

To Lisa the rest of the evening passed like a dream. She watched old Dr. Fineman helped from his chair to a seat on a big, tapestry-covered sofa. She felt dozens of hands patting her, shaking her hand, heard people repeating her words over and over.

She made her way to Dr. Fineman and dropped to one knee beside his couch. He smiled at her, a warm smile that she imagined her grandfather might have given her if she had ever known her grandfather. "You will be a fine woman," he said. "I wish I could see you in ten years, Lisa Kane. I know that will not be, but our people will be well off with you as their champion."

Lisa struggled to make the lump in her throat go away. There was nothing she could think of to say to Dr. Fineman, so she just stayed beside the old man. He placed one of his hands, old and dry and as light as the touch of a summer's butterfly, on the back of one of hers. "Fortunate Leo," Dr. Fineman said, "to have such a daughter as you."

Dr. Fineman closed his eyes and lay breathing softly, exhausted. Someone came with a blanket and covered the old man.

The meeting dissolved. Some of the older professors stayed behind. One of them said they would take care of Dr. Fineman, make sure that he was all right and get him back to his room if he needed no other help.

Outside the conference hall Marc gave Lisa a hug and shook hands with Chris, and disappeared to walk home from the university. Chris and Lisa rode back to the hotel on the shuttle bus from the conference hall. When they got there they found Lisa's father already in his slippers and dressing gown, smoking his pipe and working over his notes and papers as ever.

"Come on in, Chris," he said.

Chris and Lisa went into the room and sat down.

Lisa's dad looked partway up from his papers. In a half-distracted voice he asked, "How was the authentication group tonight? Anything interesting happen?"

Chris said, "It was a dynamite meeting, Mr. Kane. Everybody

was there from last night. We got crashed by some kind of fanatical nut who wanted to burn everybody—remember that guy we saw yesterday waving his arms and yelling?

"And when we got rid of him Dr. Fineman almost passed out and Lisa was a sensation, she was the hero of the gang. *Were is wonderful,* she said, and—"

Leo Kane had looked up, his eyes opened wide. He took his pipe from his mouth and said, "Isaac Fineman passed out?"

"No," Chris said, "he almost did, though. It was right after the woman with the big hair said her piece and then Lisa hollered 'Were is wonderful' and everybody joined in, and then Dr. Fineman got really tired and could hardly stand...."

"But he was all right," Leo persisted. "He didn't have to go to the hospital?"

Lisa joined in with "Dr. Raphael and Dr. Stewart stayed with him. They covered him with a blanket. He said he was just worn out from last night. Our whole group went up on this mountain, Dad, Mt. Tamalpais out near the ocean, you know, and—"

But Leo was out of his seat, and took off his dressing gown and put his jacket back on, heading for the door. "Did they say where they were taking Fineman?" he asked.

Lisa and Chris looked at each other. Lisa tried to remember what the professors had said. "I think they were going to bring him back here and put him to bed if he was able to do it. Otherwise I guess they'd have to call the doctor. Or take him to a hospital."

By then Leo was out the door.

"I guess I'd better get back to the other people from Stonesboro," Chris said to Lisa. "You'll be okay, won't you?"

Lisa yawned. She said, "Sure. G'night, Chris."

He looked at her and said, "Were is wonderful."

Lisa moved her lips in the shape of the same words. "Were is wonderful." Chris was gone away toward the elevator in the hall. Lisa went and undressed and got into her pajamas and climbed into her hotel bed. She turned off the light and watched the shadows and reflections from the street dancing around on the ceiling over her pillow.

Her mind was full of confusing, exciting thoughts.

She was a werewolf, yes. She and many others. And it wasn't anything wicked or shameful or bad. It wasn't a deal with the devil or a disease or anything else like that at all. It was just the way she was, part of her, like the color of her hair and her eyes and shape of her nose.

People would have to accept her for what she was, not for some twisted picture of what she wasn't but that they might want her to be. She had nothing to hide and nothing to change into something else. There was nothing wrong with her that needed to be cured.

She had to learn to accept herself for what she was, and other people would just have to learn the same lesson.

And the lesson was—*Were is wonderful.*

She fell asleep and dreamed about Mt. Tamalpais again, about having the salve spread on her and changing into a beautiful, graceful, powerful wolf. Of running up and down steep slopes on her strong, steady legs. Of sniffing the scents of a hundred different kinds of plants and animals, and of watching the moon ripple its reflection over the ocean in a thrilling silvery stripe.

She yawned and stretched.

CHAPTER THIRTEEN

Suddenly and it was morning.

Lisa sat up, surprised. Where had the night gone? Somewhere into a lovely, thrilling dream.

Her father was in the room again, walking up and down and talking to her. She didn't know how long he'd been there, but he was smoking his pipe as he walked, and the room was in full daylight again.

"Dad?" Lisa said. "Dad? Is Dr. Fineman all right?"

He stopped pacing and faced her. "Oh, Isaac. Yes, they had the medics in after all but they diagnosed simple exhaustion. That man acts like someone half his age. Wonderful thing if you can keep it up, but you have to take care of your body, too."

He stopped pacing and stood beside the window.

"You needn't trouble yourself over that, Lisa. It's something you won't have to worry about for a long, long time, eh?" He came over to her bed and she sat up and he gave her a good morning kiss on the forehead.

"Last full day of the conference, mustn't waste it. What say to another of those fine Berkeley breakfasts?"

They had a feast, just the two of them. Leo was concerned mainly with Isaac Fineman. It looked, he said, as if Fineman would have to take it much easier once they got home—cut back his student load, reduce his office work, maybe go into partial retirement. Most likely, Leo would have to take up at least part of the slack. And there was a chance that Fineman would resign as department chairman and try to get Leo into the job. That would mean a happy increase in Leo's status at Howard Phillips University, but also a lot more hours at Stonesboro and far fewer at home in Whitbridge. Those quiet days in his study, he told Lisa, might be at an end.

"But nobody in the authentication group seems to want to talk about Friday night," Leo went on. "Last night, Saturday, Isaac collapsed from exhaustion. But this conference hasn't been particularly demanding. As for jet-lag, that's more likely to hit you headed east than west—this way, the day you travel is shorter than normal and you wind up ahead of things. You tend to hit a stretched day and run into fatigue when you go the other way—it's all in how you cross the time zones."

Lisa had a mouthful of muffin with marmalade when Leo finished speaking. She chewed it doggedly and washed it down with a big swallow of cocoa, then answered. "Friday night we were all up on the mountain, on Mt. Tamalpais. The whole authentication group was. They said anybody who didn't want to go could be excused, but everyone went."

Leo shook his head. "I guess a tramp around a mountain at night could wear out an old man, but total exhaustion—there must be something more."

Lisa put down her cup and looked around the restaurant where they were seated. No one was paying any attention to them and she didn't recognize anyone familiar. "Dad, don't you remember what Dr. Raphael said about the group? About how they gave out the invitation cards? Everyone in the group had to pass that experiment with the salve that Dr. Stewart's people gave Friday afternoon. Everyone in the authentication group—" She leaned forward and dropped the level of her voice. "—everyone in the group is a lycanthrope. When we got up on that mountainside they had big containers of the same salve and we put it all over ourselves.

"It was the full moon, too. It was a day before we thought it was coming because of something about time zones too, something like that jet lag."

"Of course," Leo interjected, "Greenwich Mean Time is used

for making up ephemera, even for calendars that give the phases of the moon."

"Well," Lisa went on. She stopped to take a big forkful of bacon and fried egg and a swallow of orange juice. "Up on the mountain we all changed. Every one of us became a wolf. Chris and Dr. Raphael and Dr. Stewart and my new friend Marc. Everybody. Even Dr. Fineman."

"Of course!" Leo gasped. "Of course! It's in all the traditions, I should have known that. All the were-people, whatever they transform into, are exhausted at the end of the experience. Even the ridiculous film versions of the forties always showed the wolfman sleeping it off after his transformations. Perfectly sensible. What a strain it must be on virtually every cell in the body to alter itself from human to animal and back."

Lisa said in a low voice, looking at her plate, "That's true. That was what I meant, Dad, back before we left home for California."

Leo nodded thoughtfully. "Yes. I think I see that, Lisa. Why you said that no one could understand what you experienced. You and your mother. And Chris Simmons. But not your friend Toni and not your father."

Lisa nodded.

They passed the rest of the day quietly. Lisa didn't bother to attend any more sessions of the conference. Instead she strolled around the plaza and ran into Marc. Together they met Chris.

The three of them listened to preachers and politicians making their speeches to whoever would pay attention. Even the babbling man in the mismatched plaids was at his usual spot, shouting and waving as if nothing out of the ordinary had happened. Lisa commented on him and Marc said, "He's a Berserkely character."

Chris said, "A what?"

"A Berserkely character. A price we pay for the way this town is. Lots of freedom, lots of energy and variety. Lots of nuts, too. Maniacs like plaid-man here, or the flying saucer people down at the Revolutionary Temple."

"You know them, too?" Lisa burst in.

"Sure, everybody knows those maniacs. As long as they don't do any harm nobody hassles 'em. But that's what makes Berkeley, Berserkely."

Lisa and Chris laughed.

Chris said, "Does that apply to monsters, too?" He held his arms out in front of his shoulders and lurched forward in a stiff-legged Frankenstein shuffle.

Lisa dodged around him on one side, Marc on the other. They ran at him from the sides and began to tickle him until Chris collapsed onto the plaza with laughter, begging Lisa and Marc to stop.

They went for a walk on Telegraph Avenue—Marc said it had been named that because the telegraph lines used to run down it long ago; he'd seen photos of it showing the poles and the wires. Lisa bought a little toy cable car for Toni's brother Bruce Dan and Chris purchased a beautiful hand-tooled belt with a wolf's-head buckle for his Aunt Stella.

Late in the afternoon they stopped at the conference hall again and looked at the bulletin board. A sheet of paper on fancy letterhead asked all members of the authentication group to sign their names and addresses so that Dr. Raphael could get out a newsletter to them. Lisa and Chris and Marc all signed the sheet, then Lisa and Chris took down Marc's address and he theirs so they could exchange letters after they went home.

In the evening there was a big dinner with dull speeches and Lisa found herself dozing off long before they all returned to the hotel and to sleep.

The next day they flew back to the East Coast, and rode by bus from the airport to Stonesboro, and in Lisa's dad's Volvo from the Gamwell Library at Howard Phillips University back to Whitbridge. They cruised up the old Stonesboro Turnpike and crossed the White River Bridge outside of Whitbridge. Lisa felt happy at the approach of home—California had been fun, and her experience there had been a very important one. She would have to think a lot about it, and talk it over with people she trusted, before she was finished.

But it was still good to be home.

They dropped Chris at his aunt's house up Mountain Road beyond the empty mill. Chris shook Lisa's dad's hand and thanked him and then he took Lisa's hand for a moment too and said in a low voice for her alone, *were is wonderful*, and then disappeared through the low, rusty gate and up the path to the house.

Lisa's dad started the Volvo's engine again and Lisa slid back into her seat. They stopped again at Toni MacPherson's house. It was early evening by Lisa's body-clock, but the time zones were interfering again, and in Whitbridge it was late in the evening. The sky was dark, the moon only a little past full was providing its own illumination, and the town was settling itself for its night's rest.

Toni wanted to hear all about California but Lisa said she'd have to see her in school the next day, but that she had a present for Toni and she'd bring it with her.

Meanwhile Lucy came running out of the back room where she'd stayed at Toni's house and flew into Lisa's arms, squealing with joy and licking Lisa's face with her thin, pink tongue,

Leo Kane thanked Toni's parents for letting Toni keep Lucy while he and Lisa were gone, and then they went home and into the house. They took a snack from the kitchen and then Lisa yawned and said she was going to bed.

Her dad looked at his watch, shook his head and re-set the watch three hours ahead of California time. "Glad you came along, dear?" he asked Lisa.

She grinned happily. "It was the best thing I ever did, I think. All of those people, and now I feel as if...." She wasn't exactly sure what she was trying to say, but her father put his arm around her shoulders and she was able to lean on him for a minute. Then she said, again, "I'm going to bed," and did.

CHAPTER FOURTEEN

The next day was Tuesday. Lisa awoke early even though she had "lost" three hours because of the jet flight across the country the day before. She was too full of excitement to stay asleep even as long as she usually did on school mornings.

After Lucy had gobbled down her breakfast and had her morning romp Lisa cooked up a pot of oatmeal for her father and herself. This was nothing like the fancy restaurant breakfasts they'd shared in California, but it was a good, comforting feeling to be in her own house, her own kitchen again.

Lisa's dad said he was headed for Stonesboro. "I'm afraid it's HPU every day for a while at least," he said. "I may even have to stay for some meetings in the evenings, but I'll phone you if that happens." He put his hands on Lisa's shoulders. "You'll be all right?" he asked.

She said of course she would—she'd spend the afternoon after school at Toni's house. She was going to do that anyhow, to give Toni her present and tell her all about California. And she'd see her dad at home, at dinner time, if he didn't have to stay away.

"I'll call you at MacPherson's, then, if I'm not coming home by then."

He gave her a ride up Psalter Street to Centre Avenue, and along Center Avenue as far as Blackwood Street. Toni wasn't there yet so Lisa hopped out of the car and her dad drove on through town. Lisa waved after him as he left; she was thinking about him, what it meant to have a father, and what he must feel about her.

She hadn't thought about such things before, very much. Now she walked slowly down Blackwood toward Toni's house, her hands in her jacket pockets, one of them clutching the little box she'd brought across the country, containing the hand-wrought silver and turquoise pin she'd got for Toni. In another pocket was the toy cable car she'd got for Toni's little brother.

She looked up at the trees along Blackwood Street. Even in the few days she'd been gone they were beginning to shed their brightly-colored leaves. Soon the flaming reds and golds of the autumn leaves and the crisp, blue sky over Whitbridge would give way to winter's coloring: gray skies, black trees stretching naked limbs upward, and soon the ground, covered with white or gray.

She hoped that her dad would be safe driving to and from Stonesboro every day. He'd been doing it every winter since they'd come to Whitbridge, years before, although not as many times each week. And Lisa had never worried about him before. He was her father. He was a big, grown-up man. And she was just a little girl.

But now she was getting a lot bigger than she used to be. And Dad—Leo—seemed a lot smaller to her, far less the all-powerful, all-knowing hero he had been. Not that she loved him less. If anything, she realized, she must love him more, now that he was showing his needs and his limitations. And now that she, Lisa, was learning of her own strength and abilities.

She reached Toni's house and sat down on the wooden steps that led up to the porch. She didn't feel like ringing the doorbell. She just waited for Toni to come.

Mr. MacPherson's car was gone—of course, he was off to Parkhurst and the computer works where he went every day. Lisa hoped that her own dad wouldn't really have to go off to Stonesboro every day. She hoped even more that they wouldn't have to move to Stonesboro. Whitbridge was her home!

But actually Howard Phillips University seemed like quite a nice place to spend your days. The Gamwell Library, the faculty club where she had first met nice old Dr. Fineman, the student building where she'd listened to the juke box and looked at the magazines and the comics. It wasn't a bad place. It might be nice to be a student there some day—probably even nicer than the university in Berkeley. That had been nice too, but there was maybe just a bit too much odd activity going on.

Either was better than the computer works, she thought. In fact, she'd never seen the computer works, but she had a mental image of a terrible, great factory with giant machines clanking and crashing about, and thousands of red and green lights flashing all the time.

Her thoughts were interrupted by the sound of Toni's squeal from behind her. "Lisa! How long have you been there? Why didn't you come in the house?"

Lisa ignored the questions and just reached in her pockets and got the presents out for Toni and Bruce Dan. Toni wanted to open them then, in the house, but Lisa asked her just to drop off Bruce Dan's toy and to walk to school with her. Toni said all right.

They went up Blackwell Street and turned at Centre Avenue, and walked along the sidewalk past Dave's snack shop. Toni had been holding onto the box with her present in it and now she finally said, "I can't wait any more!" She pulled it open and her eyes popped when she saw the pin.

"It's gorgeous! Oh, it's perfect. Here, Lisa, help me put it on!" Toni unzipped her jacket and tried out the pin in different places on her heavy winter shirt. Finally, with Lisa's help, she pinned it on and zipped her jacket up again.

They continued walking. Toni said, "Tell me all about everything! Did you have a good time? Did you see exciting things? Did you meet anybody nice?"

Before Lisa could say anything Toni rattled on, "And I have to tell you all about the Harvest Moon Ball. It was terrific! Jeff gave Billy Cantor and me a ride, and Big Stew and the Studebakers were there and they were super! Big Stew has his hair like in the '50s pictures, you know, Lisa, and the band he has, the Studebakers...."

But they were at school now. Lisa said, "Let's just go to our classes, okay, Toni? Can I come to your house after school? Dad is at Stonesboro today. Lucy will be all right at home. Then we can talk about everything."

In her classes Lisa tried to pay attention to her teachers. The other kids wanted to ask about her trip and she told them all that it was nice, she had a nice time, it was fun, yes, yes, she liked California, yes, she was glad to be back in Whitbridge too.

But she kept thinking about the authentication group, about their meetings in the Maturin room. About the big meeting where she had first tried the salve that Dr. Will Stewart's helpers had brought. And about running on Mt. Tamalpais, about seeing the moon reflect off the ocean. About seeing it with the eyes of a wolf.

In a couple of classes she saw Chris Simmons.

They didn't have seats close together in either class, and Lisa avoided Chris in between. But in her algebra class she looked over at him once when the teacher was putting an equation on the chalkboard.

Chris was looking at Lisa. Their eyes locked and he said something, or moved his lips as if he was saying something. Lisa looked closely at what he was saying. *Were is wonderful.*

She blushed and turned back to the board. The teacher turned back toward the students and said, "Now, class, who thinks they can come up here and solve this simple little quadratic equation?" A boy from Thames Street who talked to Lisa once in a while put his hand up. Everybody else in the room slumped back, relaxing.

The boy went to the board and began writing a solution.

After school, as they were leaving Mr. Barton's biology class Lisa and Toni ran Into Billy Cantor and Chris Simmons. The boys wanted to talk but Toni said that she and Lisa had to go home. Billy said they had to go do their paper route anyhow and they'd talk the next day in school, or maybe call up that night.

Chris said, "You want to come over to my house again, Lisa?"

Lisa said yes, but they didn't talk about when she would.

At Toni's house they went upstairs and put on Toni's Big Stew and the Studebakers album, and Toni told all about the Harvest Moon Ball. "It was so great, I guess it would be worth missing it for a trip to California but I'm glad I was here." She told more about who was there, what it was like.

To Lisa it all sounded like fun, but not very important.

After a while, when Lisa realized that Toni wasn't going to run down, she interrupted gently. "Do you want to hear about California?"

Toni looked down at her silver-and-turquoise pin again and said, "Oh, yes!"

Lisa didn't know what to say. She wanted to tell Toni all about—everything. She tried. "We're best friends, aren't we, Toni? We've always been friends, ever since we started school, remember the first day? We sat on the floor crying together?"

Toni laughed a little.

"Well—well, I want to tell you something very important about—about me, Toni."

Toni said, "Does it have to do with your trip?"

Lisa nodded.

"Is it about a boy, Lisa? About Chris Simmons? Or some boy you met in California?" The end of the question was spoken in an excited near-shriek.

"Sort of." Lisa shrugged one shoulder. They were sitting on the carpet in Toni's room. Both of them had thrown their jackets on Toni's bed when they arrived and they were sitting in their jeans and shirts and hiking boots that all the kids were wearing this season.

Toni waited. Lisa thought Toni would ask something else, but she just waited for more of an answer to her other questions.

"Not really," Lisa said. "I mean, it's sort of about Chris Simmons and there was another boy that I met in Berkeley, a boy named Marc, but that isn't what it's really about."

"Well?" Toni said impatiently.

Lisa thought of the authentication group, of Mt. Tamalpais

and Dr. Fineman and Aloysius Raphael. She clenched her fists and squeezed until her fingernails hurt her hands. "Toni—I'm a—a werewolf!"

For a few seconds the only sound in the room was the Big Stew record. Lisa sat unmoving, the music twanging in her ears. She realized suddenly that she didn't really like Big Stew and the Studebakers very much. Then Toni laughed, and when she finished laughing she said, "You mean like the old movies on the spook show? *Grrrrr!*" She made a face so her teeth looked like fangs and held her hands up in imitation of the standard monster menace. A little like that moment in Berkeley when—

"Is that all?"

Lisa looked up. "What?"

"Is that the whole joke?" Toni looked slightly puzzled.

"That's the whole thing? You just say to somebody, 'I'm a werewolf' and that's the whole joke?"

"It isn't a joke," Lisa insisted, "It's the truth. I am a lycanthrope. I can change into a wolf. I inherited it from my mother, and it never happened before because you have to start growing up before it happens. It's like, ah, getting your, you know, period." She flushed.

Toni looked more puzzled than ever. She stared at Lisa. "It isn't a joke? You mean—you're telling the truth? You're really one of—" She made the monster face and hands again, only much less than before. It was the end of her question, the face-making and the gesture.

"Yes."

"But werewolves kill people, and then they always get killed. You know, the wooden stake through the heart. No, that's vampires. Well, you know what I mean, don't you?" Her face showed deep concentration. Then she said, "Silver bullets, that's what you need to kill werewolves. Silver bullets."

"Toni!" Lisa was close to tears. "Toni, you're my best friend! I never told anybody this before except—except other—other—"

"Other werewolves?"

Lisa nodded.

"You mean you have like a club? The werewolf club? Like the Big Stew fan club or the Magniffy Kat comic book club?"

Lisa shook her head miserably. "It's nothing like that. It's very...very serious! Don't you see? People have hunted us down for centuries, killed werewolves, told dreadful stories about us. Werewolves don't hurt people. All we want is to be ourselves, and people won't let us. They call us awful names and this crazy man came into our meeting in California and said we made deals with the devil and he wanted to burn us all and...."

There was nothing else she could say. She just sat there on the floor with tears running off her face and splashing on her shirt or on her jeans.

Toni said, "I'm sorry, Lisa. I didn't understand, I—did you tell your father about it? About—you know?"

Lisa nodded, *Yes.*

"What did he say?"

"He said not to tell anybody. But I thought I could tell you."

Toni said, "Yeah, sure." The record had ended and Toni went to the turntable.

"Please don't turn that over," Lisa said.

Toni looked at her oddly but put away the Big Stew album. She stood for a minute looking at her row of records and then pulled another album from its sleeve and started to place it on the spindle.

Lisa wiped her eyes with her shirt-sleeve and stood up. "Toni," she said.

Toni turned around.

"Do you believe me?"

Toni didn't answer.

"About the—about what I told you? That I'm a werewolf?"

"I don't know, Lisa. You wouldn't lie to me. We're best friends. And you said it wasn't a joke. But a werewolf? I don't believe in that kind of stuff. It's like—oh, I don't know, fairy tales or flying saucers or ghosts. All kind of make-believe stuff, you know? I don't, uh, not-believe you but...." She shook her head.

Lisa said, "Okay. Poor old Dr. Fineman said that people wouldn't believe."

"Who's that?"

Lisa shook her head. "Never mind. Only—please don't say anything, Toni, will you? Cause now I don't know what to do. I thought I could tell my best friend the truth, and then maybe a couple of other people, and then a little at a time.... But now I don't know. So will you promise just not to say anything?"

"Cross my heart," Toni said. She came over and hugged Lisa.

Lisa said, "I have to go home now and make dinner for my dad."

It was still early and Toni looked surprised at what Lisa had said, but she didn't say anything back.

Lisa put on her jacket and went home. She took Lucy for a long walk, all the way to the end of Psalter Avenue and then off into the fields and scrubby woods southwest of town where once-prosperous farmland had been let go back to nature.

Lucy had a fine time. She loved nature walks, or seemed to love them from the way she bounded off across fields, chasing rabbits and chipmunks, disappearing into brush and then reappearing, galloping toward Lisa like a greyhound and then zooming past her so fast that she seemed to shrink into a gray-black dot rather than really to disappear into the distance.

Except when she was ready to go home. Then she would jump up into Lisa's arms instead of zooming past on her run.

Sometimes Lisa was afraid that the dog would be lost in the countryside. Supposedly there were feral dogs in the hills— unwanted puppies, family pets that had been abandoned or that had gone astray and never returned home. They bred back to a kind of general type wild dog. At least that was what Mr. Barton had said at the Whitbridge Consolidated School when he gave a lecture one time on heredity.

All of the odd breeds of dogs that had been developed in thousands of generations simply disappeared. Tiny dachshunds and giant mastiffs, skinny borzois and massive huskies, squatty bulldogs and streamlined collies—they all bred back to a single sort of wolf-dog on their own. So much for human tampering with nature.

Lisa wondered if Lucy could survive by herself. She had her doubts. The funny gray dog had lived all her life in a house, with people around to take care of her, feed her, brush her. Could she hunt for food? Could she make herself a nest or den to sleep in?

And with a rush there was Lucy, reappearing from a little stand of trees. A gray-black dot growing as the dog rushed across the autumn-yellow field. This time Lucy didn't zoom past her mistress but took off in a great leap that looked like at least ten yards before she reached Lisa. She flew straight into Lisa's arms and crashed into her chest, sending them both sprawling onto the ground, Lisa laughing and shrieking with surprise and happiness, Lucy squealing and yelping.

Lisa dragged herself back up and yelled at the afghan, then started back toward home at a run, Lucy catching up in an instant and then running ahead, cutting back and leaping in circles around Lisa's feet as she ran.

They got home and Lisa gave the dog a good brushing, pulling whole heaps of burrs and twigs and knots out of her coat. Lucy, loving the attention, stood still better than she ever did for anything else, and when it was time for Lisa to brush her belly she willingly rolled over on her back, all four legs stuck in the air, while Lisa worked on her coat.

The only sign Lucy gave that she wasn't completely relaxed was the crazy way she rolled her eyes to watch what Lisa did, all the time she was brushing Lucy's belly.

Dad arrived home in time for dinner, although it was on the late side and he was tired, quiet, and not very hungry. After dinner he apologized and disappeared into his study, and spent hours working on papers or making long telephone calls. Lisa was sound asleep long before Dad ever emerged.

CHAPTER FIFTEEN

The days went like that. Each morning Lisa would have breakfast with her dad. He always seemed more cheerful and outgoing then than in the evenings, but somehow they never got to talk about anything serious, and Lisa wanted desperately to have a serious talk with him.

Dad would go off to Stonesboro and Lisa would walk to school. She saw Toni every day but after that one time in Toni's room they were both uncomfortable. Lisa felt that she had said something wrong, had somehow upset Toni and ruined their friendship. Not that they were enemies now; they were still friends, but—

But they only talked about little things. Everyday things. They even did homework together, and a couple of afternoons they stopped at Dave's snack shop and shared ice cream sodas. Surely they were still friends. But it wasn't the same friendship they had always had before.

And Lisa avoided Chris.

She saw him in school every day, too, and sometimes they would smile at each other across a classroom. Sometimes Lisa would see Chris move his lips as if he were saying something to her, and it was always the same three words.

It wasn't exactly that Lisa wanted to avoid Chris, either. Somehow it was the opposite of the problem she had with Toni. With Toni, Lisa had tried to talk about real, important things, and it hadn't worked. With Chris, she was afraid to talk about the really important things. She didn't know what to say to Chris, or what he might say back to her. And somehow she was frightened. And with her father...maybe it would be all right. Maybe she could talk to him about the things that really mattered to her. But there was never time in the mornings, and he was always too tired at night, or busy with work or with phone calls.

He did tell her that Professor Fineman had returned to Stonesboro after resting a few extra days in California. He'd even returned to Howard Phillips University and said he wanted to resume part of his work there, but wouldn't be doing all of it for a long while, if he ever did again.

Friday afternoon Lisa knew that a bunch of kids would be getting together at Dave's. There would be all of the chattering and playing around that took place every Friday, once the week's schooling was over and there were two days of freedom ahead. Toni would surely be there, and Lisa expected that Toni would want her to come over afterwards and watch the spook show on TV.

Lisa did not want to do that. She couldn't stand the idea of watching Gil Ghoul and listening to his crude jokes about monsters and goblins and ghosts. She used to like Gil Ghoul, but now she felt as if she would rather just go home, so she avoided the other kids. She went down Thames Street past the old dark Masonic Hall to Farnsworth Street, and west on Farnsworth till she reached Psalter, and back up Psalter to her house.

When she got there the phone was ringing. It was Toni, calling from the pay phone at Dave's. Lisa said that she just felt tired out and wanted to stay home and rest. Maybe she'd call Toni tomorrow or Sunday. No, she wasn't angry, just worn out. No, she didn't want to watch Gil Ghoul.

She took Lucy for a walk in the fields, then home again for her brushing. These days, Lisa found, that was the best time for her: those afternoon romps with Lucy, and then the times back at home when she brushed out the afghan's fur. Bedtime wasn't so good: she would lie under her quilt looking at the ceiling and thinking about herself, about her parents—Leo, who was so busy and tired these days, and her mother who had been a werewolf like herself. She thought about Chris and Marc in Berkeley, and about the crazy man in the plaid clothes and the beautiful young woman with the Beethoven sweat shirt.

And she thought about running on Mt. Tamalpais.

It was all too confusing, and she would call Lucy up onto the pillow with her and bury her face in the dog's soft coat and cry herself to sleep.

But now it was only late afternoon.

Her father arrived back from Stonesboro early for the first time since they'd returned from their trip. He came into the house and gave Lisa a smile and a kiss on the cheek, and she felt better than she had in days. Maybe she really was simply tired, and maybe after the weekend she'd feel all right.

She didn't have too much homework. The composition that she'd promised to write about her trip was due Monday, but Lisa was pretty good at that kind of thing, and she decided that she could write it easily enough. Maybe an outline and a rough draft on Saturday and her final version on Sunday.

She asked her father what he felt like having for dinner but before he could answer her the phone rang and for once he answered it himself rather than leaving it for Lisa. Instead, she went into the other room and worked on her algebra assignment while he was talking.

In a little while he came and sat by her. He put one hand on her shoulder and said, "Lisa, dear."

She looked up from her problem.

"You haven't started cooking dinner yet, have you?"

Lisa shook her head.

"We're invited out for dinner," Leo smiled. "Do you think you could be ready to go in an hour?"

Lisa said of course she could. "Where are we going?"

"Ah, we're invited to, ah, your friend Chris Simmons' house. That was, ah, Chris's Aunt Stella who called. We're both invited."

Lisa felt alternating waves of hot and cold rushing from her stomach to her fingertips. She closed her algebra book and her notebook and carried them upstairs to her room. She put them on her desk and went to her closet to look at her clothes. She changed to her best pair of jeans and put on her Magniffy Kat shirt, looked in the mirror, went and took them off and ran to the bathroom to take a shower.

After she'd dried off she came back to her room and tried a different outfit on. That was no good either. She put on her only warm dress—her father insisted on her always having at least one dress for winter and one for summer—and decided that she would wear that to go to Chris's house.

She tried her hair a couple of different ways, then tried on all her shoes and finally settled on how she would look.

She came downstairs and there was still a little while before it was time to go so she called Lucy and went outside with her, took a little walk up and down Psalter Street but didn't go very far, then came home again and put Lucy in the house. She looked at the big clock in the front room and saw that it was time to go. She called, "Dad?"

Her father appeared. He was wearing his best tweed jacket and flannel slacks, a pale-colored button-down shirt and a tie. They grinned and laughed at each other, then Lisa's dad offered his arm and she took it. They left the house almost like a couple going out on a date.

Dad drove the Volvo up Centre Avenue to Mountain Road, then out Mountain Road past the empty mill and finally pulled up in front of the old rusted gate. He shoved the gate open and then shut again after Lisa was through it. They went up the steps and rang the front door bell.

Chris opened the door. He gaped at Lisa until she almost asked what was wrong, then he said, "I never saw you wearing a dress before."

She said, "Can we come in?"

Chris stepped out of the doorway. "Oh, sure." Lisa took a few paces into the room. Her father came behind. Chris led the way into the parlor and they all sat down. Chris thanked Leo again for the trip to California and Leo made a polite answer.

Lisa could feel some tension in the room. Partly, she knew, it was between herself and Chris—they hadn't really talked about all that had happened on the trip, especially the night on the mountainside, and she knew that they couldn't be comfortable together until they did. Instead of trying to tell everything to Toni, Lisa thought, she should really have talked it over with Chris. After all, he had been there. He had had the same experience that she had. There was no way that Toni could really understand the way Chris could.

But most of the tension, Lisa realized even as she half-listened to her father and Chris talking, came from Leo, her father. It had to do with Aunt Stella—it had to.

And then the tense lines of force that had been flowing in the room snapped.

Lisa saw her father look up, then stand up. She turned her body so she could follow his eyes. Stella was standing in the doorway that led from the center hall of the house, and the stairs that went to the upper floor. The light behind her was stronger than that shining on her from the parlor, and Lisa could hardly see anything except for Stella's beautiful dark red hair that hung shining over her shoulders.

Chris stood up and said, "Aunt Stella, this is Lisa's dad, Mr. Kane. Uh—my aunt."

Stella smiled slightly. She said, "Thank you, Chris, Leo and I know each other. Or at least, we did, once." She took a few steps into the room, but before she could get very far Lisa's dad had crossed the carpeted floor to her. He stopped just a pace away from her and took both her hands that she held out to him.

They didn't say anything as they came back to the center of the room and sat on the couch facing Lisa and Chris.

Chris said, "Oh, I didn't know you had, um, met. Before, I mean.

"It was a long time ago," Lisa's father said.

Lisa was looking at Aunt Stella. Instead of the long, graceful dress she had worn the first time Lisa met her, Stella was wearing pants this time and a plain, long-sleeved shirt. She had on the hand tooled belt and wolf's-head buckle that Chris had brought her from Berkeley. Lisa thought that she looked younger this way than she had before, and just as beautiful. How did she get her eyes to look like that? Maybe she'd teach Lisa some time....

"Would you like something before dinner?" Aunt Stella asked. "Leo, a drink? Children?"

Lisa's dad shook his head, No, and Lisa and Chris, sitting side by side, did the same. Lisa thought of talking to Chris about their compositions that were due Monday. Maybe they could work on them together. Their teacher might not mind and it would be more fun that way. But she didn't say anything, waiting to see what would happen between Aunt Stella and Leo Kane. Stella was talking to Lisa's dad. "It's been a very long time, Leo. I'm—I'm sorry I didn't get in touch with you. Especially living in the same town like this. I couldn't believe it was just coincidence when you and Lisa arrived here."

Lisa's dad shrugged. "Strange things happen. I suppose I never gave up hoping. That's why I wouldn't leave this region. And then when my appointment came through at Howard Phillips, why there was never any reason to leave."

They looked at each other. Lisa thought it was odd that they didn't send the children—herself and Chris—from the room during such talk. But maybe each of them drew some kind of strength from the presence of Lisa and Chris.

"Do you get along all right?" Leo went on. "I could try to help if you—"

"It's all right," Stella cut in. "Some of that fabled Talbot fortune from Wales, you know. Part of it came to me and part of it is Chris's. From his parents. You never knew all the Talbots, Leo, did you?"

Leo said, "No, I never did. I think that might have been part of the—trouble."

"It might, yes. Well...." Stella stood up, "Won't you come in the other room, I think dinner's ready."

Chris showed Lisa the way to the dining room—she'd never been there before, in this house. Her father didn't come along with them. He disappeared with Stella, into the kitchen.

Lisa and Chris sat at the table, waiting for the others to arrive. They talked about school, about their compositions, then they fell silent. Lisa could hear voices from the direction of the kitchen but she couldn't tell what was being said.

Chris said, "What do you think they're talking about in there?"

Lisa smiled tightly. "Us. Them." She saw Chris looking puzzled. Suddenly she said, "Chris, didn't your aunt ever tell you about—all of us? Didn't you even guess?"

He only shook his head.

"Chris, my mother disappeared when I was little. My father always told me she was dead but just this year he admitted that he wasn't sure. She really disappeared when I was little. He said he tried to find her but he never could, so he thought she was dead.

"But she wasn't." Under the white tablecloth she clenched her fists on her lap. "I'm sure of it! Your Aunt Stella is—my mother!"

Chris's jaw dropped. For the first time Lisa got to watch his face grow red with emotion, then pale, then return to normal. "But why, Lisa? Why didn't they ever tell you? Or me! And why wouldn't they ever talk to each other before now? It doesn't make sense!"

"Yes it does!" Lisa challenged. "It makes plenty of sense! Don't you see, Aunt Stella is a werewolf! And so are you and I, Chris!"

"I know that," he said.

"But my dad isn't!" Lisa pulled her lower lip between her teeth and bit it. "That's why they didn't stay together! Because his people always per-per-persecuted hers! Those—those humans have murdered us and tortured us and—" She stopped and reached for the handkerchief that would have been in her pocket if she'd remembered to bring one so she chewed on her lip instead and somehow that helped her to force the tears back.

CHAPTER SIXTEEN

The two adults appeared in the doorway. Aunt Stella was carrying a long silver dish with a loaf of yellow-crusted bread on it. Leo was slightly behind her. He had a big wooden bowl of green salad in his hands. Somehow, Lisa thought, they both looked very happy. She wanted desperately not to spoil anything but at the same time she felt that she couldn't just keep quiet, she had to force this moment through to an answer.

She pushed her chair back from the table and said, "Isn't it true? Isn't it true, Dad—that my mother ran away because she was *were*—" She said it with the same sound as in *were is wonderful* "—and you weren't? Because different kinds of people just couldn't understand each other, couldn't really live together!"

Now Leo grew pale. He almost dropped the huge salad bowl, managed instead to land it on the table with a loud thump. He grabbed the back of a chair with both his hands.

He nodded, swallowed. "Yes, Lisa. That was the reason. That was why we couldn't stay together."

"But I was wrong," Aunt Stella interrupted. She had laid the silver bread tray on the tablecloth, too, and was standing with Leo. Their hands were together on the back of the chair, and Lisa saw that they had somehow laced their fingers together. "I ran away from your father," Stella said. "I was wrong to do it. I was so terrified and so filled with hatred by what had happened to lycanthropes. You can both understand that." She looked at Lisa and at Chris.

"And I couldn't really understand it," Leo put in.

"But you were willing to learn, willing to try." Stella ran her free hand over her shining hair. "And I ran away. It was my fault, Leo."

"Well, whoever." He stepped back from the chair, freed his hands. For a moment Lisa couldn't tell what he was doing, then she realized that he was holding the chair for Stella with perfect old-fashioned manners, like in the days when people thought women were so helpless they couldn't even sit down or stand up by themselves.

Stella smiled and slid into the chair.

Leo sat at the fourth place.

Chris was looking from one to the other. In a puzzled voice he said, "Then you are—married? And you're Lisa's mother?"

Stella nodded. She reached across the table and took Chris's hand with one of hers, Lisa's with the other.

"And all this time you wouldn't let him see you? That's why we had to live in this house way up here away from town?"

"Yes."

"Then how come—why did you—?"

"Why did I change my mind? It was because of what you told me about the meeting, Chris. What you all learned. About that fool in your meeting—and about what Lisa said." She turned toward Lisa and continued. "Oh, darling, I was so proud when Chris told me about what you did. And I was so ashamed of myself for running away and hiding from someone who only loved me. From your father."

Now she stopped for a moment and touched her eyes with a handkerchief that came from her own pants pocket. "I'm afraid we're not getting any dinner," she laughed.

"Stella told me about *were is wonderful*," Leo said to Lisa. "I had to learn too—to listen to you. Why, Chris had to come back here to Whitbridge and tell Stella and she told me, when you were trying to tell me yourself right there in Berkeley, and I was too busy being a scientist to listen to you. I'm sorry, Lisa. I'll try to do better."

"But *were* is *wonderful*," Lisa said, "that means that we were-people have to have our own, uh—I don't know—things." She couldn't find the right words to say what she meant.

"Yes, but we can understand other people," Stella said. "Or at least we have to try. And if they will try to understand us, we must try to help them, not send then away."

The four of them sat quietly for a time, all thinking. Then Lisa said, "Will you and Dad live together again, then? Stella? M-mother?"

Stella said, "I hope we will someday. Not yet. It's too soon. Too—we've been apart too much, too long. But I want to try. I think the time will come."

There was a longer silence. Somebody took a forkful of lettuce and began to eat it, and the sound of the crunching got them all started. In a few minutes Stella got up again. "I'd better go get the rest of our dinner or it will burn!"

"Can I help?" Lisa asked. She tensed her leg muscles to stand up, if only Stella—if only her mother would let her come along.

"Oh yes," Stella said. "Please come along and help me, Lisa. Please."

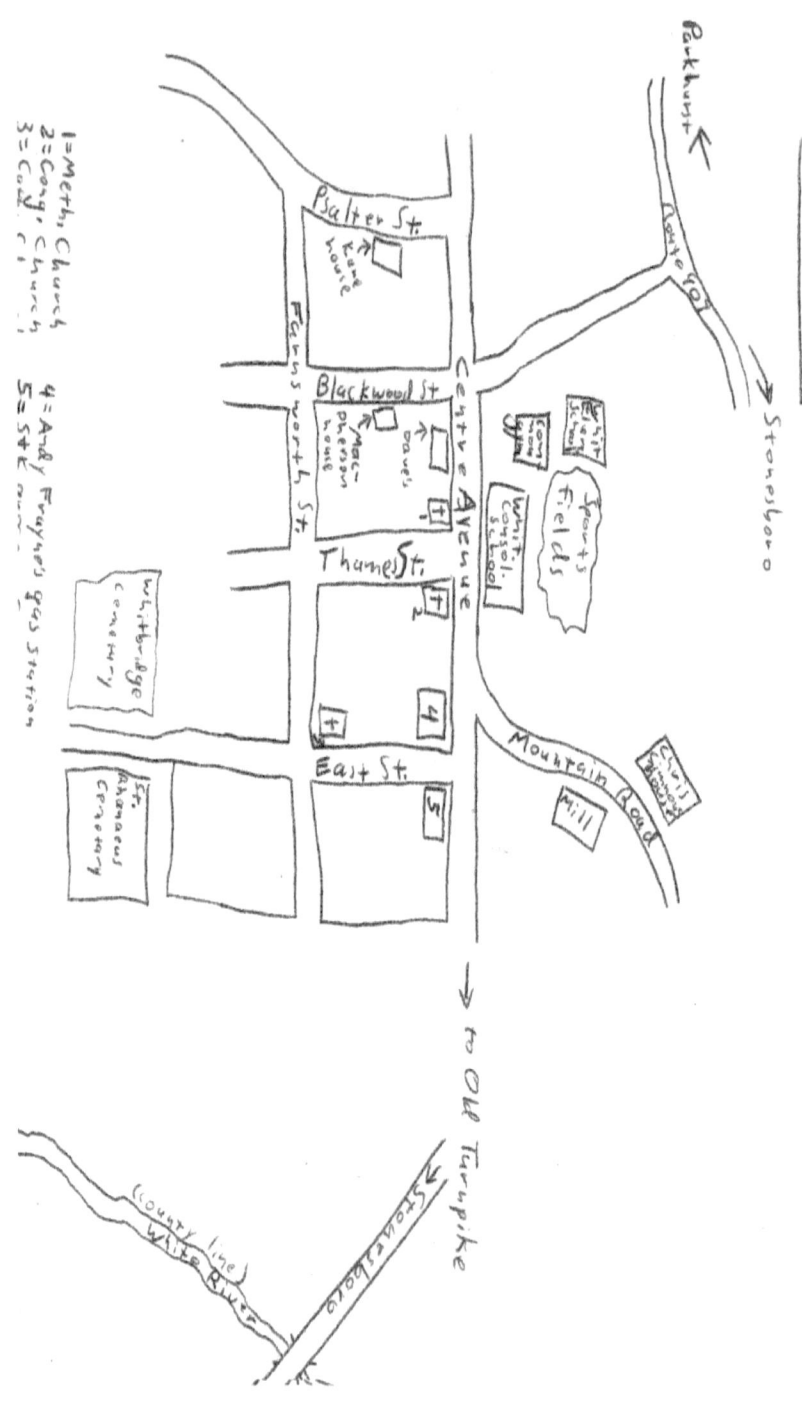

ABOUT THE AUTHOR

RICHARD A. LUPOFF is a prolific and versatile storyteller who has crossed every genre line in the world of literature. His works include mysteries, fantasy, westerns, mainstream novels, and science fiction, as well as nonfiction volumes of criticism and cultural history. His recent novels and collections include *The Emerald Cat Killer, Dreams, Quintet: The Casebook of Lindsey and Plum*, and *Killer's Dozen*. He has received many literary awards, and achieved the rare distinction of inclusion in "Best of the Year" anthologies in three separate fields: science fiction, mystery, and horror.

THE PRINCES OF EARTH

Adam Warrington is an intelligent, courageous young man from a provincial, repressive planet that has reverted to a kind of fundamentalist Puritanism. By nature a free-thinker and individualist, Adam has a tough time of it until he's accepted at one of the Empire's great schools, the University of Sol on Mars. Then he's off on the greatest adventure of his life.

His journey through space includes dining with aliens, air swimming, a hijacking, a space trial, and an attempted murder. He finally arrives on campus, where he must face further challenges before his first year of classes begins.

A Young Adult Literary Guild selection.

Borgo Press Books by MICHAEL KURLAND

The Princes of Earth: A Science Fiction Novel

THE PRINCES
OF EARTH

A SCIENCE FICTION NOVEL

MICHAEL KURLAND

THE BORGO PRESS

MMXI

THE PRINCES OF EARTH

FIRST BORGO PRESS EDITION

Published by Wildside Press LLC

www.wildsidebooks.com

DEDICATION

For Liam, Max, and Katie,
With Love...

CONTENTS

INTRODUCTION
THE MASTERPIECE
THAT NEVER WAS

by

Richard A. Lupoff

The year was 1978. Jimmy Carter was President of the United States. The best-selling novel of the year was *Chesa-peake*, by James A. Michener, followed by works by Herman Wouk, Mario Puzo, Sidney Sheldon, and Judith Krantz. The Number One song of the year was "Stayin' Alive," by the Bee Gees, followed by songs recorded by John Travolta and Olivia Newton-John, The Village People, Boney M, and the Bee-Gees (again). The Oscar for best feature film was won by *The Deer Hunter.* Other nominees were *Coming Home, Heaven Can Wait, Midnight Express,* and *An Unmarried woman.*

By 1978 Michael Kurland and I were already friends as well as colleagues, which we remain to this day. We'd collaborated on a couple of projects—a novel (that, alas, didn't sell) and a short story (that, happily, did). We had both tried our hands at what were then known as "juvies." Today they're called "YA's." Young Adult novels.

These are not children's books. Rather, they're novels with young protagonists—usually teenagers—and that deal with the process and the problems of growing up. The most successful author of this type of book, at least in the science fiction field,

was Robert A. Heinlein. "Heinlein juvies" were so popular that they were typically serialized in *Astounding Science Fiction, Galaxy Magazine,* or *The Magazine of Fantasy and Science Fiction.* Nobody bothered to say that they were juvies then, but for hardcover book sales, largely to libraries, they were so labeled. Then for mass-market paperbacks they were repackaged as straightforward science fiction novels.

So much for labels.

As for Michael and myself—I got there first, in 1976, with *Lisa Kane,* a book about a teenaged werewolf. Michael followed in 1978 with a marvelous science fiction novel, *The Princes of Earth.* The publisher was Thomas Nelson, a firm that had been around since 1798, and had a long history of publishing religious and spiritual works. By this time, obviously, they had also ventured into other realms, including science fiction.

The Princes of Earth was a first-rate science fiction novel. In the best tradition of the Heinlein juvies, Michael Kurland had created a detailed picture of the future. Humankind had explored much of the galaxy. Thanks to the development of a hyperspace or faster-than-light-speed drive, it had become possible to reach distant stars in relatively quick time, and a galactic empire had been the result.

There were human-inhabited worlds, alien-inhabited worlds, and mixed-population worlds. Laws, customs, and cultures might vary wildly but they were all held together by the concept of Empire and the universal parliament.

Kurland's protagonist, young Adam Warrington, had been raised on a planet that had reverted to a kind of fundamentalist Puritanism. By nature a free-thinker and individualist, Adam had a tough time of it until he was accepted at one of the Empire's great universities. Then he was off on the greatest adventure of his life.

No need to go into further detail in this introduction. You're about to read the book and I don't want to spoil the joy that you have coming by giving away the plot. Except—except for one

problem.

The book ends with classes about to commence at the university. It is Adam's freshman year. One of the traditional juvie formats calls for following a young man or woman through the educational process. There are countless titles like *John Doe's First Year at State* or *Mary Roe, Sophomore*. Chances are you've seen dozens of these, maybe even read some when you were in junior high—whoops, we're supposed to call those institutions middle schools now—and looking forward to your own future in the halls of ivy.

But back in 1978 the executives at Thomas Nelson decided that they should play to their strength—religious books—and not dilute their efforts any longer with things like science fiction novels.

So Michael Kurland's contract for further adventures of Adam Warrington was canceled. Yes, poor Adam was left, the eternal freshman, ready to plunge into his classes at Old Siwash, never to rise through the ranks of the Galactic Empire to whatever heights Michael had planned for him.

It's a pity, as *The Princes of Earth* is a truly splendid book, and the volumes that would have followed it—and should have followed it—would have made for a grand reading experience. In *The Princes of* Earth there are hints of things to come, foreshadowings of themes to be developed in later volumes that are nothing short of astonishing. And glorious.

As it is, we have only this one, rather short novel to entice us into anticipating the wonders that would have followed.

And yet, even after all these years, Michael Kurland is still with us, writing marvelous novels and short stories and nonfiction pieces and editing brilliant anthologies. Maybe he'll awaken in the middle of the night and exclaim, "By God, I don't care that it's been all these years! I started something and I'm going to finish it!"

And he'll climb out of bed and hit the power switch on his computer and start work on *The Return of Adam Warrington*. I can hardly wait to read it.

CHAPTER I.

One week before high school graduation I got the notice. First period in the morning, right after the bell, my work board lit up, and there it was. Under it, as on all the other boards in the room, was the Planetary History quiz we were scheduled to have, but on my board there it was: ADAM WARRINGTON, it said, the neat computer letters blurring out the test under it, PLEASE REPORT IMMEDIATELY TO ROOM 2614.

What, I wondered immediately, had I done wrong? Or, more to the point, what did the school think I had done wrong? Mr. Babdyke, I noticed, was scowling at me from his console in front of the room, so the message must be repeated on the teacher's board. Of course, it would be. I hurriedly reviewed all my recent indiscretions while I punched EXCUSE on the board. Mr. Babdyke printed *pardoned, hurry up*, in teacher's red under mine, so I got up, straightened my jacket, and walked calmly out of the room. It was the first time I realized Mr. Babdyke had a sense of humor. I wondered what I was going to be pardoned for, if at all.

Clinging to one side of the broad, empty escalator (elevators are for teachers only), I remembered one or two things. But surely they couldn't have found out who had punched the extra holes in the bell-ringing tape last Thursday before assembly. The poor, simple machine had gone crazy with an orgy of clanging during the speaker's sermon before the maintenance crew was able to figure out what was wrong. The Reverend Thrumbody—I think that was his name—was defining sins of omission and commis-

sion for us, one of the school's favorite topics. He must have added one to the list before that hour was up.

The Big Problem in school for that week was smoking. They'd caught one of the senior boys puffing on a homemade jibweed cigarette in the bathroom, and we'd been hearing about it ever since. But that let me out. The only time I'd ever tried it, two years before, I'd been sick as a dog—throwing up all over the place and afraid to go home until I stopped

When I reached the twenty-sixth floor, I saw that it wasn't an administration level, but had classrooms. Twenty-seventh to thirtieth were administration. I was saved by a floor.

There were several other students in the corridor when I got there. I recognized some of them as fellow seniors, and we were all headed for the same room. I reached the BOYS door, took a deep breath, and plunged into the room with the rest. They all, I'm glad to say, seemed as worried as I was. A guilty conscience never likes to ride alone.

The desks were all dark, the work boards not lit up, so it didn't matter where we sat. I went down to the front of the room and took a desk in the second row. It was pure habit. I like sitting where I can see the teacher without having to wait for him to project onto the desk board. If I'd thought about it, I'd probably have sat toward the rear, where whoever came in couldn't see me as easily.

Both sides of the room seemed to be filling up now, the girls' side, if anything, being slightly fuller than the boys'. I was quickly getting a lot less worried; anything this many kids had done—and over half of them girls—couldn't be that bad.

After a few minutes Principal Lowepride came in and took a seat at the desk console. My seat at assembly is at the back, so it was the first time I'd seen him up close; he looked a lot older in person. Then two other people I didn't know came in and sat beside him. One of them, a woman, wore the badge of School Administration, but the other didn't seem to be from the school at all.

The woman stood up and went to the lectern. "Courtesy,

students," she said. "Please punch your names," and the work boards lit up. I punched WARRINGTON, Ad. into mine. "All right," she said, checking the panel, "they're all here."

She sat down and Principal Lowepride took her place. "Good morning, students," he said.

"Good morning, Principal Lowepride," we all chanted back.

"You represent the top two percent of the graduating class," he told us, "and according to the Imperial Charter, as written into our binding, you're required to hear this talk." He didn't sound at all happy about it.

"Imperial Charter" sounded very impressive, and I couldn't help wondering if this was the legendary sex lecture that a school myth said we were supposed to get shortly before we graduated. But I decided it couldn't be that. First of all, it wouldn't be given for just the upper two percent, and second of all they wouldn't give it with the girls and boys in the same room. I suppose girls had to know about sex too, but they'd certainly learn in a different classroom.

The upper two percent, he'd said. Today was the first time I'd heard that, and it was good news. It meant that I was eligible to go to college, as the upper two percent was certainly part of the upper ten. My father wanted me to go to college, since only a college graduate was allowed to vote or hold office. I couldn't imagine ever wanting to become a deacon, or caring who was, but Father thought it was important. I was looking forward to Hapsburg Aggie, but for different reasons.

"Mr. Tule is on the staff of the Imperial Representative here on Jasper, and he'll speak to you this morning," Principal Lowepride said. Then he sat down and scowled. Jasper, as you've probably guessed, is the name of my planet. It isn't very big or important, as I've found out since, so don't feel bad if you haven't heard of it. It's the third planet out from the star Deuteronomy, one of the Reformation Group, if that helps.

Mr. Tule got up and faced us. You could tell right away that he was off-planet. His clothes, for one thing. Not that they were greatly different; it's only polite—and, I found out later, a regu-

lation—to dress the same as the natives on the planet where you're stationed. He wore a black double-button suit with a white shirt, a high, stiff collar, and a broad tie like every other male in the room, but they were cut differently somehow, and he looked more relaxed in them. The shirt collar, for example, was cut slightly lower than our standard.

Right off, he started speaking, without saying "Good morning," or "Courtesy," which was just enough against custom to be unusual, but not enough to offend. Anyway, he got everyone's attention, which must have been what he wanted. "I have an offer to make you," he said. "It is an offer that must be made, by tradition and law, in the name of the Emperor, to the top two percent of every graduating class of every high school of every Human-federated planet, kingdom, freehold, colony, satrapy, and League member in the Empire."

Now he really had our attention, or at least mine. The fact that Jasper was a part of a galactic empire didn't figure much in our lives or thoughts. Jasper, like all the other independent planets, is just about completely self-governing and left alone, but every kid must daydream about the Emperor and his court on far-off Earth.

I found out later that he was exaggerating. Some planets had been able to have that law written out of their bindings, and some didn't come up to standard. Then there are the planets that aren't part of the Empire, but we won't talk about those. Not right now.

"So in the name of Alexander the Ninth, Liege Sovereign of the Inner Planets, Protector of the Princes of Earth, Chairman of the Solar Hanse, and Hereditary Emperor of the Confederation of Human Planets, I extend to you this offer." The titles rolled off his tongue. Everyone leaned forward in his seat. I know because I looked around. "You are to be privileged for the next two months, standard, if you so desire, to take the tests required for entrance to the Imperial University. The tests are to be administered by Imperial personnel, and your planetary officials—in this case the administration of this school—are to

extend this opportunity to you freely. It shall not be denied to any of you for any cause. If, at the end of two months, you have not availed yourself of this offer, you will be asked to sign a waiver stating that you have freely refused." He sounded very severe. I wondered if he thought someone wouldn't want us to take the tests. I also wondered why we hadn't been told about this before; you'd think it would be used as an incentive. Heaven knows they use everything else.

It sounded like a set speech, and he wasn't using a cheat-screen. I could tell from where I sat that no words were being flashed on his retina. So he must have memorized the speech. If he'd gone to that trouble, then he thought it was important, so I listened closely to the rest.

"If you take the test and fail it"—he smiled—"and very few pass the test, so it's no disgrace—you are to be admitted without prejudice to whatever form of higher education your planet offers, in this case a branch of Jasper's Planetary College.

"If you pass the test, you are eligible to be sent, at the expense of the Emperor, to whichever branch of the Imperial University the examination shows you to be the most qualified for. The minimum time at the University, unless you flunk out," he added, smiling again, "will be four standard years. After that you may go home if you wish, go on if you're qualified, take employment with any private firm that offers it, or enter into service in whatever government branch is open to you.

"If you return home, or take private employment, you will be expected to reimburse the Emperor for the nominal cost of your education at a set rate, interest-free, over a period of time not to exceed ten years, standard. If you accept government service, the University is one of the job benefits, and you'll probably be going back for more of it over the years. I refer to the Imperium government, of course, and not any local planetary govern-ments."

He stood there for a second, and then said, "That is all. I have been informed that there is no time for questions, so if you have any, contact me at the Emperor's Freeground. My name is Tule.

Ask for me. But if you forget, anyone there will help you. I'm in the Parthenon."

The Parthenon is a small building with a lot of pillars in the middle of the Emperor's Freeground. It's bigger inside than it looks.

Tule walked out of the room, and Principal Lowepride got up and glared at us. "I'm sorry you had to hear that," he said. "If it weren't required, and they didn't insist on it, you wouldn't have." He made they sound like a dirty word. "And I put this whole talk under seal: you are not to repeat any part of it to anyone, not even to the other students with you in this room." That was laying it on kind of thick, but Principal Lowepride was good at such things.

"I'll explain," he said. He leaned over and got confidential with us, which always makes me kind of nervous.

"The Galaxy is a big place," he informed us, "with all sorts of people in it. All sorts. Most of them are pretty decent folks like you and me, maybe not as strong on morality as we are here on Jasper, but pretty decent. But many of them are not decent at all." He went into lecture 3-A on the Big Bad Galaxy, and I tuned out.

CHAPTER II.

Billy Denton caught up with me as I headed to parking lot after school. "Hey, Adam," he called, ting his arm confidentially around my shoulders, what was that meeting about?"

Billy was a sloppy-looking, heavy kid who always looked as if he had a couple of buttons unbuttoned somewhere—even when he didn't. He wanted to be buddy-buddy with everyone in the class, but he told nasty stories about people behind their backs. There was also a rumor that talking to Billy was a good way to inform the Dean of Discipline of all your latest endeavors.

"What meeting?" I asked him.

"Oh, come on," he said, thrusting his face close mine and breathing in my eye. "What's a friend for? You can trust me."

I pretended to look around nervously. "I trust you, Billy," I told him, "but I can't talk about it. You know...

"I know?"

"Sure. It was the talk about—you know." I looked embarrassed.

"Oh!" He finally caught on. "The talk about"—his voice dropped—"ess-dash-exx?"

"Billy!" I said.

"How come I didn't get one?" he whined. "I thought we were all supposed to get a—you know—talk."

"Sure," I told him. "We'll all get it before the end of the term, but in small groups."

"There's only a week left in the term," he reminded me.

"Learn from your elders and do not question them," I said,

quoting the motto above our library door. Personally, I've always wondered how you can learn from someone you can't question. "Anyway, they take only a few kids out of class at a time, but we'll all get it."

"We will?"

"Sure. Don't worry about it." I had reached my wheel, and I climbed on, stuffing my books and tapes in the junk box in back. "It's a good lecture," I told him. "You'll see."

I switched on the motor and wheeled out into the street. The image of Billy Denton waiting for the Special Lecture day after day for the next week, and it never coming, would brighten up my few remaining Study and Meditation periods.

The wheel is a vehicle peculiar to Jasper, and I should describe it to you. It's a kind of monocycle: one large rubber wheel with the motor in the middle and the seat on top. It's gyroscopically stabilized, can go about thirty kilometers an hour, and can run for about a hundred kilometers between charges. The legal age for riding a wheel is fourteen, and you hardly ever see anyone over fourteen and under twenty without one.

I took my time going home, thinking about the Imperial University and the entrance test. The idea of taking the test appealed to me, even though I had no interest in going to the University. Not that I thought the galactics were as immoral and decadent as Principal Lowepride had said—anything adults on Jasper didn't want you to do was immoral and decadent—but my future was all laid out for me, and that wasn't part of it. I was going to get a degree at the Agricultural College at Hapsburg, and go into my father's business selling farming machinery. Warrington and Son Hydroponics and Electronics was an old established firm. My grandfather was the Son. He still came around two or three times a month to tell my father how to run the business.

But I would have kind of liked to take the test. It would really be something to be proud of, if I passed. And, as Mr. Tule had said, it couldn't hurt if I failed. They would still have to let me into Hapsburg Aggie.

Principal Lowepride had stated strongly that it was not a Good Thing to take the test. He had hinted that they did all sorts of disgusting and repulsive things to you in the Parthenon. But Principal Lowepride was known for saying what he thought you should hear. Not that he ever actually lied—lying was immoral—but it was both moral and proper, when speaking to school children, to state the truth in terms that would simplify their understanding. Principal Lowepride could stretch very far from the facts to find those terms.

When I got home I did my chores, then settled down to get my homework out of the way before dinner. I did my math, ethics, and geography, and then, before getting into Problems of Morality, I punched Library: Information on my home board.

LIBRARY, the board said. CODE ? ? ?

I punched my class ID number.

REQUEST ? ? ? the board said.

Universities, I punched. *List.*

The library listed all the colleges and universities on Jasper.

The last entry was MORE, and I tapped that with my light-stick.

Now the list changed to show all the major universities throughout the Reformation Group. Again I tapped MORE.

This time when the board lit up it was covered with names, the print so small that I could hardly read any of them. There were names from ancient Earth, from the First Expansion, and from all over the galaxy. There, finally, in one corner, was IMPERIAL UNIVERSITY SYSTEM, very small. I tapped it.

THE IMPERIAL UNIVERSITY SYSTEM IS THE GENERAL NAME FOR THAT SYSTEM OF COLLEGES AND UNIVERSITIES CHARTERED OR ENDOWED BY THE IMPERIUM OR, IN SOME CASES, BY THE ROYAL FAMILY. AS VARIOUS ENTITIES OF THE SYSTEM WERE ESTABLISHED AT DIFFERENT TIMES OR ENTERED UNDER DIFFERENT CHARTER TERMS, THE

INTERRELATIONSHIP BETWEEN THE SEPA-
RATE COLLEGES AND/OR UNIVERSITIES IS
COMPLEX, AND A LARGE VARIETY OF EDU-
CATIONAL MODALITIES IS REPRESENTED.
MANY OF THESE ARE QUITE UNACCEPTABLE
TO THE ENLIGHTENED, AS THEY EMBRACE
ATTITUDES OF MORALITY AND STANDARDS
OF BEHAVIOR THAT IGNORE FUNDAMENTAL
TEACHINGS OF ENLIGHTENED REFORMA-
TION.

THE INSISTENCE OF THE IMPERIUM ON
SELECTING CANDIDATES FOR POSTS WITHIN
THE IMPERIAL BUREAUCRACY FROM GRADU-
ATES OF THE IMPERIAL UNIVERSITY SYSTEM,
AND THUS OVERWEIGHTING THE GOVERN-
MENT WITH PERSONNEL WHOSE BELIEFS
ARE BASICALLY ANTAGONISTIC TO THOSE OF
ENLIGHTENED REFORMATION, IS ONE OF THE
MAJOR CAUSES OF FRICTION BETWEEN THE
PLANETARY GOVERNMENTS OF THE REFOR-
MATION GROUP AND THE IMPERIUM.

THE OLDEST AND BEST KNOWN OF THE
UNIVERSITIES OF THE IMPERIAL SYSTEM IS
THE UNIVERSITY OF SOL ON MARS. IT IS SAID
TO HAVE BEEN FOUNDED WELL BEFORE THE
FIRST EXPANSION, BUT NO ACTUAL DATE IS
KNOWN. HEREDITARY NOBILITY OF THE SO-
LAR HANSE, LIFE MEMBERS OF THE HOUSE
OF LORDS, ELECTORS OF THE HOUSE OF COM-
MONS, AND OFFICERS OF FLAG RANK IN THE
SERVICE OF THE IMPERIUM ALL HAVE THE
PERQUISITE OF SENDING THEIR CHILDREN
TO THE UNIVERSITY OF SOL. THE UNIVERSI-
TY OF GNADA IS FAMOUS FEDERATION-WIDE
FOR ITS SCHOOL OF PLANETARY ENGINEER-
ING. LANGERT COLLEGE IS KNOWN FOR ITS

SCHOOLS OF MACROBIOLOGY AND LIBRARY
SCIENCE. UNFORTUNATELY THESE SCHOOLS
CONDONE IMMORAL BEHAVIOR, AND NO
PARENT ON JASPER WOULD BE ENCOURAGED
TO ALLOW HIS CHILD TO ATTEND.

That was all. There should have been a list of subject headings after that, so I could get whatever else I wanted to know. I punched Subjects—more. The screen cleared. The board hummed. CLOSED STACKS, the board said. AUTHORIZATION NEEDED: TEACH/AD

That meant I had to get the permission of a teacher or administrator to find out anything more on the subject. And that meant it had to be an authorized project. It seemed that the library didn't want you to think anything nice about the Imperial University and didn't want you to know anything at all beyond what every schoolboy already knew. I gave up and did my Problems of Morality homework.

Father came home late that evening, so we ate dinner almost an hour late. And he was in such a bad mood that he scared Miss Poot—she's the maid—and she dropped the roast. Then he yelled at her for being so clumsy, and she ran out of the dining room with her hands over her mouth. Mother picked the roast off the table with the serving fork and put it back on the platter. She handed it to Father to carve, and told him that if he didn't behave around the help and stop yelling, soon no girls would work for us and he'd have to buy a mechmaid. Father said this one wasn't so hot, and he'd almost rather have a robot if they weren't so expensive.

Sister Prudence, my twelve-year-old sib, said that Deacon Farthingail had a mechmaid and two maids and a groom, and that was because they had horses, and why couldn't *we* keep a horse, please?

This was pretty average dinner-table conversation for us. What with Father's temper, we went through maids pretty fast. Once we actually had a mechmaid for about three days, but

then it started throwing things over its shoulder and we had to send it back to the factory. It never came back. It was made right on Jasper. Other planets in the Reformation Group make better robots, and some planets outside the Group make even better devices, but we have such a high import tax on manufactured goods that only the landholders and deacons can afford the off-planet stuff.

By the end of dinner Miss Poot had recovered enough to clear the table and serve tea. Mother and Sister Prudence and I held our breath while she tiptoed around the table and took things off at arm's length, as though each dish were going to blow up in her face. Father affected to ignore her completely. He seemed to be in a much better mood since she had dropped the roast.

When tea had been poured, Father leaned back in his chair with his cup in both hands and stared speculatively over its rim at me. "Adam," he said. "Um, Adam."

"Father?"

"I have something to discuss with you, son—something serious."

"Yes, Father?" Now what on Jasper could this be about?

Mother stood up. "Perhaps we ladies should leave the room," she suggested.

"No, no, Clara, that won't be necessary," Father said, waving her back down. "This is not, um, man-talk."

Mother sat back down. Sister Prudence looked relieved. She hated to be left out of anything.

"I understand, Adam, that you are one of the top ten percent of your class," Father said. "Scholastically, at least. And therefore you are eligible to attend the Agricultural College at Hapsburg."

"So I believe, Father," I said. Now how did he know? The grades hadn't been posted yet.

"We might even go farther," he said, sipping his tea, "and say that you are in the top two percent."

"Yes, Father." So *that* was it. They must have called him.

Father shook his head. "How someone as bright as you can be so perpetually in trouble is beyond my understanding. Why

you can't understand that it's not to your own best interest to misbehave and provoke your teachers...or take things apart..." He allowed the sentence to die out, and just finished by staring at me.

I didn't say anything. I knew better than to answer him back. But that was unfair. It had been two years since I took the guts out of the flitterball and installed an affinity circuit. It had made it much more difficult for our team to lose when the ball just naturally preferred to go into the other goal. They'd suspended me from school for two weeks when they found out, and Father had resorted to corporal punishment for the first time since I was seven. The school authorities were particularly angry that I was reading technical material above my grade level. Everyone was supposed to know his place on Jasper.

But after all, that was two years ago.

"Now Dean Swift is afraid you'll do something foolish and take that test they told you about this morning," Father said, "so he called me. You, um, are, after all, not noted for your good judgment."

Dean Swift was the Dean of Discipline. He was not fond of me.

"What test is that, Poppa?" Sister Prudence asked.

"Never you mind," Father told her. "It doesn't concern you. Young ladies are not given this test."

There had been, as I remembered, slightly more girls in the room than boys, but I decided not to correct Father on that. On Jasper girls go to college only to become teachers or nurses, work fitting for a lady. Perhaps it was different elsewhere.

"You won't, will you?" Father asked.

"Won't what, Father?"

"Won't take that test. I can call Dean Swift tomorrow and tell him that you're not going to take it."

"Father, does it strike you as strange that Dean Swift calls *you* when he doesn't want me to do something? I mean, he could have just called me into his office and talked to me."

"You can be a very difficult young man to talk to," Father

said. "And, from what I understand, the school officials cannot forbid you to take the test because of some technicality. Even though it's clearly in your best interest."

"But *you* can," I said.

"I wouldn't want to do that, Adam," Father said. I could tell that he thought he was being very patient with me. "Not unless it were necessary."

"But that's not a choice," I said, trying not to get angry. "You won't forbid me from doing something unless I'm going to do it. But if I'm not going to do it, then you don't have to forbid me."

"Now, Adam," Father said firmly, but mildly, "I am your father, not a problem in logic. I'm not interested in who shaved the barber, only in ensuring that my son won't do something that's not in his own best interest."

It was happening again, and I couldn't help it. I was getting angry, and Father was getting mild. I always felt in the wrong and guilty for getting angry, but when Father got mad at me he didn't feel guilty, only proper and self-righteous.

I took a deep breath. "I had thought it might be interesting to take the test, Father, just to see how I placed." I said it very calmly, but I could feel my heart pounding.

Father slowly stood up. "It would not be interesting," he said. "You will not take the test. I will call up Dean Swift tomorrow morning and so inform him." He left the dining room.

"Oh, dear," Mother said.

"Excuse me," I said, getting up. "I must go and finish my homework."

For the next week Father and I exchanged very few words. And, as usual, I felt guilty.

Then, on the Thursday before graduation, the last official day of school, it happened.

There was a crew of painters in the downstairs hall when the doors to school opened in the morning. Large areas of the wall were already freshly sprayed, but they were still the same ugly yellowish-green they had been before. As I went up the escalator I noticed that several of the upper-floor corridors had also

been sprayed. I couldn't help wondering why. First, why do it in patches; and second, why not just wait two days until school was over to do it at all?

I sat down at my desk trying to figure it out. Not that it mattered, but it was a puzzle. Then the first-period bell rang, and my board lit up. ADAM WARRINGTON, it said, PLEASE REPORT TO ROOM 3031 IMMEDIATELY.

I gulped. Number 3031 was the principal's office—I had been there before. Principal Lowepride didn't send for you to congratulate you for passing spelling. I tried to think of something I had done that would interest Principal Lowepride. No sins of omission or commission for the past few weeks that I could think of. Well, there was only one way to find out. I punched EXCUSE on my board.

Excused, Mr. Babdyke printed.

It took fifteen minutes to get up to the thirtieth floor by escalator. In fifteen minutes light travels two hundred and seventy million kilometers. In fifteen minutes the average person can read nine thousand words, which would take him from the story of Creation in the Old Testament to the destruction of Sodom and Gomorrah. At one standard G acceleration, in fifteen minutes you'd travel close to four thousand kilometers. Fifteen minutes is a long time.

Principal Lowepride had a robot secretary, the gift of previous graduates to a previous principal. "Ah," it said, staring somewhere to the left of my head as I came into the outer office, "you must be the miscreant." It had a high, reedy voice that sounded as though it were about to crack.

"Excuse me?" I said.

It shifted its gaze slightly to the right of my head. "Principal Lowepride instructed me: 'As soon as the miscreant arrives, show him into my office.' You are a 'him.' You have arrived. Therefore, you must be the miscreant."

"Miscreant?" I guess I had done something.

It shifted its gaze again, and stared at my nose. "Miscreant: noun: a vile wretch; a villain; a rascal. One who has placed

himself outside the..."

"Yes," I interrupted, "I know what it means. I just want to know what it has to do with me!"

"...rules of decency and morality prevalent in society. Synonyms include: evildoer, sinner, transgressor, profligate, libertine, vandal, brute, ruffian, caitiff, desperado..."

"Never mind," I said. "I guess you'd better show me into Principal Lowepride's office."

"...rascal, knave, blackguard, delinquent, troublemaker, culprit, offender, malefactor, recidivist, renegade, apostate. See specific word for usage. This way, please, miscreant."

The creature wheeled out of its work cubicle and thumped across the floor to the door to the private office. It gave a quiver with each turn of its wheels, as though it were silently suffering from hiccups. It knocked on the door and opened it. "Student Adam Warrington is here," it announced. I guess I was the miscreant, since it knew me by name.

I went in. Anyone who thinks that being scared when you're questioned is a sign of guilt has never been a high school student entering his principal's office. At least not on Jasper.

There were four people in the office: Principal Lowepride, Dean Swift, and a gentleman and lady I didn't know.

"Courtesy," I said. "Good morning."

"Good morning, Warrington," Principal Lowepride said. "Please shut the door."

"If it isn't the young practical joker," Dean Swift said. He was sitting to Principal Lowepride's right behind the big desk that took up so much of the office.

"Hush, Swift," the lady said. She was on the other side of the desk, with her chair pulled much farther away from Principal Lowepride. "Warrington, come over here."

The gentleman stood by the window and said nothing. He had that sort of healthy, well-scrubbed, smug look of a Youth Patrol leader, but he was dressed in civilian clothes.

I walked over to the desk and stood in front of the lady. "Yes, ma'am," I said.

"You know what this is about, don't you?" she asked. She was a small lady, who was probably not as old as she looked, dressed all in black, with intense eyes.

"No, ma'am," I said. "I have no idea."

"He has no idea!" Principal Lowepride yelped, thrusting his fat chin forward and his arms in the air. "Forty men have to get up at three in the morning and spend four hours painting a few thousand square meters of corridor wall—and he has no idea!"

"Hush, Lowepride," the lady said, without taking her eyes off me. "My name is Miss Wigstaff," she told me. "I am from the Office of Public Decency."

"Yes, ma'am." She was a cop. Now they really had me worried. What was all this about?

"The gentleman by the window," she said, "is Mr. Eaststone, from the Bureau of Youth Control."

I looked at him, and he smiled at me. I didn't like his smile. "Yes, ma'am," I said.

"Have you anything to say?" she asked.

I tried to think of something. "No, ma'am."

"Really, Warrington," Dean Swift sneered from his side of the desk, "you must think we're all morons. Do you think we're morons? Do you really think we're morons?"

I was tempted to answer him.

"Let's look at the facts, Warrington," Miss Wigstaff said. "First"—she counted on her fingers—"we know that Jasper City Consolidated High School was vandalized this morning. Isn't that right?"

It was news to me. "Oh," I said. "That explains the painters."

"Explains the painters!" Principal Lowepride yelped. "Blasphemy and obscenity all over the school walls!" For a man who was in charge of a teaching staff of over five hundred and a student body of over eight thousand, he had surprisingly little control. His face was red.

Mr. Eaststone from the Bureau of Youth Control walked toward me, his step all springy and menacing and controlled. He liked his work. "Adam Warrington," he said in a voice that

was loud and commanding, and yet gentle and infinitely sad, "there is no point to this. We want to help you. And, Adam, I think you know that you need help. That childish scribbling on the walls was a cry for help, wasn't it, Adam?" The gentleness in his voice would have had me if I hadn't seen the gleam in his eye.

Then, suddenly, I realized that they thought I had done the writing on the walls. I may sound dumb, but I was so totally innocent that it had never occurred to me. I had thought that they believed I knew who had done it, and were trying to get me to spill on a friend. But they thought I was the vandal, and judging by their attitude, the writing must have been pretty nasty.

"Answer me, Adam," Mr. Eaststone said gently. "Speak with me and we'll work this out. Would you like to go into the other room, where we can speak privately?" He rubbed his hands together as though he were spreading oil. I wouldn't want to be alone in a room with him on a bet.

My heart was pounding so hard I could hear it, and there was an emptiness in the pit of my stomach. My mouth was dry. "I don't know what you people are talking about," I said. "I had nothing to do with whatever was written on the walls this morning and I don't know who did. I think it's a shame, and I hope you catch him, but I can't help. Can I go back to class now?"

Miss Wigstaff leaned forward and jabbed a finger at me to punctuate her remarks. "You seem to be upset, Warrington," she said. "Very upset."

"Of course I am, ma'am," I told her. "Wouldn't you be if someone dragged you into a room and accused you of things you didn't know anything about?"

"Not if I had a clear conscience," Miss Wigstaff said.

"Nobody dragged you in here, Warrington," Principal Lowepride barked.

"Would it surprise you, Warrington, to know that your wheel was identified as you left here at three o'clock this morning?"

Dean Swift asked, looking down his lean, bony nose at me.

"Yes," I said. "I was home, in bed, asleep."

"Would it surprise you to hear that we found your finger-prints on the walls before we painted?" Miss Wigstaff asked.

"Yes," I said.

"Do you claim that you never touched the school walls?" Miss Wigstaff asked.

"Yes. I mean, well, no. Of course I must have touched the walls at one time or another. But not last night."

"Did you wear gloves last night?" Eaststone asked softly. I could see that he thought he was awfully clever.

"I was asleep," I said.

"Have you touched the walls at all recently?" Miss Wigstaff asked.

"I suppose I must have," I said. "I don't remember specifically."

"He doesn't remember!" Principal Lowepride said.

"We're trying to be nice to you, Warrington," Miss Wigstaff said. "We have enough on you to convict you in Youth Court: your fingerprints, the fact that your wheel was seen leaving, your school record as a practical joker and troublemaker."

"We want to help you," Eaststone said softly. He had continued creeping up until he was right next to me now, looking down. "If you'll just confess to show us that you understand the error of your ways, it will go a long way toward helping you get through this unfortunate episode." A sickening sweet smell clung to him.

"But I didn't do anything," I insisted. "I was home in bed."

"That won't wash, Warrington," Dean Swift said.

After that I got stubborn, and refused to say anything. I was afraid that if I opened my mouth I'd start either screaming or crying, and I'd been taught all my life that it was unmanly to get hysterical. Besides, if they weren't going to listen, there was no point in my talking. They seemed convinced already anyway.

They kept at me for a little while longer, but finally stopped when they saw that it wasn't going to do any good. Then they

had a short conference, with me waiting in the outer office. The robot secretary ignored me.

Principal Lowepride came out alone. "You may return to class, Warrington," he said.

"Thank you, sir," I said.

"Oh, and don't bother showing up for graduation tomorrow," he added, smirking at me.

"Excuse me, sir?"

"We're holding back your certificate of completion until this is all settled. So there's no point in your showing up for graduation, because without the certificate, you can't graduate. That is all, Warrington; you may go."

"But I can't get into college without graduating," I said.

"That's true," Principal Lowepride said. "Miss Wigstaff is of the opinion that we don't have sufficient evidence of your guilt to convict you, but that a strong probability exists that you are the culprit."

"Miscreant," I muttered.

"What was that?"

"Nothing, sir."

He glared at me suspiciously. "We are continuing our investigation," he said. "When it's completed, you will either be brought to trial or allowed to graduate."

"Yes, sir," I said. "Thank you, sir. How long will that be?"

"I have no idea," he said. "That will be all, Warrington,"

"Yes, sir," I said. I went back to class to finish my last day of high school.

CHAPTER III.

My father was waiting for me when I got home. "Dean Swift called the store," he said.

"I didn't do it," I told him.

"Blasphemy and obscenity," Father mused. "All over the walls. Come into the study and let's talk."

We entered Father's book-lined study. It was one of the few times I'd ever been allowed in this room. Father looked very serious. I wondered what Dean Swift had said when he called, and what Father was thinking. "I didn't do it," I repeated.

He closed the door firmly. "Of course you didn't. If you were soft in the head, surely I'd have some inkling of it after raising you for seventeen years. Sit down." He waved to a hardback chair, which I settled gingerly down on, while he sat back in his reading chair.

"You're stubborn, opinionated, and disrespectful of authority," Father said. "I can't imagine where you picked up those traits. But you're neither crazy nor stupid. Whoever vandalized the school this morning is at least one, and probably both. Crazy to do it, and stupid to think he can get away with it."

"Principal Lowepride thinks I did it," I said. "So does the Office of Public Decency."

"They are sadly deficient in imagination," Father said. "They can't tell your sort of creative troublemaking from this sense-less, destructive act. Whoever did this is badly in need of help."

"That's what Mr. Eaststone from the Bureau of Youth Control said," I told Father, "except he thought it was me."

Father leaned forward. "You weren't out at three o'clock this morning, by any chance, were you?" he asked. "There's no chance that it really was your wheel that they saw by the school?"

"I told you I didn't do it," I said, looking him straight in the eye.

"Not the same question," he said. "I said I didn't think you were capable of pulling a stupid stunt like that. I didn't say I thought you were incapable of sneaking out at three in the morning to pull some other, uh, stupid stunt."

I suddenly realized that I didn't really understand my father. I would have bet that he didn't know about my occasional midnight trips to doctor the bell-ringing tape or conduct other social-science experiments, and that if he had known you would have heard him yelling from here to the Horsehead Nebula. But it sounded as though he had a pretty good idea of what I'd been doing, and hadn't said a word. I'd been worried about coming home to face Father, thinking he'd be sure to believe the school's accusation, and instead he believed me without hesitation. I didn't understand my father, but for the first time in several years, I was sure glad he was there.

"I didn't go out last night," I told him.

"The school custodian saw a wheel heading away from the parking lot at three in the morning," Father said.

"What made him think it was mine?"

"He didn't say it was yours," Father said, "but he did say it was red."

All wheels are black when they are sold. Most of them stay black. A lot of parents seem to think that the color of their kid's wheel is a moral issue, and that black is the only moral color. About one wheel in ten gets painted. Mirror finish was popular a few years back, but the school decided that mirror was immoral and banned mirrored wheels from the school parking lot. That was the same year a girl got expelled for coming to school in long pants instead of a long skirt. She was an exchange student.

"Red's a popular color," I told my father. "There must be a

hundred other students with red wheels."

"But they haven't got your reputation," Father said.

"The school isn't going to let me graduate," I told him.

"We'll see about that," he said.

And he did. But there was nothing he could do. He came home the next night angrier than I'd ever seen him before. And if I didn't graduate, I couldn't go on to Hapsburg Aggie. And I could never vote, or hold any elective office.

If I had been actually charged with the vandalism and officially expelled from school, I could demand a hearing to get reinstated. Father was sure they'd have to find me innocent. But they didn't charge me or expel me. I was merely suspended from classes pending investigation of the offense. The fact that I had no classes to be suspended from didn't matter. The fact that no one was doing any investigating didn't matter. The school administration thought that I had done it, and they couldn't prove it, so there was no point in continuing the investigation. They'd merely keep me suspended for the legal limit of two years, by which time I'd be too old to be admitted to any college.

Which is why, a week after my classmates graduated without me, I went to the Emperor's Freeground. I spent some time standing in front of the Parthenon trying to make up my mind whether or not to go in. I hadn't come to take the test, just to find out if I still could. The Imperial University might not want a student who had been accused of writing blasphemy on the walls of his high school.

Not that I had any intention of going to the Imperial University. My scheme was merely to take the test, after which, according to Mr. Tule, I had to be admitted to a branch of the Planetary College of Jasper, even if I flunked. Hapsburg Aggie was a branch of the Planetary College.

The Emperor's Freeground was an area on the outskirts of Jasper City that was legally not a part of Jasper. It belonged to the Emperor and was under Imperial jurisdiction. If a criminal ran onto the Emperor's Freeground, the Jasper Office of Public Decency couldn't chase him there. Of course, the Emperor's

Representative would probably just hand the criminal back to the Jasper authorities, but the point is that he doesn't have to.

The Freeground was set up like a small park, with trees and brooks running through it, and a few buildings, mostly models of ancient Earth buildings, scattered about. There was the Parthenon, the Winter Palace, Monticello, the Qua Ti, and the Opera. Few Jaspert ever play in the park, although it's open. It's just one of those things that everyone knows is not done.

A girl came down the steps of the Parthenon as I stood there, and she smiled at me as she walked past.

She was the first person I'd seen since entering the Freeground. She somehow decided me; if she could come out of the Parthenon, I could go in.

The closer I got to it, the larger it looked, until, as I climbed the front steps, the columns seemed to stretch away forever on both sides. It was very impressive. The front door was a great immovable-looking mass of sculptured bronze that parted silently and slid into the walls as I approached.

The entrance hall was a large marble-walled room with incredibly high ceilings and one small round desk right in the center. A very pretty girl sat in a hole in the middle of the desk. She was not Jaspert.

"Courtesy," I said, going up to her, "but I've come to see about taking the test. The Imperial University test, I mean."

"Go through the door over there," she said, pointing toward the far wall. One of the row of doors in it glowed red as she spoke.

I thanked her and crossed the floor casually, as though doors that glowed red on command were a normal part of my life. As I walked, it occurred to me that there was something odd about the room, but I couldn't decide what it was. Then I noticed: I was walking across a marble floor in a large marble hall, and there was no echo. None.

The door stopped glowing as I reached it, and it slid open. In the next room, a small white room that was otherwise empty, was a man sitting in a chair. The man wore a plain black suit

with just a suggestion of a red thread running through the weave. It somehow managed to look both elegant and alien to Jasper, without being visibly different from the pattern of suit I was used to seeing. The chair was an exaggerated sort of easy chair that not only provided support but seemed almost to envelop the man from head to foot.

The man, and the chair, swiveled to face the door as I came in. "Courtesy," the man said.

"Courtesy," I said. "My name is Adam Warrington."

"Of course it is," he said.

That stopped me. I took a deep breath and said, "I'd like to see Mr. Tule about the test for the Imperial University."

"That's right," he said, smiling. "Mr. Tule isn't accessible right now, but I'll be glad to help you. My name's Farb. Please sit."

I was about to comment that there were no other chairs in the room when I realized that one now stood beside me. So I sat down. "Thank you," I said. "I'd like to find out how I go about taking the test."

He produced a sheet of plastic from the arm of his chair and handed it to me. "Stick your thumbprint on that for me," he said. "That makes it official."

The sheet was clear except for my name, WARRINGTON, Adam, printed in tiny letters at the top left-hand corner. There appeared to be tiny smudges set impossibly deep in the plastic— impossibly deep, because the sheet wasn't thick enough for the smudges to be that far in. It was some sort of holographic record, I decided, trying to look as though I handled such things every day.

I was about to ask Mr. Farb whether he had any preference as to where I stuck my thumbprint when a small rectangle in the plastic glowed faintly yellow, and the words Right Thumb appeared below it. I pressed my right thumb firmly to the rect-angle. "There," I said, passing the sheet back to him. The yellow, and the thumbprint, faded from view.

"Excellent," he said. "You may go through to the next room

and begin."

"Wait a minute," I said. "Excuse me, but I just came to find out about taking the test. I'm not prepared—"

"You're as ready as you'll ever be," Mr. Farb said. "This is not the sort of examination that you can study or prepare for. Go right through to the next room, please." The door where I had come in opened again, but instead of leading back to the entrance hall, it now opened onto a long room with student desks and work boards.

"Please," I said, "just a minute. Let's go through this again." I felt as though I were being pushed. I was also a bit startled to find that the door where I'd come in no longer led to where I'd come from. But I wasn't going to let him see that. "What happens if I don't take the test now?" I asked him.

"You will be asked to sign a form stating that you were given an opportunity to take the examination and refused it of your own free will and for motives of your own."

"I can't come back later and take it?"

"There is no advantage to be gained by waiting."

I thought about it briefly, then shrugged. "Okay," I said. "Then I might as well begin now."

"Go into the next room," Mr. Farb told me, "and good luck."

I went into the next room and the door slid closed behind me. One of the work boards lit up and I went over to sit at that desk. WARRINGTON? the board asked in neat typeface in the upper left-hand corner.

Yes, I typed.

LIST GIVEN NAME AND ANY MIDDLE NAMES, the board said.

Adam Thornton, I typed.

Then the board listed a bunch of questions about my family history and health, going back about four generations. When I stalled over one question about whether my maternal grandmother had ever had Snell's disease, the machine lit up and blinked at me with: IF YOU DON'T KNOW THE ANSWER TO A QUESTION, MERELY TYPE "DON'T KNOW" AND

GO ON.

Don't know, I typed, and went on. When I had finished the list of questions, the board said, GO INTO THE NEXT ROOM, and a section of wall turned into a door and opened. The Parthenon building seemed to be constantly rearranging itself.

The newly revealed room was stark white and full of sterile-looking machines, but empty of people. I went in, and the door closed behind me. "Courtesy, Adam Warrington," a lady's voice said from somewhere around me, "please take off all your clothes."

"Excuse me?" I said, looking around. The room was still empty.

"Remove your clothes," the lady's voice told me. "This is the medical examination room."

Now you must understand that on Jasper we do not remove all our clothes for anything. Boys swim in two-piece bathing suits that cover them from the shoulders to the knees. I don't know what costume girls swim in, since mixed bathing is against custom and law on Jasper. And we were considered one of the more liberal planets in the Reformation Group. The taboo against nudity was so strongly ingrained in me that, when I got out of the bathtub every evening, I avoided looking at myself in the mirror.

"Do I have to?" I asked.

"Do you have to what?" the lady's voice replied.

"Must I take my clothes off?"

"No one will chastise you if you don't," the lady said.

"But I'll flunk the test?" I asked.

"You will not have taken the test if you refuse to disrobe," the lady said reasonably.

"Oh." That was no help. Well, by Jasper, if the only way to take the test, pass or fail, was to disrobe, then disrobe I would, lady or no lady. I took my jacket off and folded it on the table.

"Well?" the lady said after a while.

"Are you looking at me?" I demanded.

"Of course," the lady said.

"Well, turn your back," I said.

"I have no back," the lady's voice said. "I am a machine."

I should have guessed, but I hadn't. With no further discussion, I took the rest of my clothes off.

A white cylinder in the middle of the room rotated open, revealing a person-size space in the inside. "Step into the redilpopgnofarthen," the machine with a lady's voice said.

"You mean that white thing that just opened?" I asked.

"That is correct."

"What is it? Why do you call it a redilpop—whatchamacallit?"

"It is a redilpopgnofarthen. It is called that because that is its name. Why do you call that device you have tossed your clothes over a 'chair'?"

"What does it do?"

"The redilpopgnofarthen or the chair?"

"The redil—the white thing."

"It analyzes the structure and internal processes of the human body and creates a profile of the person's health, physical capabilities, and chemical and biological imbalances."

"Oh," I said, "then why don't they call it a health analyzer?"

"The people who manufacture it, on the planet Garfingle, are the ones who named it; you must ask them."

"Oh."

"Now please, step into the device."

I had been stalling, I realized, because I didn't want to step into the device, whatever it was called. I have never been particularly fond of being poked and prodded and jabbed with needles. But, like most of us, I suppose, I'm more afraid of making a fool of myself than of being hurt. And standing there in the middle of the floor with no clothes on refusing to be examined certainly seemed foolish to me. So I did as I was told and stepped into the device.

The door—or whatever—closed behind me and, to the accompaniment of a slight humming sound, the machine filled up with what felt like plastic bags filled with soft gel. Cold plastic

pushed against my body from all sides, from the neck down. A screen lit up a few inches in front of my eyes and flashed vivid colors at me in whirls and streams.

I tensed up, waiting for things to prod me or stick into me, but I couldn't feel anything but the cold plastic. "Breathe deeply," the mechanical lady's voice said from all around me. Then she told me to hold my breath. Then she said, "Do not be alarmed," and the cold plastic surrounding me heated up to something beyond body temperature and stayed there for a while. Then it cooled down again, and kept cooling until, if the gel had been water, I'm sure it would have frozen solid. Then two more plastic bags inflated around my ears, and I could hear strange beeping and humming sounds. Then all the bags deflated, or whatever, at once, and the door opened and I almost fell back into the room.

"You may replace your clothes," the lady-machine told me.

"Thank you," I said.

The door opened as I was buttoning my jacket—the same door I had come in by—only this time it opened onto a long corridor. "Follow the red line," the voice told me. I was about to ask what red line when a line of glowing red light appeared, starting at the doorway and heading off around one of the turns in the newly revealed corridor.

I followed it. It ended in a sort of small square cubicle set into the wall. I entered the cubicle, and the floor dropped out from under me. After a startled second I realized that I was in a sort of doorless elevator, which was now going down at an impressive speed. After dropping five or six stories the floor stopped and I caught up with it. I decided I liked our more primitive, more sedate versions of elevators better than the Imperial model.

The red line now led across a large room to a closed door on the other side. Leaving the elevator quickly, before it decided to do its little trick again, I followed the line. The door opened when I reached it, letting me into a small room with a chair in the middle. The chair was the only object in the room, and it was mounted on a pedestal that rooted it firmly in place. It was a padded chair with two thick armrests and a high back that

reached all the way up to support the back of the head. The room was painted a dark neutral color that just missed being flat black.

"Welcome," a pleasant lady's voice said from somewhere in the room. "You are candidate Adam Thornton Warrington?"

"That's right," I admitted.

"This is Test Booth Gamma, and I am your test guide," the voice said. "My name is Danelle."

Well. At least now it was a person. "Courtesy, Miss Danelle," I said. "What do I do?"

"Sit in the test chair," the voice said. "And it's just 'Danelle.'" She sounded amused.

I sat down in the test chair, which immediately readjusted itself to the shape of my body. I had heard about molding chairs before, but never sat in one. It's a very strange feeling the first time. "Okay," I said.

The door closed and the lights went out. A pretty girl's face appeared in the darkness in front of me. It wasn't any of the sorts of projection or backlighting that I'm familiar with. And the face didn't seem to be projecting onto anything. It was just there, in front of me, clearly visible, although there was no other light in the room. It didn't throw off any light either; there was no glow from it onto the walls or the chair or anything.

"All right," the face said, "we're ready to begin." The voice was Danelle's. She was looking at me as though she could see me, although she was just a disembodied head in front of me, cut off at the neck.

I experimented, leaning casually over to the left side of the chair. Her eyes followed me. I straightened back up. "What do we do now?" I asked.

"Instructions will be given to you from time to time," she said. "You follow them to the best of your ability. I will serve as your guide and watch you and offer suggestions when it seems appropriate. You may also ask me questions whenever you like. Some I will be permitted to answer, some not."

This sort of a test was completely outside my experience. Tests

on Jasper were either yes-no or multiple choice. Essay questions were avoided to discourage improper thoughts, except in Jaspert Composition (Our language called itself Jaspert, although it was little different from the other languages of the group. If you speak Jaspert, you can understand any of the Reformish languages, and most of the broader Anglit group), where such mind-broadening topics as "The Importance of Cleanliness," and "Jasper, Jewel of the Reformation Group" were offered for us to write a quick five pages on. Or they were "offered as topics upon which we could write a quick five pages," as my Jaspert teacher would prefer.

But anyway, the tests I was used to were nothing like the test I was about to take. I became more interested in passing, just to show them I could. It would certainly give me status in Hapsburg Aggie. "Yes, I could have gone on to the Imperial University. I passed the test, you know. But I wanted to come here to good old H.A. My father's alma mater, you know." That might serve as a balance to the nasty stories Principal Lowepride was certain to consider it his duty to spread about me.

"I can ask you questions?" I asked. "It won't count against me?"

Danelle laughed. "It depends on the questions," she said. "A really dumb question will probably count against you. Anyway, I'm not the scorer; I'm completely on your side. Are you ready?"

"I suppose so." I said. I had no idea whether I was ready or not.

"Okay. Take all the time you need, but don't waste time. Good luck." Danelle disappeared, fading out slowly like the Cheshire Cat, but not even leaving her grin behind. I was once again surrounded by total blackness.

Then a light-blue dot appeared in the air in front of me, and a deep voice said, "Open the two panels at the front of your armrests. The controls inside will, at this time, control the movement of the answerdot. Take a minute to practice."

I felt around the armrests until I found two depressions on the outsides. By pushing up with my fingers in the depressions,

I opened the fronts of the armrests. There were two toggle switches for each hand, and a series of buttons inset into each panel. The toggle switches moved the dot up and down and to the right and left. One of the buttons made the dot leave a thin line wherever it moved, and another erased the line. None of the other buttons seemed to do anything. I practiced moving the dot around and drawing squares and triangles and circles—circles were tough—and houses and stick figures, and I tried filling up the whole space in front of me with blue lines.

The test began. For the first half hour or so it was multiple choice, but of a more exotic sort than I was used to. I was asked to eliminate a shape that was unworthy of being with three other shapes, or pick a shape to join three other shapes. The shapes, which were suspended in the air in front of me, were completely three-dimensional, and they grew gradually more colorful and complex as the test progressed. I grew very adept in the manipulation of my dot as I used it to X out an unwanted shape or to circle a desired one.

Most of the time a pattern became apparent after a little staring and figuring, but sometimes the shapes were either so closely related or so clearly unrelated that no choice seemed logical. "Is it better to guess wrong or not to guess at all?" I asked the blackness at one point.

"You must answer each question in order to go on to the next," Danelle's voice told me. "In some cases 'no choice' will be one of the possible answers in front of you."

And, as she said, after that "no choice" started showing up with fair regularity as one of the possible answers, which may have been cause and effect. That is: they may have been waiting for me to ask. That may have been one of the questions I was supposed to ask.

Then the test changed. A screen appeared in the air in front of me, with my answer dot inside it. A pattern of geometric shapes crossed the screen from left to right, and I had to maneuver the dot to avoid the shapes. While I was doing this, the deep voice asked me questions on galactic history and astrography,

which I answered aloud. I got pretty good at it after a bit, but I was ashamed to realize how little I knew about the Empire that Jasper and the Reformation Group were members of. I hardly knew the names of any ex-emperors, and even though I knew the names of maybe fifty Human-inhabited planets, I couldn't tell you what almost any of them were known for. And as for what my tester called the "non-Human intelligences," all I could do was name a couple and tell what they looked like—sort of.

After a while I thought I had the pattern figured, but then it got faster and started coming from different directions. And every time I didn't get the dot out of the way fast enough, a deep voice would say "hit," and a small number in the lower right corner of the screen would get one unit larger. I had to concentrate on the dot so hard that I was missing questions, and then I overreacted by paying so much attention to the questions that the dot got picked off by every passing shape. By the time I had both things under control again, the test ended.

There was a pause now for me to rest. The chair produced a cooling drink from the right handrest, and I sipped at it. The drink was not Jaspert, but it was tart and tingly and very good.

When the test continued, it had entered a new phase. The deep-voiced tester would ask me a question about a hypothetical situation, and I would have to solve it by coming up with the best answer out of the many possible—or, at least, come as close to the best answer as I could. I could ask any clarifying questions I wanted, but sometimes I wouldn't get an answer. For example:

"You are the commander of a Thermopylae-class battle cruiser, and an enemy alien is somewhere aboard your ship. What commands do you give?"

Or: "You are appointed Governor-General to Xeebor, a new planet that is just being colonized by people from the Bergundian Federation. The colonists are killing a native creature called the Xeebor Bear, a two-hundred-kilogram carnivore, because it breaks into their fenced fields and ruins their crops. Now a group called the 'Friends of the Bear' have presented you with a petition calling for the protection of the Xeebor Bear and even-

tual recognition of the creature as rightful owner of the planet. They claim that it is sentient under the meaning of the Imperial Planetary Settlement Act of Hiram IV—7.[1] What do you do?"

Also: "You leave a building late at night carrying several very important most-secret documents. Halfway down the block you spot several rough-looking men coming toward you who may be enemy agents. It is too late to make it back to the building before they reach you. What do you do?"

I doubt if I came up with the ideal solution for any of these problems, or for the twenty-or-so more they came up with, but it was fun figuring out the possibilities. Why, for instance, would a carnivorous animal tramp around in a fenced field, no matter how smart or dumb it was? Probably chasing some herbivorous animal. That should be checked out.

After the last question, the room went black again. Then it came alive, and I was in the control bubble of a fleet patrol boat, the small five-man boats that form a guard screen around the ships of the line in a deep-space battle fleet. Off to my right was a Sun-class battleship, the biggest in the fleet. Thousands of kilometers below me was the rounded bulk of a planet, most of its surface obscured by a heavy cloud layer. The scene was more than realistic; I would have sworn it was real if I hadn't known better. The battleship was about five or six kilometers off, and was so clear and bright that it looked as if I could reach out and touch it.

"The planet below you," the deep voice told me, "is Llyra, fourth planet from the sun Pendra. The Imperial Fleet is ranged in a protective net around Llyra, which is about to be attacked by the Sendrakgh. In five minutes, approximately, the fleet of the Sendrakgh will pop out of null-E space.

"You are battle-control officer of FPB-235, charged with protecting the Rigel, which is the battleship to your right. You are sitting in the battle-control chair. You have five minutes to practice using the controls. All laser weapons and missile tubes

1. "Hiram IV—7" is the seventh year of the reign of Emperor Hiram the Fourth. Imperial acts are dated this way.

will now fire practice rounds only, so you may fire without fear of harming our own ships. You will be notified when they are activated for battle."

"Wonderful," I said. I pushed the various buttons and switches on my chair until I learned which ones did what, then practiced doing it. It was very simple. One set of controls swiveled the chair completely around, left or right, while another tilted it up and down. A red circle appeared straight ahead of me wherever I looked. This was the aiming circle, so whatever I saw I could shoot at. The buttons for the laser were on the left, missiles on the right. The missiles were for destroying enemy ships, while the laser beams were for enemy missiles launched by those ships. Friendly ships would appear to glow green to identify them. So I could shoot at anything that didn't glow green.

After I'd been practicing for a few minutes, a thought occurred to me. "Say," I said to whomever was listening, "was this a real battle?"

Danelle answered me. "That's right," she said. "It was fought over two hundred years ago."

"What happened?" I asked.

"Llyra was destroyed," she said. "Fourteen million people were wiped out by a planetbuster."

"The Sendrakgh won?"

"No, the Sendrakgh lost. Their home planet was captured and they were dispersed. They are kept on primitive planets now, and not allowed space travel."

The deep voice cut in. "The Sendrakgh fleet has just emerged. Your weapons systems are activated. Good luck."

A cluster of black dots appeared about ninety degrees out from the distant white disk of Pendra. They spread out as they approached and quickly became the vast Sendrakgh battle fleet. Beams and cones of energy crossed the space between the two fleets. The heat streaks of missiles showed in my display as red-violet lines against the black of space.

Now the Sendrakgh fleet was close enough for me to see the individual ships. Their battleships were great double spheres

connected by thick rods and covered with instrument and weapon blisters. They looked like giant diseased dumbbells. The small scouts and guard boats of the enemy fleet looked like sleek black insects.

The whole area became filled with a purple glow from the charged energy screens of the big ships. Every few seconds a missile—or a ship—would explode with a flare of white light that quickly went to black. When I had time to think about it I realized that the bubble screen around me automatically blanked out light when it got too bright. That was why I was able to look at the star Pendra, this planet's sun, which appeared only as a dim disk the size of a ten-bit piece.

I was kept busy searching the sky and shooting at everything that moved that wasn't ours. Mostly I was lasering missiles. It took a three-second beam to turn a streaking missile into an expanding cloud of bright gas.

Then, all at once, the planet below seemed to shudder slightly, and a small black cloud appeared in one quadrant.

And the sky went blank, and the light came on, and I was back in a small testing room in the Emperor's Freeground on Jasper. I found that I was covered with sweat and completely exhausted.

"The test is over," Danelle said from somewhere over my head. "Thank you."

"How long did that last part go on?" I asked her.

"Just under half an hour," she said.

It had seemed like no more than a couple of minutes, but that explained why I was so exhausted. My hands were trembling slightly, and I felt curiously lightheaded. I don't think I've ever been so completely involved in anything as I'd been the last half hour.

"Go on home now," Danelle said. "We'll notify you tomorrow as to how you did."

So I left the Freeground and went home. It didn't really matter how I did, I thought, but I wanted to do well. My object—to take the test, so they'd have to let me into Hapsburg Agricultural

College—was accomplished.

My father was at home when I got there, and I told him what I'd done.

He thought it over. "You should have consulted me," he said.

"I planned to, sir," I told him. "I just went there to get the information so we could discuss it, but when I went in they insisted that I take the test right away."

My father shook his head. "Well, what's done is done," he said. "I just hope it's for the best."

"Well, at least they can't stop me from going to Hapsburg Aggie now," I said, which just shows you how wrong a person can be.

CHAPTER IV.

The next morning a messenger delivered a red envelope addressed to Candidate Adam Warrington to the house, and I opened it. Inside was a letter on stiff pink parchment-like paper with the Imperial Crest at the top, framed by the words "Office of the Imperial Representative—Jasper."

TO: Candidate Adam Thornton Warrington Jasper

FROM: His Noble Excellency the Duke of Ley, Imperial Representative to the Reformation Group. The Emperor's Freeground, Jasper.

Candidate Warrington:

This letter will notify you that your examination for admittance to the Imperial University has been evaluated and you have qualified.

Congratulations.

Sometime within the next two months, standard, you will be notified as to which campus of the Imperial University you have been accepted at, and when you should arrive. Your transportation will be provided by the Office of the Imperial Representative.

You will have one week from your notification to accept or reject the offer. If you have any questions,

Mr. Tule of the Imperial staff will be available to answer them.

In the name of Alexander IX, Liege Sovereign of the Inner Planets, Protector of the Princes of Earth, Chairman of the Solar Hanse and Hereditary Emperor of the Confederation of Human Planets, the Imperial Representative extends his best wishes to all successful candidates.

Whether you choose to attend the Imperial University or not, may you have a life that is successful, interesting, and useful to Humanity.

I am,

H.N.E. the Duke of Ley
and by this seal, in the Emperor's Name....

The letter was signed with a scrawl and embossed with a big, elaborate seal at the bottom.

I went into the breakfast room, where my father was just finishing his morning coffee. "Courtesy, sir," I said, and held out the letter to him.

"So polite?" he murmured, taking the red envelope. "Well," he said when he'd read the letter, "as the man says, congratulations."

"I guess I won't have any trouble getting into Hapsburg Agricultural now," I said, hitching myself across the back of one of the chairs.

"I guess not," Father agreed. "And you'll be a credit to the business, I'm sure, when you graduate. Sit up straight in that chair."

"Yes, sir," I said, sitting up.

"I'll go over to the school myself with this," Father said. "I'll speak to Principal Lowepride. We'll arrange for your enrollment at Hapsburg." And he tucked the letter in his vest pocket, stood up, wiped his mouth with his napkin, buttoned his jacket,

nodded to me, and left the house.

When he came home that evening he was angry, very angry. I was talking to Sister Prudence in the hall when he came in the front door, slammed his hat onto the rack, said, "Haven't you children anything better to do than sit around the house all day?" and stormed into his study before we had a chance to reply.

It had been five years since Father had called me a child. He'd called me a lot of other things in that time, but it was agreed that if I was to act like an adult, I had to be treated like one.

Father stayed in his study until dinner. During dinner he said nothing, except for his usual grumbling about the food and service. After dinner he went back to his study and, a few minutes later, called me in. "We've been foxed," he told me.

"What do you mean, Father?"

"I had a long talk with Principal Lowepride," Father said. "I'm afraid that by the end of the conversation I had used some language that I regret using. And I called the principal several terms that I don't usually use. Not that I regret using them. Quite the contrary. But, of course, they did no good."

I would have given quite a bit to have seen Father confronting Principal Lowepride, but I didn't tell him that. "What happened, Father?" I asked. "Was it about my going to college?"

"Yes, Adam, I'm afraid that is just what it was about. After consulting several references and communicating with several people, Principal Lowepride was pleased to be able to tell me that you are not going to be admitted to Hapsburg Agricultural College."

"But they have to—don't they? I mean, I took the exam for the Imperial University."

"Yes, but you passed. According to the relevant regulation, they only have to let you in if you fail." Father shook his head sadly. "If that isn't the most stupid thing I've ever heard of," he said, "then I've never heard of anything stupid."

I sat slowly down on the straightback leather chair. "If I—if I pass?" I said. "I mean, they don't have to let me in if I pass?"

"That's right. And Lowepride let me know in no uncertain terms just what he thought of your taking the Imperial University test at all. He seemed to think that that proved you were the culprit all along."

"The miscreant," I said.

Father looked at me for a long time, but he was clearly thinking of something else. Then he shook his head, bringing his thoughts back down to Jasper, and said, "Well, what are you going to do about it?"

"What do you mean?" I asked him. "What can I do about it?"

Again my father looked at me for a long time without saying a word. Then he said, "Adam, the Universe is a large and wonderful place, and what's true on one planet or for one people is not necessarily true somewhere else. We have a set of truths here on Jasper that we live by, and they are perfectly adequate for our needs. But they are not the only possibilities. Other people live by rules that we would consider strange, or even possibly immoral, but they are happy with them, and who is to say that we are right and they are wrong?

"I think that you would have been perfectly content to spend your life here on Jasper, graduating from Hapsburg Agricultural College and taking your place in the family business. And I would certainly have been happy to have that happen. But circumstances have moved to prevent it."

"I don't have to go to college," I told Father. "Why can't I just take my place in Warrington and Son now? We could call it Warrington and Son and Son."

"I would love to have you do that, Adam," my father said. "But I don't think you realize now just how important that college diploma is."

"I can study on my own time," I said.

"I'm sure you can," Father said. "And I'm sure you would. But it's not the college education that I'm talking about—not that that isn't important. It's the diploma itself. Without it you can't vote or hold public office. And that makes you a second-class citizen. It might not matter to you now, but as you grow

older it will."

"So what can I do?" I asked, although I had a pretty good idea of what my father was suggesting.

"I think you should go," Father said.

"To the Imperial University?"

"That's right. I'm proud that you've been accepted, and I think that you should go. I don't know if you'll still want to come back here and spend your days working in the family store after you graduate—"

"Of course I will, Father," I said.

"Don't interrupt. And don't commit yourself to anything you might regret. I want you to go. I told Principal Lowepride that I was going to urge you to go. All that I ask is that you conduct yourself in a manner that will not make your mother or me ashamed of you. Think things out before you jump in, and don't ever do anything you think is wrong just because someone else tells you it's the thing to do."

"I won't, Father. I promise."

And so, due to a series of events only partly in my control, I wasn't going to Hapsburg Aggie at all. Somewhere out there, circling some star I might not even be able to see from Jasper, was the planet that was going to be my home for the next four standard years.

About a month later another envelope from the Imperial Representative arrived at the house, this one containing a stiff card saying that I had been accepted at the University of Sol on the planet Mars.

I called up Mr. Tule at the Emperor's Freeground and told him I wanted to go. He said that was good and in that case I'd leave in two weeks. He'd send me the details, and good luck.

Mars. The first planet settled when Mankind left Earth. And the University of Sol: the oldest university in the Imperial System, so old that nobody knew when it was founded. The university where the children of dukes and electors were taught to become dukes and electors. I was becoming more and more excited about going. I had a dream that night where the Emperor

was standing at the foot of the ramp to welcome me as I stepped down onto the soil of Mars.

But I also found myself thinking of my mother and father, and how wonderful they were and how much I was going to miss them. I even thought about what a great sister Prudence was, and how much I was going to miss her, something I hadn't thought before in the entire twelve years of her life. I was getting homesick already, and I hadn't even left home yet.

Mr. Tule came by my house himself to give me a small oblong disk of clear plastic with a hole punched at one end. "This is your passport, identification card, and travel authorization," he told me. "Don't lose it. I suggest you wear it around your neck." He reached into his vest pocket and pulled out a small white envelope. It held a fine gold chain. "This is from the testing staff at the Freeground," he said. "A good-luck present." He threaded it through the hole in the plastic disk and showed me how to work the tiny link, which screwed closed.

"Thank you," I said, holding it. Men don't wear necklaces on Jasper.

Seeing my hesitation, Mr. Tule smiled and stuck a finger under his own shirt collar, pulling up a gold chain similar to mine. On the end of it was a plastic disk that could have been identical. "Here's my I-disk," he said. "If you wear it under your clothes, no one will know."

I put the chain around my neck and tucked the disk in my shirt. I might as well get used to doing things differently.

"Incidentally," Mr. Tule said, "you were supposed to get an information kit, telling you what to expect at Sol and how to behave. But the kit got lost. So I'm afraid you won't have time to study that stuff before you get there, but I'm sure they'll give you one on Mars when you arrive."

"Can you give me any pointers?" I asked.

Mr. Tule shook his head. "I've never been there," he said. Then he shook hands with me very seriously and formally. "Good luck," he said. "And one thing more: Don't take much extra clothing; they'll outfit you when you arrive."

I spent the next two weeks wandering around Jasper visiting all my friends and all the places I liked to go. I stared at a lot of things that suddenly became very important to me, and hard to leave, like the creek with the small waterfall that I used to swim in during the hot summer, and Missey, my horse. I gave Missey to Sister Prudence, and she burst out crying and ran out of the room. I went after her and told her that she was making a lot of fuss over a ten-year-old mare whose only trick was kicking out the stall door every chance she got, and Prudence burst out crying again.

I made my mother promise that, barring fire, flood, or Jasperquake, she'd leave my stuff alone. If she wanted to pack it all up in a trunk and hide it down in the basement, that was fine, but I didn't want her or Father deciding what to throw out and what to keep.

And then it was the day to leave. I said good-bye to Mother and Sister Prudence in the house, and Father drove me to the spaceport. I got out and took my suitcase, and we shook hands and he wished me luck and told me not to forget to write my mother at least twice a week. Then he drove off. Neither of us likes emotional good-byes, and if he'd stayed we might have had one.

The spaceport was where the shuttle that went up to the orbit station took off. The real spaceships never got closer to Jasper than the orbit station, five hundred kilometers straight up. Inside the spaceport they looked at my I-disk in a viewer and then took my suitcase away from me and gave me a ticket for a seat on the shuttle.

The shuttle looked like a giant airplane from the outside, but not from the inside. For one thing, there were no windows on the shuttle—not for the passengers, anyway—and it was all one long area; there were no separate compartments for women in back or for deacons in front. And the seats faced back instead of front; they were soft and done in red and gold fabric, instead of hard and brown. Also, there were stewards to assist the passengers.

These differences in style and decoration puzzled me until I figured out the reason: the shuttle was run by the space-lines instead of Jasper Planetary Transportation. The shield of Imperial Transgalactic, a gold spaceship against a field of stars, was woven into the fabric of the headrest on every seat.

I was in the third row of seats, which put me right at the rear of the shuttle, since the seats were numbered back to front and boarding was from the rear. The safety webbing formed an X across my body as the two halves stretched from shoulder to waist. Then a screen in front of me showed a short cartoon demonstrating how to use the safety equipment in case anything went wrong. After that, with a jounce and a wobble, the shuttle was moving across the concrete to the far end of the runway. The web across my chest tightened and I was pushed forward in my seat as the craft took off.

After about five minutes the screen in front of me lit up again, this time with a view of the ground below as it slowly fell away. I must have sighed, or gasped, or made some sort of noise at the sight, because the man in the seat next to me turned and smiled. "First time up, ha?" he asked. He was a short, balding man with a tremendous air of self-confidence, and I saw he was obviously not from Jasper, by the cut of his suit and the familiar—on Jasper, overly familiar—way he had spoken to me.

"Yes, sir," I said. "I've been on airplanes before, but nothing like this." We were so high above the clouds now that they looked as though they were resting on the ground. I could make out the full arc of the Bay of Temperance below, with all of Jasper City forming a large dot on the lower left-hand side.

"Well, you never get used to it," he told me. "This and the view between the stars in null-E space. You just going up to the station, or are you headed on out? I'm going to Wayfare myself, and then on to the Transition Group."

"I'm going to Sol," I told him. "Mars."

"No kidding. Say, isn't that something! Always been meaning to head that way myself, but never managed it. I travel in seeds." He pushed his hand between the webbing and extended it to me.

handed me a boarding card with my name on it.

"You're in cabin G-94," she told me, pointing to the designation on the card. "The ship is numbered from the central core, ending with L-deck, which is the first one past the lock. The drop belt is just on the other side of the lock. Take it to G and walk to the left as you leave. There'll be a general meeting at sixteen hundred hours in the passenger's lounge to explain the rules and privileges of the ship: what you can't do, what you may do, and what you must do."

I had to strain a little to understand her Anglit accent. "Thank you," I said.

"In the name of *Western Star* and Imperial Transgalactic, welcome aboard," she said, making a palms-up gesture of welcome.

"Thank you," I said, as she turned to the next passenger. Her skirt, I noted, was as short in back as it was in front.

Everything in the ship was gleaming metal over soft, deep-colored plastic. It created an interesting effect of friendliness and efficiency. How an empty corridor can feel friendly and efficient I don't know, but this one did.

I stood outside my cabin for five minutes trying to open the door before a passing crewman showed me that the boarding card was also my door key. "Just till your palm print goes into the computer," he said, and walked away before I could ask him what that meant.

My suitcase was waiting for me in my cabin, I was relieved to see. The cabin was small, but very compact, with a fold-down sink, a stand-up shower, a small privy, a smaller closet, a bed, and a desk. A footlocker at the foot of the bed served for clothes storage and as a chair for the desk. They were certainly not overly generous with room. Not that I minded, but I wondered what someone with a lot of luggage would do.

It suddenly occurred to me that I hadn't brought my watch, which was calibrated for the Jasper day and would be little use on Mars, so I had no idea what time it was—or when sixteen hundred hours would be. I knew that sixteen hundred hours was

four in the afternoon, but I didn't know whether the ship was on Standard, or some special ship's time, or Jasper time, or what.

I was just about to go out into the corridor and find someone to ask, when a soft chime sounded from a speaker in the ceiling. "Attention, all passengers who just boarded at Jasper," a soft male voice said. "Welcome aboard the *Western Star*. Please assemble in five minutes in the passenger's lounge. Just follow the corridor arrows of F-deck. Thank you."

So I left my cabin, making sure I had my boarding card-room key with me, and took the drop belt to F-deck. Small red arrows glowing in the corridor wall led me to the passenger lounge, which was a fair-sized room with writing desks, card tables, couches, chairs, a small food-service area, and a great window looking out on the Universe. It was only when I saw Jasper and the space station as distant objects through the window that I realized we were underway.

There were about thirty people in the room besides me, and nobody had a clearer idea of what was happening than I did. We all milled about, waiting for someone to tell us what to do. A few more people came through the door, among them Mr. Peshnov. And then a man in a white suit with blue piping stood up on a chair.

"Good afternoon, ladies and gentlemen," he said. "Courtesy. Welcome to the *Western Star*. My name is Robel ep Dymstor, and I am second officer. Please, all of you, sit down."

We wasted another minute or so figuring out how to sit down while he waited patiently. And then, when we were all seated, he continued: "There's a voice-activated viewscreen in each of your rooms. It gives you immediate access to all the material in the ship's library and call-up of the ship's computing power if any of you want to work while on board. Typers and graphers and hard-copy devices are in the passenger library. There is also a gym, which we suggest you make use of, a swimming pool, an air-swimming domain, a game room, many ship's stores, and various other facilities for the use and enjoyment of passengers. Your room screen will give you the location and hours of each

of them.

"If you have any questions that your screen can't answer, feel free to ask any officer or crewman that you see. However, don't delay the ship's personnel or feel slighted if they excuse themselves and rush off. Schedules on the *Western Star* are very strict for officers and crew, and talking to a passenger is no excuse for tardiness.

"Each door on the ship has a place for handprint identification on the left side. Before you leave the lounge, your print will be entered in the computer. Then any door you're authorized to open will open for you. Your cabin door will open at your touch only, except in case of emergency. Any area off limits to passengers will not open for you.

"In case of emergency, obey the orders given to you by the ship's officers or crew; they are trained to handle these situations and will be acting in your best interests."

"How will we know if it's an emergency?" someone asked.

"If one of the ship's personnel gives you an order, assume it's an emergency. If it isn't, he'll hear about it. If it is, he may be saving your life.

"Speaking of lifesaving, there will be one lifeboat drill a day, and nobody will be excused from it for any reason. The drill horn sounds like this"—a rising and falling wail came out of the speaker—"and you are to respond instantly when you hear it. You go to the nearest lifeboat from wherever you are. Crewmen will be stationed in the corridors to direct you.

"Incidentally, when I use the term 'crewmen,' I am also speaking of the ladies who happen to be members of the *Western Star's* ship's company. I know you folk from Jasper are not used to taking orders from women or seeing them in positions of authority, but the space guilds and Imperial Transgalactic Spacelines do not differentiate officers or crew on the basis of gender.

"Now as to meals: breakfast will be served from seven until ten. We run on Zeta time here, a twenty-four-hour clock based on Standard Earth time. Lunch is twelve to fourteen hundred

hours. Dinner is the only formal meal. There are two seatings, one at nineteen thirty hours and the second at twenty-one hundred hours. You will be posted to one of the seatings; if you wish to change, notify your deck steward. Are there any questions?"

"I am an Esthetic Vegetarian," a short, stout woman in a red pantsuit announced.

"Just tell your food preferences to the steward," the second officer told her. "And any of the rest of you with special food needs tell the steward now, so that he can see that menus are planned for you. We are equipped to feed any of the sentient species that travel oxygen-atmosphere ships."

"You mean there are aliens aboard this ship?" a man dressed in a flowing varicolored robe asked, sounding alarmed.

"No, I didn't mean that," the second officer said, "but as a matter of fact, there are several members of non-Human species aboard the *Western Star*. There is a Betal IV alpha-male traveling with an alpha-female and three beta-males. There's a Sigmoid—it never leaves its cabin, of course. There are a group of Polypidlaq monks and a Yooserian. And, of course, we have a Greater Darwinian observer among the ship's officers. It's serving as junior astrogation warrant officer, I believe."

The man in the colored robe stood up. "I am shocked, sir," he said. "Shocked. As a member of the Humanate Congress and the Association of Greater Human Businessmen, I would like to register a complaint, in the strongest terms."

"Very good, sir," the second officer said. "With whom would you like to register it?"

"With the appropriate official."

"Courtesy, sir. The *Western Star* travels under an Imperial charter, which regulates and specifies the conditions under which we are obliged to grant passage. Your complaint, sir, is with the Emperor."

"Oh," the man said, "I—"

"There is an Imperial legate on board, traveling, I believe, to Wayfare or Comstock. If you will give me your name, I will

have him contact you."

"Thank you," the man said stiffly. "Allow me some time first to put my complaint into the proper form, and then I shall do as you suggest."

"Of course," Second Officer ep Dymstor said. "Are there any other questions? No? That's all, then. Thank you for coming. As you leave the room, stop by the door and Junior Lieutenant ep Liztom will verify your handprint for the computer. You'd better do this now because the boarding pass will no longer open your cabin door. Courtesy, my friends. Have a good trip."

Junior Lieutenant ep Liztom was the girl who had given me the boarding pass. She had changed out of the short skirt into a pair of slacks and a jacket, still white with red piping, very much like Second Officer ep Dymstor's, except for the color of the piping. She had one band around her right sleeve, and he had four, two wide and two narrow. I thought she looked very good in the uniform. She probably looked very good in the short skirt too, but when you're embarrassed to look at something it's hard to see past your own embarrassment.

A line quickly formed in front of Junior Lieutenant ep Liztom. I hate standing in lines when I don't have to, so I sat down on the couch to wait. Mr. Peshnov, the seed dealer, plumped himself down next to me. "Well, the great adventure has started, ha?" he said. "I bet you're pretty excited. On the way to Mars. First time off Jasper. Quite a day, ha?"

"Yes, sir," I said politely.

"If there's any way an old, experienced traveler can guide you over the next few days, feel free to call on me," Mr. Peshnov said. "I expect you'll be surprised, shocked, and astounded quite a bit over the next little while. Nothing to be ashamed of. There's quite a variance of style and behavior in the Human Race these days, not to speak of the aliens. A lot of things I wouldn't do if you offered me the Imperium are being done every day by perfectly respectable people. And the most Human-looking alien—not that any of them are too Human-looking, if you ask me—probably has habits that would shock a horse. Don't see

many aliens on Jasper, ha? Forbidden, aren't they?"

"No," I said, rising to the defense of Jasper for some reason, "not at all."

"Ever see one?"

"No."

"Well, then, they're not exactly encouraged, let us say."

I couldn't argue with that. "What was the man in the robe talking about?" I asked. "All that about greater humans and the like?"

"He doesn't like aliens," Mr. Peshnov said. "There are a lot like him around. It used to be a lot of people felt like that kind of inside, you know, only they were ashamed to say anything about it. But it seems to have become a popular viewpoint over the last few years. The Humanate Congress is a sort of political party that's spreading through the Empire. They have seats in the parliaments of many local planetary governments, and I think they recently elected an Elector to the House of Commons of the Solar Hanse. Their whole policy is isolation from any non-Human people. The funny thing is, they don't seem to go over big on any of the mixed planets, only on the mostly Human ones."

I didn't even know there were any mixed planets. "It sounds kind of silly," I said.

"To you," Mr. Peshnov said. "Not to them. That Association of Greater Human Businessmen—I've dealt with them. 'Humans first' is their motto. They don't want me to sell my ultra wheat to the Yooserians, or my hybrid pintop maize on Polypidlaq. And they won't buy rasherfruit or tintail because it didn't originate on Earth. What can you say to that, ha? I say nothing. I sell to who will buy."

"We're not that bad on Jasper," I said.

"No," Mr. Peshnov agreed. "You don't like anybody from off-planet. Human or alien; all in equity. Not you personally, you understand, you of Jasper. You personally seem to show a surprisingly non-Jaspert open mind."

I couldn't think of anything to say to that, but I was spared

the need. Mr. Peshnov noticed that the line had dwindled, and he excused himself and joined the end. I waited a minute, staring out the viewpoint at Jasper as it dwindled in space. Since the day side of Jasper was below, getting smaller, we must be heading toward Deuteronomy, I realized in a flash of brilliant deduction. Deuteronomy is our sun. Jasper is Deuteronomy III. Jennings and Job, Deuteronomies II and IV, are also settled; both are colonies of Jasper. Nothing much interesting happens on them.

"It is beautiful, isn't it?"

I turned. Junior Lieutenant ep Liztom and I were now alone in the lounge. "I never get used to it," she said, "and I've been spacing for six years now."

She looked hardly old enough to have been doing anything for six years. "Courtesy, ma'am," I said. "I've never seen my planet from space before."

"They all look different," she said. "Proxima, Tantalis, Eddrey's Planet, Sandsmarch, Finnigate with its blood-red moon, Jasper, Wayfare, Betal IV, the Great Perseii Station, Mars, Earth, the Thousand Planets; you could never mistake one for another, but they're all equally beautiful from space. None of us ever tires of it."

"It is quite a sight, ma'am," I agreed.

"Don't call me ma'am," she said.

"Then what should I call you?"

"Either Junior Lieutenant ep Liztom, or just Lieutenant, or just Nancy. But not ma'am. Please."

"Your name is Nancy?" I don't know why that surprised me.

"My name is Junior Lieutenant Sarah-John Maydeath Nancy Tenn f 'Ivan ep Liztom. I'm a fourth-generation space brat."

"I'm Adam Warrington," I told her.

"I know," she said. "Come give me your hand."

"Excuse me?"

"Your hand. We have to get your handprint registered with the computer—that is, if you ever want to get into your cabin again."

"Oh." I crossed the lounge over to her. "I'm sorry. I didn't

THE PRINCES OF EARTH | 67

mean to delay you."

"Don't be silly," she said. "Somebody has to be last. Besides, I have a message for you."

"For me?"

"Yes. The captain requests the pleasure of your presence at the captain's table at dinner tonight. Second seating. You'll find a note to that effect on your message service when you get back to your cabin."

"Oh," I said. "That's nice. Thank you."

"Nice!" she laughed. "Do you know how many of the passengers would give their right arms up to the waist to sit at the captain's table? That's the greatest bit of egoboo there is on one of these liners, to be invited to eat at the captain's table."

"Egoboo?"

"Right. Slang. It means, roughly, a boost to the ego, a raise in status. Everyone on the passenger side of one of these trips is more concerned about status than anything." She took my hand and pressed it against an opaque read-screen. "Warrington," she said clearly at the screen, "Adam."

"Confirmed," the ship's computer said, storing the pattern of my palm and fingerprints in an appropriate slot.

"Why would the captain want me to sit at his table?" I asked. "I mean, if it's such a big thing?"

"You don't know?" she asked. "Or are you merely being humble?"

I laughed this time. "I wish my father could hear you calling me 'humble,'" I said. "No, I don't know. I have no idea."

"You are going to Mars?" she asked.

"That's right."

"You are a student at the University of Sol?"

"Well, I will be. That is, I haven't got there yet."

"And you didn't know that that makes you a celebrity?"

"No. And I still don't. Why does that make me a celebrity?"

"Beans! You sure put on a good humble act, for somebody who's not humble. Sol is just the hardest school to get into in the entire Confederated Imperium, that's all. I'll bet you don't even

know about your I-disk, is that right?"

"What about my I-disk?"

"Here," she said, flipping open the top of the handprint screen. "Stick it in this slot, it's a reader. I'll show you."

I pulled at the gold chain around my neck and brought the I-disk up from under my shirt. "Here," I said, taking it off and handing it to Junior Lieutenant Sarah-John Maydeath Nancy Tenn f 'Ivan ep Liztom. "Show me."

Nancy put it in the slot and the reader screen lit up. It had my name across the top, and my picture from the shoulders up and a thumbprint sharing the rest of the screen. I wondered when they'd taken my picture. I didn't remember its being taken.

Nancy touched a button, and the reader went one level deeper into the I-disk. This leaf said that I was attending the University of Sol on Mars; that I was born on August the third in the twelfth year of the reign of Alexander IX; that my blood type was A neg, sig, kappa, 334, mono, sig; that I had no dangerous allergies; that none of my organs were artificial; and that my rating was alpha-alpha-alpha.

"That's as deep as I go," Nancy said, sliding the disk out and handing it back to me.

I put it back around my neck. "What is that alpha business?" I asked, pushing the I-disk back under my shirt.

"Alpha-alpha-alpha," Nancy said. "That means you have unlimited credit, unlimited travel, and unlimited access."

"Wow," I said. "Access to what?"

"Information. You ask a computer a question, and you won't get 'I'm sorry, but that information is closed.' Not often, anyway."

"Now I am impressed," I said, remembering all the times I'd been shut off by the terminal at home. "And say—unlimited credit. You mean money?"

"That's right. You really didn't know?"

"The outside Universe is not very popular back on Jasper," I told her. "It's kind of hard to get information."

"Not anymore," she said.

"That credit business—you mean I could buy anything I wanted with just my I-disk?"

"That's right. But remember, that's credit, not money. I mean you'd have to pay for it sometime. The disk just tells people that you can be trusted for it."

"Now why would they do that?" I asked, sort of just talking aloud, not expecting an answer.

"I suppose it's to see if you can handle it," Nancy said. "Graduates of Sol get the most important jobs in the galaxy, so they want to find out early if you are up to the responsibility."

"You think fast, Lieutenant," I said. "That sure sounds right to me. So having a high credit rating makes me a celebrity?"

"Beans!" she said. "You still haven't got it? Look: how many people are there?"

"Where? And why do you keep saying 'beans'?"

"We're not allowed to curse. 'Beans' is as close as we get—on duty, anyway. It's short for Beans' Simplified Algorithmic Handbook for Computing Planetary Orbits and Approaches. All space officers have to learn how to use it—and it's the closest thing we have to a curse word."

"I thought the ship's computer did all that stuff."

"Of course it does. But if a meteoroid punches a hole through the computer's cpu just as we're entering a system, we have to be able to."

"Oh."

"How many people are there—all together?"

"I don't know. Let's see. There are...how many?...fourteen hundred peopled planets, more or less. They range from planets with no more than a couple of thousand up to Earth, which has about twenty billion."

"Not counting Earth," Nancy told me, "the average is about two hundred million per settled planet."

"Okay," I said. "At two hundred million per, times fourteen hundred, that makes"—I closed my eyes for a second and let my subconscious do the math—it's better at math than I am—"two-point-eight times ten to the eleventh. About two hundred eighty

billion people. And with Earth, that makes about three hundred billion. That's a lot of people."

"A lot," Nancy agreed. "And now figure that ninety percent of them would cheerfully let all their teeth be pulled out if they or their children could go to the University of Sol. And the only way to get in, unless you're born to it, is by competitive examination. And you made it. That makes you a novelty, anyway."

"Swell," I said.

"Think about it," she said. "I must go now. See you at dinner."

CHAPTER V.

When I thought about being a celebrity, all I felt was silly. So I decided not to think about it. I certainly wouldn't be any sort of celebrity once we got to Mars; I'd just be another freshman. But it would be fun to eat at the captain's table. As far as I was concerned, the captain of a null-E ship was the closest thing to a celebrity that I could ever hope to meet. It was considered one of the most responsible jobs in the Empire. The captain was in complete charge of forty thousand tons of ship and four thousand crew and passengers as they journeyed through the collapsed light-years of null-E space. He had complete life-and-death power over the crew and passengers in case of any mutiny or insurrection, and his decisions could only be countermanded by the Lords of Space, none of whom were usually on board.

I found all this out from the ship's computer when I returned to my cabin. I also learned that the *Western Star* was going to Sol Terminus by way of Wayfare, Comstock, the Great Perseii Station, Dandry, and Betal Moonstone. From Sol Terminus I would go by inter-system liner to Mars, while *Western Star* would continue on her route from Sol to Sandip, Kol, the Andromeda Free Port, Nancel, and out to the Fringe stations. And these people, who were going to places whose names I had never heard of until the computer rolled them off, thought I was a celebrity. Well, it all goes to show that no one ever thinks that what he's doing is nearly as interesting as what someone else is doing.

The ship's computer also told me that I was supposed to dress

for dinner.

"I was not planning to go unclothed," I told the device.

The computer snorted. I don't think they should make devices that snort or laugh or make other disrespectful sounds at Humans. "Dressing for dinner, young man, entails more than putting on a clean shirt and that dreadful Jaspert black suit," it said.

There is something very disconcerting about having a wall speaker tell you how to dress. But the ship's computer knew more about this than I did. "My wardrobe is extremely limited," I told the device. "What would you suggest I wear?"

The screen lit up, with a sketch of a costume that on Jasper you see only in the history books—and even then the colors are much more somber. This one was gold and scarlet: gold leggings tucked into scarlet knee breeches, a ruffled white shirt with a scarlet cravat, an embroidered gold jacket, and a gold-and-scarlet cape. "Very conservative, very good taste," the computer told me.

"I own nothing like that," I said, "and I wouldn't wear it if I did." I was half convinced that this was a practical joke. Computers on Jasper were incapable of joking, but who knew what this star-crossing bubble-brain was capable of.

"As you wish," the device said smugly.

"Maybe tomorrow," I said.

"You are not sitting at the captain's table tomorrow," the device told me. "Tomorrow it will not matter what you wear."

"It won't?" I said.

"Of course not. First night for celebrities. Second night for important people. Other less important people other nights. Last night of any leg guests are invited at the captain's choosing, regardless of rank or importance."

"I see," I said. So I was only a celebrity, not an important person. A fine distinction, and one that I approved of. I hoped that someday I would graduate to the status of important person. "How would I go about getting proper garb for sitting at the captain's table? Or is it too late?"

"You may acquire the proper attire from the Gentlemen's Clothiers and Roughwear Outfitters Shop on Level One. No, it is not too late."

"Well!" I said. "So the ship's stores are really stores on board the ship. I thought they meant storage rooms or something like that."

"Storage areas aboard ship are called 'bins,' or 'tanks,' or 'lockers,' or 'closets,' or 'cabinets,' or—"

"Enough!" I yelled at the wall speaker, and, wonder of wonders, it stopped in mid-sentence.

I went down to Level I and found the G C & R O Shop. I still wasn't convinced that I was going to wear the strange-looking garb the computer had sketched for me, or anything like it. Besides, they probably didn't have anything in my size.

I stood outside the shop for some time, watching the hologram in the window switch from pose to pose and costume to costume. There were several that were a lot like the one the ship's computer had sketched, and they were all labeled "Formal Wear."

Finally I made up my mind and went in. The proprietor of the shop was tall and thin and kept wringing his hands together. He was dressed in orange pantaloons that ballooned out on both sides, a horizontally striped blue-and-white puffy shirt, and an orange-and-gold vest. He had long black hair, which was tied behind his head with a short gold string. "Ah!" he said as I came in. "A young Jasperian venturing abroad into the Galaxy. And what may I do for you, young master?"

"I have been invited to eat at the captain's table this evening," I told him. "I require appropriate garb."

"You certainly do," he said. He tilted his head sideways and examined me up and down like a bird eyeing a worm. "Something," he said, "to emphasize those broad shoulders, that manly chest. Something to draw attention away from those big feet, those protruding ears. Something to exaggerate the adventurousness of youth and minimize the awkward gawkiness. Yes, I think I can do that."

"Thank you," I said, "I think."

"I am an artist," he told me. "My canvas is the human body. You will see." He took a stylus and a thin light panel and started sketching rapidly, glancing back and forth between me and the panel. After a few minutes he put the stylus down with a flourish. *"Mercrimi!"* he said. *"Pwissimi!* It is finished. Observe."

I looked over his shoulder at the light panel, and saw a stick figure with numbered geometric designs plastered over it. It didn't look much like a person and nothing at all like clothing. "Very nice," I said doubtfully.

"You are polite," he said. "A good and useful trait. But it is not at the figure board that I wish you to observe. You are not trained to read the creative code. Here, I show you." He pushed a button on the side of the board, and a full holo display lit up on one wall of the shop. "You see, I inform the fashion computer of what I have designed, and it displays the creation on a manne-quin for you."

The holo was a three-dimensional version of what the ship's computer had sketched for me, but more elegant. This one was in bright green and deep black, with large cuffs and slashed pockets outlined in rolls of fabric. The hologram figure danced slowly in space, so I could see how the suit moved. The holo figure, I thought, was much better looking than I was—the sort of square-jawed, waistless hero type who could get away with wearing such outlandish (to my Jaspert mind) garb.

"That's very pretty," I said, "but it's a bit much for me. Remember, we're a lot more somber on Jasper. It's going to be a while before I can wear anything like that in public without feeling that everyone is laughing at me."

"I assure you that nobody will laugh if you wear this creation. On the contrary, your present outfit will provide much amuse-ment."

"That may be so," I said, "but I want something more, ah, somber. Something in brown, perhaps. I like brown."

"Brown?" he said, staring at me and wringing his hands together. "Quite a challenge, brown. Perhaps I could do some-

thing. Let me think. Yes, perhaps so." He took up his stylus and board and went to work again. "Earth colors," he said. "Simple lines. What an idea. Yes." He pushed the display button and waved his hand at the holo. "Observe! *Mercrimi!*"

The new display was more like the suit I was wearing, but even more simply cut. The pants were still converted into knee breeches, but this time they tucked into black boots that came up to the knees. I've always been fond of boots. The cape—a cape seemed to be essential—was brown with a deep-red lining, and the jacket and breeches were the same brown outlined with red stitching. I wouldn't have been seen on the street with it on Jasper, but I had to admit that I actually liked it. And I wasn't on Jasper.

"I think I like it," I said.

"I think you do too," the proprietor told me. "I, Clemensal Brobagnak, never fail twice to please a customer. Step into the sizing booth."

"How do I pay for this?" I asked him, stepping into the indicated booth. "I have almost no money."

"What?" For the first time he seemed taken aback. "You come in here with no money? For why do you do this?"

"They told me something—that is, I was told that my credit was good. How does that work?"

"Let me see your I-disk," Clemensal Brobagnak said suspiciously.

I took it off and handed it to him, and he put it in a reader. "You jest with me, sir," he said, handing it back to me. "Your credit is good here, of course. Your credit is good anywhere in the fourteen hundred and twenty-six planets of the Imperial Confederation, and on all the ships that travel the space between them."

An orange light filled the little booth for an instant and then was gone. "You may step out now, sir," Brobagnak said. "Your new garments will be delivered to your cabin in about a quarter of an hour."

"Thank you," I said.

"It has been my pleasure to serve you," he told me. "If you visit Earth, Brobagnak Cie. and Frat., the firm of my relatives, will be pleased to serve you." And he bowed me out the door to his shop.

The clothes arrived back at my cabin shortly after I did, and they fit me like my epidermis. It took me a while to figure out what went where, and how to close the places that were supposed to be closed. There were no snaps or buttons and no rough patches that mated, but when you put two edges together that were supposed to stay closed, they stayed closed. Then it took me a while to figure out how to take off the clothes. I finally discovered that if you twisted the seams in opposite directions while pressing together, they would open at that spot and then slide open along their length. It's very easy to do once you've done it a couple of times, and almost impossible to do by accident.

Now I was all set to go to dinner.

By the time the chimes sounded for the second seating, I was really ready to eat. I didn't care where I was sitting, just bring on the food. I followed the signs that glowed softly in the corridors to show the way to the main dining room on J-deck.

The main dining room was large—much larger than I had expected. There must have been a hundred tables in the room, some for only two people, some seating as many as twenty. Figuring a quick rough average of ten people a table, the dining room sat about a thousand people. And the diners weren't all people. For the first time in my life I was in the same room as members of an alien intelligent life form—several, as a matter of fact.

The only one I recognized for sure was the Yooserian, a three-meter-tall brown pole with a large round head at the top, a bunch of four short legs at the bottom, and a bunch of four short arms somewhere around the middle. The eighteen giant blue grasshoppers in brown robes crouched around a large table were probably the Polypidlaq monks. A small ball of red fur was squatting on a table waving its two thin, spindly arms about

as it engaged in earnest conversation with a scantily clad very Human young lady sitting across from it. And what looked like a large bear with a long neck and fangs ten centimeters long was sitting at a table by itself.

The captain's table was a long table, seating about twenty, on one side of the room. At each seat was a little card with a name on it. I was placed at one end between a very portly man in a red-and-silver costume, with heavy, ornate rings on almost every finger, and an elderly lady dressed in pure white robes and a white turban. She wore a deep-blue jewel the size of a hen's egg on her bosom, but was otherwise unadorned.

The seat I would like to have had was at the other end of the table, next to a humanoid alien who looked like a friendly two-meter-tall house cat dressed in pink coveralls. Several of the places, including the captain's in the center, were still empty when I arrived at the table, but the stewards started serving dinner anyway. We were all brought a thick soup, except the lady with the jewel to my left, who got a salad, and the alien, who was addressed as "Madam," and must also have been a lady, who got what looked like a plate of crunchy breadsticks. The lady used chopsticks, and the alien lady used pointed prongs that slipped over the three stubby fingers on each hand.

A junior officer in the white uniform, but with blue braid instead of red, came over to the table. "The captain regrets her absence," he said, "but we are about to transit to null-E space, and it is traditional for the captain to be on the bridge during transit. She should be with us in time for the main course." Then he sat down at one of the vacant seats.

A tall man in a bright-red cape came to his place at the table, looked down at the other end, and said loudly, "I will not eat at the same table as any alien." Then he strode off and found an empty seat across the room.

"That was Lord Higar," the red-and-silver man on my right told me in a hushed whisper. "He is chairman of the League for Human Rights."

"Why are you whispering?" the lady on my left asked in a

high, precise voice. "It is no secret. Lord Higar is proud of his part in founding that despicable fanatical group. Although why they call themselves the League for Human Rights has never been made clear to me, since they aren't for anything, but are merely against the rights of every other species."

"If we don't keep Humanity on top," the man said, no longer whispering, "then we must surely and inexorably sink to the bottom! Even you must see that, Dame Proud."

"Bah!" Dame Proud said. "Slogans in place of thought. Human history is full of little people peering around corners and under beds and finding imaginary bogeymen to frighten everyone with and make themselves bigger. What are we to be kept on top of? And what must we sink to the bottom of? Bah!"

"We have a right to consider ourselves first," the man said. "Forces are at work in the Galaxy—there to see if you're not too blind to look—that do not have the best interests of Humanity in mind."

"True enough," Dame Proud said, banging her chopsticks down on the table. "And most of them are Human. This race we are a part of has the widest spectrum of any I know. More geniuses and more idiots. More artists and more clods. More saints and more—Lord Higars. I think the only way in which we humans don't show the greatest diversity is sexually, and even there we give it a good try. No, I really don't know why we spend so much time and so much effort in looking for external bogeymen; they exist so clearly and frequently within the serried ranks of Humanity. We are our own worst enemy."

I was beginning to feel as if I were the net at a tennis match. "Courtesy," I said, "and excuse me, but I don't understand. Who is Lord Higar, and what is the League for Human Rights?"

"Courtesy, young sir," the man said. "Allow me to introduce myself. Citizen Pieter Sensa-Togert, at your service. Surely you jest, asserting that you don't know of Lord Higar or the League. Why, everyone in the Hanse must know..."

Dame Proud laughed a light, silvery laugh. "You are mistaking the costume for the man, Sensa-Togert," she said.

"This youth dresses like a young Hanse lord, but his speech betrays him. Surely he is a Jasperian or Jasperite, or whatever they call themselves." She looked at me, her clear hazel eyes seeming to see deep inside my brain. "Courtesy, lad," she said. "I am Susanna Proud, Dame of the Hanse. Which ending is proper for a citizen of Jasper?"

"Courtesy," I said. "My name is Adam Warrington and I am a Jasperian. We also say 'I am Jaspert,' if you like that better."

"Gracious," she said, laughing again. "By choice, I shall never say either. But thank you for the information."

"Even you of Jasper must surely know of the League," Sensa-Togert said, "and of the great period of crisis we Humans are now entering and the great dangers that confront us?"

"I'm afraid that, on Jasper, we are not encouraged to know of anything that goes on in the great Galaxy outside our own planet," I told him. "We know something of the politics of the Reformation Group, of which we are a part, but little else."

"Why, the Parliament of the Stars is to be convened next year, and we Humans hold but the barest majority. And there are those in positions of authority—not to say power—in Human affairs who would give away positions we need for our own growth and defense. That is what Lord Higar is trying to prevent, and he deserves the support of all loyal Humans throughout the Solar Hanse, indeed throughout the entire Confederation!" Sensa-Togert had a small mustache, which twitched as he spoke, making him look like a plump, worried rabbit.

"The position that Citizen Sensa-Togert is explaining," Dame Proud said, "is held by only a very small, if extremely vocal, minority within the Hanse. It has always fascinated me how those who are the most wrong-headed always yell the most loudly and stridently, and how many people are always fooled by the noise."

"I am not yelling, Dame Proud," Sensa-Togert said stiffly.

"No, Lord Higar is doing your yelling for you, insulting that perfectly sweet Lysertling matron. How unmannerly of him."

The main course was slid in front of us by red-coated stew-

ards, and Sensa-Togert turned to his food, clearly glad of a chance to break off the conversation. We were served halves of some bird covered in a rich sauce except for the Lysertling, who got a whole bird and no sauce, and Dame Proud, who got a ceramic pot of mixed vegetables and grain.

"What is the Parliament of Stars?" I asked, in between bites of sauce-covered bird.

"The Parliament of Stars meets for five hundred days once every two hundred and fourteen years," Dame Proud told me. "All recognized governments of all inhabited systems send delegates. All intelligent species are represented. At the Parliament the rules of governing the intercourse between the systems and between the Human and non-Human peoples are formulated to stay in effect until the next Parliament."

"I remember reading about that," I said. "But I thought it was ancient history."

"Well, the last one was two hundred and thirteen years ago," Dame Proud said, smiling, "and you might call that ancient history, although there are those of us who are old enough to remember it. The upcoming one will be the fifth, so that means they have been held for over a thousand years, standard."

"Yes," Sensa-Togert said, looking up from his food, "since the first atrocity."

"Citizen Sensa-Togert is referring to the destruction of Hope by Greater Vand," Dame Proud said.

"I've heard of that, too," I said. "Hope was a Human planet...."

"And there is no record of what the Vand were," Dame Proud said. "They may even have been Human too."

"Not likely," Sensa-Togert said, holding a bird leg like a midget club and glaring at Dame Proud.

"Nobody knows," Dame Proud said. "After they destroyed Hope, Greater Vand emigrated to an unknown location. The whole planet just picked up and moved."

"To escape a just retribution," Sensa-Togert said.

"As may be," said Dame Proud. "At any rate, the first Parliament of Stars was held shortly after that. Since then,

all intelligent peoples of all races have tried to achieve what harmony they can in order to, at the very least, avoid killing each other."

"Yes, and what has happened?" Sensa-Togert said. "The Catarrhy wars and the destruction of Llyra."

"Two tragedies," Dame Proud agreed. "And I could cite others. What of the Lippener Border Dispute, or the War of the Sandusky Cessation?"

"But that was Human against Human," Sensa-Togert said.

"Exactly," Dame Proud said. "We Humans have never needed any outside help in killing each other. But since the destruction of Hope by Greater Vand and the Emigration of Vand, we have at least tried to prevent the destruction of whole planets and whole peoples, of whatever race. Who is to know what the Great Plan intends for any of us?"

"The Great Plan!" Sensa-Togert said, snorting. "I should have guessed. Pacifism and vegetarianism and The Great Plan. You're a Causalist!"

"You say that as though it were a dirty word," Dame Proud said. "As a matter of fact, my vegetarianism is purely functional; animal protein makes me ill."

There was a sudden lurch, as though the ship had been kicked sideways. Then I realized it was a loss of orientation in my own mind. Nothing had moved on the table, and the water glasses didn't even jiggle. "We have entered null-E space," Dame Proud said calmly. "This ship and all in it have just, in a mathematical sense, become imaginary."

"Imaginary?" I asked, not sure I liked the sound of that.

"In order to compute where we are in null-E space, and where we will emerge, or transit back, into normal space, astrogators must use a class of mathematics involving what are called 'imaginary numbers.' And it is more than just a mathematical conceit. One could say that when we enter null-E space we cease to exist in a very real physical sense." Dame Proud nodded thoughtfully and chewed on her dinner. "Furthermore, the physics of null-E space indicate that there is a finite probability that a ship tran-

siting back to normal space might be removed from its intended point of emergence both in space and in time. We might come out of null-E parsecs away from our target, and thousands of years in the past."

"Really?" I asked. "I've never heard that before."

"Just a slight chance," Dame Proud said.

"It never happens," Sensa-Togert said firmly. "Never."

"You'd know, of course," Dame Proud said.

"I would have heard. I would know if such things happen."

"A ship that was thrust into the past would just disappear as far as any outside observer was concerned," Dame Proud said, "And ships do disappear."

"Seldom," Sensa-Togert said. "Very seldom."

"What about the Quatti?" Dame Proud asked.

"That proves nothing," Sensa-Togert said. "Or, rather, nobody can say what it does prove."

"The Quatti?" I asked.

"A people that were found about ten years ago on a newly discovered planet," Dame Proud told me. "They are humanoid to so many points of similarity that there seems no doubt that they are Human. And they leave a myth of having come to the planet on a big ship thousands of years ago."

"Many civilizations have had such a myth," Sensa-Togert said.

"Correct," Dame Proud agreed. "And perhaps that should be looked into."

Sensa-Togert shook his head in disgust and went back to his dinner.

Just then the captain came in and took her place at the center of the table. She was a tall, slender lady of middle years, with an air of competence and authority that marked her rank more surely than the golden sunbursts she wore on her collar. "Good evening, honored guests," she said in a calm, soft voice. "I am Captain Lady Tara ep Tzinn. I'm sorry I couldn't be with you at the start of the meal, but tradition placed me on the bridge at that time. We are the servants of tradition, we of the space

service." She sat down and turned to her lieutenant. "But there are two places empty. Mqdrekkor the Divornian and Lord Higar are both absent. Did my tardiness offend them?"

"Mqdrekkor has not appeared for dinner, Captain ep Tzinn, and Lord Higar chose not to grace us with his presence." The lieutenant nodded his head toward where Lord Higar was eating his solitary meal. "The Noble Lord was offended by the presence of Madam M'Yar."

"Oh, I see," the captain said. She turned to the Lysertling. "I hope that Lord Higar's attitude did not, in its turn, offend you, madam."

The Lysertling shook her fuzzy head violently back and forth. "Not," she said. "No. Not. Most notly." She put one three-fingered hand delicately to her face. "He smell bad."

"Ah! Then reciprocity is, as ever, observed. He would not have you and you would not have him. Enjoy your dinner, madam."

"Most reply suitable," the cat woman said, nodding firmly.

"Good," the captain said, and turned to her own plate.

When we had finished the bird, the plates were cleared away and hot, moist squares of towel were handed to each of us to cleanse our hands. Then three different sorts of teas were served with a variety of small pastries. "You have not been in space before, Citizen Warrington?" Dame Proud asked. I knew that this was her version of polite conversation, since it must have been ultimately clear to her that I had never even been off Jasper before.

"No, ma'am," I told her. "This is my first space voyage."

"I trust it will be merely the first of many," she said. "There is much to learn in the Galaxy, and knowledge is the only true riches. Continual learning is the only way to keep your mind young. The cosmeticians can keep the body young for hundreds of years, but what good is that if you have an atrophied mind?"

"You travel a lot, Dame Proud?"

"I have that fortune," she said. "My profession keeps me on the move."

"What do you do?" I asked her.

She touched the jewel on her robe. "I am an observer," she said. The deep blue of the jewel seemed to lighten slightly and sparkle from inside as she touched it.

"An observer," I repeated. "Is that like a reporter? Do you work for the news networks?"

"I have, on occasion, worked for the news networks," she said, "but an observer is more than a reporter. Evidence presented by a member of the Guild of Observers is accepted as factual in any court of law or equity. We are recognized as being completely impartial and truthful."

"You sounded pretty partisan to me," Sensa-Togert said, stuffing another pastry into his mouth.

"We are required to be accurate only as to fact, my dear Citizen Sensa-Togert. No one should be prevented from having—or voicing—an opinion. But if you hire me to witness any transaction, you know that nothing can cause me to alter or shade the facts."

"I know, I know," Sensa-Togert said. "Don't be so sensitive."

"I am not in the least sensitive," Dame Proud said.

The captain did not speak with anyone while she finished her dinner, but when she was done she spent a few moments talking with each of her guests. I found that I was at the table with some very interesting people. A tall man at the far end was a master cosmetician-synthesizer, who could create whole new artificial limbs and reshape any part of the body to new specifications. His companion, a woman who looked to be in her early twenties, was a concert librettist who was going back to Earth to celebrate her two hundredth birthday.

A man sitting across from the captain was the finalist in an Imperium-wide play contest who was going to Earth to arrange for his play to be put on for the judging committee. The captain asked him what the play was about, and he told her it was a dark drama of a Human-alien-Human triangle that took place seven kilometers deep in a vanadium mine in the first act and with its characters marooned on a comet in the second. "It's full

of subtle nuances and secondary motivation," he told her. She seemed impressed.

An archdeacon from Jasper was at the table also. He was on his way to the missionary college on Wayfare. Next to him was a scientist who spent most of his time on a research ship floating stationary in the deep space between the stars. He was on his way to Mars to have a piece of scientific apparatus repaired by the Physics Lab Repair Shop at the University of Sol.

The other people, including Madam M'Yar, the cat-lady from Lysert, were connected in one way or another with the coming Parliament of Stars, which was to take place on Earth's Moon, in a special city being built just for the delegates. Citizen Sensa-Togert turned out to be a caterer, who supplied specialty foods from far planets to the exclusive restaurants of the Hanse. He was going to see if he could get the contract for the restaurants of Parliament City.

When the captain talked to me, everyone at the table turned to look at me. For a moment I was very nervous, but Captain ep Tzinn immediately put me at ease. I think it was because when she spoke to you, you felt that she really cared. She was delighted that I was going to the University of Sol, and told me that she had graduated from there herself many years before. "Don't even ask how many," she said with a laugh. "But the University is timeless, and I'm sure it's the same today as it was the day I left."

The captain asked me whether I'd like to visit the bridge, and I told her that there was nothing I'd like better. "I'll send Junior Lieutenant ep Liztom for you," she promised, and she rose from her seat to indicate the end of dinner.

But for the next three days nothing happened. Not that I was bored—the ship was gigantic, much larger than I'd realized, and most of it was open to passengers. The central core had no pseudogravity, and a large part of it had been turned into a giant air-swimming area. There were sheets of rubberized fabric called "bounce sheets" stretched periodically around the hall and, by bouncing off them at the proper angles, you could go through

complicated high-speed maneuvers, like a living billiard ball.

There was a two-hour course of instruction before you were allowed to go air-swimming—mostly practice in how to use the flippers and how to make turns, and giving stern warnings about keeping out of everyone else's way. Working with a partner was great fun, if you had a partner, but one of the two of you had better be an expert or you both were going to end up with broken bones. Or so we were warned.

I found the attitude strange after growing up on Jasper. On the ship they taught you how to do something if you wished, warned you of its dangers, and then left you alone to do as you chose. On Jasper if something was dangerous they would simply forbid it.

The third time I went air-swimming, Junior Lieutenant Nancy ep Liztom was there doing a complicated air-ballet routine. She seemed really pleased to see me. "Come on in," she called as I put my flippers on. "The air's fine!"

"I'm not very good at this stuff," I told her, adjusting the straps on my feet. "If man were meant to fly, he would have been born with flippers on."

"I practically was," Nancy said. "I was born in a free-fall tank on board the Major Barbara. Weightless birth was in for a while back then, but nobody's doing it anymore. It was supposed to make the baby mature faster."

"Did it?"

"Only if you consider the ability to do triple flips a sign of maturity. Come on out here, and I'll take you through a couple of the simpler moves."

I bounced myself off the wall and out to where Nancy was, but when I reached her I couldn't stop until she grabbed me with one hand and the edge of a bounce sheet with the other. "First lesson," she said, "is always know where you're going to end up—and which end is going to be up when you do. And be very careful with those flippers; that gossamer fabric tears very easily."

I looked down at the meter-wide span of fabric at the end of

each foot flipper. "Why is it so thin?" I asked. "Won't thicker fabric hold the air?"

"Sure, but if some booby plows into you, we want the ends to break off instead of clubbing or jabbing you."

"Right," I said. "Of course. Good thinking."

"Say, you're pretty good," she said after I'd tried the same simple turn three times and then finally got it almost right. "You ought to consider a career in space; you have a natural affinity for it."

"You," I said, "are making fun of me, and that's not nice."

"I'm not," she insisted. "You should see the way most lubbers do out here. They never learn, and never can."

"Well, thanks for the compliment, anyway. And, speaking of that, whatever happened to my invitation to visit the bridge?"

"I don't know," Nancy said, looking troubled. "We're on amber alert right now, and no passengers are allowed in any operational areas while an alert is on. When it's over, I'm supposed to invite you up."

"What is an amber alert?" I asked.

"It's the first stage of alert. It means there's a chance something may happen that's detrimental to the welfare of the ship, so we all have to be extra careful."

"What may happen?"

"Nobody knows but the captain, and she didn't say."

"Can't you ask her?"

Nancy looked at me "You don't ever ask the captain why she orders something. If she wants you to know, she'll tell you."

"Oh."

"And listen. Please don't tell any of the other passengers what I said. I mean, about the alert. Passengers aren't supposed to know."

"Why not? Maybe we could help."

"Well...passengers behave very unpredictably unless they have something specific to do. That's why we have lifeboat drill every day, so that it has become a habit if you ever need it."

"Okay," I agreed. "I won't mention it. But when it's over, I

really would like to see the bridge."

"I won't forget," Nancy said.

That day we came out of null-E space in a wide arc around a distant star. We slowed down enough to match speed with a snatch boat that had come out to take off the passengers for Wayfare. Then we sped up again, and by late evening, ship's time, we reentered null-E space. I was lying on my bunk in my cabin when I felt the psychic jolt of reentry, and I suddenly remembered that Mr. Peshnov the seed salesman was leaving at Wayfare, and that I had forgotten to say good-bye to him.

CHAPTER VI.

For some reason I couldn't sleep that night, so I went to the passengers' lounge. Nobody else was there—it was already very late—and I settled myself in one of the soft, high-back chairs and stared out the large window, which was all that separated me from the Universe.

In null-E space the stars all look strange. First of all, fewer of them are visible, although trying to count them all would still take quite a while. Then the color differences are more pronounced. The stars shine in every color the human eye can see, and probably in a few that it can't. They are the same stars as in regular space, but different parts of their spectra are visible. None of the light photons that usually make the stars visible can reach the ship, since in null-E space the ship is effectively traveling a lot faster than light. Other particles emitted from the stars do reach the ship, and they behave like photons when they strike the screens—or the window, which is a special boron-silicon-yttrium glass over half a meter thick to keep out dangerous radiation.

In null-E space you can see great coronas and sweeping bands of coruscating color, like star-spanning rainbows, sweeping and whirling, growing and changing, appearing and disappearing as you watch. In a matter of minutes the shape of space through your window will distort and change, never the same twice and never still. It was the most glorious show I had ever seen, and one that I will never tire of, no matter how many times I see it.

I sat and watched the ever-changing display of the Universe

through the window into space for perhaps an hour or more. Then I dozed off in my chair and fell into a deep sleep. I dreamed I was flying through space, soaring between the stars, a great gaseous creature who could put his hand through planets and stare close-up at the insides of stars.

I don't know why I woke up. Perhaps I heard something, but more probably I shifted position in my chair and my head fell off the backrest. At any rate, I did wake up, and it was very late. I decided that I'd spend the rest of the night securely in bed. So, yawning and stretching, I got up to go back to my cabin.

But when I got there, my cabin door wouldn't open. I pressed my hand firmly against the identity plate and ordered the door to open, and nothing happened. I tried again, with the same result. I tried controlling my voice and saying "open" in different tones. I tried wiping my hand clean on my trousers before pressing it against the plate. I tried using my left hand. Nothing I could think of would open the door. I checked at the stairwell to see if I was in the right corridor, on the right level, and as far as I could tell, I was. The only thing left to do was to get access to the ship's computer and find out why it wasn't letting me back into my own cabin.

Then all the corridor lights went off.

I was now convinced that there was something wrong, but still couldn't think of anything better to do than head back to the passengers' lounge and use one of the computer terminals there. I walked slowly, my left hand gently touching the wall, toward the stairwell. I am not ordinarily afraid of the dark, but I am not ordinarily locked out of my cabin in an interstellar spaceship either. I thought I heard voices ahead of me. Then I was sure: two people, at least, whispering quietly.

"Hello!" I called. "Who's there?"

There was a scuffling noise, and the whispering stopped. I got the impression, don't ask me how, that one of the whisperers was now silently headed toward me. That idea didn't appeal to me. Who could they be? What were they doing in the corridor in the middle of the night? All sorts of half-formed notions

crowded into my head involving pirates, masked murderers, secret smuggling agreements, and all the other plots from the adventure stories my father had never liked me to watch. But mostly I thought I should get away from these people until I found out what was happening.

Just then my hand found the corner of the stairwell. The drop belt was right beyond, but I didn't feel like trying it with the lights off. I quickly entered the stairwell and started downstairs, going as fast as I could in the dark without making any noise. Something else strange was happening, and I didn't know what it was. It was getting harder to walk, and my muscles were responding strangely. I held on to the railing, using it as a guide and a support.

I reached the level below, where the passengers' lounge was, and started out into the corridor, when I heard a faint snik! in front of me. I paused, listening, straining my ears and trying to suppress my already overactive imagination. The snik! was repeated, closer than before.

I turned back to the stairs, heading down. I felt curiously light-headed, and my feet were having a hard time gaining traction on the carpeted steps. I was down another full flight before I realized what it was that was happening: the pseudo-gravity was slowly being turned off. I went into the corridor and jumped, pushing myself off the floor very lightly. I not only touched the ceiling overhead, but I was able to flatten my entire body against it before I started slowly drifting back down.

There was a noise from the stairs—someone was following me down. I headed off down the corridor, half running, half air-swimming, pushing off from the walls or ceiling as often as from the floor, keeping my hands feeling the way in front. Now that my eyes had become adjusted to the dark, I could see a thin strip of fluorescence running along the upper margin of the left-hand wall, and I followed that as best I could.

A pair of legs scissored around mine, flipping me over, and a slender arm went around my neck, neatly locking my right arm in the process. I tried to fight, instinctively, despite my surprise,

but I had no leverage and no place to go.

"Don't move," a familiar voice whispered, "and don't make a sound, or I'll break your neck!"

"Nancy!" I whispered hoarsely. "Lieutenant ep Liz-tom!"

The hold on my neck was cautiously loosened, and I sensed a small head peering around over my shoulder. "Adam Warrington!" she said. "What in the Imperium are you doing here?"

"I don't know," I said. "The lights went out, and someone was chasing me. Or I thought someone was chasing me. How can you tell who it is in the dark? And let go of me. Please."

"I have infrared goggles on," Nancy said. "From up close I can make out enough detail to tell who it is." She let go of me, and I started massaging my neck and shoulder.

"Boy, you've got some grip on you, for a lady."

"Don't you forget it," she said. "And whisper!"

"What's going on?" I whispered.

"I'm not sure," Nancy said. "We think pirates are trying to take over the ship. Somebody sure is. They attacked the bridge without warning. Killed the wheelman, the second officer, and an astrogation warrant."

"Then they have control of the ship?"

"No. The bridge is now sealed off and turned off. The ship is being conned from the battle bridge. But there are some of these pirates still loose in the ship. The computer estimates twenty to thirty."

"Pirates?" I asked. I always pictured pirates as swinging aboard sailing ships with wicked curved swords in their teeth.

"There are planets that support themselves by hijacking null-E ships," Nancy said. "But Lady Tara says she thinks these people are political."

"Lady Tara?"

"Captain ep Tzinn."

"Oh. That's right. What are you doing here?"

"Guarding this corridor. Why are you out?"

"I couldn't sleep. I went to the passengers' lounge. Then my

door wouldn't open when I tried to return to my cabin."

"Right. Computer has sealed all the doors. And there's no safe place I can send you in the dark. You'll just have to wait here with me."

"Maybe I can help you," I said.

"Don't be silly," she said sharply.

That did it. I completed the transition from scared to angry in record time. "I'm not completely useless," I said. It came out sharper than I intended. And louder.

"Keep your voice down," Nancy said. "Better yet, don't talk. I didn't mean to insult you or hurt your pride. It's just that this is my job, and I'm trained for it. That's why we turned the pseudo-G off, to give the ship's company the edge."

"That makes sense," I whispered "I'll just stand—or float—here quietly."

We remained silent for a while. Nancy kept her hand on my shoulder, which I found reassuring. I kept hearing, or imagining I heard, noises in the distance. But nobody came down our corridor.

"Are you armed?" I whispered to Nancy.

"No. We keep the number of internal weapons on the ship very low. If I'm not armed, no one can get a weapon by taking it away from me. And I have the advantage in unarmed weightless combat, because I practice it every day."

"Are they armed?" I asked.

"The group that took the bridge had a handgun. I have no idea how they brought it aboard. They may still have it, but they're locked in the bridge. The rest of them have tanglewebs, but nothing else as far as we can tell."

"Tanglewebs?"

"Little round pellets they either throw or shoot through a slingshot. If one hits you it bursts, sending a sticky web all over you and making it very hard to move. If one hits you in the face you might suffocate."

"Cute," I said.

"They probably can't throw them very well in no gravity,"

Nancy said.

There was a noise at the end of the corridor, where the stairs were. We waited silently, but the sound wasn't repeated. "What is on this level?" I asked. "I mean, what are you guarding?"

"A duplicate passageway to the battle bridge," she said. "Kind of a back way. They probably don't know it's here."

The passage lights suddenly came on full, then dropped to about a quarter brightness, which was still too much for a pair of eyes used to total black.

"Well," I said, "it must be finished. Maybe the door to my cabin will open now."

Nancy lifted her feet and floated a half meter off the floor. "No," she said.

"No?"

"No gravity. The first thing we'd do if the ship's emergency were over is gradually restore the pseudo-G. You'd feel it by now. Think of all those passengers asleep in their bunks who are actually floating a few centimeters over their bunks. Think of the ones who are awake and can't get out of their cabins— and can't keep their feet on the floor."

"You mean—it's them?"

"Somebody has found one of the emergency light switches, but still hasn't figured out how to gain access to the computer. And one of the emergency light panels is in the battle bridge." She turned and kicked off down the corridor, bounced off one wall, and came to a slamming stop at a cabin door. Fitting a ring she was wearing into a notch in the side of the palm-plate, she opened the door and went inside.

I followed more slowly, pulling myself from doorway to doorway so I wouldn't overshoot and have to work my way back. When I got to the door I could see that it wasn't a cabin, but a disguised corridor that went down at an angle into the innards of the ship. Nancy was already well on her way down. I bounced and kicked my way after her, working up a set of bruises that I felt for weeks afterward.

At the end of the corridor was an armored door that looked

like the outside of a space hatch. Nancy had it slightly open by the time I reached her. I was right; it was a space hatch, and just inside was an airlock. "This is called the battle bridge," she told me, pulling the massive door the rest of the way on its track. "It's supposed to be completely independent of the main ship's life support in case of attack." Sweat stood out across her face as she pulled.

"Let me help you," I said, and tried to add my strength to the pulling effort. The door massed over two tons, and was usually opened by machinery. The problem was, there was no place to hold on to when you pulled, and without gravity there was no weight to supply friction against the floor. But finally we had it open, and Nancy—Junior Lieutenant ep Liztom—went into the airlock.

"Let me come with you," I said. "Maybe I can help."

She thought about it for a second. "Come on in," she said. "But stay behind me and keep out of the way."

"Okay," I agreed.

Closing the outer door to the lock was easier than opening it. We had to pull again, but this time we had the wheel for the inner lock to hang on to. In a minute or so we had it closed and sealed. A small panel glowed red, showing that the automatic interlock was activated, unlocking the inner door, since there was no pressure differential between the room inside and the lock.

"I'd like it better if the lights were still out," Nancy whispered. "I'm going to open this door as quietly as possible, so don't make any noise."

I stayed stock-still while Nancy pushed the inner door open. It opened steadily and silently onto the battle bridge. All we could see was a row of red panels in front of us, but in the room on the other side of the panels we could hear a man yelling orders and a lot of bouncing around.

I started to go around the panels, but when I saw Nancy floating silently to their top, I followed. From on top of the panels, which were about two meters tall, we had a clear view

of the rest of the battle bridge. It was an eight-sided room, with great screens taking up four of the sides. The command chair was in the center, raised up, and four control chairs faced each of the large screens. The screens showed the universe around the ship in various views and at different magnifications.

The rear four sides of the room held instrument complexes, mounted on desk consoles or racked in panels like the ones we were on top of. The main entrance was a large space lock high on the wall behind us and to the right. Steps came down from the lock to the floor.

In the center of the room, standing—or rather, floating—at the command chair, was Lord Higar, dressed in black. Four of Lord Higar's henchmen were at the control chairs, while the six *Western Star* crew members in the room, including Captain Lady Tara ep Tzinn, stood together to one side of the room with their hands on top of their heads.

In Lord Higar's hand was a wicked-looking slug-throwing handgun, and he was waving it at Captain ep Tzinn. "If you don't quickly order your men to help us," he yelled, "I'm going to have to shoot someone to show you I mean business!"

"I have no doubt that you mean business, Lord Higar," Captain ep Tzinn said, her words glacially calm. "You would have to be a complete fool to do this merely as a prank."

"Well, then, which of these controls is for the pseudogravity? None of us can read the markings."

"You should have taken linguistic differences into account before you began this insane venture," Captain ep Tzinn said. "You can't expect me or any of my people to aid you in an act of piracy." She seemed to be staring past Lord Higar right to where Nancy and I were lying.

Nancy raised her hand from the wrist and then dropped it again, and Captain ep Tzinn gave a barely perceptible nod.

Taking her goggles off and dropping them behind the panel, where they hung suspended in the air, Nancy rolled over to face me. She took a soft-tip pen from the pocket in the arm of her jacket and wrote on the panel top between us, "When I move

you go to main lock and undog it."

I looked over to the main lock and could see the large U-shaped dog that was keeping it locked, and I nodded at Nancy. I wasn't exactly sure what she meant, but I thought it would become clear as I saw what happened.

Lord Higar was trying to control his temper. He was clearly not used to being thwarted, even in piracy. "We do what we do for a good and sufficient reason," he said, "and if we must do it without you, why, then, so be it." And he leveled his handgun at Captain ep Tzinn's breast.

"You cannot control or astrogate this ship at random," Captain ep Tzinn said, staring him in the eye. "If you kill us you will be doomed to travel null-E space to the farthest corners of the universe, unless you first contaminate the life-support system or blow up the ship in your ignorance. There will be no salvation, there will be no escape."

"First I will kill you," Lord Higar said, "and then the next in command, and then the next, and so on down the line until I find someone who would rather astrogate for us than die."

"The chain of murders will be for nothing. There is no such person in this crew. For the last time, give yourself up."

"You don't seem to understand who's in command here—"

As Lord Higar spoke, Nancy launched herself into space, pushing off from the wall-ceiling intersection in a tight spin aimed at Lord Higar's back.

One of Lord Higar's men spotted her hurtling through the air, and yelled a warning. Higar turned and tried to level his weapon at the spinning ball that was Nancy, but before he could, she extended, arms high toward the ceiling, feet smashing out into Higar's face.

Everyone started moving then. I headed flat-out across the room to the lock. There was the sharp sound of the handgun firing twice. I reached the lock, harder than I'd intended, and had all the air knocked out of me by smashing up against it. Something twisted in my shoulder, and my right arm didn't want to work. I rotated the locking dog with my left hand and

pushed the door release. The door immediately swung open and armed ship's officers pushed in one after the other until about twenty of them were through the lock.

There was a little scuffling until all the pirates in the room were secured, but with the loss of their leader they quickly gave up. And Lord Higar had proved no match for Junior Lieutenant Nancy ep Liztom in weightless combat.

The rest of the ship was methodically searched, and twenty-six more plotters were taken into custody by the ship's crew. But I took no part in any of that; I was down in the ship's hospital having a broken collarbone set and treated.

CHAPTER VII.

Four people had been killed in Lord Higar's assault on the *Western Star:* three crewmen in the bridge and one of Lord Higar's men, who was shot by Higar's own handgun when he tried to hit Nancy. Three crewmen, two of Higar's men, and one passenger—me—were injured.

The next day at eleven hundred hours, deep-space burial services were read, and the four dead were puffed into space on jets of air that would carry them away from the ship.

"And so these voyagers begin the endless journey," Captain ep Tzinn read from the ages-old service of the Space Guild as each body left the ship. "They go where time has no meaning, where space has no limits. They join the company of all those who have died in space, and of all those who shall die in space, to meet in the eternal, limitless Valhalla that is the space between the stars." She closed the book.

"Let it be written in the Great Scroll of the Guild that Second Officer Robel ep Dymstor and Qualified Spaceman Billup Stermatt died in the performance of their duties, and let their people be notified. Warrant Officer"—and here she made a series of sounds I cannot spell or pronounce—"an observer from Greater Darwin, died in the performance of its duty. Let its name be entered in honor in the Great Scroll, as it was in the service of the *Western Star* that it gave its life, and let its people be so notified.

"As for the other dead man, another will have to speak for him."

And Captain Lady Tara ep Tzinn turned and walked out of the room.

At thirteen hundred, Deep Space Court was convened in the passengers' dining room. The tables were removed and rows of chairs were set out facing the front of the room for the passengers and crew who wished to watch the proceedings. At a small table at front center sat Captain ep Tzinn, who was the judge. To her left, at a slightly longer table, sat the ship's purser, the first officer, and Dame Proud. To her right, on a double row of chairs, sat the thirty accused. The machine shop had manufactured shackles for them, and they were all shackled together, each one's right foot to the next man's left, with Lord Higar first in line. The witness chair had been placed between the two tables. On the middle seat of the front row of observers sat a ship's officer with a holo camera to take an official record of the court proceedings.

"Are we ready?" Captain ep Tzinn asked. "Good. Then let this court be open. We are inquiring into the events that took place aboard the *Western Star* on the night of April sixteenth, in this twenty-ninth year of the reign of Alexander the Ninth, leading up to and including the deaths of three ship's officers and one passenger. Let the names of the dead be entered into the official minutes."

The officer with the holo camera whispered something into his whisker mike and then nodded to Captain ep Tzinn.

The trial started with a series of witnesses to establish all the dull, procedural things that had to be established: the course of the ship, the probable location of the ship at the start of last night's events, the true names of all passengers concerned as entered on the ship's manifest, the ship's doctor's certification of the fact of death of three crew members and one passenger.

I sat in a corner watching, getting used to my neck brace, and waiting to be called as a witness. I found even the dull stuff to be fascinating, as slowly a chain of fact was woven around last night's events, pinning them down and making them real.

At one point, after the doctor left the witness chair, Lord

Higar stood up and asked, "Am I to be allowed to speak?" in a haughty voice, as if the answer were of little concern to him.

"Of course," Captain ep Tzinn told him. "And you will be heard."

"This court has no jurisdiction," Lord Higar said.

"The *Western Star* is in null-E space," Captain ep Tzinn replied. "If the captain or other senior officer of a rated ship in null-E space decides that an offense or an event is serious enough, the officer can convene a court. I am, and it is."

"No one on this ship has jurisdiction over a lord of the Solar Hanse," Lord Higar said.

Captain ep Tzinn nodded to the purser. "You are serving as law officer," she told him. "What do you say?"

The purser opened a thick book which lay on the table in front of him and riffled the pages until he came to what he wanted. "Deep Space Act," he read, "Hiram the Fourth, Year Three, and ratifying the appropriate Order of Confederation." He ran his finger down the page until he came to what he wanted. "As a ship in null-Einsteinian space, by the known laws of nature, cannot communicate with the outside universe and cannot emerge except at precisely planned nodes, such a ship must be regarded as a world unto itself for the duration of such a voyage. The legal master of the ship is responsible for the health and safety of the crew and passengers and the safe transport of the cargo, and must be the sole arbiter of fact and justice, with power of summary punishment, confinement, and, if necessary, death over any sentient beings aboard.

"Any later review of such actions taken under this act may reprimand the master only if it can clearly show that the actions were unfounded, capricious, or vindictive.

"No person is immune to the authority of the ship's master by reason of hereditary position, elective office, status, or title."

He closed the book. "I think that covers it."

"I believe," Lord Higar said, "that the Solar Hanse, and, indeed, the Confederation, frowns upon a ship's master imposing the death sentence. Is that correct?"

"That is correct," Captain ep Tzinn said, staring coldly at Lord Higar. "It is seldom done."

"And I have a procedural point," Lord Higar said. "The court recorder is working for the, ah, prosecution. How can I be assured that a fair record is kept of these proceedings?"

"I have asked Dame Proud of the Observer's Guild to sit in," Captain ep Tzinn said, nodding at Dame Proud, who nodded back. "She has graciously agreed. Of course she will receive her usual Guild scale. Does that suit you?"

"You are recording?" Lord Higar asked Dame Proud.

"I am."

"Then I guess I have to be satisfied. You may proceed with this farce," Lord Higar said, sitting back down.

Now we got down to the incidents of the attempted takeover. A spaceman testified that he was tricked into opening the door to the bridge by Lord Higar, and that Lord Higar and his men rushed in, killed three crewmen on watch, and took over the bridge. Other testimony then established that Lord Higar left the bridge in charge of five of his men who were space-trained (on private yachts) and went off to secure the rest of the ship.

The first officer told how he isolated the bridge and cut it out of circuit, so control was transferred to the battle bridge, where Captain ep Tzinn reestablished command of the ship and cut off the lights and pseudogravity. But Lord Higar stormed the battle bridge before the crew could arm themselves to capture him, and isolated himself in there. The members of his scheme who could run a spaceship were locked off in the main bridge, so he tried to coerce his prisoners in the battle bridge to run the ship for him.

Then my turn came, and I testified to what I'd heard Lord Higar say while I was hiding on top of the panel.

Through all this Lord Higar remained calm and unruffled, acting as his own attorney and as attorney for all those accused with him. He seldom interrupted and seemed almost uncon-cerned with what was being said on the witness chair.

Then it was all over, all the evidence had been introduced,

and the captain went off with the first officer and the purser to discuss their findings. Lord Higar turned to talk to his men while they were gone, and whatever he said seemed to cheer them up greatly, even to the point of laughing at a couple of his commerits. The audience was told that they could leave and would be recalled when the court was called back to order, but only a few people left. Most of them stayed in their seats as though frozen in place, awaiting the outcome.

After a few minutes of waiting, a general discussion of the trial and the crime broke out in the audience. I found the talk very interesting. Some of the people brought up things that had little relation to what had actually happened, as though they were of utmost importance, and some others seemed to have witnessed an entirely different set of events from those I had just lived through. One woman thought it was criminal that that uppity lady captain dared to try a member of the Hanse nobility. Another thought it disgraceful that the word of an alien was being taken over that of real Human beings—although no alien had given evidence. A large, red-faced man insisted that the rules of the Space Warfare Convention of Alexander III, 7, should apply. When I asked him who was at war with whom, he told me to have respect for my elders.

Less than half an hour later Captain ep Tzinn and her two aides returned with a verdict. The first officer and the purser took their seats, and Captain ep Tzinn stood behind her desk. "We find as follows," she said. "Qualified Spaceman Jonas ep Alain...."

The spaceman, who had given evidence, stood at his name.

"...you are guilty of neglect and bad judgment in that, during an amber alert, you allowed a passenger to talk his way past you onto the bridge. It is my decision that, upon reaching your home port, you are to be grounded at the pleasure of the Guild, but for at least a year."

The spaceman sat down. He didn't look very happy.

"Junior Lieutenant Sarah-John Maydeath Nancy Tenn f 'Ivan ep Liztom," the captain called.

Nancy stood up.

"You have acted in the best traditions of the service. A comment to that effect shall be appended to your record."

Nancy sat down.

"Citizen Adam Warrington."

I stood up. I had no idea what this was about, and found that my heart was pounding as badly as right before I launched myself at the airlock.

"You have been of material aid to the crew members of the *Western Star* in the performance of their duty," the captain said to me. "The Guild Hall and the Lords of Space will be so notified. And you have my thanks."

I sat down. I had no idea what that meant, but it sounded nice. And to be thanked personally by Captain ep Tzinn was reward enough in itself.

"Will the following persons please stand?" the captain said, and read a list of names starting with Lord Higar. All the prisoners stood.

"We find you all, separately and collectively, guilty of these crimes," the captain said. "Assault, criminal trespass, piracy under the meaning of the act, interfering with the operations of an Imperial Transgalactic Spaceliner while in null-E space, kidnapping, and murder. Have you, any of you, anything to say before I pass sentence?"

Lord Higar stood up. "We do not admit to the competence of this court to judge us," he said.

"That's as it may be," she said. "Nonetheless, I do judge you, in the name of this court." She sat down. "You are guilty, all of you, of murder. It is the most heinous act imaginable, the taking of a sentient life: heinous because of its absolute finality; once taken, a life cannot be given back. You are also judged guilty of two other offenses that are considered capital crimes: piracy and kidnapping.

"But I shall not sentence you to death. I can no more return your life than you can return the lives of those four people you killed, and I am reluctant to take away that which I cannot

return."

Lord Higar leaned back and said something to the man behind him, who snickered.

"You imagine that, as I do not kill you, you will soon be free, because this voyage cannot last forever and I must soon turn you over to some planetary authority," Captain ep Tzinn said, "and because your money and influence will soon combine to have you released.

"Well, I have thought about that, and that would be wrong." Captain ep Tzinn stood up again. "I hereby sentence you to eternal banishment from the Hanse, the Confederation, and all the planets of Humanity. This judgment is to be carried out immediately, as soon as the astrogator can find a proper planet to release you on."

Lord Higar jumped to his feet. "What! You can't—"

"I can," the captain said. "I have. You will be released, with all your personal gear and your hold baggage and enough supplies to sustain you for a time, upon a planet suitable for human habitation that contains no sentient race. The location of this planet shall be known only to me and the astrogation officer, and a sealed document with the coordinates shall be placed in the vault of the Space Guild, not to be opened for two hundred years, at which time a search party might come out to see what became of you.

"If any of you are so inclined, I suggest keeping a diary; it should be fascinating reading for those who find it." Captain ep Tzinn looked around. "Is there any other business to put before this court? No? Then I declare this court closed." And she turned and strode from the room.

Lord Higar stood where he was. His mouth worked, but no words came out. Then the security guards took him and the rest of his men away.

Two days later we pulled out of null-E space above a beautiful blue planet that circled a yellow-white star. Two small moons chased each other across the planet's sky. A chain of islands ran across the planet's equator, and one big continent spread across

the southern hemisphere.

The winged shuttle was loaded with the involuntary settlers and all the equipment it could hold and set out on the long glide path to a water landing by a natural bay on the east coast of the southern continent. Eighteen hours later it returned to the *Western Star*, and we headed back out into deep space. Six hours after that we reached a node and flipped back into null-E space.

A week and a half later we reached Sol Terminus, and it was time for me to leave the *Western Star*. I was invited to the captain's table on the last night, and Lady Tara—she asked me to call her Lady Tara told us stories of space and what it meant to sail the ocean between the stars. She talked of a cold planet circling a distant star where the people look like silver beetles and build crystal lattices high into the thin air. She talked of Humans so long isolated from their race that they could no longer produce fertile offspring when they interbred with the rest of mankind. She spoke of the warm friendship and trust that grows in the cold of null-E space. And then she shook hands with me and wished me spacer's luck. And she turned to the far end of the table and said, "Number One, the toast!"

And the first officer at the far end of the table lifted his glass and said, "Air, Water, Space, and Land."

"Air, Water, Space, and Land," the three other officers at the table repeated, while we lubbers sat silent.

"Junior!" Lady Tara said.

And Nancy, as the junior officer present, stood and drained her glass, and then put it upside down on the table. "Air we breathe," she said, "water we drink, space we cross, and land we never."

And the dinner was over.

From a distance Sol Terminus looked like a giant set of children's blocks spilled out haphazardly into space twenty million kilometers past Mars's orbit. Here and there over the surface, null-E passenger and cargo ships as big as the *Western Star* were resting like flies on a cow's back. As we approached Sol Terminus it loomed ever larger until, when we had docked, it

stretched off in all directions, the featureless metal plain of a mechanical planet.

The *Western Star* didn't actually touch down on Sol Terminus, but rather the port extended a flexible quarter-kilometer-long umbilical for passengers. The cargo pods were offloaded by great telescoping arms that extended to grab a pod and remove it from the ship.

Nancy came off the ship with me and saw me over to the check-in for the intersystem liner. Sol Intersystem Transit Monopoly took my bag and told me I had four hours to wait for the next departure for Mars, so Nancy and I went over to the Solview Lounge to say good-bye to each other.

One whole wall of the Solview Lounge was window— about three stories high and a hundred meters wide, the largest window into space I had ever seen. A sheet of four-centimeter krys glass twelve hundred meters square was all that separated the room from the vacuum, radiation, and utter cold of space.

Nancy and I sat at a table right next to the window, which made me extremely nervous for the first few minutes. Looking out the window from right next to it made you feel as if you were falling off the edge, and it was a long way to fall. Out the window on the far left you could see the port facility, where the *Western Star* was still being serviced. Way off in space on the left you could see the vast array of mirrors that gathered the Sun's energy for the use of Sol Terminus. On the right was a strange-looking space dock, a network of lacy beams and wires that twinkled with a myriad of tiny light sources in alternate circles of blue and gold, like some gigantic target.

"Do you have any idea what that is?" I asked Nancy, gesturing toward the scintillating space target off to the right.

"Sure," she said. "It's the clubhouse for the most exclusive club in the universe, the Windjammers."

"Windjammers?"

"Tiny ships with giant sails of gossamer-trymar that ride the solar wind. The ships are balls with a four-meter diameter, pulled by sails four to six kilometers across. To join the club you

have to have sailed a windjammer from Earth to Sol Terminus and back."

"Alone?"

"Solo," she agreed.

"I wonder how it feels."

"I asked a windjammer once what it felt like to be alone in space for months at a time," Nancy said, "and he quoted one of the first astronauts of ancient Earth. 'Ninety percent of the time you're bored to death,' he said, 'and ten percent of the time you're scared to death.'"

I thought about that for a while. "I think I'd prefer the scared to the bored," I said. "Of course, I imagine you could get a lot of books read."

A long, skinny metal pipe extended up from the side of the table about thirty centimeters, and a round metallic eye on top looked at each of us in turn. "Courtesy," a tinny voice said. "Welcome to Sol Terminus, O strangers from far lands and distant stars. I, who am screwed in to the base of this table, envy you your visual experiences. How may I serve you, O honored guests?"

"What are you?" I asked, while Nancy giggled softly.

"I am the waitbus robot, at your service. Would you like to see a menu?"

"Waitbus?"

"I wait on the tables. I bus the tables."

"And you're screwed in to the base of this table?"

"True. The eye that is I at this table is so screwed. The eye of I is also screwed into each of the other tables in this copious room, and three other dining rooms in this great complex. The brain of I, or the I that is my brain is in the unitized kitchen, in immediate proximity to the small food freezer. Which is why I get headaches. Would you like anything else?"

"We haven't had anything yet."

"Would you like to see a menu? Here is a menu." Two thin plastic-looking cards appeared on the table, one in front of Nancy and one in front of me. When I reached out for mine, I

found that it wasn't really there; my hand went right through it without disturbing either the card or my hand. "Very showy," I said.

"The Thousand Planets is famous for manufacturing high-quality robots and projection devices," Nancy told me. "High-vacuum precision-controlled picodot circuitry devices."

"What is, or are, the Thousand Planets?" I asked her.

"Between Mars, which is Sol Four, and Jupiter, which is Sol Five, there is a band of space occupied by asteroids, rocky plan-etoids from the size of a grain of sand to tens of kilometers in diameter. They are the rocky remains of a never-quite-formed planet, and there are millions of them. Over the years—over the centuries—many of them have become inhabited by various small groups that wanted to get away and be by themselves."

"Away from where?" I asked.

"Earth," Nancy said, "the most overcrowded planet in the Confederation. These groups are too small to be independent of Earth completely, but they sure have what they want, which is privacy. They are called the Thousand Planets, although nobody really knows how many of them there are, and they do things their own way out there. Sol Terminus is right on the rim of the asteroid belt, although it isn't properly one of the Thousand Planets, since it's run from Earth and for the inner planets as a business by the Sol Intersystem Transit Monopoly."

"Have you decided?" the food robot asked, turning its bulging eye from side to side.

"Um," I said, quickly reading over the menu. "Bring me a Mars Metropolitan Sandwich."

"I'll take a flight salad," Nancy said. "And bring us each a caffé Mars."

"A wise choice," the robot assured us, and then dropped back into the table.

"How is your neck?" Nancy asked me.

"Fine, I think," I said, moving my head around gingerly. "It still aches a bit, but that's all."

"It used to take months for broken bones to knit," she said.

"You're lucky. One week in a neck brace, and it's down to an ache."

"I'm not complaining," I told her. "Your ship's doctor is a very good man."

Nancy nodded. "And he has a lot of electronic and chemical help," she said.

A wheeled tray with a central eyestalk brought us our food and served it with mechanical claws. "Tasty," it said, "very tasty."

Nancy stared at me from across her salad. "You are my friend," she said positively, then attacked the food in front of her.

I was already well into my sandwich—it had been four or five hours since I'd last eaten—but I stopped and looked at her. "Of course, we're friends," I said.

"You don't understand what I mean," she told me. "Spacers make good friends, but usually only with other spacers. There seems to be some sort of gulf that separates us from lubbers. We think differently. Even passengers who travel regularly are still lubbers. You almost have to be born in space to think like a spacer."

"And I do?" I asked.

"No," Nancy said. "But the differences are not in the important things. I'm glad we're friends, and I'll look forward to seeing you again."

"Me too," I said. "I think it's good to have friends who are in different professions or have different lifestyles. It helps keep you from getting in a rut; it keeps you aware that other things are happening. Besides, I like you."

"And, most important, I like you," Nancy agreed. "Not that you're not right about the advantages of having friends from all over. It's hard to do, but if you can, it's worth it. Lady Tara seems to have friends all over the Galaxy, but the first officer doesn't know anyone not in the Guild, it seems."

Now that we had decided that we were friends, we munched our food silently and thought about things. I thought about how

exciting it would be to be a spacer and travel on a great passenger ship and have friends all over the Galaxy. I don't know what Nancy thought about.

A large round object appeared around one corner of the port facility and slowly occluded a larger and larger section of the sky. It seemed to be black, except that patches of it sparkled in the reflected work lights of the facility as it passed.

"What in the Imperium is that?" I asked, staring out at it.

"That's a windjammer coming in," Nancy said. "It's farther away than it looks; that sail spread is probably at least four kilometers across. Somewhere right in the center is the cabin."

"What happens now?" I asked.

"First he furls the sail. Then two or three hogs from the club will float out and fasten killer rockets to the cabin."

"Hogs?"

"Spacehogs. Anyone who works in space with just a suit between him and the vacuum is called a spacehog."

"Why?"

"Because that's what he's called. It's an ancient term."

"Oh. What are killer rockets?"

"That windjammer has built up a high outward velocity with its sail. The velocity has to be killed so it can dock," she explained, clearly being very patient with my ignorance.

"I guess every profession has its own, specialized vocabulary," I said. "Sounding like a spacer is more than just speaking Anglit with a spacer's accent."

"We don't have an accent," she said indignantly. "We speak Universal Anglit, the common language of all people. It is very carefully centered so that everyone, wherever we go, can understand us if they speak any sort of Anglit-derived language at all."

"It sounds like an accent to me," I said.

"I won't tell you what that Jaspert you speak sounds like to me," she said. We glared at each other, and then went back to finishing our food.

The sail started closing in on itself as we watched, cutting

a strange series of geometric shapes in black across the bright starfield.

"That's what I call fascinating," I told Nancy.

"You want to get a closer look?" she asked.

"You mean go out there?"

"Well, I meant drag a telescope over to the table, but if you want to go out there, why not?" She dropped a ten-solar-bit piece into a tray on the side of the table. "Lunch is on me," she said.

The tray digested the ten-bit piece and coughed up three bits fifteen in change, which Nancy scooped up. "Let's go," she said.

We scooted down a slidewalk and back over to the port and docking area of Sol Terminus. Nancy palmed open a couple of doors that would have been off limits for me, and we ended up in a small locker room on the wrong side of a big safety airlock.

"I'll sign out a couple of worksuits," Nancy said. "They'll be charged out to the *Western Star*, so don't worry about it. I'm sure Lady Tara would say we owe it to you."

"Thanks," I said. "I sure appreciate it. I've never been outside in a suit before."

The checker ran a gauge over me when I told him I didn't know my size, and handed me a worksuit. It was like a one-piece coverall with built-in gloves and shoes and all sorts of little fitting connections coming off from strange places.

"Don't I need some sort of training or something to use one of these?" I asked Nancy, looking over the various valves and fittings.

"The thing is pretty idiot-proof," she told me. "The life support slides into those brackets on your back, and it takes care of monitoring your oxygen consumption and demand. The helmet faceplate automatically shields you from staring into the sun. Of course there are a lot of stupid mistakes lubbers seem to delight in finding, but I'm sure you'll avoid most of them. Besides, I'll be with you. The only thing you need to know about is your radio. This button controls it. Suit-to-suit frequency here. General call here. Emergency here. Don't push emergency unless it is. Okay?"

"Okay," I said. "I'm reassured. How do I get into this thing?"

"Just pull it on over your clothes. Take your shoes and jacket off first and stick them in a locker."

I hung my jacket up in one of the blue lockers along the wall and stuck my shoes in the bottom. Then I pulled the space worksuit over my legs and slid my arms into it. There were two clasps to close on each foot, locking the inner shoe in place, and then the suit zipped up the front. The helmets were all of a standard size, and clamped onto a ring around the neck of the suit. The material of the suit was about half a centimeter thick, except at stress joints and work areas like the knees, where it was doubled. The whole thing weighed about five kilograms and was kind of baggy all over. The helmet was another five kilograms.

Nancy checked out a pair of backpacks that were marked 4 HOUR: NO RECYCLE, checked to see that they were full, and connected mine up for me. There were about a dozen little nozzles and wires to fit up. I started to put my helmet on, but Nancy stopped me. "Don't put it on till we're in the lock," she said. "No point in wasting suit air until you need it."

"Thanks," I said.

"Also," she said, "always check up your own suit connections, no matter who puts it on for you. It's your own life, and you're responsible for it."

"Right," I said. I went over each of the connections that Nancy had made in my suit while she was installing her own backpack. They looked fine to me.

We went into the lock and Nancy showed me how to lock my helmet down. The life-support system automatically went on, and air veins in the suit filled up, pressing it tight against my body. It didn't sag anymore, but filled out and felt hard and resistant to the touch.

The lock cycled, and the air was bled out. Nancy opened the outer door. "Be careful outside," she said, her voice sounding very natural through the helmet phones. "There's a red line outside the lock that marks the gravity terminator. On this side

of it the station's pseudogravity will hold you down, on the other side of it you're weightless."

"Completely? What about the real gravity of the station?"

"Well, let's see; Sol Terminus must mass a few tens of millions of kilograms. Let's say twenty-five million, just for an estimate."

"Okay," I said.

"And you must mass about seventy-five kilos."

"Right."

"Well, then, Sol Terminus pulls you toward its center with a force of about point oh one two five dynes, which means that you have an effective weight of about a hundredth of a gram. One good muscle twitch and you'd be headed out for an orbit of your own."

"I'm convinced," I said. "I'll be good. How do I make sure I stay down?"

"The bottoms of the shoes are coated with a special resin that will stick to the metal plates of the station. Just don't lift both feet at once." And with this final helpful hint, she went out the lock ahead of me. I followed close behind, and the lock door automatically cycled closed behind me.

There is no way to describe the feeling of standing on a small, airless body surrounded by the Universe, of knowing that the only thing between you and a hundred thousand kilometers of vacuum is the thin bubble of krys glass that is your helmet. I was frozen in place, not by fear, but by the immensity of the Universe and the smallness of me.

"Come on," Nancy said, "shake a leg. You can't see anything from there."

"I can see about a hundred thousand stars," I told her. But I followed her on out to the curving surface of the station. And then, after about six steps, I fell off the side of the station and kept falling—or that's what all my senses but my eyes told me. My eyes said I was still right where I had been, but I had just stepped over a wide red stripe painted on the surface. I was on the pseudogravityless side of the barrier, and it took me a few

seconds to get used to it.

Walking with sticky shoes proved to be easier than I'd thought. I had a tendency to lean at strange angles as I walked and to take much larger steps than I should, and the only thing wrong with that was I looked funny. But I didn't really care how I looked.

We rounded a corner of the station—something like climbing a hill with no feeling of climbing and no hill—and were facing the side of the sky that we had seen through the lounge window. There, flat in the sky ahead of us, was the windjammer, with its sail almost completely collapsed. It was now space side of the station (there are two basic directions in space: sun side and space side; they are the equivalent of up and down). Two men in suits like ours, but bright red, with maneuvering jets on their backs, were closing in on the cabin of the jammer, towing four silvery cylinders.

Off to the left, at an angle that made it invisible from the lounge window, was the strangest sight I'd ever seen in space: a white ball about ten meters across with hundreds of varicolored rods sticking out from all angles. It was tethered to the far side of Sol Terminus by long cables, which kept it floating free in space a few hundred meters off the station.

I pointed it out to Nancy. "What in the Imperium is it?" I asked.

"I've never seen anything like it before," she said, staring speculatively at the strange construct. Then she snapped her fingers, or tried to through the space gloves. "Of course," she said. "I know what it is."

"Don't tell me," I said, as she slapped her hands together gleefully. I could see her laughing through the krys-glass helmet.

"It's the Emperor's birthday present," she said.

"Courtesy?"

"It's a gift from Emperor Alexander the Ninth to the citizens and subjects of the Solar Hanse on the occasion of his one hundredth birthday."

"Alexander the Ninth is going to be one hundred?"

"So are we all," Nancy said, "if we wait long enough. But Alexander will achieve that distinction this year."

"I see," I said, "and so he is giving his subjects a present."

"Right."

"A ten-meter ball."

"Right."

"Great. Just what I always wanted. How did he know?"

"The present comes when it is launched from here," Nancy told me.

"Launched?"

"Right. That construct is a comet-ball. When launched into the proper parabolic orbit around the sun, it will provide a splendid display for everyone in the Solar System. As it dips in and gets closer to the sun, the solar wind will push particles off to form a tail millions of kilometers long. It should be a glorious spectacle."

"What's it made of?"

"Mostly ice, I think, doped with various organics to provide spectacular colors."

"Wow," I said. "That little ball?"

"It's as big as most natural comets. It's all a question of composition and orbit. And if they get this one just right, it will swing around on the far side of its orbit just in time to come back for Alexander's two hundredth birthday. Is it not, indeed, an age of wonders we live in, as some ancient Greek once said?"

"I'm impressed," I said.

"That's funny," Nancy said, staring off into space.

"Not really," I told her. "I'm easily impressed with all the things we didn't have back on Jasper."

"No, not that," Nancy said. "That is, not you. Those two spacehogs."

"The ones at the windjammer?"

"Right. They're fastening four killer rockets to the sides of that cabin. Usually it's only two."

"The jammer is going faster than usual?"

"I suppose. Only, since it's powered by the same sun every

other windjammer uses, where'd it get the extra velocity?"

"They're only half as powerful as usual? The rockets, I mean."

"No," Nancy said. "They're the standard model."

"I don't think I need another mystery," I said. "I just got my cast taken off from the last one."

"Don't worry," Nancy said. "Accidents in space don't break bones—they kill you."

"Thanks," I said.

We were standing in the shadow of a large unloading arm, which meant that the two spacehogs couldn't see us, although they were clearly outlined by the reflection of the port's work-lights off the shiny windjammer cabin. Nancy stared at the hogs and their work for about half a minute, and then I heard her whistle, a long, drawn-out sound.

"What is it?" I said.

"Those rockets," she told me, "are being installed backward!"

"What does that mean?"

"It means that when they're fired, instead of killing the 'jammer's forward velocity, they'll double it. And then the two extra rockets will double it again. Whatever those two men are doing out there, it isn't right, and I have to stop it." She fingered the general call button on her suit radio. "Here, you two space-hogs out by the windjammer. This is Lieutenant ep Liztom. What in the Imperium do you think you're doing?"

There was no answer, and the two kept fastening the rockets backward onto the cabin without looking around.

Nancy thumbed the emergency-channel button.

"Hello, emergency monitor," she said. "Trouble at the wind-jammer that's docking now. This is Lieutenant ep Liztom of the *Western Star.*"

The two men finished their installation as Nancy talked, and started running connecting wires from one killer rocket to the next.

"What sort of trouble?" the emergency monitor asked.

"Two men are hooking up four killer rockets, and they're on

backward. Can you get a security team out here on the double?" She turned to me. "I'm going to have to jump for it," she said. "If they get those rockets hooked up and set them off, we'll never see that cabin again."

"There isn't anyone suited up right now," the emergency monitor said. "It'll take about ten minutes to get someone out there."

"Well, get started," Nancy said. She ran, in a measured lope, toward the jumping-off point for the windjammer. I came behind her as fast as I could. It was sort of like trying to ice skate without touching the ice except to push. "I'll have to try to stop them from firing those things," she said.

And she jumped. She did it like a perfect swan dive, but up instead of down. There is no up or down in space, except toward or off the sun, but she went up from where I was.

So I followed. Lining myself up with the cabin of the windjammer as best I could, I squatted down to the deck and then pushed myself off with the sides of my feet, so the sticky bottoms wouldn't hold me down.

We moved very slowly between the station and the windjammer. It was a few seconds before Nancy noticed that I'd followed her. "What are you doing?" she called.

"Floating," I told her.

She looked critically at me and back at the 'jammer cabin. "You're going to miss," she said. "Don't panic. I'll come after you as soon as I disarm those rockets."

I checked the line I was moving in as best I could. She was right. I'd pushed myself off center somehow when I jumped, and I was going to miss the cabin by several meters at least. My throat closed up, and I felt as though I were going to choke. I was heading out toward the endless black Universe, with nothing ahead of me for as many light years as I could see. I had done the ultimately stupid act. I had rushed in where only a well-trained angel would dare to tread. It had never occurred to me that I might miss, or what it would mean if I did. And here I was, headed toward eternity.

One of the two spacehogs at the cabin spotted Nancy and me heading at him—or, in my case, not quite at him—and tapped his buddy on the arm, gesturing in our direction. The two of them spoke helmet to helmet for a few seconds; then one of them quickly finished a set of connections and left a gray box dangling from one of the rockets. With that they both pushed off and headed toward the other side of Sol Terminus, where the Windjammer Club entrance was.

"Didn't want to stay and fight, eh?" I said. I would gladly have fought anyone, or anything, rather than face the fate that was rapidly and inexorably going to be mine. Sure, Nancy would come after me as soon as she could commandeer something with jets, but by then I would be awfully hard to find: a tiny dot growing ever smaller in the vastness of space.

The emergency monitor came back on. "I've been in touch with Prince Michael," he said, "and he has no air for his emergency suit. He had to use it to repair some cables on the windjammer about two months ago, and it ran out of air just as he finished the job. He has been confined to his cabin ever since."

"Prince Michael?" Nancy asked. "Of New York?"

"Yes. I can't put you in touch direct because his radio doesn't work on your suit frequencies, but he says he'd be very grateful if you could disconnect those rockets. Computer says that it'll be at least two weeks before we can catch up with him if they go off, and his life support has been acting strange for the past month. It might not last another two weeks."

"Well, the two who hooked the rockets just blasted," Nancy said. "So they've probably got the rockets set to go in a few seconds. But I'll see what I can do. Get someone out on a scooter, will you? My partner has overshot the cabin, and he may need retrieving."

"Will do," the emergency monitor said, without adding, "That idiot," or any other comment that I felt he was probably entitled to make.

I spent some time wondering who Prince Michael of New York was, and why someone would want to kill him. It then

occurred to me to wonder how long my air supply would last.

Nancy reached the windjammer cabin, right on the nose. I was now clearly going to miss it by about five meters, and there was nothing I could do to change that. It was so near, and yet so impossible to reach.

A bright cone of flame appeared at the tail of one of the rockets, and then the second, and then the third. Nancy quickly ripped a handful of wires out of the fourth, and that one failed to ignite. One of the three that was burning slowly yawed out from its position against the side of the cabin, until it was pointed nose in at about sixty degrees. The ship began to move away and ponderously started to spin around the axis formed by the three rockets.

Suddenly I saw a large black shape hurtling toward me, one of the collapsed vanes of the windjammer sail, and it was going to pass no more than a meter away from me. This, if I could use it, was a reprieve. All it would take was for me to stretch out enough to grab the vane and manage to hang on.

I practiced everything I had learned during the week in the *Western Star's* air-swimming tank. I pulled myself into a ball to spin around faster until I was oriented the way I wanted to be. And then I reached, stretched in a taut, straight line from the tips of my toes to the tips of my fingers.

The vane hit at my wrists and I grabbed, ripping the bubble-thin material of the solar sail. A thin supporting rod whipped into my fingers, numbing them through the space gloves, and sprang free before I could grasp it. But slowly, by pulling on the constantly ripping material, I swung my body into the sail. Then, fighting the centrifugal force that kept trying to throw me off again, I crawled toward the center. It was like climbing a flagpole covered with tissue paper. But as I got closer to the center, the gravity effect of the centrifugal force lessened, and the framing supports got larger and easier to climb.

The cabin was a small globe studded with large portholes. The three rockets attached to it were still firing, causing it to go about in large, spasmodic spirals, headed roughly away from

Sol Terminus but in an ever-changing direction. Nancy was lying flat against the cabin, her right arm wedged between it and one of the rockets. She didn't move. As I worked my way over to her I could that her eyes were closed and her head was forward in the helmet. When I touched my helmet to hers, I could hear her breathing, so she must just have been knocked out. I pulled her free of the rocket and fastened her safety link to one of the rings on the outside of the cabin so she wouldn't float away.

I looked through one of the ports and saw a man inside the cabin. He had long hair, fastened in back, and a neat spade beard around a thin face. He was wearing a loose-fitting white shirt with ruffles around the cuffs and a pair of puffy-looking deep-red pantaloons. He was talking on the radio when I saw him, and he paused to wave to me and smile. He seemed very unconcerned about the fact that he was going in an erratic spiral farther and farther from the station with a life-support system that promised to give out on him at any moment. He said something to me, and I put my helmet against the glass to try to hear it, but couldn't.

I had no idea how long the rockets would burn, or how to shut them off—or, for that matter, whether you could shut them off. The only thing I could think of doing was to disconnect them from the cabin. I examined the closest one and saw that it was fastened in place with a double latch, one at the top and one at the bottom. I unsnapped each of them, and the rocket leaped off into the distance, burning my glove as it passed.

The removal of this one rocket increased the speed of rotation of the cabin and almost flung me from the surface. But I steadied myself against one of the masts that jutted out from the sides of the cabin. Slowly I worked my way around to the next rocket, which was pushing in on the cabin and causing most of the rotation. The rear clamp was already loose, as I had guessed, but the front clamp was wedged tightly in place by the body of the rocket and didn't want to open. I took the rocket in both hands and worked it from side to side until finally the metal of the clamp gave way and the rocket jumped away from

my hands and chased its sibling.

Nancy had come to while I was working on the second rocket. As I turned to the last one I saw her already at it, and only a second later it joined the other two in a race to the ends of the Universe.

The motion didn't stop with the rockets gone—there is no friction in space to slow anything down—but it ceased being erratic and became a slow, steady tumble in a direction tangent to Sol Terminus. Nancy waved at me and said something, but I couldn't hear her. My radio had been broken by one of the jolts my suit had taken in the past few minutes.

The security people at Sol Terminus swear that it was less than half an hour until their scooter reached us and pulled us off the windjammer, but as far as I'm concerned it took at least a week. They sent a space tug out to pick up the 'jammer's cabin, since its motion was too exotic now to stop with killer rockets.

And I missed my flight. First, the security service of Sol Terminus questioned us about what had happened and about the two men we had seen, and then an inspector of the Solar Hanse Space Police asked us the same questions all over again. Then we were told to wait until a representative of the Special Branch of the Imperial Protective Service could talk to us, which would be right after he'd seen to the safety of Prince Michael.

"He's just going to ask us the same questions," I complained to Nancy.

"None of them want to take the responsibility," Nancy said. "After all, somebody tried to kill Prince Michael."

"Who would want to kill him?" I asked. "And what is this New York that he's a prince of?"

"Prince Michael is one of the five Princes of Earth," Nancy told me. "Don't you people on Jasper know anything of what's happening in the outside Universe?"

"As little as possible," I told her. "The Princes of Earth are the Emperor's sons?"

"His adopted sons. No direct descendant is allowed to take the throne. The Emperor's real sons are known as Princes of

the Blood, and they keep the title prince all their lives, but they can't ever become emperor. One of the Princes of Earth will be the next emperor when Alexander dies. Prince Michael of New York might someday become Michael the Second, Liege Sovereign of the Inner Planets, Protector of the Princes of the Earth, Chairman of the Solar Hanse—and like that."

"I'll have to learn all that stuff," I said.

"I should think so," she told me.

The man from the Special Branch came in, asked us the same set of questions over again, and told us that the two phony spacehogs had disappeared. He then told us that Prince Michael wanted to thank us personally, and in another second, before I had a chance to be nervous, Prince Michael of New York, who might someday be the Emperor Michael II, walked into the room. He looked very pale and weak, and he had a limp, but there was something in his eyes and his voice that commanded your attention when he spoke. He thanked us and asked personal questions about who we were and where we were from and what our interests were. He told Nancy that he had met her mother, who was a famous admiral, now retired (which should not have surprised me, but did), and he told me that he had a daughter who was going to the University of Sol. He told us both that our names would be given to his doorkeeper, and that if we ever wanted to see him for some reason, we were welcome. Then he shook hands with us both, and left.

Nancy had to get back to the *Western Star* to go on duty, so we shook hands very formally and promised to see each other again whenever possible. But we both knew that it wouldn't be possible for quite some time. I wanted to kiss her, just a good-bye kiss, but on Jasper boys and girls don't do such things and I hadn't been off Jasper that long, so I didn't.

Then, at the door, Nancy turned and smiled and blew a kiss at me, and said, "See you, Adam." And was gone.

CHAPTER VIII.

It works like this:

The Emperor reigns for two hundred years, unless he dies before his term is up. During this time he selects between five and ten people he deems worthy to succeed him to the title. They are known, regardless of sex, as the "Princes of Earth," and are formally adopted by the Emperor and anointed to the succession and given titles. Then they spend their time training for the job of Emperor.

When the Emperor has served his people for two hundred years, or if he should die in office, the Princes choose by lot among them who shall ascend the throne and take up the mantle of office.

The general belief is that the office of Emperor is largely a figurehead job with no real power, but it has been noticed by historians that when a strong, good Emperor is in office, things generally go much better for the Solar Hanse and the Confederation than when a weak, poor Emperor sits on the throne. Several emperors had said, during speeches or when interviewed, that they consider it their major duty and most sacred obligation to prevent the human race from destroying itself, or any large portion of itself, in a war. The tenuous threads that hold together the Imperium are woven of the compelling need to eliminate the possibility of one planet's destroying another in the insane furies generated by a major war. Ever since the destruction of Hope by Greater Vand and the Emigration of Vand a millennium ago, all Emperors have conceived it to be

their particular responsibility to keep the whole Human family under the one blanket of the Imperium, and under the watchful eye of its agents.

I read up on all this as soon as I got to Mars and gained access to a library board. That was right after I arrived at the dome and they assigned me a room.

I should describe the dome. First, I guess, I should describe Mars. Okay. It's red and it's cold. There's not enough atmosphere to breathe, but there's just enough atmosphere to whip up giant sandstorms that obscure the sky for days and clog all the machines and get sand into everything that isn't sealed, and into a lot that is.

Most of the people on Mars live in plastiskin domes, some as small as a tent, some as big as a city. The dome that houses the University of Sol, or most of the University, is a good-sized one, about twelve kilometers across and half a kilometer high. Since it is round, that makes for an area of just about one hundred thirteen square kilometers, which is a lot of land to stick under a dome.

The dome is made of a very light, very thin, extremely strong plastiskin, which is held up by air pressure from inside. Sandstorms can't break through the plastiskin, although they scour the outside to the point where sections are periodically replaced.

All the land under the dome belongs to the University of Sol, although all of the University isn't under the dome. The Physics Department has a vacuum lab on Deimos, the larger of Mars's two moons. The Department of Prehistory has all sorts of projects going on Earth itself. Prehistory is defined as the study of what took place on Earth before Humanity expanded to the other planets: Ancient Greece and Rome and the Dark Ages and the False Peace and the Age of Exploration and all of that.

The University is divided into twelve colleges. On Jasper the college represents the general subject, like the College of Agriculture or the College of Religion. But at the University of Sol the colleges represent the twelve independent universi-

ties or colleges that came together to form the University back almost in prehistory. They are Berk, Bonn, Clay, Gill, Hyde, King, Mars, Mech, Ox, Pen, Vard, and Yale.

It used to be considered very important which college you went to. Certain planets, certain professions, certain families were associated with each college. You went to the college your parents went to, or at least an uncle or aunt. If you had no relative to "stand for you" at one of the colleges, then your parents' professional guild would do it. If you had neither parents nor guild, then getting admitted to the University of Sol could be a difficult experience. Each college would accept a couple of "weeds" just to show how liberal they were, and the rest would be considered students at large, which carried no status. And at the University of Sol status was all.

Then, about two hundred years ago, Emperor Hiram IV changed the rules himself. Saying that the graduates of the University of Sol formed the "nerves of the Imperium," and that the university and its colleges must be interested in "quality, not heredity," he made the colleges pick by lot from the freshman class.

The colleges still maintain a rivalry, and each student feels a strong identification and pride in his college and fellow students, but now this pride is founded on continuing excellence and accomplishments, and not on the snobbery based on an accident of birth.

Or so they told me.

I was by lot assigned to Hyde College. I was given a pamphlet titled "Welcome, Incoming Freshmen," and told that the bursar at Hyde would take care of all my needs.

One of the marks of distinction of each college was the individual architectural style of its buildings. The main university buildings were either domes or babyblock functional, but the colleges pulled from all eras and all styles in their desire to be unique. Bonn was all Greek columns and open spaces. Ox was all weathered sandstone, which was quite a trick considering that there was no sandstone on Mars and no weather inside the

dome. Vard was red brick. King was all glass and steel. Hyde was flowing concrete, done in swirls and rounded angles, with round doorways and small, porthole-like windows. There were three buildings like that, one large one between two smaller ones. They looked like a flotilla of ships from some elvish kingdom that had been long stranded on the red sand.

The bursar of Hyde College assigned me Room Red-Green-Violet, which was about halfway down the second corridor on the second floor of the large building. The doors were all color coded with three large diamonds, in a number of different colors. He also took my size for everything from socks to hats and said that a bundle of Hyde College-authorized clothing would be delivered to my room. Everyone at the college was required to wear clothing picked from a narrow assortment of approved garments. It was a wide enough assortment so as not to be called a uniform, but still a narrow assortment. I asked him why the clothing restriction, and he said, "For our convenience." I couldn't think of any comment to make to that, so I went off to my room.

The rooms were not exactly monastic, but they were not exactly luxury hotel either. Each room was a double, with a bed at each end and a twinned pair of desks acting as a partition. Each desk had an elaborate built-in work board with a provision for printing out hard copy. Above the desks and all around the walls were bookcases and cabinets, and there were two long, skinny walk-in closets. There was a shower-and-sinks room that was shared with the room next door, and a separate lavatory that was not shared.

I settled in as best, and as quickly, as I could. I had the room to myself, at least for now. Later that day the bundle of clothing was delivered, and I put some of it on. It was heavy into pinks and grays: gray jackets and pink slacks and pink jackets and gray slacks. Shirts were white. Shoes—three pairs—were black. Everything, except the shoes, was loaded with pockets. All the jackets had the Hyde crest over the breast pocket on the left side and my last name neatly embroidered over the right side.

I had almost two weeks to wait before I started my first class. The University of Sol didn't run on the quarter or semester system, as the schools back on Jasper did, but operated on a computer-assembled schedule of fits and starts—mostly, it seemed, fits. Courses began at random, ran for however many weeks they needed, and then stopped. A student was supposed to work his way up gradually to five courses, and then stay between four and six. Taking a vacation involved a lot of prior planning to arrange courses that all ended at about the same time.

The first year's classes (roughly) were assigned to you by the computer; after that you were pretty much on your own. My first year's classes were to be, according to the computer printout:

ANGLIT (1). How to use the language as a tool to understand and be understood. Many papers.

PREHISTORY (1). Earth before spaceflight; our common heritage.

PHYSICS (1). The basic physical laws that run the Universe, and how most of the gadgets in your everyday life work. A lab course.

HISTORY (1), THE DISPERSION. What Mankind has become.

ETHICS (1). How to act—and why. A lab course.

HISTORY (4), A HISTORY OF THE IMPERIUM. Covers the 45 major currents of planetary history of the past 2,000 years.

ALIEN ETHNOLOGY (1). How the major sentient alien species differ from Humans in culture, sex, mores, and behavior patterns. What to do and not to do when communicating with an alien.

BIOLOGY (1a), HOW LIFE WORKS.

SPECIAL (22), THOUGHT PROCESSES IN HUMANS, ALIENS, AND MACHINES.

MATHEMATICS (2), ELEMENTARY MATH. From Boolean Algebra to Topological Calculus.

GOVERNMENT (2b). What works, and why; and what does not work, and why. A lab course.

These were the credit courses. Along with them, for the first three months, I'd be taking a non-credit course called "How to Use the University for Fun and Profit."

So here I was—at the University of Sol, on the planet Mars, with no friends, no acquaintances, and the accent of an outworld hick, ready to conquer the Galaxy and start my rise to fame and fortune.

The room next to mine, Room Red-Green-White, was inhabited by two girls. This was the room that shared the bathroom with mine. There was an automatic lockout that prevented any door from opening when someone was in the room, but I still found the idea of sharing a bathroom with two strange girls to be rather unsettling.

I saw them going into their room several times in the next few days, and they affected to ignore me completely. I couldn't complain about that since, according to the manners I was taught as a child on Jasper, I also had to pretend to ignore them.

Anyway, for the next few days I was kept very busy. The University spent some time giving me a variety of obscure tests of both mind and body. Then the Freshman Interviewer for Hyde College talked to me for two hours, trying to find out if I had any redeeming social virtues at all. I think he decided not; at any rate, he didn't ask to speak to me again, and nothing at all came of the talking as far as I could tell.

Then, on the third day I was at Hyde College of the University of Sol, my roommate arrived and changed my life.

CHAPTER IX.

His name was Galahad de Roth, and his friends called him "Gilly." His father, as I found out within the first ten seconds of meeting him, was Larch Beaugrift de Roth, Duke of Parthia. Galahad de Roth was very rich, very noble, and very doubtful that we would become friends. His first move, after coming into the room and seeing me, was to call the bursar and try to get his room changed. That didn't work.

He was short and thick-necked and had a face like a bull terrier, which made him appear very masculine and rugged-looking. He also looked older than he was by about five years, despite the fact that he was a good ten centimeters shorter than I. He had an air of jaded knowledge about him and a group of friends who followed him around, mouths open, to see what witticism he would come out with next.

"It looks as though," he told me when the bursar had turned him down, "despite my earnest entreaty, you and I are to be roomies for the term. Well, just don't impose upon the relation-ship."

"What do you mean," I asked him, "impose?" It is amazing how quickly you can dislike someone you hardly know.

"I choose my friends very carefully," he told me, "and not on the basis of an accident of proximity."

"I also choose my friends carefully," I said, "and not on the basis of an accident of birth!"

His eyes got wide and his mouth dropped. For a second I thought he was going to have a stroke. "You barbarian!" he said.

"You utter barbarian!"

"Listen," I said, "maybe if we both appeal to the bursar together, they'll move you."

He shook his head. "No," he said. "I thought of that. I already told him that it was your idea."

"You what?"

"Well, he asked me what you thought about it, so I told him it was your idea."

"Well, de Roth, you've certainly got a lot of nerve. But I suppose a boy in your position grows up with a lot of nerve."

"You'll have to tell me what it's like sometime," de Roth said, "growing up on one of the far-flung outposts of the Imperium, without any civilizing influences. No idea which fork to use. You do use a fork, don't you?"

"For what?" I asked.

De Roth gave a great sigh and went over to his side of the room to unpack. "This is going to be a trying year," he said. "I can tell. Very trying."

About fifteen minutes later, while we were both lying on our respective beds and trying to figure out what to do about each other, there came a knock on the door. "Gilly?" It was a girl's voice.

De Roth swung his feet over the side of his bed and sat up. "I have that tomato," he said.

"Why, man," the outside voice said, "he doth bestride the narrow world like a tomato."

De Roth went over and opened the door. Two girls were outside. "Welcome to my humble tomato," he said. "Come on in."

They came in. They looked at me curiously. "Is this your roomie?" one of them asked.

"Does he speak tomato?" the other inquired.

"He barely speaks Anglit," de Roth said. "Ignore him."

"Why, we couldn't do that," one of the girls said. She was tall and slender and had ringlets of brown hair cascading down her back. Her companion was shorter and slightly stouter and

had waves of blond hair piled on top of her head and fastened in place with golden spikes.

"Who are you?" the blond girl asked me.

"Courtesy," I said. "I am the ghost of tomato past."

The brown-haired girl clapped her hands. "You will be visited by three tomatoes," she said.

"And you must be tomato yet to come," I told her.

The blond turned to her friend. "Who is he?" she asked.

"Reformation Group," the brunette said. "Samuel, perhaps, or Jasper."

"He is but an uncultured barbarian," de Roth said. "Pay him no heed."

"Adam Warrington," I said. "From Jasper. Is it written on my forehead?"

"No, it is sounded in your speech. I study accents. I am Melisa Trina-Jones, and this lady is Delicate O'Shaughnessy. We've been friends of Gilly since he was even younger than he is now."

"It is, indeed, a pleasure to meet you," I told her. "And that's the first time I've been able to say that since I arrived on this rusty planet."

"Say," de Roth pouted, "isn't anyone going to pay any attention to me? How come this barbarian gets all the attention?"

"Gilly! Shame on you. You must get over these attacks of self-importance."

"I am important," de Roth said. "My father is one of the most important, influential men on Earth."

"This isn't Earth," Melisa told him, "and you're not your father. Gilly, just because a lot of sneering idiots follow you around thinking you're somebody because your father's the Duke of Parthia is no reason for you to be as consistently snotty as you succeed in being. We all have parents, you will remember."

De Roth shifted uncomfortably. "This is not fun," he said. "I'll put up with this barbarian if we go do something that's fun. My youth is fleeing before my eyes, and soon I shall be an old

man and a sober one, hobbling with bent back over to the study boards."

Melisa shook her head. "I don't know why you came here anyway," she said.

"The Duke insisted," de Roth told her. "I wanted to stay home and race hundred-meter yachts. But here I am tied to the books."

"There isn't a book in this room," Delicate said.

"I speak metaphorically," he said.

"We'll have to get you some books," Melisa said. "They'd look so nice on that piece of furniture over there. It looks almost as if it were made to hold them."

"You mean the bookshelf?" de Roth asked.

"You've got it," she said. "What about some of the classics? 'Romeo and Tomato'?"

"'Portrait of the Artist as a Young Tomato'?" I suggested.

"Good. 'The Tomato of the Baskervilles.'"

"Dante's 'Tomato,'" said Delicate.

"'I, Tomato.'"

"'Space Tomato.'"

"'Huckleberry Tomato.'"

"'A Connecticut Tomato in King Arthur's Court.'"

"'The Last of the Tomatoes.'"

"Promise?" asked de Roth.

"Cross my tomato and hope to sprout," Delicate said. "Let's go down to dinner. I'm starved."

"You're always starved," Melisa said. "You must learn self-control."

Ignoring Gilly de Roth's dirty looks, Melisa invited me to join them at dinner, and I accepted.

Within about three days de Roth and I had fallen into one of those strange friendships where it is against the rules of the game to say anything nice—or even polite—to or about the other person, but the friendship bond is slowly forming. He was now "Gilly" to me, and I was "Adam" to him. But he was still as firmly convinced as ever that I was a barbarian, just as I was

utterly sure that he was a useless snob.

The great secret about Gilly, which I didn't realize until I'd known him for some time, was that he was a very lonely person. He had sailed yachts on the seas of Earth and in space, and had three homes on Earth and a dig on the Moon, but he had few friends. He despised the people who flocked around him on Earth, trying to bask in the doubly reflected glory of his father's title and position. But it was all he had.

Three days before our classes started, Gilly's father, the Duke of Parthia, showed up at the college and offered to take us both out to dinner. "You see that?" Gilly complained as we walked down to Brown-Black-Black to meet the Duke. "Everyone assumes that if you're roomies, you've got to be close friends. So my father asks you out to dinner with us. Now when he sees you grubbing the food up with both hands and stuffing your face, he'll blame me."

"If he did, he'd be right," I told Gilly. "I've watched you eat. If your head were any closer to the plate, you'd have your nose in your food. How you can manage to get a fork between your mouth and the plate is a puzzle to me."

"How to button your shirt is a puzzle to you," Gilly said. "Which pants leg to stick your foot in is...Father, I'd like you to meet Adam Warrington, my roomie. He's from the Reformation Group. He doesn't speak Anglit very well, but I'm doing my best to teach him. Adam, this is Lord de Roth, my father."

"Courtesy, my lord," I said. "It's an honor."

"On the contrary," Lord de Roth said. "It's an honor for me to meet the lad who saved Prince Michael's life."

That stopped me for a second. "That's an exaggeration, my lord," I said finally. "And besides, Lieutenant ep Liztom had a bit more to do with it than I. And how did you know?"

"Prince Michael and I are good friends," Lord de Roth said, "besides sitting on the same side of the House in Lords. He told me all about it. The young lady is going to get a commendation or some such to go on her permanent service and Guild record. You get a notation on your University record—which,

I'm afraid, doesn't mean a thing. Grade point average is all; it is beyond rank or merit or status or relations. In the great Galaxy of Imperial service that lies beyond the University, your class standing is more important than your social standing, and your ability is twenty times as important as your parentage—as I keep trying to tell Gilly here."

Gilly shook his head impatiently. "And, as I keep trying to tell you, Father, I'm not at all interested in a career in the Imperial service, or in politics, or in any other profession I might be suited for. Winning the trans-Pacific would give me all the glory I'd ever need."

Lord de Roth sighed. "You're eighteen," he said to Gilly. "With a modicum of luck and care, you've got something over two hundred years more of waking up every morning and looking forward to the day's events. Yacht racing will not occupy you, body and soul, for the next two hundred years. As an avocation, fine, but it won't do as a vocation. You need something more meaningful."

"Why can't I do what I want?" Gilly said. "Why must you try to live my life for me?" This was obviously just the latest installment of a continuing discussion, in which Lord de Roth seemed to be ahead in points. Gilly, after all, was at the University.

We stepped into Lord de Roth's groundcar, which immediately started off, heading toward the dome's nearest exit. "It's your life I'm talking about," Lord de Roth told Gilly. "You must believe me. Personally, I don't give a damn whether you pilot a sea yacht all your life or become president of the Confederation, if what you're doing makes you happy. You certainly don't have to earn money; we have money. But I think that when you're older, probably somewhere between thirty and forty, you'll find that you want something more from life than standing behind the tiller of the *Golden Roth*. If I'm mistaken it will always be on my head and you'll never forgive me for it. If I'm right, you'll probably never forgive me for that. So let's just settle on what we've both got. I'm stuck with you for a son, and you're stuck with me for a father. And the bonds that tie us together will

certainly weather out whatever emotional strain is put on them by my forcing you to go to the finest university in the known universe."

Our groundcar left the dome and headed due west. It was late afternoon of the Mars day, and the crater rim of Bulmar Crater was casting long shadows along the silver guide rail, which stretched off into the distance. "Where are we going?" I asked.

"To Lowell Cavern on the other side of Bulmar," Lord de Roth told me. "A restaurant called Osto's is built right into the cavern wall, with great windows overlooking the drop. It's quite a sight."

Gilly transferred his attention back to me. "You saved Melisa's father's life?" he asked. "How?"

"Prince Michael is Melisa's father?"

"You didn't know? Michael Trina-Jones, Prince of New York, is Melisa Trina-Jones's father."

"I never heard his last name," I said.

Gilly laughed.

Ten minutes later the ground car went around a tight curve and entered a tunnel in the face of Bulmar Crater wall. After a few seconds the car slowed and then stopped. An airlock opened to admit the car and then closed behind it. In a short time a green light went on in the compartment and Gilly opened the door.

We were in a small, dimly lit chamber. In front of us was a door with a bronze plaque that said "Osto's—Martian Cuisine."

When we were all out of the car, Lord de Roth slid the door closed, and the car went off to park itself. The robot brain in that ground car was as good as the best robot in the most exclusive piece of equipment in use anywhere on Jasper. I was properly impressed, and, properly, did my best not to show it.

Osto bowed and scraped us into his restaurant, and gave us a private booth all decorated with dark woods and shiny brass studs, and one mirrored wall. Lord de Roth ordered for us: Mars table for three, and Osto bowed twice more and left.

Lord de Roth closed the booth curtain and dimmed the light.

And the mirrored wall turned into clear glass. For a minute I couldn't make out what was beyond, as my eyes adjusted to the light. Then I could see. We were on the lip of a chasm that seemed to stretch off forever into the depths of Mars. A faint phosphorescence from the rocks lining the gigantic hole provided the only source of light, and they effectively outlined the hole but faded quickly to pitch-black as the hole receded.

"Wow," I said. It seemed an inadequate comment, but I had to say something and that just came out. "What is it?"

"It's called Lowell Cavern, after a prehistoric astronomer," Lord de Roth said. "It's about three quarters of a kilometer wide, and goes down at a sixty-degree angle for about fifteen kilometers. It's capped at the top by the stone ridge of Bulmar Crater. Nobody knows what it actually is, or how it got here, or when. It's old; very, very old. It was probably here before the meteor hit that caused Bulmar Crater and sealed off the top."

"What's at the bottom?" I asked.

"Same as at the top," Lord de Roth said. "More rock. And occasional traces of water vapor."

"Mars table" turned out to be little dishes or cups filled with an incredible variety of foods. There were dozens of them, and each was a special Martian version of an Earth food, or a hybrid grown only on Mars. Baked, braised, puffed, glazed, sweet, sour, salt, tart, crisp, limp, some dishes that might once have been chicken, and some that I couldn't identify at all; the food kept coming, dish after dish.

After the last dish of the dinner had been served and removed, Lord de Roth turned the lights in the booth entirely off, and we sat warming our hands over little steaming cups of cafe Mars. The only light came from the faintly glowing rocks of the cavern walls. Gilly and his father sat silently, expectantly, although what they expected I didn't know.

There was a flicker. I just saw it out of the corner of my eye. Something moved outside the window. I turned to look where I thought I had seen the motion, but there was nothing there. I stared, looking carefully out the window all around the area

where I had seen motion, but still nothing moved.

Then again the sense of motion, this time right where I was looking. I felt that I had seen motion, without seeing the thing that moved. Then something else moved, and I almost saw it. It was as though I were looking at ghosts, or at images created by my own mind, but not yet given shape.

"What's happening?" I asked. "What am I seeing?"

"You do see them," Lord de Roth said. "Most people don't the first time." He was staring out the window with a strange intensity, as though there were some secret that would be revealed to him if only he knew just where to look.

"What do they look like to you?" Gilly asked.

"It's hard to say," I told him. "I'm not even sure there's anything there."

"Neither is anyone else," Lord de Roth said.

A weird creature, like a parody of a human being drawn in green sparks, floated into my view, grinned at me, and then disappeared—if it was ever there. Then just a head,—if it was a head—expanded from a spark the size of a pinpoint to a couple of meters around and immediately winked out. "What is it?" I said.

"What you're seeing are called 'Lowell's creatures,'" Lord de Roth said. "Some people see them sometimes, and others never do. They cannot be photographed by any known technique, or detected by any known instrument but the human eye. Most aliens cannot see them at all. Yooserians, on the other hand, claim to be able to communicate with them. But Yooserians are known as the galaxy's greatest, ah, storytellers."

"Does anyone have any idea what, or who, the creatures are?" I asked. "What do the Yooserians say they are?"

"The Yooserians maintain a respectful silence on the question," Lord de Roth said. "Some people say they are caused by random variations in the light intensity in the rock, and an overactive imagination; some say that they are the spirits of longdead relatives; some think that they are the Martians—that is, the indigenous Martians; still others believe that they are hallu-

cinations caused by some strange organic gas emitted by the rock."

"What do you think?" I asked.

"I think they are very interesting," Lord de Roth said.

"I think they're people from some alternate universe trying to contact us," Gilly said.

"You certainly have an active imagination," his father said, "for someone who wants to spend the rest of his life sailing hundred-meter yachts."

A face grinned at me through the glass.

CHAPTER X.

The next morning I got up late. Gilly had gone to breakfast. Gilly would eat anything that wasn't tied down, and would even get up early to do it. After the meal I had had last night, I didn't think I'd be eating for another three days, anyway.

I showered, standing extra-long under the water until the automatic timer shut it off. Water is treated with great respect on Mars. The drying cycle blew gusts of hot air at me until its sensors told it that any more would dry out my skin instead of just drying it off, and then it shut off. I was beginning to feel alert enough to go out and face the world—or the University, anyway.

When I got dressed my shoulders felt cramped in the jacket, and my arms stuck out about five centimeters too far past the sleeve cuffs. My first thought was that I had miraculously grown five or six centimeters overnight. Then I realized that I had put on Gilly's jacket, and that he, clearly, in his rush to get down to the dining hall and stuff his face, had put on mine and never noticed. I looked in the mirror. Sure enough, there was the **de Roth** staring back at me in reverse mirror writing from over the right breast pocket.

Gilly was probably still in the dining hall. I left the room to go down and switch jackets with him, and get a glass of milk as long as I was there.

When I rounded the corner on the first floor I saw two men standing in the corridor. One was very tall and thin and had a small bushy mustache; his partner was short and fat and had a

weary, sad expression. They were both dressed as businessmen, but somehow the clothes looked wrong on them, as though they were costumes or disguises. The short one had a small hand case of the sort barely large enough to hold a sandwich dangling from his left hand.

"Galahad de Roth?" the tall one asked.

"It looks that way," I said, "but actual—"

He raised a slender styluslike cylinder, and a green vapor spurted from the end and spread around my face in a fine cloud. Slowly, as though in a dream, I fell over. I could still see and hear and think, but I could no longer control my muscles to move or talk.

The ground took a long time to reach me, but finally I was there, with my cheek pressed into the carpet.

The short one opened the hand case and unfolded it in a series of surfaces and angles that rapidly became a good-sized trunk. It was quite flexible as he unfolded it, but when it had reached its full size it quickly hardened and became rigid.

The two of them picked me up, shoulders and feet, and placed me inside the trunk. "Don't worry," the skinny, tall one said, "you'll be all right."

"Yeah," the short one added, "for now."

They closed the trunk, and for a long time after that all I know is that I was bounced around a lot and left alone a lot. There was air in the trunk so I could breathe, but that's all I could do. The drug didn't even begin to wear off. And I was getting colder and colder.

Finally, after what seemed like more time than there was left until the Sun became dark and cold, the trunk was opened again. Then the two men tipped it over and I was dumped out on the floor. A very tall, haughty man, dressed in the height of fashion, peered fastidiously down at me. He wore a small domino mask to cover his eyes, but his nose was long and thin and sloped in the middle and curved up at the end: altogether an unforgettable nose. Despite his mask, I would know him if I ever saw him again.

"Well!" he said, his voice a satisfied whine. "My little Lord de Roth. You must not take this personally. I—you see—I had need of your services and, being an impetuous man, I availed myself of them. I would not brook no for an answer. Indeed, I would not brook any answer at all. So here you are. You have arrived. I hope this does not too badly inconvenience you."

I wanted to hit him in the face. I wanted to kick his shins and punch his nose. I wanted to sneer at him and tell him he had snatched the wrong kid, that I was not very ransomable. But I couldn't move. My heart beat, and my breath continued, and my eyes could focus, but beyond that, nothing.

"You will be of great service to me," he said. "Your very— you see—existence will benefit me greatly. You will be my guest—yes, guest—for a little while. I hope this does not inter- fere too greatly with your—if I may say—studies, which, I am given to understand, are not of particular urgency to you anyway, Master Galahad."

He made some sound with his throat that might have been a chuckle or a gurgle, and turned away. Right about then I had an interestingly frightening thought: If he found out I wasn't the real Galahad de Roth, I would be of no use to him for whatever he was scheming. And he might just burn me where I lay, or cut my throat, or—I decided not to think that one through.

The two men who had kidnapped me picked me up and carried me through a door and down a narrow corridor that was all fitted out in gleaming metal. I then realized we were in some sort of small spaceship. They brought me into another room, which had four acceleration couches, and I knew I was right. Someone was in one of the couches already, and I was strapped down with a sticky webbing into a second one. Then they left, and I heard the door click locked behind them.

"Gilly?"

It was a girl's voice, and I thought I recognized it.

"Can you talk yet, Gilly?"

It was Melisa Trina-Jones.

"In a short while the drug will wear off," Melisa said. "You'll

tingle all over, and then you'll be able to move."

Wonderful. Where I could move to, tied down in this couch, she didn't say.

"Oh, Gilly, I'm scared," she said.

There was a great roaring noise, and a giant hand pushed down on my chest. The ship was taking off at high acceleration. They must have been in a hurry to get somewhere—or, it occurred to me, away from somewhere.

I started to tingle all over. Then I started to itch all over, with a burning intensity. For a few minutes, which seemed like hours, all I could do was itch without scratching. Then I started to regain control of my muscles. I was strapped in, so I couldn't use my hands, but I could partly relieve the itching by twisting my body against the restraints.

"You didn't say anything about the itching," I said, in a voice that didn't sound at all like mine. It was all hoarse and stretched-sounding.

"You can talk!"

"Sort of. I wouldn't be much of a conversationalist yet with this voice.'"

"It doesn't sound like you at all," she said.

"It isn't me at all," I told her.

"Gilly?"

"No, Adam."

"Adam! Yes, it does sound like Adam. Where's Gilly?"

"As far as I know, he's probably still eating breakfast. And wearing my jacket."

"What are you doing here? I mean, they said they were going to take Gilly."

"I'm wearing his jacket."

"Oh."

"What's happening? Do you have any idea? Have they told you anything? I assume they kidnapped you too."

"I go for a morning run around the campus for exercise," she said. "I had just turned the corner of the Non-Human Religions building when a tall man in jogging coveralls caught up with

me and squirted me in the face with some stuff that smelled like peaches, and I fell over. They carried me to a waiting groundcar concealed in a wheelbarrow with a canvas over me."

"That's about what happened to me," I said, "except that I was just jogging down to breakfast."

"They think you're Gilly?"

"I assume so. They keep calling me Galahad."

"Why don't you tell who you are, and maybe they'll let you go."

"They'd probably just kill me and shove me out the hatch. If I'm not Gilly, then they don't need me."

"Oh." She thought that over for a second. " Then I guess you'd better be Gilly."

"Have you any idea what they want?"

"Sort of. They—actually he—wants to influence our fathers—actually mine and Gilly's—in their votes in the Parliament of the Stars."

"By he you mean that gentleman with the mask and the nose?"

She giggled. "Certainly his most outstanding characteristics," she agreed. "He represents an organization that calls itself the Humanate Congress."

"I've heard of them."

"Well, my father and Lord de Roth are full delegates for the Solar Hanse at the Parliament of Stars. The Humanate Congress wants to control their votes by controlling us."

"I'm sure your father would agree to anything to protect you," I said. "But how can they know he'll keep his promises?"

"By keeping us until after the voting. And I'm not at all sure that he will agree. It's an awful responsibility."

"But can't he just change his vote when you are returned? You know, demand a recount or something?"

"All votes at the Parliament of Stars are final. At least for the next two hundred and fourteen years. That's the rule. No excuses, no recounts, no changing your mind."

A gong rang in the ship, and then the hand stopped pressing

against my chest. We were now in free fall, somewhere off Mars, and headed out. "Where do you suppose they're taking us?" I asked.

"I wish I knew, Adam," Melisa said.

"I'd better be Gilly for the next little while," I told her, "unless you want to see my body floating by outside this boat."

"Gilly," she said.

A few minutes later the short, round man came into the room. "I will release you from the webbing," he said. "Do not attempt to leave the room. Shortly food will be brought. I hope you are acquainted with the techniques for eating in free fall."

He unsnapped the webbing and left before I could think of anything clever to say.

We spent the next three days in the small cabin, Melisa and I, a time punctuated only by occasional escorted trips to a bathroom down the corridor, periodic meals in suck-bottles, sudden bursts of the course-correcting rockets, and one long lecture from the masked man on the importance of Humanity first, and how we would all thank him for this someday.

We talked a lot, Melisa and I. She told me about little girl-hood as the daughter of the Prince of New York, and I told her of youth in a small town on Jasper. At first I was worried about saying anything that would reveal to listeners that I wasn't Gilly, but then I realized that they'd have no reason in the Universe to listen to us. We found a box of beads in a wall locker, and Melisa taught me to play Go on a grid she drew on the wall.

Late the third day the tall masked man came into the cabin. "Strap yourselves down," he told us. "We have some velocity matching to do, and I don't want to have to yell down to you every time we're going to fire the rockets. Wouldn't want to— you see—damage either of you. Prematurely, that is. So for the next hour or two I want you to stay strapped in. It's—as they say—for your own good." And he left, locking the door behind him.

"Where do you suppose we are?" Melisa asked.

"Three days' travel from Mars, at whatever velocity we had

when they stopped blasting. And they were blasting at something over one G for a quite a while." I thought for a minute, remembering some things that Nancy had taught me about in-system space travel. "We must be heading away from the Sun," I finally concluded.

"Why?"

"Because we picked up a tremendous velocity with that continuous blasting. And heading in toward the Sun would have increased the velocity, and we'd have to blast for quite a while to neutralize the speed and match velocities with whatever we're arriving at. But heading away from the Sun would cause us to slow down, so we'd have less blasting to do to match orbital velocities."

"Of course!" Melisa said. "The Thousand Planets. Where else?"

"What do you mean?"

"The Thousand Planets are as isolated and mysterious as though they were in a different system, light-years from here. Nobody knows anything about them. Each one is different, and they don't even communicate with each other, much less with the outside Solar System."

"I thought they sold exotic electronic equipment," I said.

"The Thousand Planets' Exploitation Group sells exotic electronic and robotic equipment," Melisa said. "But nothing is known about any of the individual planets. Not even what they do with the money. They have a right under Earth law—they are protectorates of Earth—to their individuality, and they interpret that right as the right to maintain complete secrecy. Except for Eunomia, which is a health resort, and Victoria, which is a giant gaming complex, nobody is invited to visit any of them."

The ship's rockets blasted, pushing us both down to the deck. We pulled ourselves into couches and strapped in. "Why not?" I asked.

"They're weird," Melisa said. "They were all settled—if that's the word for digging into a hunk of orbiting rock—by little strange groups from Earth who didn't want to be like anyone

else. And now those groups have been there for centuries, and they are most definitely not like anyone else. Not anymore."

The ship blasted again, and then swung around on its axis to blast once more. "Well, we're certainly arriving at somewhere," I said.

It took about an hour and a half for our captors to maneuver their ship into whatever orbit they wanted. Then came about ten minutes of thudding and banging while they docked.

Then the masked man came back into our cabin carrying a hand recorder. "I want to get you both on crystal for your fathers to see," he said. "We—our group—has heard from them both already, and they say they will discuss—ah—the terms as soon as they see evidence that you are both all right."

"Both?" I said. I couldn't help it; it just came out.

The masked man turned his nose toward me and stared for a minute. "And why not?" he asked.

"Oh, I, uh, didn't think my father really cared what happened to me," I said.

"Ah, the fledgling bird," the masked man said, "ready to fall from the nest on his own. Youth will never change." He pointed the recorder toward Melisa. "Speak, young lady, and move about, so that your father, Prince Michael, can see that you are in good health and have been not unduly poorly treated."

Melisa sat up on the couch and waved into the recorder without enthusiasm. "Hi, dad," she said. "I'm okay." Her voice sounded dull and listless.

"A little more enthusiasm, young lady, if you don't mind," the masked man said. "I don't want your father to think—you see—that you've been drugged or otherwise mishandled."

"I was drugged," she snapped. "That's how you got me here."

"That's what I meant," he said, keeping the recorder going, "a little life—a little animation."

"I'll give you animation!" Melisa said, in a sudden fit, and she launched herself across the small cabin at him.

"Good! Good!" he said, giving small yelping cries of satisfaction as he slapped her aside with the flat of his hand and kept

recording. Melisa spun away from him and came up sharply against the metal wall of the cabin.

I jumped toward him, but was suddenly grabbed by my feet and hauled back to the couch. My hands were twisted behind my back and bent inward in a very painful hold. "Simmer down, small Duke," the voice of my fat abductor sounded in my ear.

"Keep your head down, Karls," the masked man said, swinging the recorder around to face me. "It's the young gentleman's turn to speak to his father. Go on, young gentleman."

I stared into the recorder's eye. "We've just docked at one of the Thousand Planets," I said.

The masked man stopped the recorder and pulled it down to his side. He stared at me with his mouth open. Then he closed his mouth and set it in a hard line. Finally he laughed. "Very clever," he said. "Indeed, very clever. But it is—you see— useless information. They are called—after all—the Thousand Planets because there are thousands of them, spread out over millions of kilometers of space.

"And now, I think, that will do. I have—I do believe— evidence that you are both alive and well at the present moment, which is all I need or desire. I will leave you two alone for another few moments." He backed out the door. Then Karls pushed me across the room, and he was out the door before I could get back.

Melisa was crouched in a corner of the cabin, holding her head and crying softly. "Are you okay?" I asked, going over to her.

"No," she snapped, glaring up at me, "I'm not okay. I'm locked up in a small cabin millions of kilometers away from home, kidnapped, and my head hurts. A lot."

"I'm sorry," I said.

"And you, the big hero," she said, "just sit there while Big Nose throws me across the room and cracks my head against the wall."

"I'm sorry," I said.

"I'll just bet you are," she said.

They came and took us away, and brought us through an airlock and into a round reception chamber of some sort. It looked as though it had been carved out of solid stone. "This is where I'll say good-bye to you," the masked man said. "They'll be out to get you sometime soon. You'll be here until your parents come for you. You won't like it much, but one must— you see—take the bitter with the sweet."

"When will our parents come for us?" I asked.

"They will be notified of your location as soon as they have done what we wish. A matter of a small change in their vote in the upcoming Parliament."

"But," Melisa said, "the Parliament of the Stars runs for almost two years, and it's not due to start for a couple of months yet."

"That is true, young lady. Those, then, are the parameters of your—you might say—confinement. It depends upon just when the issues we are concerned with come up for a vote. Right now the agenda isn't firm yet, so I cannot tell you better."

"Where are we?" Melisa demanded, her voice edging toward the hysterical.

"Why," the masked man said, gesturing around him, "you are here." He and his companions left through the airlock.

CHAPTER XI.

There was what must have been pseudogravity on whatever asteroid we had been left on, since our weights were about normal. The room we were in was lighted by five large naked bulbs placed high above us next to the ceiling. Aside from the airlock, there were four other exits from the room, all of which were securely locked.

I explored what there was of the room while Melisa sat on the floor with her arms wrapped around her and rocked slowly back and forth. I thought she was crying, but whatever she was doing she didn't want me to interfere, so I didn't.

There were many signs chipped, or etched, or something, into the wall. They seemed to be slogans or mottoes.

WE ARE EACH ALL AND THAT IS ENOUGH
THE ONLY GOOD ANG IS A RELEASED ANG
THE PAST HAS NOT HAPPENED YET,
ONLY THE FUTURE IS DONE
THE HIGHER THE LEVEL,
THE LONGER THE FLOAT

There was nothing else in the room, save the doors, the lights, and the signs.

HEAVY
TO BELIEVE IS TO KNOW
WHAT CAN BE, IS: WHAT CANNOT BE, IS NOT

UP YOUR ANGS

"Adam."

It was Melisa. I went over and knelt by her side.

"I'm sorry. For what I said. It's just—it all became real for me all of a sudden. I mean, being kidnapped and all. It's not a game anymore."

"No," I agreed, "it's not a game."

"I don't want to be here for two years."

"Don't worry," I said. "We won't." My thought was that we'd starve to death long before the two years were up, but I didn't say it.

"You think they'll find us?"

"I think your father is smart enough to figure out a way." Of course it might take a year or two....

"Where do you suppose we are?"

"Your guess is as good as mine. Better, because you know something about the Thousand Planets.

Melisa dried her eyes on her sleeve and looked around. "I know what everybody knows," she said, "which isn't much. They're supposed to be strange people in the Thousand Planets. Each planet is different, and each people is stranger than the last. I don't think I want to be here."

There was a loud creaking sound, which continued for some time, and then one of the four doors slowly opened outward. A thin young man with a brushy mustache and a toothy smile came into the chamber. "Welcome, seekers," he said. "You are here to find the truth, and it shall be offered." He was wearing a light-blue shirt, silver pants, a red-lined gold cape, and had on one gold boot and one red boot.

"We are here because we were kidnapped!" Melisa said. "Are you part of the plot against us? Where are we? What are you going to do with us? Will you let us go? Will you call my father? He'll pay you well."

The man held up six fingers. Then he folded one of them down. "No," he said.

He folded the next finger over. "You are on Aegle."

The third. "No human can do anything with another human, that is illogical."

The fourth. "No."

The fifth, his right thumb. "No."

The sixth (the first finger on his left hand). "I do not require or use money. Money is an illness."

"What is your name?" I asked him.

"I am Meta-Doremus, in this incarnation," he said.

"I am Adam, and this is Melisa," I told him, in an attempt to be friendly, which was not what I felt like being.

"You will be named henceforth," he said. "You have come here seeking, and your ang knows your true name."

"We were brought here by kidnapers," Melisa said.

"That is but an exterior cause," Meta-Doremus said. "The interior knows no such boundaries." He raised a finger. "Come!"

Melisa looked at me, and I shrugged. "We'd better follow him," I whispered to her. "Staying here won't help us at all."

The planetoid Aegle was laid out like the inside of a ship, with a complex series of decks and stairs and rooms and cabins, interwoven with another complex web of pipes and wires and ducts. It was painted in a variety of bright colors, that had no seeming relation to any object being painted. A red stripe might wander up one wall, across half a duct, then turn right and smear across a doorway. The other wall might be large yellow circles in a blue field, and the remaining half of the duct might be purple. The effect was to make you unsure of the shape of anything until you'd stared at it for a while.

Meta-Doremus led us up stairs and along corridors and down stairs and through rooms and around corners and through hatches until we were thoroughly confused—not that we weren't pretty confused to begin with. There didn't seem to be anyone else around; all the corridors and rooms were deserted. "Do a lot of people live here?" I asked him.

"The number of angs present at any time is indivisible," he said. "The number of bodies at the present moment exceeds

twenty thousand."

"Where are they all?"

"It is the hour of watching."

I nodded as though I understood. He seemed to think I should, and I didn't want to disappoint him.

He took us to a small room with no furniture, but with a lot of wires coming out of one wall and disappearing back into the ceiling. "Wait here," he said, and went through another door.

Melisa promptly sat cross-legged on the floor. "I don't think I like any of this," she said. "What do you suppose it's all about?"

"I don't know," I said. "I think the kidnapers left us here because they know these people, whatever they are, won't let us go. But I don't think these people know anything about the kidnaping, or are a part of it."

"Why?"

"Well, if Meta-Doremus is a representative example, they're not together enough to do anything in the real Universe. You don't have any idea what sort of people live on Aegle?"

She shook her head. "Never heard of it before," she said.

Meta-Doremus came back in. "The Op will see you now," he said.

"The what?" Melisa asked.

He didn't seem offended. "The Op," he repeated. "Op-eight, to be precise. He awaits."

"Well then, I guess we'd better see him," I said. "It would never do to keep an Op waiting."

Meta-Doremus took us through into the next room, which was larger but equally devoid of furniture. A tall man with a long white beard, dressed all in gold, was lying stretched out on the floor, as though he had collapsed in midstride.

"This is Op-eight," Meta-Doremus said, indicating the fallen man. Then he folded his arms and stood calmly a couple of meters away from the body.

"Shouldn't we help him?" I asked.

"Help him what?" Meta-Doremus replied.

"Never mind," I said.

"Oh," Meta-Doremus said. "I don't mind. It is bad for your ang to mind."

"Are you just going to let him lie there?" Melisa asked.

Op-eight sat up and opened his eyes. "I was called away," he said calmly, standing up.

"You are the seekers?"

"We were kidnapped and brought here against our will," I said. "Are you going to hold us here?"

Op-eight nodded. "I am aware that you were brought here unknowingly," he said. "But it is clearly part of the plan."

"What plan?" I asked. Maybe I was wrong; maybe they were in on the kidnapping.

Op-eight gestured, a wide, all-embracing gesture. "The plan of all," he said. "It is done, so it was to be done. The past has not happened yet; only the future is done. It is not your will that brings you here; it is the will of cosmic accident. You are seekers because you are here; it is enough. You will be trained. Your angs will be released. It is right. To believe is to know."

"You're not going to let us go?" Melisa demanded.

Op-eight shrugged. "What can be, is," he told her. "What cannot be, is not."

"What does that mean?"

"These things cannot be explained to those who do not understand," he told her. "You must begin as an egg, and progress up to flight, releasing ang as you go."

"What is 'ang'?" I asked him.

Op-eight gazed at me placidly through half-lidded eyes. "You are ang," he said, "and ang is you. And I am ang, and ang is me."

"I don't understand," I said.

"Soon you will convey what is to be conveyed. After a mere twenty or thirty years your ang will be lucid, and you can join the waiting ones, which is the first plateau."

"Waiting for what?"

Op-eight smiled and absentmindedly placed the tips of his thumbs together, palms apart and open. "Mother Hubbard," he said. Then he collapsed back onto the floor in an undignified

heap.

"Come," Meta-Doremus said.

We followed Meta-Doremus through another maze of corridors and rooms to a large door that had a sign over it reading APOLLONICS I + ENTER YE WHO WOULD KNOW.

Meta-Doremus pushed the door open, and a loud booming voice said, "Do you know?"

"No," Meta-Doremus said.

"Do you know that you do not know?"

"No," Meta-Doremus said.

"Who knows?" the voice asked.

"I don't know," Meta-Doremus said.

"Enter," the voice boomed.

Meta-Doremus went into the room behind the door, with us close behind. "That was Mother Hubbard," he told me in a solemn voice.

I looked around. There was no one else in the room. "It was a man's voice," I objected.

"Mother Hubbard is a man," he said. "He is the founder of Apollonics and Angistics, and it is he for whom we wait. We settled here on Aegle to await his return and practice his religiositic teachings."

"When did he leave?" Melisa asked.

"Over a thousand years ago."

"Where did he go?"

"No person knows. He promised to return, and so we wait."

"But," I said, "that was his voice?"

"Yes."

"Anglit has changed so little in the past thousand years?"

"We have a computer analyze the recording and correct it for cogency periodically," Meta-Doremus explained. "But every syllable is Mother Hubbard's voice."

"Ah!" I said.

"Sit," Meta-Doremus said. "We must begin your teaching."

I looked around the room. There were two long tables with benches on each side running the length. The tables, which

seemed to be wooden, had parallel strips of white tile inlaid crosswise into their tops, dividing them into meter-wide segments. "What are we supposed to learn?" I asked.

"That which cannot be put into words," Meta-Doremus said. "You are to learn the way. You are to learn to free your ang. You are to learn your true name."

"Oh," I said.

"While you are learning," Meta-Doremus said, "I will have you assigned bunks. A pallet in boys' org for you, and a pallet in girls' org for you."

"But we—"

"Good-bye for now," he said, and slumped forward and fell to the floor.

"What, um, do you suppose causes that?" Melisa asked, pointing to the supine body of our host.

"I don't know," I said. "But I hope it's not catching."

Two men dressed in white robes came into the room from another door. One of them took me to a seat at one table, and the other took Melisa. The whole process, everything that was going on, seemed bizarre and ridiculous, but very frightening. It would have been easy to run, but there was no place to run to. The white-robed man sat opposite me, the other one opposite Melisa, and Meta-Doremus lay still on the floor with no one paying any attention to him.

Set into the tile top of the table in front of me was a black circle about twenty centimeters wide with a red cross inscribed in its center. The man opposite me took from his robes a triangular piece of clear plastic with what looked like intricate electronic circuitry imbedded inside it and a fine silver chain attached to one end. The device looked new, but the design was clearly centuries old, since the electronics inside were of a type that hadn't been used in hundreds of years.

"This is the symbolizer," the man told me. "It is used to release your angs. You will be using this a lot over the next few years. As soon as you get out of primary process, you will be given your own."

"Wonderful," I said.

"Here, take it," he said, holding it by the chain and extending his hand across the table. I reached for it. "No, no," he said. "Not by the symbolizer. Never touch the symbolizer. Take it by the chain."

I took the end of the chain, as directed, and held the symbolizer directly over the center of the cross with my right hand. "You are right-handed, aren't you?" he asked me, and I assured him that I was. "That's good," he said. "I once wasted a lot of time processing someone who didn't bother telling me he was left-handed. It was my fault, of course. I should have asked."

"What are we doing?" I asked him.

"You are starting process," he said. "I'm going to ask you a lot of questions, and you answer them the best you can, and the symbolizer will tell us whether we have reached an ang hangup or just a process bar."

"Oh," I said.

He started asking me questions, while I held the symbolizer over the cross. They were mostly rambling questions about my childhood, without any apparent point or purpose. The tip of the symbolizer moved in a small circle above the table as I held the chain. Sometimes the motion of the gadget would change to a figure eight or a back-and-forth line, and then his questions would get more intense, digging into whatever we were talking about. One time we got hung up for a while on what color socks I wore to school, and another time we discussed the length of my sister's hair for quite a while. I couldn't make any sense out of the whole thing, except that he clearly thought that the motion of the gadget revealed some deep secrets about my innermost thoughts.

"Enough for today," he said after a while. "If we go on for too long, all we get is tired." That was the first sensible thing I'd heard since I arrived on this strange planetoid.

I looked around and saw that Meta-Doremus must have recovered, since he was no longer lying on the floor. As a matter of fact, he was no longer in the room. "Say," I said to my teacher,

or whatever he was, "why do you people all sometimes just fall over onto the floor?"

"We don't all," he said. "Only those of us of level three or above can dislocate."

"Dislocate?"

"Yes. When your ang is called to a different time or place, your temporal body is dislocated and out of control."

"Oh," I said.

Meta-Doremus came back into the room. "Your bunks are assigned," he said. "I see that you are finished with your first teaching. Was it not exciting? Did you not feel the release, as your mind and ang began to sever their bonds?"

"I feel tired," Melisa said, turning from her bench to face him.

"Of course," he told her. "That is a good sign, a sign of great progress. Come with me now, and I will take you each to your assigned bunks. Your new clothing will have to wait until tomorrow, as the clothes org is closed for the day."

As Meta-Doremus led the way, Melisa took my hand and held me back until we were far enough behind him for her to be able to whisper to me without being overheard. "We have to get out of here," she whispered. "I can't take this. These people are going to drive me crazy! I don't understand what they're talking about. I don't think they understand what they're talking about."

"Have you got a watch?" I whispered.

She nodded.

"Okay then. In exactly five hours meet me back here. Don't forget the way. They should be asleep by then."

"What are you going to do?"

"I don't know," I told her. "But I will by then. You're right, we've got to get out of here."

"Okay." She squeezed my hand.

We reached the girls' org first, and Meta-Doremus called out a lady, dressed all in gold except for red boots, to take Melisa. "They'll take care of you in there," he told her.

"Yes, come on in, dearie," the lady said, smiling with the

same forced smile that Meta-Doremus wore. "We'll take good care of you here."

Melisa gave me a quick panicked look, then composed her face and followed the golden lady inside.

Meta-Doremus took me two corridors and three bends farther, then pointed to an unmarked door. "Pallet seven by the right leg," he told me. "I go now."

He went on and I went in. The room was very strangely shaped, with zigs and zags and odd angles and corners. It was full of beds, which were indeed pallets: canvas mattresses full of straw on sixty-centimeter-wide planks, set about a meter apart. There must have been a couple of hundred of these pallets in the room. At the foot of each pallet was a wooden box, open at the top, full of neatly piled clothing.

The occupants of the room were boys who looked to be about four or five years younger than I was. There was just about one for every pallet, and they sat cross-legged on top of them. The low murmur of conversation that had been going on ceased when I entered the room, and every face turned to stare at me.

"Courtesy," I said. "My name is Adam. I am to take pallet seven by the right leg."

They kept staring, silently. This made me even more nervous than I already was. "Would one of you show me where it is, please?"

Without a word, they all pointed to an empty pallet far down the room. I went over to it and sat down. If they didn't want to talk to me, fine. I had a lot of thinking to do for the next five hours.

I had promised Melisa that I was going to get us out of here. And, for that matter, I thought it was a pretty good idea myself. Too much longer with these people who left their temporal bodies collapsed on the floor while they traipsed around time and space in their angs would probably not be very good for my sanity either.

As I sat there making up all sorts of wild schemes for attracting the attention of Mars by setting off giant flares or

altering a radio to broadcast a rescue beacon, the conversation around me slowly picked up where it had left off.

And I heard the answer, or what I hoped would turn out to be the answer.

One of the boys across the room from me was telling the boy in the pallet next to mine that his group was going on an expedition the next day. They were going "outside" to visit the "mother ship."

Outside.

On the surface of this planetoid, somewhere, there was a ship. And it couldn't be that hard to find; you could probably walk all around the planetoid in a couple of hours.

All we had to do was find out where they kept the vacuum worksuits, and go steal the ship.

Of course I had no idea how to pilot a spaceship, but maybe Melisa did. Or maybe the controls were clearly marked, with instructions printed neatly above the panels. Anyway, it was certainly better than staying here.

Lights out was announced in the easiest way possible: the lights suddenly went out. Luckily the watch I'd picked up at the University on Mars had a button to light up the numbers, so I just lay down to wait.

CHAPTER XII.

I couldn't wait five hours. I arrived at the meeting place almost half an hour early.

Melisa was already waiting for me. "Did you meet anyone?" she whispered. "I think they're all asleep."

"That's what I think too," I said. "They don't seem to have any guards out or anything, for, after all, what is there to guard?"

"How are we going to get out of here?"

"Thank you," I said.

"For what?"

"For your faith in me. I have an idea we can try, and it may get us away from here and it may not. Can you pilot a spaceship?"

"I've piloted a dome-class yacht," Melisa said, "but all you do is tell them where to go, and they do it. Very intelligent ships."

"Well," I said, "let's hope this one is a dome-class, or something like it."

"Which one?" she asked. "What are you talking about?"

"I'm not sure," I said. "Somewhere on the skin of this planetoid there is the mother ship. One of the boys in my org is going to visit it tomorrow. Sort of a class expedition, I guess. Well, my idea is we should visit it first."

"You think it's fueled up and ready to go?" Melisa asked. "You think you can run it?"

"I hope it's ready to go," I said, "and I was hoping you could run it. But maybe there's an instruction book around somewhere."

"That's not incredibly hopeful," Melisa said.

"It's the best I can do," I said sourly.

"Oh, I'm not criticizing you," Melisa assured me. "You did better than I did. The girls in my org—I wonder what an 'org' is—wouldn't talk to me at all."

"The boys didn't do much talking to me either," I told her. "Well, let's get out of here, and we won't have to worry about it."

"Fine," she said. "Which way?"

"Now that is a good question. I have no idea. And I have no other ideas either. If you keep going in any direction you're bound to come to the outside. But this place is designed so it's hard to keep going in one direction. And, besides, just any place on the outside won't do."

"Can't we just walk around until we find the ship?" Melisa asked. "Aegle can't be very big around."

"True," I said, "but we have to find vacuum suits before we can go out at all. And they're probably all together beside the official exit, wherever that is."

"I imagine there'd be some in a room by each exit," Melisa said. "What good is an exit into space without handy vacuum suits?"

"That's true," I said. "But my idea is that they don't encourage people to leave. They'll have emergency ports to get back in, or for authorized people, who already have suits, to use—but probably have only one controlled port where suits are supplied."

"You might be right," Melisa agreed. "How do we find out?"

"I don't know," I admitted. "But I guess we'd better do something. Say, do you think we can find the room we were left in?"

"The stone one with the doors?"

"Right."

"I don't know. There weren't any suits in there."

"Right. But there is a lock. I'll bet they keep suits nearby. That's probably the main entrance to this place."

"And a very gloomy main entrance it is. But that fits. I think it's back this way."

Melisa and I spent the next two hours looking for the lock we

had been left in. The maze of corridors doubled back on itself, and they all looked alike. But finally Melisa stopped in front of a door I could have sworn we'd passed by only a few minutes before. "I think this is it," she said.

"It looks like all the rest," I said.

"Yes, but it's got a snap lock from this side," she pointed out. "Remember all the doors were locked from the outside?"

"That's right!" I stared at the door. "Of course, this just might be where they keep the deadly rattlesnakes."

Melisa put her ear to the door. "I don't hear any rattling," she said.

"Okay," I said. "It's worth a try. Let's see if we can open it."

The lock was a strange one: a large round lump on the side of the door that went a few centimeters over the jamb and had all sorts of little bumps and knobs sticking out at odd angles.

"Here, let me," Melisa said, crouching down to bring the lock to eye level. "Picking locks is a hobby of mine." She slid a piece of straight plastic stiffener from the collar of her shirt and attacked the lock with it. For three or four minutes she prodded, twisted, and jiggled.

"Well?" I said.

"Have patience," she told me. "Picking locks demands, above all else, infinite patience."

"That's all very well," I told her, "but we don't have infinite time."

The lock clicked, and the door swung open. "Well, there," she said. "If I'd known you were in a hurry—"

Just then we both heard footsteps from down the corridor. We quickly pushed through the door and closed it behind us. "You have a point," Melisa whispered.

"Good timing," I said. We waited until the footsteps had passed. "Now I just hope we haven't locked ourselves in," I added, looking around. We were in the large room that had been our first introduction to Aegle, having just entered through the door with HEAVY carved over it.

"No fear," Melisa said. "I slid the plastic thingie between the

door and the lock."

"Good," I said. "Now, if our logic is right, behind one of these other doors is a roomful of vacuum suits. Can we get through from this side?"

"No," she said. "I need to be on the lock side of the door to pick the lock; that's only common sense."

"Right," I agreed. "Let's try the corridor side of the doors around that way." I pointed to the left.

Melisa cautiously pushed the door back open and looked out. The corridor was clear again. We went down it and took the first branch that headed in the right direction. About three doors down I paused. "Here," I said, "try this one. It feels right."

Melisa set to work on the strange lock and opened it slightly faster than the first one. The room was full of odd pipes and valves with no labels. But there were also interior doors that led to the rooms to either side of it, and they were not locked.

"Here," I said, "I'll go this way, and you go that. The first one to come to suits goes to get the other. But no yelling."

"Believe me," she said, "you didn't have to tell me that. I'll be as cautious as an early worm."

The first room I went in had oxygen pressurizing equipment, which was encouraging. The next one was a repair shop for things that looked like mechanical grasshoppers. Just as I was going through to the next, Melisa came in. "I found them!" she whispered.

"Great!" I said, following her back to the room she had found. The vacuum suits were all neatly lined up and hung from special rigs so the wearer could just step into them from behind and the rig would seal the suit and release it. The life-support backpacks were lined up on shelves along one wall. It wasn't until we were both suited up, and had helped each other put on and adjust the backpacks, that I realized the one thing missing: there were no helmets in sight.

For over half an hour we searched for the helmets, getting more and more anxious as the minutes passed. In a couple of hours the first early-morning people would probably come in to

open the rooms. Finally I opened a little cabinet with a mirrored front that was behind the counter. It looked as if it probably contained a first-aid kit. It was certainly too small to hold more than one helmet.

There, sitting on the shelf, was one helmet. When I took it out, the shelf slid silently down, and another helmet came into view. "I found them," I said. "It's some sort of trick."

We crossed the large stone room to the lock and went in. Putting on our helmets at the last minute, the way Nancy had taught me, we cycled the lock and walked out onto the surface of Aegle.

The ship was in sight outside the lock, maybe a half kilometer away. After five steps in the ship's direction, the gravity suddenly dropped to almost zero, just barely enough to keep one from floating off into space. For some reason the effect almost made me sick this time, and I had to stay still for a few minutes, fighting down the nauseous feeling in my stomach and throat.

Melisa walked over to the ship while I was being sick. We didn't dare turn the suit radios on, so it wasn't until she had returned and touched her helmet to mine that I got the word. "It's no good," she said.

"What's no good?"

"The ship. Are you feeling better?"

"Yes," I told her. "I'm okay now. What's wrong with the ship?"

"From here it looks like a spaceship," she said. "From up close it looks like what it is: the gutted shell of something that used to be a spaceship maybe two or three centuries ago."

"You're sure?" I asked, knowing that it was a stupid question. She merely nodded. "What now?"

"Well, I guess we've got almost four hours to find another ship."

She smiled through the helmet. "Did you ever hear the story of the three men who had to go tell their families that a great flood was going to wipe out their houses in exactly four hours?"

"No," I said.

"Well, the first one ran into his house and said, 'We've got just four hours to live. The second one announced, 'We've got just four hours to make our peace with the Universe and prepare to die.' "

"And the third?"

"The third one told his family, 'We have just four hours to learn to breathe under water.'"

"Do you want to go back inside?" I asked.

"No, no, I agree with you," she said. "We have just under four hours to find another ship, and we'd better start looking."

"And we'd better stick together," I said. "We could cover more ground—if you can call this ground—separately, but we'd never find each other again."

"Right," she said. "We'll hold hands. Or gloves, anyway."

"Which way shall we walk?"

Melisa looked around. "That bright red planet in front of us is Mars," she said. "Let's walk toward Mars."

"Very good."

The planetoid was so small that the horizon fell away practically under our feet, and the farthest point you could see on the surface was probably no more than two to three kilometers away; anything farther than that was under the curve of the horizon. We walked toward Mars until it was overhead, and then kept walking, keeping it at our backs. The sun came into view—merely an extra-bright star with a barely discernible disk at this distance.

"It's no good," Melisa said. "These strange people probably have nothing that can leave this horrible place."

Just then the Sun went out. Even though, at this distance, the Sun was merely the brightest star in the sky, its sudden disappearance was very frightening. It took me a few moments to realize what must have happened: some dark body had interposed itself between us and the Sun.

Stars on both sides of the Sun started going out, a good sign that the dark body was getting closer. Melisa and I stood and watched this happening until we were able to tell the shape of

the approaching object by the changing pattern of black in the sky.

"It's a windjammer," I said. "It must be way off course. I wonder what could have happened."

"Look," Melisa said, pointing toward a corner of the dark object that was slowly filling the sky. "That side of it seems to be ripped. It must have had an accident."

"I wonder if the skipper is all right."

"Is it going to hit Aegle?"

"I hope not. If it does, it will certainly kill anyone on board, and probably do us in, too; we'll be knocked off into space."

We watched with growing apprehension as the kilometers-wide spread of the windjammer sail approached the planetoid. It looked as though it would hit for sure, and we had no place to hide and not nearly enough time to get around to the lock we had left from, which seemed to be the only lock on the whole surface.

The 'jammer sail covered the whole sky, blotting out the universe, and then contacted with the surface of Aegle. The bubble-thin trymar skin of the sail parted as though it had never been, and only the struts and reinforcing crosspieces absorbed any of the impact, which they did by crumpling and twisting. The windjammer cabin missed impacting Aegle by over a kilometer, but the sail had grabbed a firm hold as it crumpled. The cabin section slowly wheeled around Aegle, spiraling in as the struts crumpled, and giving up energy. By the time it finally reached the surface of the planetoid it hit with no more than the impact of two hands clapping.

Melisa and I ran practically halfway around Aegle to reach the point where the cabin had landed, but the length of the leaps you can take on a body of such small mass is impressive, so it didn't take long. We just had to be careful not to jump too strongly, or we might never come down.

There was a man in the windjammer's cabin, and he seemed to be all right. He was strapped into an impact webbing that stretched across the cabin, and he wore a black hood over his

head. I tried to attract his attention through the port, but didn't succeed.

"What place is this?" a voice asked.

I turned, and the man was standing next to me on the surface of Aegle, clad, as he had been in the cabin, in but a thin coverall with no helmet. I looked back through the port, and he was still strapped into his webbing.

The man—or the apparition of a man—standing beside me laughed. "Don't be afraid, boy," he said. "This is merely a projection. Pure science, nothing mystical about it. The projector is that black gimcrack you see me wearing over my head. You can see into the cabin, can't you?"

"Yes," I said. "Can you hear me?"

"Of course. A complete two-way gimcrack, this is. Where am I? Courtesy, young lady, I didn't notice you standing there until just now. I don't think the vision scan on this is adjusted wide enough."

"The name of this planetoid, apparently, is Aegle," Melisa said. Her voice sounded clear in my helmet—probably a side effect of the gimcrack. "Can we help you? I don't know how much help we can be, since the inhabitants of Aegle probably don't feel too friendly toward us right now."

The man—or the projection—stared at Melisa. "Courtesy," he said, "but you're not the Lady Melisa Trina-Jones, are you?"

"Yes," Melisa admitted.

He turned to me. "Then you must be Adam Warrington."

"That's right," I said.

"Well," he said. "Fancy that. My name is Otis Smith, and it's a pleasure to make your acquaintance. Prince Michael will be delighted. There must be half a million people looking for you two. And I, trapped alone in the least efficient means of transportation in the Solar System, with a broken sail quadrant at that, find you. Wait a second and I will get the word out."

The apparition disappeared abruptly. A couple of minutes later it reappeared. "A message is now beaming its way Earthward. Actually Moonward, I suppose, since at last report

Prince Michael was on the Moon. Congratulations; you are rescued."

"I hope so," I said. "Whenever they can get here. But for now, probably you are captured along with us. They're not going to let us leave, and they have no way off anyhow."

"It's a lucky thing for you," Otis Smith said, "that I happen to be something of a communications enthusiast. Most of those who take windjammers out for the six-month journey to Sol Terminus wish to be quite alone, and carry only an emergency beacon. But I've been playing chess with a professor on Mars and writing political articles for an Earth periodical during my trip. That's why I have this helmet, which is somewhat experimental.

"That's also why, when a random meteor ripped off the right axial tendon of the 'jammer sail, I was able to call for assistance immediately. Right now the rescue cutter is about five minutes behind me, on full deceleration."

Six or seven vacuum-suited figures appeared from around the horizon of Aegle, heading rapidly toward us. "I'm afraid that the Aegle rescue committee will beat them to it," I said, watching them come.

Otis Smith—or his projection—turned to look at them. "They are your abductors?" he asked.

"That would be too strong," I said. "It would take a while to explain. They didn't abduct us, but they are certainly our captors, in that they are keeping us here against our will."

"They will hear about it," he said. "As for their present approach—watch this!" He stretched his arms and floated slowly into the air—although there was no air. When he was about ten meters off the surface, he stopped rising and headed toward the approaching group of Aegles, flapping his arms slowly.

They all stopped, frozen, and watched him approach until he was about twenty meters from them. Then, with one motion, they turned and went racing off back around the other side of the planetoid.

Otis Smith popped out of existence where he was, and

appeared next to us again. "Rah, rah," he said. "Cheer the victor, boo the vanquished. As long as people believe in magic somewhere deep in their souls, they can be fooled by such tricks. And here, I believe, comes the rescue clipper."

A slender silver ship put down about fifty meters off, and two men popped out of a hatch and came loping toward us. One of them fed a special collapsed vacuum suit through the emergency hatch of the windjammer cabin, for Otis Smith to put on and be led to safety. The other one escorted Melisa and me into the ship.

An hour later we had on clean clothes, were sipping hot soup, and were on our way back to Mars.

"And just in time," Melisa said.

"How's that?" I asked.

"First day of classes tomorrow," she said. "I'm looking forward to that."

"School will seem awfully tame after all this," I said.

Well, I've been wrong before.

ABOUT THE AUTHOR

The author of over thirty novels and a melange of short stories, articles, and other stuff, MICHAEL KURLAND has been writing professionally for over three decades. His stories are set in epochs and locations from Ancient Rome to the far future—anyplace where the reader won't spot the anachronisms too easily. His works have appeared in Chinese, French, Italian, Spanish, German, Swedish, Polish, Portuguese, Japanese, Czech, and some alphabet with a lot of hooks and curlicues. They are believed to be the fragments of one great opus, a student of the *Untermensch*. He has been nominated for a Hugo, two Edgars, and the American Book Award, and various book clubs have picked up various of his books. More can be learned at his website:

www.michaelkurland.com